Entice

Brenda -
Thanks Av
all the
Shrimp!
Xo
Oskar

Entice

S.E. HALL

Love is like a butterfly, it settles upon you when you least expect it.

—AUTHOR UNKNOWN

TABLE OF CONTENTS

Prologue

WHERE DO DREAMS COME FROM? No one knows, and that's what makes them cool; some are random as fuck, some stem from recent events, but never knowing what you'll dream each night, how weird or erotic they'll get, gives you that time with your mind to look forward to.

When your dream's the same every night, it becomes a god damn nightmare.

I know, every single night, what I'm going to see from the time I close my eyes to the moment I drag my sorry ass out of bed in the morning. Without a doubt, I'm going to toss and turn in frustration, a rerun marathon of that night this past summer taunting me.

This bachelor party, for Parker, who I've known maybe eight weeks. God, I'm jealous as hell of him. That Hayden of his fucking adores him, and she's even hotter knocked up than she was before. And she dotes on his ass in a very independent, non-bloodsucking leech kinda way. Why can't I find a girl like that?

Obviously I've had too much tequila since I'm hosting my own little titbag party over here, feeling sorry for myself. Fuck this. I hold up two bills in my hand, I think they're twenties, and Silver Cowboy Boots comes over, way too eagerly.

Challenge me, dammit! Engage more than my dick!

"What's this get me?" I slur, shoving the bills at her.

She kicks one ankle, then the other, getting my legs just as far apart as she wants them and climbs over them, onto my lap. "This," she croons and starts to grind. Her attempt to pet my chest all sexy-like is an epic fail, snagging one way too long silver nail on my nipple ring. She better not rip my fucking shirt—I love this shirt.

"How much to go in the back?" Two months on a farm is damn lonely.

She cuts quick, nervous glances around, then leans into my ear. "Not my usual club, so not in here," she whispers. "But for a hundred, I'll meet you outside, after."

Just when I'm about to finalize the exact details, "Shook Me All Night Long," my favorite song ever, starts blaring. Now this dance I gotta see, moving Dracula Nails off my lap and outta my view to the stage, aka the flat area in this place.

Spank me and put me to bed…who the fuck is that?

"Zach?!"

Nothing.

"Zach?!" I yell louder.

"What?"

"Who. Is. That?" I point to the, um, we'll go with "dancer" for now.

"Cause I know her? I think they said Karma or something, but I doubt you'd find her in the phone book under that. Why?"

Look at him, trying to be all smartass... Well, he fucked it up, who the hell uses a phone book?

"No reason." I bounce my shoulders in what I hope looks like casual nonchalance, never taking my eyes off her. That may blow my cover, but damn if I could look away even if I tried.

I'm thinking it's the beer, strike that, tequila goggles; has to be. I was just dogging every chick who came near me, ready to pay for a meaningless quickie, a scratch to an itch, and sheer perfection happens to strut in to my favorite song?

Yeah, and when I'm done here, I'm gonna ride home to the Playboy mansion on the flying fucking dragon that I bought with my lottery winnings.

This isn't real; up close she's probably a big mess with bad breath and a whiny voice...and herpes. Gotta be.

But here's what I do know, no guessing, no wishful thinking, no maybe to it—take it to the bank: her hair is so dark and shiny that you can damn near see reflections in it and it has purple streaks in it—hot as hell. AND, wait for it... IT. IS. IN. BRAIDS.

Usually two braids or ponytails are known as "handlebars" in my language, but on this girl, they're cute; cute, wet dream-inducing braids.

Her eyes are as dark as her hair, and hold the fear and anxiety of a kitten stuck in a drainpipe when it's raining. I may never know where

3

it came from, this instinct that up until this point I would have sworn on a stack of Bibles I didn't possess, but I swear I hear her mind screaming to mine, "You're big and strong, protect me, Sawyer, take care of me, hold me and make me unafraid!"

That body of hers is tiny. Not frail, just petite, and tan and muscular…and her own. She turns it to the side and away from the onlookers and keeps her hands over her barely-covered breasts like the tease is part of the dance, but it's not. I'd bet you a nut this girl has never danced or stripped before in her life. And if she has, she should stop immediately, because she absolutely sucks at it.

Those come fuck me heels she's wearing? They're two sizes too big and she's never walked in them before. Also something she should stop doing immediately. If the teetering and wobbling didn't draw attention to her shapely legs, it'd just be sad, but the legs are worth the painful show. Oh and fuck me, she's skipping around in a circle. I hope she doesn't think that's a good cover for her lack of dance skills…skipping, for crying out loud.

And lastly, she loves this song. She's mouthing the words, keeping her eyes unfocused and on the back wall, dying for everything but the song itself to be over. And when it is, she runs like she's on fire for cover behind the curtain.

"Who was that?" *I ask Dracula Nails, still standing beside me.*

"New girl," *she answers snidely.* "First night, can't you tell?" *she laughs.*

"Yeah, I can."

"So, I'll see you later?" *she curls those inflated lips at me.*

"Maybe. If I see ya I see ya." I get up, walking over to Dane. "Where'd you get these girls?"

"Hell if I know; Brock hooked it up."

"So the company, it's local to us, like in Statesboro?"

"I think so, why?"

"Find out for sure. I'm gonna hit the can. Be right back."

I really do need to take a leak, but somehow I veer off course, peering behind the curtain like the Great and Powerful Oz will be waiting to hand me the 411 on this girl. I don't see him, or her, only several other scantily clad women who only remind me how different she was. I want to bust in a demand they tell me her name and where she is, but I'm forced to duck out and shove the curtain back when their escort/bodyguard/whatever guy spots me.

No worries, Dane can find out for me, that man has scary ways of digging up the buried. I hurry back from the bathroom and catch him just as he's hanging up his phone. "Well?"

"Local company, kinda off the radar, Brock isn't sure they're on the Better Business Bureau, if you catch my drift."

"I don't."

He leans into me, talking low and discreetly. "I know nothing, and I'm going to say this, walk out of here and never speak of it again. I may also fire Brock for being a dumbass. It's some on the side thing for one guy, mostly underage college girls needing money."

"Fuck," I mumble.

"Fuck is right. My name is never to be associated with this, ever. I had no idea and I'll kill Brock if he jeopardized any of us in any way.

5

You hear me?"

"Wait, so college, as in our college?"

"Yes," he sighs, running his hand through his hair, mad as hell.

"My old job ready at The K?" Wait, better yet... "I'll replace Brock even."

"You always have a job with me, Sawyer, you know that. Just say the word."

"Word. I'm heading back early. Don't fire Brock until I say, okay? I need to talk to him first."

"You just fire him when you have what you need. My hands are washed of this whole thing. Now get the fuck out of here and pay for the party in cash. No paper, you hear me, Sawyer?"

"Got it. Go, man."

Look out, Skipper, Daddy's coming home.

Chapter 1

SLEEPLESS IN STATESBORO

—SAWYER—

"WHY ARE WE HERE AGAIN?" Zach questions me, looking around.

"Put your pussy back in your pocket and shut the fuck up."

Since all my boys keep getting lost in the Bermuda Bush—as in they dive into her bush once and I never see them again—I've nominated Zach, the only single one left, as my new partner in crime. Though if he doesn't quit his fucking whining, I'll go solo.

I'm a man on a mission; there's no time for bellyaching. After spending the last few weeks scouring every club within fifty miles of school, in all directions, my patience is wearing thin…and I've run out of clubs. If this isn't the one, and I'm guessing this isn't the one, I'm out of brilliants ideas. All Brock had to do was take Dane's money and throw together a bachelor party for Parker. No one even said send dancers, but he did anyway, and because he can't get ahold of the shady fuck he did business with, I'm plagued by the image of a girl who's proving to be more elusive than Bigfoot.

"I don't think this is a strip club, bro. Look." Zach nudges my shoulder and points to a small stage with a wall of chicken wire wrapped around it and several different colors of broken glass littering the surface.

The flashing sign outside says Unbuckled—how is it not a strip club? Disappointed doesn't even begin to describe how I feel watching Meemaw and Peepaw slow dance amongst the peanut shells on the floor. I'm not sure if I should sue for false advertising or thank God they're not going to actually unbuckle anything.

"Come on." Zach gives me a slap on the shoulder, his face not hiding his pity. He knows this was it—the last place on the list. "Let me at least buy ya a beer."

Since there's nothing better to do and we're already here, I accept his offer and we grab two stools at the bar. Zach orders our drink and within minutes we're approached by two girls who are way below Social Security eligibility, so I'm more than a little surprised they're here.

"You wanna dance?" the blonde asks me, strategically placing herself between my chest and the bar, her tit grazing my arm.

I wouldn't even begin to pretend I know how to dance to the twangy, inbred music coming from the jukebox…and if we're doing this, I want her brunette friend anyway. I shake my head slowly and take a swig from my beer. "No, but Zach here has dance fever, don't ya, buddy?"

"Yeah," he stands, extending his hand to her, "show me your moves."

And he's back in the game, ladies and gentlemen! Now it's me and the friend. I blatantly move my eyes down her body and back up even slower, giving her a one-sided grin when I get to her wide, hungry eyes. Not bad. "You got a name?"

"Carmen. Yours?" She smiles shyly. Nice try. Her eyes tell me the truth; she's anything but shy.

"Sawyer. Have a seat," I pivot toward her and spread my legs, patting my thigh, "right here."

"Sawyer!"

Don't open your eyes, just keep going. She'll go away, you'll finish and fall asleep; another day down.

9

Her fist thuds on the door so hard this time it shakes. "Sawyer!"

"What?" I scream back, aggravated. Whatever my sassy ass roommate Laney lacks in good timing…she doesn't make up for in subtlety, either. Must we talk while I'm buried nine inches deep in…? I spare a one-eyed peek at…the brunette under me. That's right—the friend. The girl I picked solely for the color of her hair.

It may always be a raven-haired beauty, for the rest of my life, if I don't fuck her image out of my head. The thought of the clumsy-yet-captivating lil' stripper has me pumping feverishly into Miss Not Her, screams of "Oh Daddy!" bouncing off my bedroom walls again.

Which explains the complaining spitfire banging on my door. This bitch is loud!

"You are not her daddy and I have to be up and on the field at 6 am! Finish or shove a sock in her mouth!" Laney calls out, the thin plywood door, the only thing between us, not even close to a barrier if Laney decides to come shut this girl up herself.

"Yup," I answer, eyes squeezed shut again, no break in the rhythm of my thrusts. "You heard her," I grunt to my guest, "quiet down, sweetheart, and no more Daddy talk."

"Hmph." She starts to pout, but it easily morphs into an open-mouthed groan when I switch from teasing her with only the tip to slamming home again.

"Yes, oh God, yes!" she screeches beneath me, totally faking it.

Yes, I'm sure. You see…loose chicks, or basic bitches, can get away with the fake orgasm when they're fucking a needle dick. As long as she fluffs Pencil Dick's ego until five seconds after he comes, he's okay with ignorant bliss because of the unspoken understanding that he's anatomically equipped to get off regardless of the fact that he's a suck fuck and she got nothing. Not only can he not tell, since he's sporting a twig, but most guys don't give a shit if she's really getting off or not, so they've never made a study of the signs.

I have a different handbook; feel free to follow along.

I'm built. It's not ego, just a fact. So if I can't touch the sides, the elasticity in that thing is shot—Ben Wa, kegels, duct tape, and electrical wire be damned—there's no hope, sweetie. Buy a double-wide dildo and a lifetime supply of anti-depressants and wait 'til some unlucky bastard's too drunk to care.

For the rest of you—guess what the fact that I'm packin' means? I can feel, or not feel, the ripples, the natural quivering in the lining of your pussy that you can't make happen anymore than you can make it stop when you actually get off. So save the fake screams and use your big girl voice to tell me left, right, up, or down instead. There's a 100% chance I will come by the time we're done, and since you went to all the trouble of letting me in, you should get yours, girl...no shame in that game!

It never ceases to amaze me, really. A woman in the passenger seat won't shut the hell up. It's all "turn here, slow down, stop and ask," but she'll fake her way through mediocre sex, unfulfilled, and never say a word. What is that?

If only this one would do something to snap me out of the monotony, do something to engage me enough to stop these damn vagina monologues currently running through my head. Slap me, take charge, tell me how this shit's gonna go down— do something, girl! But she doesn't. Just like the one before her and I'm sure the one after her, she just lays there with the false moans and occasional twist or squirm. So I answer accordingly, banging into her like a jackhammer, not so much as using one finger to tickle her fartbox (which they all like, though they'd deny it if asked). Sorry, Senorita. No extra effort, no surprise ending.

Showing some life, she tries to grab my face and raise herself up to kiss me, but I turn my head, resting my forehead against the pillow. I'm ready to finish, not prolong the niceties.

"Almost there," I growl in her ear. "Wrap your legs around my back."

She does so immediately and I find myself wishing her pussy gripped as tightly as her legs do. But, since it's not even close, I scoop both hands under her ass and tilt her pelvis, angling myself to drag along the upper wall inside her for at least some friction. That really amps up her moans now, so I'm forced to use one hand to cover her mouth, lest we have a second visit from Laney. After a few more slides in and out, my eyes closed, my ultimate fantasy skipping through my head, I finally find my non-climatic climax and she feigns the same.

I don't take time to relax or fall down beside her. I don't even catch my breath, not wanting to send her any fucked up signals. We're done, so I jump out of bed and walk to the bathroom, disposing of the condoms. Yes, condoms. I always wear two.

Unfortunately, I catch a glimpse of myself in the mirror as I walk past it. When I turn to examine my reflection, I realize I look as shitty as I feel. My eyes are vacant and hollow, my heart damn near visible on my sleeve. I've never done relationships with all the snuggling and kissing, but I've also never been quite the callous ass I've become. I'd be lying if I said I wasn't a bit ashamed of myself, yet I can't seem to pull myself out of my funk. Even the women willing to forego being wined and dined, or even sweet-talked, before they jump in bed and spread their legs to help ease my ache and tension don't deserve the level of asshole I've become.

I'm not completely in denial; I know I'm idealizing her in my head and building up a fantasy perhaps a million times greater than what it would actually be like in real life. I haven't stopped the idealistic comparisons, imaginings, what ifs in my head ever since that night. There's a tugging in my gut that tells me, more certainly than anything ever before, that together, we'd be something special. Maybe it's all the "true love" bullshit around me, everyone pairing off, my friends adored by some of the hottest, coolest girls you'll ever meet, but I'm starting to feel like anything but the lucky bastard who escaped the claws of a woman. I feel like something's missing.

Oh, fuck me, I'm a goddamn chick, dreaming of my skipping, extraordinary Princess Charming. Gidge and her Disney bullshit are rubbing off on me and shriveling my nut sack into a vag. Is there a razor here? I'll go ahead and slit my wrists right now and call it a day.

Sighing, I wrap a towel around my waist and open the door, ready to try and at least behave cordially, which I know is only right. "Listen, can I—"

"She's gone."

I look up, startled by Laney's voice and even more shocked to see her sitting on my bed. Thank God I put on a towel. "Where'd she go?"

"Home, I guess." She shrugs. "I didn't ask. I heard the front door slam and got up to see what the hell was going on. Since you're here and she's not, I'm assuming it was her."

How did I not hear the door slam? Not that I would've chased her. "All right, she left. So what're you doing in here?"

She stands, grabbing some shorts off my floor and

throwing them at me. "Go put those on and we'll talk. Since I'm up," she reminds me with an evil glare.

I head back in the bathroom to change, and stay in there, locking the door and taking a deep breath. I'm over six feet tall and lift almost every day, but yes, I'm scared to face Laney. Not only is she a hellcat when she wants to be, but I don't want to see the disgust or disappointment in her eyes. She's one of my best friends, even more so after becoming roommates, and her opinion means a lot to me.

"Get out here!" she yells when she finally realizes I must be stalling. "Take it like a man."

I might as well go out there or she'll undoubtedly come in here, kicking in the door or taking it off the hinges in what I have no doubt would be less than five minutes.

She pats the bed beside her when I open the door. "Come sit down. We're doing this now."

I hesitantly take a seat, my knee bouncing as I wait for her to speak.

"First, and of the utmost importance, you know I call my father 'Daddy,' so hearing your visitors scream it repeatedly in the middle of the night freaks me out. I wake up thinking I'm in some bad Lifetime movie."

Fighting my smirk, I agree. "Okay, got it." Maybe this little chat won't be so bad after all.

"Second," she stands and tucks my extra pillow between the headboard and wall before sitting back down beside me, "on school and game nights, booty call curfew is eleven. That work for you?"

"Yeah." I sigh and run my hands along my head, wishing I had some hair to pull. "It won't happen again, Gidge. I'm sorry."

She places a hand on my shoulder with a small smile. "Don't be sorry. This is your house too and we hadn't talked about it. Now we have, so we're all good. Any rules you want to put in place?"

"Nah, I'm easy."

"Made crystal clear by the parade of women coming in and out of here." She laughs and scoots away quickly, ducking the pillow I grab and swing at her head. "Speaking of which, been busier than usual lately—you trying for Guinness or Gonorrhea?"

Here we go—this is what she really wants to talk about. It was a nice segue, funny even, but I'm on to her.

"I mean, you used to at least walk them out and kiss their cheek at the door. I know you said you'll come to me when you're ready, but I can't watch you self-destruct much longer and not say anything." She ducks her head and looks up at me, forcing my eyes to meet hers. "You're trying to fuck something, or someone, out of your system, Sawyer, and it's killing you." Care to share with the class?"

"I would've walked her out. She left before I came out of the john."

16

"What was her name?"

"Molly," I answer immediately.

She sighs heavily, flopping backwards on my bed but jolting right back up like the mattress shocked her. "Oh, God! Gross! I just laid on your bed o' brothel. Ewww," she whines.

"Relax," I roll my eyes at her, "I double wrap and she faked it. There's nothing on this bed but some sweat and regret."

She stands, waving me up with her hand. "Still, better safe than sticky. Ew, yuck, not a good joke." She pulls the blanket all the way up, covering the sheets, then sits back down right on the edge. "Now then," she again pats the spot beside her and I sit, "her name was Carmen. You weren't even close!" She slaps my back. "And by the way, I read or heard someplace that double wrapping isn't recommended."

"If I triple wrap, I won't feel a damn thing! And just one? No fucking way. I'll take my chances."

"Fine," she huffs, defeated.

"And how in the hell do you know her name? Are you sure it wasn't Molly?"

"I'm sure it was Carmen. You were still in the hall, that thing that runs right in front of my bedroom, when she said, and I quote, 'don't worry, Daddy, Carmen's gonna make you feel real good.'" Her breathy imitation and finger air quotes are hilarious, but I bite back my laughter, knowing she wants me to take this whole conversation seriously. "Highlight of my day, really, thank you."

What am I doing? I'd kill any man that treated one of my girls (and by my girls I mean Laney, Bennett, and Whitley) the way I've been treating women lately. There's a big difference between trying to have a good time and straight up being a dick. I don't want to be the latter, but damned if I can find the cure for my fucked up head.

I lie back, mesmerized by the ceiling fan blades whirling above me. "I'll try to be better, be nicer. I swear I'm not that guy."

"I know you're not, which is why I'm worried."

"Don't be," I reply with a resigned sigh. "Eventually I'll get happy in the same pants I got mad in."

"What? You'll get in someone's pants again and then you'll be happy?" She turns her head to look at me, face full of confusion.

I chuckle at her and shake my head. "It's a saying: 'you'll get glad in the same pants you got mad in.' As in, wait the woman out and she'll be over it quicker than she changes clothes. I didn't write it. Ask Confucius' ass to explain it. And by the way," I poke her in the side, "don't you chicks usually veg out and eat when you have problems? You haven't offered to make me shit. I should be surrounded by junk food by now."

She mocks me, poking out her bottom lip and batting her eyelashes. "Aw, does Sawyer need a hot fudge sundae?"

"Now you're talking, woman! Geez! You were holding back on me. What kind of friend are you?"

She stands, pulling me up by the hand. "My bad. How about I give you extra sprinkles? Will you forgive me then?"

"Maybe. You better hope you've got chopped nuts and chocolate ice cream though or we're through."

Chapter 2

LOST BOY

—SAWYER—

"YOU WANT A HIT OF THIS before I kill it?" CJ tries to hand the creepy-looking wizard bong to me, the end of his staff the bowl.

"No, man. I'm good," I mumble, rolling my eyes. I don't need to take an actual hit, the contact buzz is more than enough. If I had to guess, I'd say the air in his rat-hole apartment is currently two parts oxygen, ninety-eight parts bong smoke. CJ's definitely not the most upstanding citizen, nor is he my friend.

The only reason I keep him around is because he's the go-to guy for ammy motorcross. Ammies, or amateurs, are the lower level events allowed at the track on "off" times. No one's sponsored, things are unofficial, and money changes hands under the table since betting's technically not allowed.

At one time, I'd been an up-and-comer in the motocross scene, getting better and better with every race, but it had been left behind when Dane and I made a pact to quit all the bullshit partying and head to Georgia to be near his brother.

But now?

Dane has his holy grail of happiness, his refuge from the storm, Laney. Same with Tate—he and Bennett are happy as hell. Hell, even Evan, who definitely looked to be the last dog in the race, is now all wrapped up with Whitley.

So Imma get mine where I can.

"You got any races booked soon?" I ask him.

"Your bike even ready?" He coughs, blowing out a cloud of smoke as big around as my head.

I'd recently dipped in to my savings to tweak up the racing bike I'd just bought. Dane pays me well for working at The K, or doing whatever else he needs done, and what the fuck else do I have to spend it on?

"Yep, got it ready to ride, slicker and quicker. I rented storage for it at the track, even taken it out couple times. So, when's your next race?" I ask again, annoyed. I'm here for one reason and one reason alone; tell me race time, sign me up, exit stage left. Enough with the stoner-speed conversation; if he doesn't get to the fucking point soon, I'm walking out of here, straight to a skin peel. His place, this couch…it's all suspect.

CJ digs through the wrappers and God knows what else on the table until he finds his phone. He's on it about ten minutes before finally looking back at me. "Friday night, 10 o'clock. You're in."

I nod curtly and stand, way past ready to get the hell out of here.

"Aren't you forgetting something?" His lip curls up, baring yellow, crooked teeth. "I don't do this shit for my health. Fifty bucks," he sticks out his hand.

I digging around in my wallet and slap sixty in his palm. "Keep the change."

IT'S BEEN A LONG ASS WEEK with nothing much to look forward to, and I've been just going through the motions. I'm glad it's race night for no other reason than the guaranteed five minutes of pure adrenaline rush, an escape from the mundane. Tonight's crowd is decent, the screamo music blaring as loud as the engines keeping them amped up, ready for the real show. I watched the first heat and it looks like there's some stiff enough competition to keep things interesting.

I'm leaned against the fence, already in way-too-hot-for-Georgia gear and waiting for heat two of four to start, when I feel a small, warm hand on my arm.

"You racing tonight?"

I turn my head to the sultry voice, lined with invitation. "I am."

Sticking merely the tip of her index finger in her mouth and giving me the classic doe in heat eyes, she asks, "Are you all warmed up?"

I know this is the part where I'm supposed to walk away, especially after my talk with Laney about being a better guy, but if they put it in your face…it's rude not to take it. "No, ma'am. You got any suggestions?"

"I can warm you up." She moves closer up against me, her hard nipples poking my chest.

"How's that?" I don't even attempt to hide my perusal down her top.

Fake.

They're nice, and most guys live by the motto "if I can reach out and touch 'em, they're real enough for me," but I'm not a cardholder to that club. I like real tits and I cannot lie. The more they bounce when she rides me, the better. Doggy style, the natural ones sway back and forth like pendulums, damn near hypnotizing me. And when I titty fuck her, I want the "give" of natural flesh to mold around my cock like a glove.

HALL

"However you want," she says in her best 900 number voice. "I'm Mariah, by the way." She trails her finger along my forearm. "And you're Sawyer Beckett."

I should probably be concerned with how she knows that and the way it's screaming STALKER at me, but much like any other guy (you know, those brainless things with dicks), I'm not.

"Well, Miss Mariah," I run my gaze and fingertip from her neck down to the dip in her cleavage, lifting one brow and eye only, my head still dipped, "that's an awful sweet offer."

Her breathing hitches and the once-ivory skin exposed by the low cut top flushes under my touch. She darts her eyes around and I watch them settle and come back to me when her plan's decided. Taking my hand, she practically runs as she leads me across the gravel lot and in between two random buildings.

Once we're out of blatant sight, she's on me, her frantic, seeking hands barely able to decide what to unzip or lift first, her mouth sloppy and unskilled on my chin, then my neck.

"Hey, hey," I chuckle, using slight force on her shoulders to still her. "You're gonna hurt somebody, woman." I lean in, letting the tip of my nose graze her neck up and down a few times in a soothing rhythm. "Little calmer?" I murmur.

She whimpers, almost as if she's in pain from being settled, but her touch is more controlled now as one hand

24

sneaks into my open coveralls and under my sliders. "Ahhh," she hums, like she found the prize without having to dig all the way to the bottom of the cereal box. In a flash, she's on her knees in front of me, one hand moving clothing out of the way, the other gripping my dick like a vice.

"Easy," I soothe her, running one hand along her hair. I'm actually apprehensive of having her so excited...and so close to my dick. I'd like to leave this makeshift hideaway unscathed. "Slow, sugar," I croon. "I want it sweet and slow."

That does the trick. Her eyes lock on me, seeking praise as she sucks as much as she possibly can down her throat.

"There ya go, just like that," I mumble.

I'm about six licks away from the creamy center of my back alley blowjob when a sweet voice rings out, "Mariah?"

Ahhh, fuck. I squeeze my eyes shut, blocking out everything but the directive I'm mentally sending my cock to detonate before the owner of the voice calling out for my "new friend" finds us. I take over now, not usually one to force feed, but desperate times... I start face fucking her like a man with an hour left to live, cause I'm damn sure I'm gonna die coming. "Almost," I pant, "don't stop."

"MARIAH?" Shit, the voice is much louder this time. Friend found us.

The first shot fires down her throat as my eyes fly open, head turning towards the sound of a surprised gasp. NO! No fucking way! This is an ejaculation hallucination, it's gotta be.

25

With odds like this, no one would bet on the races, the fortune to be had is in my bad fucking luck. I try to pull out, but Mariah latches on with a threatening hint of teeth. "I-I," is all I manage, squeezing my eyes shut in humiliation.

"Oh, by all means, finish." She snickers.

Shamefully, I do. In my defense, it's not one of those things you can just stop. Mariah takes it all, an audible "pop" echoing against our surrounding walls when she pulls away and rises. I'd rather go blind, but I open my eyes, seeing her proudly beam as she wipes the corner of her mouth.

"Good thing I got you a drink, huh?" She mocks, stepping forward and offering one of the drinks she's holding to Mariah. Then she looks down at my dick and back up at me and winks. "Not bad."

I'm in shock, mentally willing my hand to stop shaking like a puss as I tuck myself back in, zipping up in embarrassment.

There she stands, the apparition of my every recent dream come to life at the most inopportune time imaginable. In all the scenarios I made up in my head about how, when, and where we'd finally meet again, I assure you this was not one of them. She looks even more incredible than I remember, far more perfect in real life than my dreams. I'd remembered a dime; she's a fucking quarter and I don't need change.

The purple streaks in her ebony hair are gone; she has

long, deep brown locks with dark red tips now. She's a bitty thing, maybe 5'3" tops, but her jean shorts, pockets hanging out, make her tan legs look deceptively longer than they are. On her feet are black cowboy boots that match a wide black belt that pulls my eyes to her rockin' fucking hips.

Badass hair, cowboy boots and the face of an angel… she's fucking Skittles—one package, every fucking flavor!

When I make it back up to her eyes, an almost unnatural dark green, like lush grass wet with morning dew, she's got me locked in her crosshairs. She cocks her head at an angle and raises her eyebrows, silently and incredulously saying, "can I help you with something?" louder than actual words.

"I gotta go." I duck my head and start to move past her, feeling hands pulling me from behind.

"Wait! Don't you want my number?" Mariah calls out desperately.

I turn around but continue my steps to the track backwards. "I'll um…I'll catch ya around later, okay?" I sling my thumb over my shoulder. "I gotta hurry. Race time."

Chapter 3

HOPE SINKS

—SAWYER—

SHE'S OUT THERE, somewhere in the crowd, watching the race. I can feel the grit in my eyes and between my teeth, the balmy heat and the motor's vibration coursing through me, but I don't feel her eyes on me. I know it, as sure as the sun will rise in the east and set in the west, that if her eyes were on me, I would feel it.

As we line up, I steal a quick glance to the crowd, trying one last time to pick her out—nothing. The place is packed with hordes of college guys seeking the rush and even more college girls seeking those guys; it's a big ass meat market. There are more female heads of dark hair than not and exactly how many people are wearing a yellow fucking shirt?

Know who I do see? Laney Jo Walker.

When you climb onto the bleacher rail and wave your hands in the air, people tend to pick you out in a crowd.

I give her, and Dane, who's standing beside her shaking his head and laughing, a wave. I'm surprised that he's here at all. What happened to the whole "stop with the destructive behavior" speech?

I turn my attention back to the flag, the familiar surge of exhilaration taking over. When the flag drops, the flight of ten bikes takes off, slinging up dirt and clouds of dust. It only takes me three laps to gain a huge lead, so I use it to my advantage. I will get her attention.

I'm having a fucking blast, taking the hills a tad faster now that I'm out of the pack and adding some kick twists when I'm airborne. Purposely allowing some fishtailing, flying sideways around the corners, I keep my eyes on the track, despite the need to check the stands. Thoughts of her race through my head as fast as the testosterone through my veins. Is she watching yet?

The last foothill before the finish line, I go all out and turn out a flip…easily landing it and crossing for the win. The horn blares and I rip off my helmet, lines of sweat dripping down the sides of my face. A flip. She had to have noticed that, right?

I don't know how or when Daney, my clever

combination of their names a nod to the single person they've fused into, make it across the track, but here they are beside me. That had to be like a real life game of Frogger, and I wouldn't be surprised if he carried her across the traffic.

"You won!" Laney screams. "The shenanigans at the end scared me a little," she slaps my arm, "but you won!" She's gushing, literally bouncing up and down. See—the electricity of a race is contagious, 'cause Laney Jo Walker doesn't bounce.

"Nice job, man," Dane chimes in, holding up his fist for a bump.

"Thanks." I flick my eyes to him for acknowledgement, but just as quickly back to the stands. Get a pattern, one row at a time, left to right… It's the best way to make sure I don't miss her. Back and forth I scan as quickly as possible, getting disoriented every time a group moves. "Damn it!" I yell, throwing my helmet on the ground.

Laney gasps. "What? Are you okay?"

I sigh, running a hand down my face. "Nothing. It's nothing. Come on, let's get the hell out of here." I lean over to pick the helmet back up, still unable to stop my eyes from wandering around hopefully.

"Don't you have the finals?" Dane asks, curious arch of his brow.

He's right, I had advanced to the big race, but I couldn't care less about it at the moment. Add racing to the list; one more thing getting the fun sucked right out of it. Sucked out of it. Damn. I shake my head at the ironic pun that peaked my misery in the first place.

"Fuck the finals. I suddenly don't give a shit," I grumble, fiddling with the snaps on my helmet.

"You want to go out or—"

I cut Dane off, tired and frustrated. "I'll meet you guys at home later. I've got some shit to do."

"You sure? I have at least one beer in me," he offers.

"Nah, man," I pull Laney into me and kiss the top of her head, "but thanks for coming. I thought you hated me racing."

"Yeah, well, your roommate can be pretty persuasive." He chuckles, pulling his woman from my arms to his own.

"Saw, what's wrong?" Laney asks, her brows dipped with a worried frown.

"Not a thing, Gidge. I'll see you later, okay?"

"Okay." She looks back as they walk away and I give her the best smile I can muster.

"SAWYER, your phone's ringing."

So answer it, dumbass.

"Sawyer, it's Dane. You want me to grab it?"

I think I manage a thumbs up.

"Hey, drink this, Dane's on his way to come get you."

I lift my head and see that I am... Huh. I'm shitface plastered, sitting at The K. "What?"

Kasey's behind the bar, pushing a drink towards me. "Drink up, man. Dane's on his way to come get you."

"What time is it? Who called Dane?" My mouth tastes like ass, my voice a gravelly inconvenience much like sandpaper across my skin.

"He called ten times and I finally answered it," he explains. "And it's three in the morning."

I grab the glass and down it, bubbles tickling my nose. "What the fuck did I just drink?"

"Homemade hangover cure. You'll thank me in the morning." He laughs, turning to make me a refill.

Maybe it's a play of the drunken mind, but I actually start to feel less fuzzy halfway through the second serving. "You should patent this shit, man. You'd be rich."

"Alka Seltzer and Aleve might not like that. Finish it, your ride's here." He looks behind me and offers a shaky smile. "Hey, boss!"

"Thank you, Kasey," Dane says through clenched teeth. "I'll lock up, go ahead and head out."

"Thanks, Kasey," I mumble, turning to face my angry friend. "What's up?"

"You tell me." He pulls up the stool next to me. "Laney

and I offer to take you out for a drink and you decline, yet you went and got hammered at your place of employment? Your phone broke? It's three in the fucking morning; Laney cried herself to sleep, she was so damn worried!"

"Ugh," I groan, letting my forehead drop on the bar. "I'm fine. I'll apologize to her."

"Yes, you will. Right after you tell me what the fuck is up with you. I'm done, Sawyer," he says firmly, slamming his hand on the bar. "Start talking."

"Can you even remember what you felt like before you met Laney?" I turn my face up to him. "Empty and meaningless and jealous of every happy motherfucker you knew?"

He nods, waiting patiently for me to go on.

"She was there, at the race. Now she thinks I'm shit before we even really meet."

"Who is she?"

"Skipper Stripper, the most beautiful girl on Earth. And her voice, ahhh," I moan, letting my head fall back and my eyes drop closed. "Her fucking voice, those lips—my God. And she's cool! I knew it!"

"Why would she think badly of you?"

I rub my both my hands furiously over my head. "She may have walked up on me gettin' a blowjob."

"At the race?"

"At the race."

33

"Only you." He shakes his head back and forth. "So we're talking about the girl from Parker's party, right?"

"Yeah."

"Sawyer, that was months ago. That's some serious pining time you've put in, bud. What if she's not everything you've built her up to be?"

I turn to him, thinking about it for a minute. "What if she is?"

He stands, giving me a knowing smile. "What if she is? Come on," he pats my shoulder, "let's go home."

Chapter 4

INTERVIEW WITH A VIXEN

—SAWYER—

I'M STACKING GLASSES, "Hurt" by Johnny Cash cranked up, when Dane comes strolling into The K. He reaches for the panel and turns down my soundtrack.

"How's life? Any better?"

"Well, I fired Brock, the douchebag," I grumble. He's lucky I didn't kick his ass while I was at it. "So I moved Kasey to security with a raise and myself behind the bar. Oh," I snap, "and I finally figured out what the fucking fox says, so yeah, I'm golden."

Chuckling, he hands me some papers. "Good to hear. I forgot I had this interview and Laney's waiting for me. Could you do it?"

I skim over the resume he's handed me. "What are we hiring for?"

"Waitress for nights and behind the bar for lunch if she wants it."

"Yeah, I got it," I assure him, not feeling like looking at his happy-in-love face. "Get outta here."

"See ya, brother." He slaps the bar and winks at me.

Why the fuck is he winking at me? God, I hope he gets some…from his WOMAN.

I start to make my way up the stairs to Dane's office, not at all in the mood to play nice through an interview, when Dane calls out and stops me. "Sawyer?"

"Yeah?" I say as I turn. What the fuck does he want now?

"Do you trust yourself?"

"What?" I back down the two steps I'd taken and close the gap between us. "Dude, you're winking at me, asking weird shit…did someone leave glue open around you or what?"

"Do. You. Trust. Yourself?" he repeats, quirking one brow like he does when he's challenging someone.

"Of course I do. Why? Do you trust yourself?"

"Absolutely." He nods. "Which is why when naysayers give me shit or try to plant doubt, I have no problem ignoring them."

I just stare at him, trying to discretely discern the size of his pupils; I honestly think he sniffed glue.

He puts one hand on my shoulder and grins. "You and I, we're go with our gut kinda guys. Don't change."

It takes me a minute to file all that gibberish away and head up to the office. If I thought he'd just thrown me for a loop with that weird talk, then what happens next is a full-out circle around the fucking globe. When I open the door, I'm dumbstruck.

Her name is Emmett L. Young, and I finally know this because that's the name on the resume I'm holding and she is sitting in Dane's office.

I told you—that guy has scary ways of making things happen. And he can wink at me and sniff glue any fucking time he wants, 'cause I kinda love him right now.

"Hi," I manage as I walk further into the office and offer her my hand. "Sawyer Beckett."

She stands with a subdued smirk, her wide, shocked eyes quickly grazing over me. "Emmett Young," she says as she shakes my hand. "Nice to see you again, Mr. Beckett." Her voice pours out like warm honey as she retakes her seat.

"What's the L stand for?"

There's a slight flinch of her face—she's as thrown off by my question as I am. It just came out.

"Louise?"

"You sure?" I flirtingly challenge her as I take a seat

behind Dane's desk.

"I'm sure, uh, it was kinda weird you asked. Not what I was expecting."

"Mine's Landon, also an L. That's why I noticed." That is so not why I noticed. Much like the fact that I know she had cinnamon gum recently, that she tried to cover the small butterfly tattoo behind her left ear with makeup, and that she used to bite her nails but she's trying to let them grow back… I noticed.

"So, um," she fidgets, "this is kinda awkward. If you want to cancel, I'd understand."

"Do you want to cancel?" I refuse to look away, forcing my eyes to stay on hers despite my embarrassment and mortal fear she might say yes.

Her head shakes back and forth rapidly. "No, not at all. I really need this job. Mr. Kendrick said it pays fifteen dollars an hour. That's unheard of for a waitress. It's more than I make at both my current jobs combined."

"All right then, Emmett." God, her name tastes good in my mouth. "Let's talk."

A smile as timid and sweet as a baby deer takes over her gorgeous face and I have to grip the arms of the chair to keep myself in it. Fuck, she's hot. I want to know what she tastes like everywhere. Are her sighs high or low, quiet or loud? Which curls and digs into the sheets first, her fingers or her toes?

"Mr. Beckett?"

"Hmm?" Oh. "Sorry. And call me Sawyer, please."

She nods and looks down, her cheeks slightly flushing. I've never gotten hard just from looking at a girl before, but I could lift this desk off the ground with my dick alone right now.

"Let's get it out of the way, okay? I manage The K, so you'd be working more for me than Dane. Mr. Kendrick, I mean." I cough. "We both know what you saw. Will you be able to take direction from me, respect my authority, after that?"

She crosses her left leg over her right and pulls at the hem of her shirt. "Absolutely."

I lean back in the chair and steeple my fingers under my chin. "Are you sure? I can't have you thinking poorly of me. How can you listen to someone you don't respect? You can't even look at me right now."

Her head snaps up, eyes defiant and locked tight on mine. "It was just a blowjob." She slaps her hand over her mouth, her entire body (every inch I can see, at least) blushing furiously. She lowers her hand and whispers, "I mean, it wasn't a big deal. Not that it wasn't big, it was…oh my God." She drops her head and covers her face with both hands, talking through them. "Please kill me."

My laughter can't be stopped and soon she's joining me, peeking at me through her spread fingers.

"I'm gonna try this one more time." She graces me with her unencumbered face once again. "While your choice of public venue may have been a tad shocking, the fact that you get blowjobs was not, especially from Mariah. It's fine and will not affect my ability to work for you."

"Good," I reply with a straight face. "And for what it's worth, I'm very sorry you witnessed what was not one of my proudest moments."

"Can you tell me about the job?" she asks sweetly, fidgeting just a bit.

She means this job, not that job, right? Right. Pull it together, Beckett.

We sigh together, both relieved that conversation is finally over. I'm still worried what she really thinks of me, but I'll have plenty of time to prove myself to her soon enough.

I briefly describe the job, which isn't complicated, and ask a few questions. "So tell me about what you're doing now, Emmett." I notice exotic dancer is not listed on her resume.

"I wait tables at Granny's Kitchen and hostess at The Crossbow."

Interesting…she's either lying to me or changed jobs and I was looking in all the wrong places. I assure you, I never went looking for my stripper at Granny's Kitchen. Maybe they fired her because she's such a horrific dancer. I can't tell ya how happy the thought makes me.

"So you're 21, right? Do you know how to make drinks?"

"I'll be 22 soon, and yes, I can make almost anything. I've tended some before."

"Are there any hours you can't work?"

"I take one class at Community, Wednesdays from noon to one. Other than that, I'm all yours."

Oh, sweet Emmett, how you taunt me so.

"I'll take all the hours you're willing to give me, any job, any shift."

The anxiety in her voice, along with her imploring eyes, triggers some baser instinct in me. Something is off, my gut telling me this girl needs me. I want her to need me. I already need her, after all.

"That's great," I answer. "I'll keep it in mind. So, how much notice do you need to give your current jobs?"

"Will you think badly of me if I say none? I wouldn't do that here, but I need the increase in pay to start as soon as possible. They only give me about twenty hours a week each anyway. How bad could they possibly miss me?"

"All right then." I smile, letting her know I understand her standpoint.

"Does that mean I'm hired?"

"Yes," I nod, "I'd love to have you."

"Oh, thank you!" She leaps from her chair and runs over to hug me.

Very pleasantly shocked, I'm already standing when she gets to me, more than happy to return her embrace. She's so tiny in my arms, barely reaching the middle of my chest, her arms struggling to reach around me. Far too soon, she pulls back and looks way up at me.

"I'm probably out of line," she starts, her voice soft, "but you don't understand how much this means to me. Thank you so much. I promise to do a great job for you!"

"It's my pleasure, Emmett." I clear my throat and step back. "How about you come in Sunday? We can do all your paperwork and go over a lot of logistical stuff when no one's here to interrupt. I think we'd get more accomplished that way, so you can be on your own faster."

"Perfect. What time?"

"Nine?"

She nods, her huge smile contagious.

"All right, I'll see you then. Let me walk you out." My hand reaches for the small of her back, itching to touch her, but I pull back quickly, actually contemplating my pursuit tactics for perhaps the first time ever. "Unless you're hungry?" Even I can hear the hope in my voice; I'd kill for more time with her. "Can I feed you?"

The sweetest giggle reaches out and sucker punches me in the chest. "No, thank you, I'm fine."

Disappointed our time together is in fact ending, for now, I turn to walk her out, moving slow and battling the hint of a shot-down scowl. Daney meets us at the bottom of the stairs, the blonde of the duo eyeing Emmett anxiously as my boss and awesome friend smiles coyly.

"I'm guessing you're our new waitress? Emmett, is it?" Dane offers his hand.

"Yes, sir, Mr. Kendrick. Thank you so much for the opportunity. I promise you won't be sorry."

"I'm sure I won't. This is Laney, my beautiful girlfriend," he introduces. "Laney, this is Emmett. Sawyer hired her."

Laney looks at him like he's a circus sideshow, probably wondering why he reiterated what she'd already heard. "Hi, Emmett, welcome. You'll love it here. Everyone's wonderful, even my weirdo boyfriend here."

"I can't wait to get started. I'm so excited." Smart girl; breeze right over the owner being weird part with a grin to the girlfriend.

Laney's too sharp for her own good, her eyes smiling at me as she nods at Emmett's response. "I can see you're in good hands. Sawyer will take excellent care of you."

I air kiss her over Emmett's head and laugh when Dane growls audibly and pulls on her arm. "Come on, Emmett," I say to my newest employee, "Mr. Kendrick's gonna blow."

Oh shit. Bad choice of words.

Emmett looks back and up at me, choking down her amusement. "Um, yes, okay. Nice to meet you both."

I hold the front door open and she brushes past me, the

slight hint of some wonderful scent I could never name teasing my nose.

"Red. It's my favorite."

"Wh—"

"You sniff pretty loud," she teases. "My body spray is called Red. Do you like it?"

I gulp pretty loud too, 'cause I hear it myself. "Sorry. Sniffing you probably seems kinda weird." I run a hand over my head and shrug. "But yeah, I like it a lot."

"Thank you. Me too. I'll see you Sunday."

"See you Sunday, Emmett."

TWO DAYS DOWN, two to go until I get to be alone with Emmett Young. It's all I can think about and I'm proud to admit that I feel like an utterly brand new version of myself. I've never looked forward to anything more in my life.

I kinda feel bad, kinda, for every time I gave Dane or Tate or Evan shit about being pussy whipped, thinking they needed to grow a pair. I'm starting to understand a completely foreign word…anticipation.

"What are you smiling about?"

Damn sure not you.

"Hey?" I look behind the girl who spoke, wracking my

brain as much for her name as to how the hell she got in. "Mariah, what're you doing here?"

It can't be more than six o'clock and we're clearly not open, so why is she standing across my bar? Oh, and then there's the whole how the fuck did she know I work here thing, but I snort aloud as soon as I think it—chick wants to find ya, she will.

"That other guy let me in. I told him it was really important." She smirks and I grumble, noting to have a talk with Kasey. "Soo," she props her elbows on the bar top and pushes up on her feet, "I wanted to invite you to my birthday party tomorrow!"

My mouth is open, "now why in the fuck would I—" on the tip of my tongue when a flash of brilliance snags me. Mariah is friends with Emmett.

"Your birthday, huh?" I say. "You having a big blowout with all your friends?"

"Of course!" Her lashes bat feverishly, body leaning closer. "It'll be so much fun. Will you please come?"

No, but I will attend, for the chance to see Emmett. Or is that a bad idea? Will she think I'm there for Blowjob Betty? I could explain I'm not... Jesus, I am so bad at this. I have no idea what to do or not to do—my only known territory is nut and bolt. I'll feel my way through it to spend some time with Emmett, though. She's worth it.

Could I sound more like Evan "Romeo" Allen? Fuck.

45

"Yeah, I could probably swing by. I've got a friend I could bring too." I concentrate on the rag in my hand, wiping the bar aloofly. "What about your friend from the race? She gonna be there? He'd probably like her."

"Emmett?" She laughs viciously. "Probably, I invited her. But they'll be plenty of other girls there for him to choose from. Fun girls."

Sad, really; she can't possibly buy that—that it's more fun to fuck a stranger and be forgotten than to be the one girl who's sought out for so much more than what any girl could give.

I gotta write that shit down! My mind never thinks that profoundly and might never do so again.

"Yeah, okay." I slide her a napkin and dig around under the bar for a pen. "Write down the address and I'll see what I can do. But then I have to get back to work."

As in amscray, oozieflay.

MUSIC IS BLARING, drunks are all over the yard and in the street, and this house is packed sardine tight. No way a neighbor's not gonna call the cops soon. I'm figuring I've got an hour, tops, before this shit show gets busted. I've got to find Emmett fast.

I scramble through the droves of bodies, only pausing on dark heads of hair to scan the faces attached. No luck in the front, so I find the kitchen and stand in the farthest corner of it. This spot offers me a straight view of the only two doors into this place: front and sliding glass to the backyard. If she walks in, I'll see her.

One glimpse, a single, "hey, funny seeing you here," is all I need to tide me over until Sunday. I can taste my anxiousness.

Thirty minutes later, that stank flavor in my mouth is disappointment, turning rapidly into the hint of vomit as the birthday girl spots me. Awesome.

"Why is your fine ass hiding in the corner?" she slurs, blowing vodka breath in my face as she pretends to lose her balance and falls into my chest.

"Easy there." I grip her shoulders loosely and place her upright and off me, immediately removing my hands. I really do hate to lie flat out, so I stare at the floor as I force out the necessary bullshit. "I'm watching for my friend, we're gonna have to go soon. I was hoping he could meet your girl, Emily was it? She here?"

"Emm-ett," she annunciates. "No, she couldn't come. But where is he?" She looks around, drunker than I thought or simply missing the fact that she has no clue who she'd be looking for, even if he was actually with me. "I could hook him up with any other girl here, then you and I could—"

I latch on to her wrist, stopping her hand's progression up my chest. I've heard all I need to—Emmett's not here and she's not coming. There's 47 minutes of my life I'm never getting back. "You know what? Everybody's here to see you. Why don't you go be the birthday girl and I'll go look for him. K?" I end on the low "talk to them like they're a child" voice that works every time.

Such as right now.

"M-kay." She grins, twisting her hips back and forth. "But come find me later. You can spend the night with me."

"Go on." I turn her, giving her a gentle push forward. "It's your party, have some fun."

She's made it all of five steps before I've slid out the back door and jogged to my bike.

Make that 54 minutes down the fucking drain.

Chapter 5

There's Something About

Emmett

—SAWYER—

"WHERE ARE MY KEYS? Fuck!" Four never-ending days, the longest of which was that dumbass, waste of time party where she didn't show, I'd waited, and I oversleep? You have got to be kidding me!

My head jerks at the sound of keys jingling, and I see Laney dangling them from the end of her finger. With her other hand, she offers me a thermos. "Drink this coffee on the way or you'll be grumpy."

I snag both items, frozen in shock that Laney is both

awake and efficient this early in the morning. "And chew this gum after, smelling coffee breath sucks." She shivers. "I don't know how you people drink that crap. She leans in and kisses my cheek. "Just be yourself, Sawyer. That's more than enough."

"If Dane didn't adore you," I wrap her in a hug, "I'd—"

"Get your ass kicked?" Dane rumbles, appearing around the corner. "Go train your girl and let go of mine."

"Yeah, okay, I'll see you guys later."

She's standing out front when I pull up, the slight breeze blowing her dark hair up to tease her face, giving me a cheerful wave.

Hurriedly parking the bike, I jog up to her. "I'm sorry I'm late. You been waiting long?"

"No, not long at all. Good morning."

"Good morning, Emmett." Is it ever. "Shall we?" I ask, unlocking and holding open the door for her. When she passes, I inhale my dose of Red and then turn to lock the door behind us. "I doubt you'll ever open, but just in case, the lights are here." I begin flipping the switches one by one, bringing The K to life. "Let me show you the break room. We can get you a locker and you can put away your bag."

She walks beside me, her eyes taking in every nuance of the club. "I really like the layout and décor. Such a modern, trendy feel. How long have you worked here?"

"Since the day it opened. I moved here with Dane from

Connecticut. Here we go," I open one of the unclaimed lockers, "you can put your stuff in here for now. I'll grab you a new padlock when we go upstairs."

"Thank you." She takes her purse off her shoulder and sets it inside. "Do you mind if I use the ladies' room before we get started?"

"Of course not, let me show you where it is. We have separate ones for patrons and employees. You can use either, and we keep them super clean, but I'd suggest the employee one all the same."

There's her giggle again, a soft and dainty sound that I already adore. "Thanks for the tip."

"Speaking of tips, we don't share here. What you make is yours."

"And the fifteen an hour?" She bites her lip, eyes tearing up.

"Yeah."

She pounces into me like a puma, hugging the breath from me. "Oh my God, thank you! That's just…amazing!"

I rub her back, soaking up the clean, crisp scent of her hair. "I'm glad you're happy, Emmett." And I am. Glad isn't even the right word. For some reason, making this sweet angel's day has instantly become my priority.

"I really need the ladies' room now," she says with a laugh. "I'm so happy I could tinkle!"

I laugh, really laugh, at that. "Well, we wouldn't want

that. Come on." I usher her through the hall with a hand to her back.

Once she's tinkled, we head up to Dane's office to do her paperwork and I can't help but ask, "So, how've you been these last few days? Do anything fun?" Cause you missed a certain birthday party.

"No, nothing fun. Read a book or two, wrote a paper. You know." She shrugs.

I don't know...and I don't know where you were that night and I want to. But for once, I bite my tongue before blurting out the complete truth. Something tells me mentioning being at that girl's party is not a good idea.

Her voice pulls me from my haze and I focus back on her across the desk where's she's been filling out forms, her little tongue peeking out in concentration. "Oh, I guess you need my cards. They're in my purse." She sets down her pen and starts to stand.

"I'll go get it." I jump up, trying to be a gentleman. "You can keep working on the rest of the stack."

She studies me, twisting her lip. "That's awfully nice of you?" she almost asks, as though surprised.

Why would it surprise her that I'm a nice guy? Ah, back to the BJ—she thinks I'm a dog.

"Emmett," I hitch myself up on the corner of the desk, "I am a nice guy. I'm single and she offered. Have you ever done anything you regret? A chance was there so I took it kind of thing?"

A glance to the left, right, finally back to me. "Yes, I have."

"Okay, so you understand. I'm not depraved, Emmett, I'm young and unattached. First impressions aren't always the right ones. At least not all-telling anyway."

For instance, you don't seem like a stripper.

"As a matter of fact," I continue, "you seemed so sure and cocky then, but the sweet, shy violet I see now seems more like who you really are?" I raise my brows in question, challenging her.

"Sometimes you have to own the situation or it will own you," she replies. "Never let 'em see you sweat, right? I didn't want to go to a rowdy race, or walk up on typical Mariah, but I did," she shrugs, "so I went with it."

So did I, I think to myself, but decide not to say it. "I'll be right back." I hear her start to say something as I leave the room, but she must think better and stops herself. I want so badly to turn around and rush to her, to pull her out of that chair and make her forget everything but right now. Instead...I go get her purse.

She doesn't bring it up again when I return and the rest of the morning goes smoothly, me rambling out boring instructions, her soaking it all in with enthusiastic questions and answers. I have no doubt, from her exuberance over HR bullshit, that she'll do a fantastic job.

Here and there, through the natural flow of conversation, I find out a few new facts about her and offer some of my own in return. She's so easy to be around, with an ease to her voice that seeps through your pores and soothes your soul. I'm enraptured, inundating her with information just to hear her laugh or whisper a small gasp across her lips, both so intoxicating that I don't even care that she now knows I take blatant advantage of free sample stands and am not above wearing mismatched socks with my boots. She thought both those facts were funny, not weird, and shared that she refuses to write in red ink (something about everything written in red is bad news) and still has all her sticker albums from when she was a kid.

At one, I ask her if she's ready to call it a day. Her coloring has changed to a pasty white and the speed of her gait has slowed significantly.

"Are you feeling okay?"

She sighs and drops in the nearest chair. "I haven't eaten in while is all. Can we take a quick break for lunch?"

Well shit, I've been so selfishly basking in her little noises that I've starved her! "Emmett, you should have said something. I'm sorry. I'll go grab us something. What do you want?"

"No, no, I have something in my bag. Let me—"

I saw her tiny purse; she'd be lucky to get a fucking cracker pack in there. "Then what am I gonna eat?" I smile at her. "I'm going anyway. Please let me get you something. My treat."

"A salad would be great, thank you."

"Salad it is." I tap the end of her nose instinctively and regret it when she flinches. "I'm sorry, I didn't think before—"

"I'm just hungry," her smile is placating, "you don't have to apologize. In fact," her eyes scrutinize me cooly, "you've already said sorry to me more times than anyone ever has. Are you always this polite?"

"I don't know." My head bows and I rub the back of my neck, peering back up at her. "Maybe I'm overdoing it a bit. Kinda like you thanking me." I pop my brows, questioning her with a cocky smile.

A brilliant idea of how to get to know this girl even more without begging on my hands and knees for any information she'll spare forms in my head. "I'll make a deal with you," I say. "Every time you say thank you, you have to tell me something about yourself."

Her mouth twists as she considers it. "Fine, but same goes for you every time you apologize."

Then there's that comfortable silence where her deep green eyes widen in sincerity and search mine for the same. She'd make a great interrogator; no one could hide from that look or that face.

"All right," I agree with a nod and pull out my keys. "I'll

be right back. You fine to stay here for a minute?"

She looks around hesitantly. "Oh, um, sure."

"I'll lock the door behind me. Unless you want to come with me?"

"On your motorcycle?"

"Yeah." I give her a knowing grin. Chicks can't resist a bike.

She shakes her head rapidly. "No, thank you. I'll stay here."

What? I try to hide the shocked disappointment in my voice. "Okay, I'll be right back then."

"I snore."

"Huh?"

"I said no, thank you, so I owe you a fact. I snore," she shrugs. "Not like lumberjack snore or anything, more like a teeny tiny," she holds up her thumb and finger in measure, "sound other than breathing."

Most adorable thing I've ever heard in my life. It takes strength I didn't know I possessed to only chuckle and keep walking. "Good to know. Be right back."

—Emmett—

A BREAK, FINALLY. New, fresh, focused. My chance to really make a dent. Thank you, aligned stars; thank you, ray of light shining down upon me. Take it, scared girl. Take the chance to do great things. Pave your path and walk it, head high.

"What's that?"

"Oh!" I shriek, startled and frankly, scared. "My God, I didn't hear you come in."

"I'm sorry, I didn't mean to scare you." His kind face now wears a frown of remorse.

"It's my journal. I like to free write; sometimes I get lost in it and forget the world around me." I quickly tuck the small spiral notepad in my back pocket. "You owe me a fact."

He chuckles, a deep, mesmerizing sound, and rubs his chin. "I guess I do. Okay, let's see..." he ponders, "I have seven tattoos."

"Seven?" My eyes search frantically over what of him I can see... nothing. "That's a lot of tattoos." I have to find as many ways as possible to get him to apologize. This man and the mystery rolling off him is my new fascination. I could so easily breathe him in and let myself become intoxicated. This enigma becoming my reality, but no…no regrets, Emmett.

"I got you ranch." He hands me my salad and unwraps my silverware for me. "Everybody likes ranch, right?"

Forgive me for the trickery.

"Eh, it's okay. I'll eat around it."

"Oh shit, I'm sorry, you didn't say, so I guessed."

"Why seven?"

He looks at me, puzzled at first, but when he sees the coy smirk of my own, realization hits and a grin the likes of which I've never dreamt catches up to his dancing sapphire eyes. "You like ranch, don't you?"

I nod, biting back a giggle. "Why seven?"

"All right, sneaky girl, but remember you switched it up when I start deciding what facts you get to reveal."

"Fair enough." I take a bite, full of ranch and delicious. "Mmm, so good." I wipe my mouth. "Thank you."

"Oh, you are sooo welcome, Miss What Were You Writing In That Little Notepad?"

Well shit, the teacher became the student.

"Free writing. Whatever falls out. I put the pen on the paper and go numb. Sometimes I can't even make sense of what it says."

"Do you write anything else? Poetry?"

"I dabble." I take another bite to excuse myself from saying more.

He lets my answer settle in, nodding as his mind wraps

around it. "You know that game in school, Heads Up Seven Up?"

I shake my head no since I've never heard of it and continue my assault on my salad.

"Seven people go to the front of the room and everyone else puts their head down with their eyes closed and their thumb poking up. The teacher says go, and the seven chosen ones go tap a thumb. When everyone's done, the class lifts their heads and if your thumb got tapped, you try to guess who did it. If you're right, you get to go up and be one of the thumb tappers next round."

Mouth full, I wave my hand for him to continue.

"I hated that fucking game. No one ever picked me. So, I like to do things in seven, kinda like my big "fuck you" to all of them."

"No one ever picked you? Not once?"

"Nope," he pops his answer, refusing to meet my eyes.

"Why not? Were you a bully, a mean kid?"

"Not at all." He pauses for only a second, seemingly instinctually. "I was a poor kid."

I picture Sawyer as a sweet little boy anxiously waiting, with his thumb up, praying that would be the round someone finally picked him. Kids are so cruel, and yes, that hurt sticks with you forever—Sawyer was the proof of that. I don't even realize tears are welling up in my eyes until Sawyer reaches over and gently rubs my arm with his timid fingers.

I didn't flinch. Odd.

"Hey, don't cry for me, angel. It's not a big deal; just bullshit kids. It's stupid actually, a weird hang-up I have. Shhh," he dips his head to catch my watery eyes and pleads with me, "dry those eyes. You're breaking my heart."

"I would have." I sniffle, somewhat embarrassed. About to cry in front of the boss on training day, nice, Emmett. "I would have picked you. I promise."

"You think so, huh? And how can you be so sure?"

"Because my friends were in my books. We'd have been the perfect pair. I could've tapped your thumb at least once a day and told you wonderful stories of the lands we could disappear to where everyone was nice to everyone. And you, you could have said you thought my glasses and buck teeth were beautiful and helped me climb that huge tree behind the library. That thing was so big and tall and strong and all I ever wanted to do was disappear way up in it and read."

"Emmett?"

"And I'm not a crybaby, I swear. I don't know what came over me, really."

"Emmett?"

I lock on his gaze, no other words needed from me. Of one thing I'm sure; this is the part where he talks and I listen. One certain look from this man, the one he's giving me now, makes that crystal clear.

"I'm going to kiss those beautiful lips of yours."

Don't let him, Emmett. Say no, turn your head. You need this job and things will get real messy real quick if you kiss him.

"Now?" I squeak, obviously forgetting the pep talk I just finished having with myself.

"Right fucking now." He leans his face into mine and brushes his words across my lips. "I'd rather die than wait another second. Are you gonna kill me or kiss me?" His pools of midnight blue flick nervously waiting for my answer, which never comes. "I'll take my chances," he grumbles and then kisses me. No, not kisses me. He reaches in and steals every ounce of strength I had left with his soft, strong lips. It's slow and tastes like all that I can't have and I whimper. "Emmett," he opens his eyes and sucks as he slowly pulls away, "you may have just been the death of me anyway."

"Sawyer, I—"

"You what?" he husks out, face still very close to mine.

"I need this job," I whisper, staring straight into his eyes, hoping like hell mine are conveying to him all I can't say. "I'm sorry and not sorry at the same time, but that can't happen again."

"Why not?"

"The fact that I work for you should be reason enough. The other pertinent tidbit, the fact that I barely know you, should excuse me from any other explanations, not that I'm even saying there are any."

"There are." He sounds positive; smart guy.

"Maybe." I again try to plead with my gaze only for him to leave it be.

"Are you sick?"

"No, I'm not dying, Sawyer."

"Are you married, in the witness protection program, and/or scheduled to have a sex change operation in the near future?"

"No," I snicker, unable to stop it.

"Then I'm liking my odds." He tries for another kiss, but I stop him with a finger against his lips.

"Eat your lunch, boss."

Chapter 6

MISSING THE SCENT OF A

WOMAN

—SAWYER—

"WHERE ARE YOU GOING? We're doing Crew Night here." Laney catches me before I make it out the door.

"I have to work tonight."

"No, you don't. I specifically had Dane check the schedule before I planned it." She pouts, hands on hips in a classic Laney pose. "David works tonight."

"Who the fuck is David?"

"The other guy," she argues. "As in, not you."

"David? Do you mean Kasey?"

"Okay," she holds out her hands, palms up, and shakes her head, "Kasey works."

"I think I'm caught up. And Kasey bounces, which means I tend bar. Dane knows this."

"I know what?"

Where the fuck is he always hiding that he keeps popping up like a creeper? This place isn't that big.

"That I work even when Kasey does. Gidge is mad I'm missing Crew Night."

"Baby," he wraps his arms around her, "leave him be. He's smitten."

"No!" Her jaw drops. "Are you really? You?"

"Fuck no," I laugh mockingly. "It's her first night on the floor. I need to make sure she's all right. That's my job." Truth be told, I've thought of nothing but the taste and feel of her kiss since it happened and how I can make it happen again. I've retold her cute little stories in my head a thousand times, recapturing the image of her big, curious eyes alight with fascination as I told her mine.

Let the record show—I knew the minute I saw her that she was amazing and I was right. Oh, and I've definitely edged precariously close to actually growing a vagina. I can't help it and, to tell the truth, I don't want to help it; I fucking like her. A lot. I think about talking to her as much, if not more, than I think about sliding into her sweet body. Even I know that means something.

Dane scoffs into Laney's neck, which he's currently eating. "Doing a helluva job, man. Very thorough."

"All right, go on, Saw Saw, be happy. But next Thursday night there are no excuses." Laney points at me and glares. "You will spend time with us."

"Promise." I air kiss her. "Have fun tonight. You too, Daney."

He flips me off, never lifting his head.

Evan and Whitley are coming up the walk as I'm heading down it. "Hey, stranger!" Evan gives me a bro hug and then I kiss Whitley's cheek. "Where you been?"

"Same place I've always been; here, work, or school. How are you guys?"

"Real good. Are you not staying tonight?" Whitley pops out her bottom lip.

"Nah, I gotta work. But I'll be there next Thursday, I swear. This fool taking care of you?" I punch Evan's shoulder when I ask her.

"You know he is," she snuggles into his side, "and I'm taking care of him right back."

All right, I've had enough. I'm starting to get a fucking toothache.

"I'm late, so I'll see you later." I start walking and wave behind my head. "Thursday!"

I adore my friends, but if one more of them blocks my path to Emmett, I may lose my shit. If you're not part of the solution, you're part of the problem, people! I haven't seen her in three days, and...I miss her? Shit, I really do. I want to talk to her, ask what she's been doing, what does she need, did she miss me too?

At least two traffic laws are broken by the time I pull up to at The K in perfect time to see Emmett climbing out of a cab. The driver watches her walk away and I'm making my way to claw his fucking eyes out when Emmett steps in front of me.

"Hi!"

I give Shit Sack a glare, memorizing his cab number, then lower my eyes to her. "Hey, Shorty, your car broke down?"

"I don't have a car. And I'm not that short," she punches my chest, "you're just really tall."

She is that short, but I like it. She's tiny and precious...and not taking a taxi ever again.

"You don't have a car? You must spend a fortune on cabs." I open the door for her, using one hand on her back to guide her in. As she brushes by me, I take my sniff, immediately missing my dose of Red. Did she forget or is she out?

"Not really. The bus runs everywhere I need to go but here. The raise in pay more than makes it worth it, though."

I give Kasey a quick nod as we walk in, still listening to her. "I'll meet you at the bar in a minute if you wanna put your stuff up."

"K." She hurries toward the break room, turning back once to catch me watching.

I'm not ashamed I was caught gawking, but I'm curious as hell what made her look back. Could it be possible that I dented that fucking wall around her? A big enough dent that I can lecture her on how I feel about her mode of transportation?

Yeah, probably too soon.

Stomping up the stairs, I take deep breaths and start shooting Laney texts. If she took a taxi here, that means she'll take one home. At the end of her shift. At two in the fucking morning. Hell. No.

Sawyer: Do you know a spray or perfume or wtf ever called Red?

Sawyer: How much for that Accord you never drive?

I'm pacing, watching my phone like it holds the meaning of life. The thought of that angelic creature in a cab at 2 am being eye fucked by a greasy driver like the one who dropped her off has me wanting to smash shit.

Laney: Bath & Body Works. Y?

Sawyer: Where's that?

She does know who texted her, right? She may as well have answered in Chinese.

Laney: The mall.

Sawyer: Thnx G.

Laney: **SMITTEN. I think it's great. Bring her Thurs?**

Sawyer: We'll see.

Dane: If you need a car, it's yours.

Sawyer: I need a car. Take $300/month from my check.

Dane: Or you can have it. Her car a POS?

Scary fuck. He's freakier than that Copperfield guy on TV. He's a lot like me; when we decide it's ours, God help anyone who stands in our way or "tells us how." Except he's much worse and damn near crazy with it, so I know I don't have to explain to him why the bold play so early in the game. In fact, Dane's probably wondering what took me so long. I can almost hear him screaming "interweave all the fuck up in there and conquer!" at his phone.

Sawyer: Or non-existent.

Dane: **All yours. I'll give Laney the key. Do not demand sexual favors in return for helping her.**

Sawyer: **No? Damn, Plan B then. Lil credit, fuckwad?**

Dane: He was kidding. Love you! xo Gidge

Sawyer: One more favor?

Dane: Anything

Sawyer: **Will you go get the Red and maybe a bag? I'll owe you.**

Dane: **Yes! We can give it to her Thurs. night!**

Or not, crazy woman.

Sawyer: Easy Gidge...we'll see.

Dane: Go talk to your own woman. I'm taking mine back.

Sawyer: Last thing...Dane?

Dane: It's me

Sawyer: When did you first catch yourself missing Laney?

Dane: Remember the night we met her and B and they ran into the bathroom to strategize their exit?

I think back...was that before or after Laney threatened to take a bat to Whit? I shake my head and chuckle, knowing it doesn't matter.

Sawyer: Yeah

Dane: Then

Yes! Mine was three days, his three minutes. So even if I'm a whipped pup, tail wagging, with his tongue hanging out, Dane's worse!

"HEY," I SAY as I sneak up behind her.

She jumps and spins around to face me. "You have got to quit that!"

"Sorry. Listen, I'll drive you home tonight, okay?"

She tilts her head in the way I've seen her do before, trying to figure me out. "Why would you do that?"

"Cabs aren't safe, especially at 2 am."

"Oh, stop. I'm fine. But thank you for caring."

"Why won't you let me drive you home? What are you afraid of? And don't even think about not answering, because you just thanked me."

"And you said sorry." One eyebrow goes up, challenging me.

"Driving ya' home."

She growls and grabs my hand, pulling me into the break room. Looking around and finding it empty, she starts in. "I need you to quit being so considerate and irresistible. This," she flicks her finger between us, "can never happen. I'd love nothing more than to fall into you and get lost, but it can. Not. Happen. I need this job, so go find Mariah and quit making me feel special!"

"Whoa there, Shorty, simmer down." I grab her shirt and tug her back when she attempts to get the last word and storm out. "Look at me."

"No," she answers softly, facing the wall.

"Emmett, please turn around and look at me."

"Sawyer, I'm not what you think I am. Let it go and be my friend. I could really use one." She pulls away and I let her, watching as she walks out. Her shoulders are slumped, and there's no pep in her step.

I can't leave it like this, plus I owe her a fact.

"When I was eight, I wanted to be a cowboy!" I call out behind her, waiting.

She stops on a dime, remaining stone still and facing away from me. "When I was eight, I wanted to move to Green Gables."

I'll worry about figuring out where the fuck Green Gables is later; right now, I have a more pressing question. "I think you're fascinating and beautiful and as unused to whatever this is as me. That's what I think you are. Tell me I'm wrong."

I wait as she remains standing in the same spot. There's not the slightest movement for long seconds, before she finally walks away without answering.

Not what I think she is? Does she think I care that she is, or was, or what the fuck ever, a stripper?

We've got about thirty minutes before we open and I'd say some warm up music is exactly what we need. I walk out of the break room and over to the sound panel, turning up the volume before starting the song. I want to see her face with the first unmistakable riff.

"Shook Me All Night Long" comes through the speakers in every room, since I don't know where she's run and hidden. Angus is already singing about American thighs before she comes around the corner, eyes bugged out of her head.

When she finds me across the room, our eyes meet and I mouth to her "I don't care" and crook my finger for her to come to me. She shakes her head violently and disappears again, full speed. Dammit! Not the reaction I was hoping for at all.

Out of nowhere, Kasey saunters over and turns down the music. "You know," he slaps one hand on my shoulder, "you can chase and chase a butterfly and never catch them. But if you stand still, they may decide to land right on you." He walks away whistling the AC/DC track, seemingly pleased with his own philosophical wisdom.

Butterfly? If he's gotten close enough to see behind her ear, that's too fucking close and I will lay him out like carpet. Her secret tattoo…that she didn't mention when we'd discussed mine. I wonder if she's hiding any more…and when I can find them.

I decide to leave her be for a bit, seriously contemplating Kasey's advice. We open to a line and I'm busy, but not so much so that I'm not keenly aware of her non-appearance. She only comes out of hiding after the crowd really starts picking up, probably thinking all the bodies will shroud her. But she has to order from me at the bar, so soon we're sharing awkward silences, far louder than the pulsing beat, as she waits for me to fill her tray each visit.

How long does it take a butterfly to land? She's not even talking to me now and it's driving me insane! Desperate times call for desperate measures, so I initiate plan You Better Talk to Me, Woman and wait for the effects of my brilliant masterminding to kick in.

She slides the glass my way a few minutes later. "This got sent back."

Imagine that—I made the perfect you're not in Alabama Slammer...with grapefruit juice. "Really? Huh. Okay. I'm sorry, I'll fix it." She looks down at her nails, far too sweet for the "hurry up, I'm put out" façade she's attempting. "Emmett, did you hear me? I said I'm sorry, I'll fix it."

Ask for your fact, Angel, don't leave me hanging.

"If you mess with my drinks, it'll hurt my tips, Sawyer."

"I. Said. I. Was. Sorry."

"I. Heard. You."

I slap both hands down on the bar and lean over, right into her face. "You agreed to the game. Play with me, Shorty, please."

She sighs, defeated, and rolls her eyes. "Where'd you see me dance?"

There she is. Relieved, I lean closer, resting my forehead on hers, and she lets me. "At a buddy's bachelor party. You were terrible at it."

She laughs softly. "Thank you, I'll take that as a compliment. Not really my thing, obviously."

"You're welcome and it was a compliment. Do you do it anymore?"

She shakes her head back and forth, those bewitching green eyes staring at me. "I need my orders."

"I'm driving you home."

"I figured."

I smile, happy we're back to talking, even happier she's going to let me give her a ride home and ecstatic that she and I have a cohesiveness all our own; it's just a matter of finding the moment and a few words to put us back to good. I finish filling her tray, all made right this time, then pull out my phone. I shoot Dane a quick text that I really need the car tonight and slide it back in my pocket. I don't have to wait for a reply; I know he'll come through for me.

The rest of the shift goes more amicably than it started, Emmett gifting me with a few sentences or a smile every time she comes back up. By last call, she looks dead on her feet, but still breathtaking, and I can't wait to be alone with her. We all pitch in to wipe tables and stack chairs, then I tell everyone they can head out, which will leave Emmett and I alone while I finish drawer counts.

She flops down on a bar stool in front of me and slides off her shoes. "I don't think I've ever been so tired in my life," she groans, lifting one leg and starting to give herself a foot rub. "Totally worth it, though. I made over a hundred dollars tonight."

"Emmett, you want to walk out with us?" Jessica stops and asks on her way out with Kasey and Darby.

"No, I'm okay, but thank you. I have to wait for Sawyer to finish counting so he can give me a ride home."

Darby's face wrinkles up. "Why would he do that? I'll give you a ride home. Where do you live?"

Ahh, isn't that nice? Fuck no! Darby's do-gooder act isn't fooling me. If she thinks cock blocking Emmett is gonna get me to fuck her again, she's got another thing coming, or not coming, I suppose. I quit it almost before I even got done hitting it, a regret I live with every shift she works.

"Briarwood Apartments, right off Daline," Emmett answers her.

Oh fucking hell, she lives in CJ's complex? That place is...well, saying it's sleazy would be like saying Miley Cyrus has kinda lost her damn mind. This keeps getting worse; she was going to take a cab at 2 am to Briarwood. My smokin' lil' butterfly has got herself one helluva life.

"That's on my way." Darby tips her head. "Come on."

Emmett turns back to me and flashes a smile full of either sarcasm or defiance, which one, I'm not quite sure. "Looks like I've got a ride. Goodnight, Sawyer."

"Night," I grit out, giving Darby the stink eye.

Once they're all filed out, I finish the count, my mood souring with every minute. Darby better not run her mouth about us, it was over a damn year ago...just get Emmett home safe, watch her walk to the door. What if she doesn't? That neighborhood, the late hour...I'm up the stairs before I know it, grabbing the folder with her name. The beauty of management—access to the personnel files.

I program her phone number into mine, assigning it the perfect ringtone, then dial. "Hello?"

"Emmett? Hey, it's Sawyer."

"Hi?"

"Hey." You already fucking said that, dumbass. Jesus, why not fly a banner over her house that says, "I never call girls"?

She fills the painfully awkward gap in exhilarating conversation with a giggle. "Sawyer, did you need something?"

"I, ah, wanted to make sure you got home all right. It's late and all, so did you make it okay? Inside?"

"I'm sliding my key in the lock as we speak. You're too sweet, thank you."

"Go ahead and get inside, turn on the light. Everything look in order? Nothing out of place, right?"

"No, looks the same as when I left it. I'm fine."

I sigh, relief flooding me all at once. The thought of something happening to Emmett makes it hard to breathe, the protective instinct burning in my chest unlike anything I've felt before, certainly different that the protectiveness I feel for my female friends. I love Laney and the girls and I'd take a bullet for them, but with them it feels like instinct and with Emmett…it feels like will.

"Okay, wanted to make sure. I can let you go."

And I just lied to her—I don't think I could let her go if I tried.

"Goodnight, Sawyer," she whispers.

"Sweet dreams, Shorty."

Chapter 7

DRIVING MISS EMMETT

-*Emmett*-

NINETY-THREE! I roll my eyes at the thermostat on the wall and try to call my landlord for the tenth time; voicemail again.

Opening the windows might have actually made it worse as this is late summer in Georgia. I'm drained, dizzy, and nauseous from the stifling heat and lack of moving air in my box of an apartment. This can't possibly be good for me, but I have no one to call, nowhere to go...not that I have the energy left to walk to the bus stop anyway.

The knock on the door sounds like angels singing—maybe it's the landlord! I fling open the door, ready to tear into his ass or faint, whichever comes first. Faint, definitely faint, becomes the obvious choice as I take in the sight of one very large, very sexy Sawyer Beckett leaned up against the door frame.

"Morning, glory," he says with a smirk, chipping away at my resolve with those teasing, deep blue eyes and perfect white teeth uncovered by a beaming smile.

"Um, morning?" I'm sure my face expresses my confusion at his presence.

"Can I come in?"

I do a mental check, cataloging in my head. Unless he sneaks away from me and goes digging through my closet, we're good. "Be my guest." I put out my arm and step aside. "Hope you like saunas."

He steps in and immediately feels it, turning to me with an angry scowl. "It feels like hell in here, Emmett. Pretty sure my eyebrows are singed. What the fuck?"

"The air's broken and my landlord won't answer." I blow the hair out of my eyes, a complete waste of effort since it's plastered to my forehead with sticky sweat. "Don't!" I hold up my hand when his mouth pops open. "Dressing me down won't fix it. What are you doing here, anyway? How'd you know which apartment was mine?"

"Brought you a car, checked your resume, get your shit." He stomps over to the window, slamming it closed and attempting to lock it, figuring out quickly the latch is broken. He turns his head slightly, one eye glaring at me. "Your air doesn't work and your window doesn't lock. Lemme guess, you have to walk down to a well and pail out water?"

I glare at him. "Not helping." So it's not the Hilton, but it's mine.

He's clomping through the place like an angry bear, flipping light switches on and off, grumbling something about "lazy slumlords" when I step in front of him.

"Stop it. You're making me feel worse than I already do."

"I'm not trying to, but shit, woman, no dishwasher, no microwave." He sighs, clamping a hand on the back of his neck. "Where do you do your laundry?"

I shrug. "Laundromat."

"Emmett, I really don't want to lose my shit in front of you, but so help me God, woman, if you do not grab whatever you need in the next five seconds and head to the door, I'm gonna do it for you."

It's official, I'm suffering heat exhaustion. I'm obviously hallucinating him talking to me like that. Who does he think he is?

I'm still trying to figure it out, frozen in place in open-mouthed shock, when my arm is damn near ripped from its socket.

"Got your purse and phone, that about it?" he asks as he pulls me toward the door.

As much as I don't want to let him boss me around and

get any bright ideas that I might actually be the kind of girl who lets a man tell her what to do, I really don't want to stay in this hot box another second. "That's it," I concede, still at odds with my own cooperativeness.

He ushers me out the door with his hand, so large it spans it almost completely, on my back. "How long were you in there like that?"

I shrug again, complacent and exasperated. "Since I woke up. I'm sure the landlord will call me back soon. I would've been fine."

He takes his hand from my back and lifts all my heavy hair off my neck, the fresh air on my overheated skin refreshing. When he leans over and blows on it, I'm no longer hot, but covered in goosebumps, chills coursing through me. "You have anything you need to do today?" he asks in between blowing upon my neck and shoulders.

"No," I hum, immersed in every wonderful sensation his breath is causing.

"Okay, let's go." He leads me down the stairs to a shiny red four-door car that looks brand new.

"Did you get a new car?" I ask him, thankful he's not about to try and force me on his bike.

"Actually," he grins, digging a set of keys from his pocket and dangling them in front of me, "it's yours. Will you give me a ride?"

"No, no, no." I shake my head, backing away from the

keys like they're a live snake. "I'm not accepting a car from you! It's too much and I'm not a charity case. I told you not to get too close, Sawyer! Would you buy your other friends a car?"

"Simmer down, Shorty, wouldn't you trust your other friends? Gotta say, you don't seem to trust me any more now than the day we met. I didn't buy you the car. It's Dane's, on lease, until you've saved enough to get one." By this time he has boxed me in against the side of the car, my back against the warm metal as I look up and up into his eyes.

"Lease? I can't afford to pay to rent a car, Sawyer. You have to stop. You can't—" Too frustrated to even finish a thought, I let my head sag, tears welling up in my eyes.

In another life, I could have a great friend who happens to makes me feel funny in every part of my body with his endearing, hot as hell, sexy way…but this is this life. I'm no fool. Men don't arrange for your job, a car, or check to see if you made it home all right if they don't want something more.

And I have nothing more to give. At least not anything anyone in their right mind would want. I have to tell him, to stop this madness before I hurt an innocent man who doesn't deserve the pain my life can bring.

"Sawyer, I appreciate it, I really do, but—"

He leans me back over the car, using his sizable body to make my own do his bidding. "Okay, don't panic on me,

Shorty. We'll talk about the car later. For now, let's get out of the heat, get you in some air, and figure everything else out later. Sound reasonable?"

His nose brushes the end of mine, his huge, finely-toned arms surrounding me in comfort. Nothing could get past Sawyer, and for once I pinpoint one of the new feelings that's been stirring ever since I met him—I feel safe.

"Fine, but it's not my car. You drive."

"My pleasure," he whispers in my ear before standing back to release me and taking my hand to help me in the car.

"Where are we going?" I ask him as we zip down the highway.

This car is very nice, better than anything I can ever hope to have, and Sawyer looks like my knight in shining armor behind the wheel of it. Behind those sunglasses, I know his eyes are full of pity, brimming with sympathy for the scattered woman he sees when he looks at me.

He turns to me, his full mouth pulling up at one side. He has to quit doing that. And grow long, gross hair, rather than tempting me with that dark, cropped look. And take out that damn eyebrow ring, you wicked man. And what is the name of that cologne you can't stop wearing— Tempt Emmett Off

Track in a bottle?

"My house, that cool?"

"No, no that is not cool. Sawyer, I can't go to your house."

He chuckles...he has to stop doing that, too! It's a mesmerizing sound, like my ears have been blessed by the gods, my nerve endings plugged into electricity.

"And why is that, Short stuff?"

Nicknames—the devil's tool, created to help men make woman feel special. A clever word or phrase they created only for you, because of you, having devastating effects on your ability to walk, talk and or breathe regularly. I gotta get out of this car, far away from him, my will power is waning and my mind is racing, succumbing to his trickery.

"Because," I groan, pinching the bridge of my nose, willing the tears to stay at bay.

"Because why?"

"Because you..." Deep breath, Emmett. "You—I—we can't. Take me to The K. I'll do inventory or something. Or the mall. I'll people watch in the air conditioning."

"Not happening."

"Yes, Sawyer!" I yell, tired from the heat, overwhelmed by my thoughts, and just plain beat down by life. "Please don't do this! Don't be so goddamn wonderful, reminding me every time you smile at me, and rescue me, and do something amazing for me, that I can't have you!"

He reaches over, taking my small hand into his own large one, swallowing it up all at once like everything else about him, swallowing me whole, taking over, taking control, making my small stature and weakness seem like an attribute, a compliment to his differences. "You can have me," he whispers onto the back of my hand, placing a kiss behind his words. "All you have to do is take me."

"You can't possibly mean that." I sigh, pulling my hand from his. "You don't even know me. I-I have to tell you something, Sawyer, and then you'll understand."

"I've never meant anything more." The car stops in front of what I'm guessing is his house, well, duplex, but adorable and a castle compared to my ratty apartment.

"Sawyer," I turn in my seat to face him, "I'm—"

Loud thumps on the top of the car interrupt me and I look past Sawyer to see a pretty face shining behind him. "Hold that thought." He taps my nose and rolls down his window. "Hey, Bennett."

"Hey, stranger, get out and hug me!" The pretty girl steps back from the door so he can open it.

He wraps her up in a hug, twirling her around then setting her down. "Bennett, this is—"

"Emmett?" she cuts in, giving me a friendly wave. "Nice to meet you. I'm Bennett Cole. My boyfriend, Tate, and I live next door to Sawyer."

I climb out of the car and walk over to her, extending my

hand, thankfully not shaking anymore. "It's nice to meet you. I am Emmett."

"Tate's at work, but I think the rest of the Crew's gonna take a dip, maybe grill some burgers. You guys gonna join us?"

Sawyer looks to me, thoroughly enjoying this, waiting for me to speak for us.

"I don't have a suit," I manage, "and I'll only be here for a little while."

"Pssh," she waves her hand at me, "Laney or I can loan you a suit. Come on, stay. You'll have fun, I promise."

I can't get in a bathing suit in front of strangers, in front of him. I give Sawyer a look, pleading with him to get us out of this, but he doesn't. Instead, he moves his eyes up and down me, then licks his lips. "Yeah, Em, grab a suit from Ben here. A cool swim sounds real good to me."

Hiding my aggravation, I force a smile and look back to the welcoming redhead. "Sounds great, thank you."

"Yay!" She grabs my hand and pulls me towards the other side of Sawyer's duplex, flowers and flags of all colors decorating the walkway and porch. "Come on, I'll get you fixed up. We'll be over in a sec, Saw."

"Looking forward to it," he says with a chuckle. "Pick a bikini," he whispers in my ear, placing a soft kiss right below it.

86

Chapter 8

ANOTHER SWEET DAY

−Emmett−

THESE ARE THE GREATEST PEOPLE in the whole world, almost unreal. Each one of Sawyer's friends is more kind, welcoming and down to Earth than the last. The girls aren't catty, gossiping and whining, but rather fascinating, interesting and funny. I'm having a great time, but I can't help feel a bit sad, knowing I won't become a permanent fixture in this "Crew" as they call it; which will truly be my loss.

Sawyer walks over, slinging one leg over the chaise I'm sitting on and placing himself behind me, his legs surrounding me on both sides. "Having fun?" he whispers into my ear.

"So much," I reply honestly, turning my body slightly back towards him. "You?"

"I always have fun with them," he nods his head to his friends, "and with you here? In a bikini? Yeah, I'm feelin' good."

I try not to look at his bare chest, especially not the dark trail leading down to his swimsuit or any further. "WXYZ," I hear in a breathy moan inside my hormone-induced brain.

"Now you know your ABCs?" He laughs, making his whole glorious chest shake.

Crap, I should've stopped at his V and certainly not have finished out loud.

The glare of the bright sun off his tanned, ripped abdomen and pecs has my mind spinning in circles. I've never seen anything like him, not even close. I hope he doesn't notice that I notice the miniscule holes that tell me his nipples are pierced, or his rock hard biceps, or my anything-but-ambiguous examination of his tattoos.

Truly, his ink is amazing, the canvas of his body a work of art in itself. His right bicep proudly boasts a compilation of colorful, merging tattoos that almost dance before my eyes, starting at the slope of his shoulder and ending right below his elbow. The main focal point is a gothic cross with faint wings behind it, thick black tribal lines branching down his arm. To the left, the lines seamlessly transform into tree roots. To the right, the thinnest line breaks into a scripted

"Semper Fidelis," which I already know means "Always Loyal." It fits him perfectly.

On his left bicep, as large and intimidating as the right, is a lone "7," surrounded in big "fuck you to them all" flames.

And then there's his ribcage. The left side says, "Beckett," and the right, "Courage." I can't quite put my finger on it, but there's something…

"They're ambigrams. Check it out." He's careful to swing one leg over and around me to get up and stand in front of me. He turns and contorts, bending down and placing one hand on the lounger, and his "Beckett," upside down, becomes "Sawyer."

"Holy—" I gasp, fascinated.

"And," he stands and swivels, bending once again to show me the "Courage" is now "Strength."

It's the coolest thing I've ever seen in my life. I decide right then and there, an ambigram tattoo is going on the bucket list. I reach out my hand, looking up and seeking acceptance, which he readily gives with his eyes, before running my fingers over the words. I hear him suck in a hiss of a breath when I make contact, his muscles tensing under my touch.

"I love them," I whisper.

"So now you've seen them all." He takes his place behind me and I shift to face him. "Cross, wings, roots," he's pointing as he lists them, my eyes eager to keep up, "seven, flames, and two ambigrams."

I don't know if I ever consciously thought tattoos weren't sexy, or never thought about it at all, but I officially have a stance now. Hot. As. Hell. Yeah, I tried not to notice any of it, or at least convince myself over and over in my head that my chemical reaction is simply that, but I think the fact that I'm still staring back and forth between every tattoo and inch of his body, maybe panting, might have blown my cover.

Time to pull it together. I close my eyes and shake my head. Ground zero, Emmett, knock it off. What were we even talking about? Oh yeah, he asked if I was having fun and I may have answered him. "It's beautiful out today, and everyone's great. Thank you for bringing me."

"You're welcome, Shorty pants. And with that thank you," he lifts a finger to my face and slowly traces my jawline, "I would like to know, why a butterfly tattoo?"

Ah, seems I'm not the only one with wandering eyes…and we're back to tattoos.

So he had seen it; I didn't even think of makeup today. "Butterflies have very short lives. The minute they reach their full potential, become what they were meant to be, their clock is ticking," I explain. "If they'd never emerged, never taken flight, they'd have postponed their end. So technically, their quest for life kills them."

"Emmett." He searches my eyes back and forth, his

thumb resting now on my chin to hold my gaze in place. "If you're sick, I'll help you," he whispers. "Please, let me help you with whatever you need. Whoever it takes, the best in the world, I'll find them."

I cup his face, the words caught in my throat, my thoughts momentarily lost to his beautiful face. "I already told you I'm not dying, Sawyer, I swear. But my destiny's been chosen and I've accepted that as my path and happiness."

"What does that even mean? Just tell me, Emmett. Wherever you're going," his lips brush my own, flavored with longing and hope, "I want to go with you."

"Oh yeah, is that right?" My green eyes glitter with mischief as I throw his words back at him. "How can you be so sure?

"Because from the day I first saw you until the day I saw you again, I didn't like where I was. Now you're here and I do. So it stands to reason that staying with you, wherever it is we're going, is my best course."

"You got any ideas?" I touch his arm. "Cause I'm a little lost." I am getting lost, every minute I spend with him making it harder to remember why I'm not allowed to enjoy it, crave it, need it like my next breath. Maybe I'll start leaving myself sticky notes or put a snap band around my wrist as reminders of why it's simply a bad idea to think he's a good idea.

A splash of cold water on my back makes me jump with a loud shriek. "Damn, that was cold!" I laugh, turning to see who got me.

Evan is pointing at Zach, who's pointing at Laney. I think they all three pushed each other in the pool in one giant jumble.

"Sorry." Evan smiles at me. "Ya'll wanna play Chicken? Hummingbird, get in here, woman, let's take these punks down."

I feel like I've fallen into the Planet of the Hot Guys...none of them are anything short of perfection physically, and they all treat these women like queens. I want to stay in this world, build a small cottage and move in forever...why can't I stay?

I'm saved from having to talk myself out of playing when Laney pipes up. "Punks, huh? Oh, we got you, come on, Dane!"

I lean back against Sawyer, his hands rubbing up and down my arms, as we watch the teams go all out in some merciless games of Chicken. The methodic slide of his hands on my skin, coupled with his solid form, the perfect back pillow, and the hot sun, and I'm soon fighting to hold my eyes open, even amongst all the commotion.

"Hey," he leans over me, his hot, smooth voice in my ear, "let me carry you up to my bed for a nap."

"I'm fine, really. Little longer." I turn to my side and curl into him shamelessly. I can't help it, his skin is hot, and there's enough of it with his enormous body to warm up every part of me. "Tell me something else, without the game, because you want to."

"Like what? Gotta tell ya, this is a lot easier when you tell me the question. I'm a guy; I don't store up random facts and memories."

"Yes, you do; you've already proven that's a lie several times. But I'll let you slide this once. Tell me about your parents."

"No, pick something else."

That refusal was adamant and I want to know why, my head perking up. "You don't have to tell me," I run my hand gradually up his chest, warm, slick with suntan oil and hard as stone, "but will you tell me why you won't tell me?"

"Too ugly. I don't ever want you to look at me like the people who know do. Ever." He takes a few deep breaths, so deep from such a large body, and I feel my body lift up and down with his lungs. "What about your parents?"

"Very ugly." I lay my head back down but leave my hand beside it. "Man, we need some happier questions." I chuckle, and he joins me.

"Em, you're almost asleep. You ready for me to carry you up now?"

Wiped out, I nod and curl my arms around his neck. He lifts me with one arm behind my back and the other under my knees and I can't help but feel cherished.

"Bye!" a myriad of voices call out from the pool as we leave.

"Don't forget, Thursday night Crew Night!" Laney calls from the water. "You better come too, Emmett!"

"Mhm," I answer her with a mumble into Sawyer's neck, where my head rests on his shoulder.

He walks us down a hall and then lays me, as though I am made of glass, onto the softest bed I've ever felt. My body sinks into the mattress and I turn on my side, snuggling my face into a pillow that's saturated with the smell of Sawyer.

If I can't have him, at least I can see him in my dreams, and smell him now too.

I hear the buzz of the fan he must have turned on, then feel covers being tucked tightly around me.

"Get some rest, Shorty," he whispers, kissing the top of my head, "and when you wake up, we'll figure out how to make you mine."

Pretending to be already so deep in sleep I don't hear him, I will my breathing to remain even, concealing the panic his almost irresistible words stir in me. The lights go out and he pulls the door silently closed, with one more whispered, "Sweet dreams, Emmett," before he retreats.

WHEN I FINALLY PRY MY EYES OPEN, the room is completely black, no light offered from the window. I'm not surprised I slept into the night; not only was I exhausted, but sinking into this glorious bed was intoxicating.

I try to sit up when I'm stopped by a large arm slinking around my waist and tightening its hold, begging me to stay close. I slowly push out my butt, seeking reconfirming contact with an actual body, proof that this isn't some wonderful dream I never want to awake from. Oh my!

"You keep doing that and we're gonna be talkin' bout a whole new ball game, woman," he mumbles in a sleepy voice.

I flip over and gasp. "Sawyer, why are you in this bed?"

"Well, Shorty, that's an easy one. It's my bed."

"And the little surprise poking me?"

"If by little you mean gargantuan, then it's my dick. He likes you too."

Sitting up abruptly, I cross my arms with a huff. "Do you have a lamp or something? I can't see a thing."

"You can feel your way," he suggests with a chuckle, fumbling around and knocking things over before finally switching on a light. "Nice nap?"

Oh, God. Sleepy Sawyer is even more tempting than usual Sawyer. He's lying on his side, looking over at me with one arm stretched above the pillows and one down his side. There's already a slight dark stubble on his jaw and his blue eyes are downright sinful.

"Wonderful, thank you." I look away, down at the fascinating sheets. "For carrying me and letting me sleep, I mean. But…but I didn't think you'd get in here with me."

"Why not?" He scoots over, sliding both arms around my waist and kissing the outside of my thigh. "I've never slept with a girl before," he drops a kiss on my knee, "though I definitely understand the appeal now."

I lay one of my hands over his at my waist and rub circles with my thumb. I'm not sure whether I want to soften the blow for him or soak up the feeling for myself. "Sawyer, I told you many times that this can't happen. We barely know each other and the stuff you don't know—it's pretty big."

"Then tell me." He lifts up, kissing my shoulder then letting his tongue linger and trace small circles near my collarbone. "I don't think there's anything you could say to make me not want you."

"Is that it?" I turn my face to his. "You want me? So if I sleep with you, you'll listen and go be happy? Fine." I flop back, flat against the mattress with my arms out to my sides and speak in monotone. "Oh. Yeah. Take. Me. Now."

He rolls and lays his body on top of mine, keeping most of his weight on his forearms, which are deliciously bracketed on either side of my head. "Don't insult me, Emmett, I don't deserve it. Yes, I've fucked a lot of women. Yes, I would love to get lost inside of your sweet little body, but not like that. I want to know you, everything about you. I want to make love to you, which I've never done before. Never. When I take you, it will be because you can't wait another fucking second, and you'll be begging me to take you to a place where only you and I exist, a place where only I can show you I love your heart as much as your body, your mind and everything else that makes you you." He gets rights in my face now, our noses bumping and his plump bottom lip grazing mine. "And you'll never want to leave that place. You'll feel me here," he rubs a hand over my heart, "you'll ache for me here," he traces a circle around one nipple, bringing it to painfully pointed life, "and you'll beg for me here." He brazenly cups between my legs and I whimper, biting my bottom lip in a futile attempt to stop my panting. "You'll feel me in every part of you, every day, until we're together in our place again."

I shake my head back and forth, shrinking into the mattress. "I won't. I can't."

"Why. Not?" he growls, his voice harsh but his eyes still kind.

This is it—this is where I tell him...and lose him. My mouth is open, my eyes squeezed shut, ready to finally blurt it out when he speaks again.

"Emmett, look at me. Don't shut me out. I'll pick the

lock, baby."

Against any judgment, I slowly open my eyes, shuddering in actual physical pain at what I see. His face looms over me, filled with agony, asking me to take the leap with him.

"Hey, you're shaking. Never mind. Shh, new plan. Don't tell me yet. If you don't have complete faith in me, I haven't earned your secrets. When you trust me, trust that I mean it when I say I won't run, no matter what it is, then you tell me." He lays a finger over my lips. "That's it, end of discussion, so stop worrying about it. Tell me other things."

"L-like what?" I'm dazed; nothing's up or down, round or square anymore. He's pleading with me not to tell him and I'm berating myself for considering taking the coward's way out. "I really think I should tell you, Sawyer. Just let me get it out, then I'll get out."

"Nope." He laughs, rolling over onto his back. He takes me with him, tucking me into his side. "Surely you can think of something else to talk about. Stimulate my mind, woman," he teases, chuckling to himself.

Our friendship or whatever we have is baffling and confusing, but I don't want it to end. So for now, I curb the nagging guilt and soak up Sawyer.

Fascinated, I lift one finger to his nipple, examining it. "Why pierce them if you're not gonna wear a ring in it?"

"Do you have ADD? Is that your secret?" He smirks at his own cleverness, kissing my head, as seems his developing habit. "I'm fully prepared to have my mind challenged and you touch my nipple? Playing with fire, Shorty."

I blush, but simply can't look away from his chest. Suffice it to say, his physique piques my interest.

"If you want me to wear them, I will. I'll wear all of them, just say the word."

"All of them?" I raise my head, my mouth agape as I stare at him. "How many piercings do you have? No wait, I bet I can guess." His words come back to me, and the feeling of...I have no idea what to call it, washes over me. I know, without a doubt, the answer, and somehow I feel closer to him, special, that I do. "Seven, right?"

He nods, his dark blue eyes boring into my own. "Very astute, Ms. Young. Now, can you tell me where they all are?"

"Two in your ears, two for your nipples, your eyebrow; that's five." I look him over gradually, letting my eyes shamefully take in his large, hard body, every defined line a thing of beauty. He lets his tongue slide from his mouth and wiggles it at me. I lean in, getting a closer look, and sure enough there's a small hole. "Okay, that's six. One more," I tap my chin thoughtfully, eyeing his belly button.

He laughs out loud, his stomach muscles tightening under my stare. "I didn't pierce my belly button, Emmett." Still staring at his tummy, his hand glides down the ripples, one finger tracing over his dark happy trail. "Lower," he taunts in a rich, tantalizing voice, no longer holding even the hint of a laugh.

I don't even know my own body, shivering yet burning hot at the same time from the thought of his. And my eyes, they roam lower, following the trail of his finger, taking in the outline of one very large, very hard penis through his light blue basketball shorts. Like a brazen hussy, I squint, searching for the hint of any jewelry.

"I don't have it in. I usually don't." His raspy comment startles me, and I look up at him. His eyes are smoldering, filled with the same lust I feel between my legs.

"Why not?" I whisper, licking my lips.

"Nobody gets that, Emmett, nobody." He sits up, putting his face inches from my own. "I did it on a dare, and it hurt too bad not to keep it. But it's all yours if you want it, Angel."

"Why? Why can I demand I want it and get it?"

"'Cause I said you could. Listen," he holds my face between his palms, one thumb outlining my jawline, "I have no idea why it takes some couples years to fall in love and some only a day, or if any of them even know. But I do know that I like you, so much. I want to know you, and I think you want the same thing."

This went from the kinkiest conversation I've ever had in my life, my mind's eye conjuring up fantastic images, to the sweetest. My heart is banging against its own walls and the tingles that started in my belly have now turned into sharp, sporadic twinges much lower.

Holy mother, I want him. I mean, I want him like I want air.

No, no, Emmett. Tears threaten in my eyes and I quickly turn my head, starting to climb from the bed. "I have to go," I stammer, trying to untangle myself from the sheets, but only getting stuck further. Grappling, swinging limbs and sheets in a tizzy, I finally free myself and stumble to the bedroom door, still embarrassingly in a bathing suit and shoeless. I don't know how, but I have to get the hell out of here and away from him. I can only torture myself so much.

One arm comes over my head, bracing the door shut. I feel every hard inch of him against the back of my body as his other hand moves my hair to the side. "Don't leave, please. I'll be good." He runs his nose up the side of my neck, whispering against my skin. "You're just so beautiful, Emmett, and in my bed, still in that damn bikini. I wouldn't be a man if I didn't want you."

I lean forward, letting my forehead rest on the door, but it's no escape as he leans with me, pressing the length of his hard body against my own.

"I'll get you some shorts and a t-shirt to change into if it'll make you feel better," he says. "Come back to bed, it's late. We can talk about astrophysics and grandmas just as long as I can hold you."

I can't help but snicker, the desperation in his voice as he invites me to discuss grandmas with him is so cute, and charming. "I don't want to leave, but we can't have it both ways. You say not to tell you, that we'll be friends, but then you make me feel…"

"I know, I know, my fault." He rubs my shoulder and kisses behind its wake. "Don't spook on me, Shorty. I understand."

No, he doesn't, but it's good enough for now. It's late, I'm tired, and he's warm and inviting.

"Okay, some clothes would be nice," I admit. "Maybe I'll hop in your shower real quick?"

"Uhh," he growls behind me, pressing his body into me more firmly. "Don't tell me you're going to shower, woman. Tell me you're gonna go poop and blow your nose."

And the moment is officially gone… I die laughing, turning to face him. "Gross!" I slap his chest, still giggling. "Go get me the clothes, ya big nasty!"

I take my time in the shower, praying he falls asleep before I come out. The cold shower thing doesn't work on me. I lather my hair twice, regretting it when I realize he has no conditioner in here, and double soap every inch of myself before finally turning off the water. I dry off and slip on the way oversized clothes he gave me, towel drying my hair to an acceptable sleeping dampness and creep back in to his bedroom on tiptoe.

"Are you asleep?" I whisper to his back as I climb in

behind him.

"No." He rolls over, smiling at me widely. "Nice try with the marathon shower, though. Why are you avoiding me? I told you I'd be good."

"I'm not," I say over-exuberantly, burrowing down under the covers. "I'm just not used to spending the night in a man's bed, I guess."

"You haven't ever done that?"

"God no!"

"Oh, Em, you keep making me happier every time you let something slip out."

"So glad I could help." I use my thumb and finger to flick him in the chest. "Go to sleep. I'm wiped.

"Night, Shorty."

"Night, Seven."

Chapter 9

THEN HE FOUND ME

-Emmett-

THE DIGITAL FACE on the alarm says 9:24 when I wake again, now alone in the bed. Or not alone…for there's a note on his pillow with my name on it.

> *Em,*
> *Maybe not exactly like a lumberjack, but definitely a snore. Good morning, lovely.*
> *-S*

I fold the note back up, searching aimlessly for a place to tuck it. I have nothing with me, not even my own clothes, so

I hide it back under the pillow I slept on last night, secretly hoping I'll be back there soon to pick it up. I check his bathroom, stealing a quick tryst with his toothbrush, and then go back to sit on the edge of his bed. I can't stay in here all day, but the thought of wandering out, in his clothes, mortifies me. I refuse to do the walk of shame when the dirtiest thing we did was talk about pooping.

Ten minutes later, I can't sit idle any longer. I have too much to do today. I stand, tightening the drawstring of his shorts that hang past my knees despite my efforts and make my way down the hallway. I wince as a floorboard creaks beneath my cold, bare feet, but I forge onward.

"Morning, Sunshine," Laney greets me in the kitchen.

"Hi, Laney," I duck my head, crossing my arms over my braless chest. "H-how are you?"

"Good, considering it's morning. I hate them."

"Uh, where's Sawyer?" I mutter, still looking at the floor.

"He had a class, but he told me to tell you he'll be back at ten. And," she comes around the corner, holding my clothes and purse, "he went and grabbed these from Bennett's for you in case you woke up."

"Oh, thank you." I sigh in relief and take them from her. "I'll, ah, go get changed."

"Emmett," she places a hand on my shoulder, "don't be embarrassed. I know Sawyer, therefore I know you have nothing to be embarrassed about."

"What do you mean?"

"You slept, all night, in his bed, and he let you. And you're still here in the morning. You're different for him. I'm not trying to be nosy, I just want you to know you don't have to feel weird. No one's going to think less of you, okay?"

I swallow down the disgust I taste at the thought of Sawyer's revolving door, flashbacks of him and Mariah in the alley playing in my mind. "Okay, thank you." I give her a fake smile and scurry down the hall, his clothes now burning my skin.

Shutting the door and changing as quickly as I can, I'm not sure which bothers me more, the thought of all his conquests or the fact that I'm not one. Am I deficient? Can he smell the baggage on me?

Wait, what the heck, Emmett? You told him it wasn't an option and now you feel rejected? See, this is what happens when you get too close to the fire…you go completely insane from smoke inhalation. I have a plan, a clearly laid path that I must stay on, and no one will lead me astray.

I grab my phone, dialing the cab company. I realize I don't know the address here as soon as they ask. "Hold on," I grumble in his ear, walking back out to the kitchen. "Laney, what's your address?"

She spouts it off and I repeat it into the phone, confirming a fifteen minute wait before hanging up. "Why?" she finally turns around to face me and asks.

"I needed it for the taxi."

"What? Why? No, please don't leave!" she shrieks, her arms flailing wildly out to her sides.

I back up, slightly concerned for her sanity. I think she might actually be tearing up right now, and I'm more than a little freaked out.

"Is it because of what I said? I meant it as a compliment, Emmett, like you don't have to hang your head, afraid we all think you slept with him. Not that it's bad if you did, but, God!" She fists her hands, holding them to the sides of her head. "I didn't mean anything. I'm so sorry. You just looked embarrassed. Shit, he's gonna kill me!"

And she seemed so normal yesterday.

"Laney, I have to go because I have a lot to do. I'm not upset. I know what you were trying to say and I appreciate it, really."

"Sawyer will be back any minute. Why don't you wait and let him drive you? He'll be so upset if he comes back and you're gone. You didn't see his face this morning, Emmett. I haven't seen him smile like that in months."

"I like him too." I grin despite myself, thinking of the way he makes me laugh, the feel of him holding me close all night. "He's a good friend. It'll be fine, I'll see him at work."

Her head drops and she shakes it back and forth. "You'll destroy him."

"I won't," I say sternly. "He knows we can only be

friends. I promise, he'll be all right. His headboard will be rocking again before you know it." I snicker facetiously, trying to convince myself as much as her that everything's just great.

A horn sounds outside. Thankfully, the cab's early.

"That's my ride, I gotta go. Everything's cool, Laney. Promise."

"Yeah." She swipes her hand under her nose, sniffling. "So, I'll see you Thursday night? You promised to come to Crew Night."

"I'll be there," I nod and turn to get out the door as fast as my legs will carry me.

She knows as well as I do that Sawyer and I have already happened and collateral damage is inevitable.

I just pray I can bear the brunt of the pain and he's spared.

OBVIOUSLY HE WASN'T HAPPY that I left before he got home, since he's refusing to walk up to my door now.

Sawyer: I'm downstairs, come get the car keys please.

If this makes him feel better, like he's punishing me, I'm going to let him have it. As I walk down the stairs, approaching him, I lose my breath. He's propped on one hip against the side of the car, aviators covering the eyes I can feel on me. Dressed in dark washed jeans and a white muscle shirt, white ball cap riding backwards on his head; he's absolutely the sexiest man I've ever seen.

"Hey," I mumble, fiddling with the leg of my shorts. It hurts to look at him any longer, the tugging on my heart more than figurative, it's downright painful.

He startles me by shoving his hand under my hair at the base of my skull. "Your hair's wet. How hot is it up there?"

"Not bad, I just have thick hair," I pull the tie off my wrist and make quick work of a ponytail. "Thank you for letting me use the car. I shouldn't accept, it's too much," I peek up at him with a small smile, "but I will."

"Why'd you leave me this morning?" His grip on my neck tightens and he pulls my head to his, resting his forehead on mine.

"You actually left me," I snicker, "but I had to go. I work tonight, so I needed to do laundry and try to find my landlord, stuff like that. I didn't mean to make you mad."

"I wasn't mad." He sighs, his fingers on the side of my neck now massaging the muscles under them.

"Liar," I smirk, "that's why you made me walk down here to you. Doling out your big punishment." I poke him in the stomach playfully.

"Come with me, please." He presses his lips against

mine, sliding them sideways back and forth. "At least until your air's fixed. We can drive to work together, eat first. Let me take care of you, Emmett."

I struggle to breathe steadily, consumed by the feel of our lips feathering one another. "We can't keep going in circles, Sawyer. I'm only so strong. I can't take this," I whisper, my traitorous voice squeaking with the urge to surrender.

He drops his grip on me, backing away and lifting his arms in the air. "All I fucking see is you! All I'm asking for is a chance, Emmett! I don't care about your past, everyone fucking has one woman!"

"Don't yell at me!" I gulp back the sobs, but can't stop the flow of tears. "You said you didn't want to know, so you'll just have to trust me, Sawyer. I'm not worth it!" I turn and run back up the stairs, slamming my door and throwing myself face down on my bed. How quickly things turned, his soft mouth and warm breath caressing me one second, lashing out in pained harshness the next.

I hear him coming, a man his size can't sneak up on anyone, so I don't even flinch at the sound of his voice, leaving my face down.

"Here's the key, drive the car."

I feel the key bounce on the bed beside me right before he slams the door behind him and I listen to his heavy, angry footsteps plod down the stairs.

Good—I hope he stays angry at me. I'd rather have him mad than hurt.

—SAWYER—

I'M REALLY ON A ROLL TODAY...I'd left Emmett in tears, was a complete dick to the cab driver (probably should've planned how I'd get home after leaving her the car) and now I'm scaring Laney. I crash through our front door, putting the knob through the wall, causing Laney to jolt a good four inches off the couch.

"Shit, Sawyer!" She clutches her chest, shrinking me on sight with her scathing glare. "What's on fire?"

"Sorry." I pull the door out of the wall, slamming it closed. "I didn't mean to scare you. That woman is driving me crazy!"

"She's scared." Her face now dissolves into a sympathetic frown. "I don't know of what, but she's petrified. I hate to say it, but you may need to back off."

"Oh, I've backed off all right. I just screamed at her and left while she was crying. Fuck!" I grab my head with both hands, scrubbing furiously back and forth. "Why the fuck don't I have longer fucking hair! Shit!"

"Okayyyy." Laney walks over to me, pulling down my

arms. "Come sit down before you blow a blood vessel." She guides me to the couch. "By the way, you need to work on your angry words. The f-bomb is only powerful if you don't drop it every other word."

I can't help my lip curl, smiling at my girl; she always knows the right thing to say. Her slick wit gets me all the time. "You were scared shitless when I first met you. Tell me what to do, Gidge."

"I told you, I honestly think you should back off. Let her come to you."

"Like a butterfly, let her land on me," I mumble to myself, thinking of Kasey's advice.

"That might be the coolest thing you've ever said," she looks at me in wonder. "Have you been camping out in the greeting card aisle?"

"Something like that." I shrug. We're talking about me here, not Kasey, so screw giving him credit.

"She's coming Thursday night, she promised. Stay away from her until then, and POW!" She slams one fist in the other palm. "When she gets here, show her what's been missing all week. Be aloof but flirtatious, dress to kill and let your Gidge take care of the rest." She winks at me.

"Have I told you lately that I love you?"

"Seriously, stay out of Hallmark. You're creeping me out." She shoulder nudges me. "And I love you too."

Chapter 10

YOU, ME AND THE CREW

—SAWYER—

MONDAY NIGHT I WENT TO THE GYM and worked out until I could barely lift my arms. I downed three beers in one episode of Miami Ink, CJ called about a race this weekend and I hung up on him, and then I went to sleep. Actually, then I laid in my bed and tossed and turned, typed and deleted about four texts to Emmett, then I feel asleep.

Tuesday I went in to The K before the lunch shift, took care of all my stuff at lightning speed, and got the hell out of there. I waited for Zach outside the field house and forced him to go on a two-hour ride on our bikes. I ate in my room then jacked off twice in the shower. Three guesses, and the first two don't count, who I pictured in my head while yanking myself.

Wednesday I skipped classes because honestly, right now I fear for the safety of anyone who crosses my path sideways. I can't remember ever being this wound up in my life, not even when I couldn't find her. I'm fucking exhausted because I can't sleep, starving because I've barely eaten and sore as hell from the marathon gym trips. Not to mention, I've never gone so long without sex in my life and I'm a little worried backed up cum may start seeping out my eyeballs any second.

I can't go in to work for obvious reasons and Dane's probably about to kick my ass for all the overtime he's about to have to pay Kasey. I worry about her non-stop, especially not being at the bar to watch her, but I trust Laney's advice and I've come too far to fuck things up any further. The only reason I find restful sleep Wednesday night is because I know she only worked until nine, has a car now, and tomorrow is Thursday, Crew Night, and she'll be there.

When I walk into the living room Thursday morning, Dane's adjusting his tie in the mirror by the door. "Could you be any more obvious?" he asks without meeting my eyes.

"'Bout what?"

"Why all of a sudden, after three days, you're functional and spunky-tailed. Where's your 'don't give a fuck' attitude?"

"If it was up your ass you'd know it."

"Testy." He chuckles. "You ready for tonight?"

I glare at him, at the nerve of the smug bastard. I taught him game. "Pretty sure I got it, but thanks for your concern."

"Don't get it twisted, Sawyer." He turns, face now serious. "I am concerned. If you're upset, Laney's upset. If Laney's upset, I hire fucking clowns. Now whatever's up your ass—fix it." He heads back to the door, picking up his briefcase. "Saw her at The K the other day," he comments nonchalantly. "She asked about you. Said to tell you 'hi' since you haven't returned her calls or texts?"

"Hmm," I reply, shooting for unconcerned.

"And for what it's worth, I think she'd be crazy not to see what a great guy you are."

"Thanks, Daney," I give him shit, "did you take care of the other thing for me?"

"Should go down sometime this afternoon."

"My man." I walk over and fist bump him.

"And the place?"

"Sent the cleaners in today; all yours."

"I meant to ask, not that I'm not glad as hell you did, but why'd you buy that duplex too?"

He turns and looks at me like I'm one beer short of a six-pack. "Is that a real question? I'm controlling the perimeter. I have to make sure guys don't live on either side of Laney."

"Tate lives right there," I point, "and I'm pretty sure he's a guy."

"He's my brother."

"Tucker, also penis-packing, lives right there," I point to the other side of the room. "Really pulled off that plan," I jibe. "Good job."

"You're right, he is penis-packing. Packing it right into his boyfriend."

"How could you possibly know that?"

"If you live with, beside, or anywhere in the vicinity of Laney, I know."

"Does it bother you at all that you're psychotic?"

"You say psycho, I say careful...and Laney says she loves me." He winks. "I'm sleeping just fine at night." He claps me on the shoulder and gives it a squeeze. "Key's on the counter."

I shake my head, laughing to myself at that douche. Can't help but love the kid, though. I assume Laney's already left or she would have accosted him on his way out the door, so with the house to myself, I crank up my Emmett song, "In Luv Wit a Stripper" by Somo. I do the dishes and clean my room like a good boy. When all that's done, I head to the store, following the list Laney left for me with a ton of help from the guy at the store, who also had no idea what half the shit she wrote was. Hell, I bought it and I'm still not sure what the fuck hummus is.

Crew Night starts at seven, so at six, I jump in the shower, wanting not only to be clean but as relaxed as possible. A man with a loaded gun can be a very scary thing, and I can't afford to "scare" Emmett tonight. Jumping on her the minute she walks in the door and humping her leg probably wouldn't be conducive to the whole "I'm a sensitive guy, Emmett, I swear" fact that I desperately need to her to understand. So now scrubbed head to toe, I squirt more shampoo in my palm and wrap it around my dick. I close my eyes and lean my head against the tile wall, like I've done so many times this week, and picture her in my head. More often than not, I use the still frame in my mind of her in that little red bikini, but today...today I envision her big green eyes looking up at me as she lies beneath me in my bed. She sucks on her bottom lip and slowly lets her knees fall open before me. "Take me, Sawyer" she whispers, using her hands to spread herself wide open for me. Ah, Goddamn, that's it, my hand moving rapidly up and down my length, squeezing tighter around it.

"What do you want?" I actually pant out loud, totally vested in this fantasy.

"You, inside me," my dream girl sweetly begs. "Please, Sawyer."

My cum spurts out of me and I grunt, pulling and tugging on my dick with no mercy. I can almost feel her soaking it up, all I have to give her, and I remain bent against the wall, my chest heaving long after I've finished.

Now I'm ready to see her tonight. With that pressure

alleviated, surely I can go at least five minutes being in the same room with her without imagining myself buried in her. I get dressed like Laney instructed, a white button down with the sleeves rolled to my elbows and low riding jeans. I put both diamond studs in my ears, slide my eyebrow ring in, and brush my teeth three times, finishing up with a dash of Usher cologne.

I'm filling the kitchen sink with ice and drinks when the first of the crowd starts to arrive. Because they only have ten steps to make, it's, of course, Tate and Bennett.

"What can I do?" Bennett asks, and I turn, hands full, and give her a kiss on the cheek.

"Everything Laney had me get is in the fridge. Maybe you'll know what to do with it."

Tate beats her to it, reaching in for a beer. "She specifically said she wanted me to taste test the beer. Duty calls," he says as he tilts back a Dos Equis. "So, I hear we're plus one tonight." He hitches a brow my way. "I'd be lying if I said I wasn't dying to meet the girl who's sprung Sawyer Beckett, Esquire."

"Don't say shit like that when she's here." I turn and point at him, my cheeks beginning to flush. "I mean it, vag bag."

"I won't, relax," he grins, "but think about this. If you have to be someone else around her, then you're not letting her get to know the real you. Why would you want to be someone else? If she falls for the wrong version, she's not really falling for you."

"Makes sense," I ponder it for a minute, "but I'm not doing it on purpose, it just is. The person I am around Emmett, it's the me I want to be. It feels natural."

"Ahhhh," Bennett gushes. "That was a perfect answer, Sawyer."

"I can buy that." Tate nods. "Good for you, man."

Dane hedges around the corner and into the kitchen as usual. Swear to God, I'm gonna strap a bell around his sneaky freakin' neck. "If ya'll are done with the slap and tickle, Laney needs you in your room, Sawyer."

"And now it's official," Tate chuckles, "the world is ending. Sawyer's prophetic and Dane's telling another man to go in a bedroom with Laney. Drink up, kids, we're in the midst of the apocalypse."

"Tate's just pumped you're all sappy now so he gets to be the one slinging out the smart ass comments. And I'm going with you, of course." Dane slings an arm around my shoulder. "Come on, Romeo."

Laney's waiting in my room wearing a cat that ate the canary smile. "Here ya go!" She hands me a pink bag with all kinds of shit sticking out the top. Even if I didn't know what was in it, I would know. The essence of Emmett hints from the bag, treating my nose to all I've missed for too many days.

"Thank you, Gidge," I kiss her cheek, "you're the best."

"Give it to her alone, at the perfect time," she advises.

"Which is?"

"You'll know." She winks. "You're probably better at this than you think."

I stand there holding the bag like a goon long after they walk out. If I rip into it and spray my pillow, do I have to turn in my balls at a counter somewhere? The door creaks behind me and I turn, dropping the bag like I stole it.

"She's here," Laney whispers. "Remember, aloof but flirtatious."

I nod, wiping my palms on my jeans and following her out. Emmett's atop a stool at the kitchen bar laughing with Tate and Bennett. Her short, little legs look glorious, bared by the gray dress thing she's wearing. Her dark hair is down around her shoulders and I immediately notice the red tips are gone, about two inches have been trimmed off. All heads turn to me as I enter, but her eyes divert quickly, instead choosing to focus on Laney.

"Emmett!" Laney exclaims. "I'm so glad you came."

"Thanks for having me, Laney. Hi, Sawyer," she says quietly, not looking at me.

Rushing to her and wrapping my arms around her probably isn't aloof, so I force my feet to remain planted. "Hey, Emmett, how are ya?"

"Fine." Now she tilts her head and sneaks a peek at me from under her dark locks.

120

"Hey, hey, hey," Zach booms in, "what's good?"

Not your timing, for damn sure.

Noticing Emmett sitting in the room, Zach makes his way over and opens his arms. "Hey, Emmett, nice to see you again."

She stands and accepts his hug. "Hey."

Well, aren't we all friendly motherfuckers?

I turn at the sound of a chuckle behind me and see that Evan and Whitley have joined us. Evan smiles at me and shakes his head. "It was only a hug, killer, calm down," he says. "Don't let her hear you growl like that, either. Might scare her."

The room gets way too crowded for me, so I head into the living room and plop down on the couch like a redheaded stepchild, feeling miserably out of place in my own home with my own crew. Truth is, it's only really about her. Being this close with so much in between us, shit I don't even understand… I've never felt more alone in my life.

Dane grabs a seat beside me, too close for male comfort, handing me a cold beer. "Stop pouting, Nancy, you're not going to attract a straight girl by acting like one."

"Worked on you, though, huh? How's about you scoot the fuck over, fag?"

He throws back his head and gut laughs, moving away from me. "Nice one. Welcome back." He raises his voice above the ruckus to be heard. "So Emmett, how are you liking The K?"

As I'm sure he'd planned, she walks over and joins us, taking the chair. "I love it, thank you again, so much."

"And this guy?" He tilts his head at me. "He hasn't scared ya off yet?"

Her green eyes find mine and hold as she answers him. "I would never be scared of Sawyer. He's been wonderful. I owe him so much."

"You don't owe me anything," I answer, making the conversation my own.

"Oh, Lord—incoming," Dane mumbles beside us seconds before Laney starts clapping her hands for our attention.

"Okay, Pictionary time! Team up!"

All the couples pair off, leaving me, Emmett and Zach sitting around like the lone idiots. "The three of us can be a team," Zach suggests.

I thought it sounded like a reasonable solution. Laney? Not so much.

"No, that won't work, then it's three against two. Hmm..." She glances around as though if she looks hard enough, another person will appear.

"Laney," I start in but am abruptly cut off by the most competitive person in the world.

"No way, okay, so we can—"

"Baby," Dane's voice of reason comes in, "it's not the

Hunger Games; we're just friends playing Pictionary. One team of three is fine."

"But—" she starts, her pout hysterical to everyone but her.

"But nothing, you competitive thing," he holds out a hand, "come here."

We all watch in amazement as he literally hypnotizes her. She chews on her bottom lip, looking to each of us to take her side, rubbing a hole in the carpet with her toe. Then she looks back up at Dane slowly and he nods, wiggling the fingers of his outstretched hand…and a calmness comes over her face as she accepts it, making her way to him and into his lap.

I chance a glimpse at Emmett and yes, she felt it too…that "connection" two people have, a push and a pull 'til they meet in the middle. That's what I'd been dealing with for months, the force of the relationships all around me. I want it too, and I want it with Emmett. She's staring right back at me, an understanding in her eyes. Yes, Shorty, we have the makings to be that great. "I'm sorry," I mouth to her.

"Me too," her shiny pink lips mouth back.

PICTIONARY—an age old game where everyone laughs and

has a great time with friends and family.

HA! You need to flip the box over and read the other description…the directions for when the Crew plays it. Evan and Whitley, Mr. and Mrs. Can't Stand Any Controversy, already left. Tate and Dane are now a team, and out for blood, since they pissed their women off and Laney declared a switch. Basically, Team Trio is kicking serious ass and it's causing meltdowns amongst the others. And Laney is funny as fuck when she's losing; she gets so damn flustered she can't even speak in full, rational sentences.

The great thing? Emmett hasn't quit laughing all night, excusing herself to the "ladies room" at least four times. I love watching her face light up and hearing the sweet sounds of her amusement. Or my favorite, when her eyes bulge out at some of the crude comments flying around. It gives me an even bigger sense of comfort, some rightness, knowing she'll fit in with the Crew like she's always been there.

Zach lumbers slowly up from the floor. "As much fun as you guys have failed miserably to provide, I gotta be up early. Try not to kill each other," he jokes, grabbing his helmet and heading for the door.

And then there were six…

"All right!" Laney practically screams, all that adrenaline coursing through her turning her more into Crazy Game Laney. "Now that the teams are even, we're starting over on the score."

"No, ma'am," Dane stands, "I'm done. Let's clean up and go to bed, baby."

"I'll clean up," Emmett offers, using my thigh to help push herself up. "You guys hosted; it's the least I can do."

I'm right behind her, my chin resting on top of her head and hands on her shoulders. I've been yearning for contact of any kind all night and I know she won't chastise me in front of them. Probably a dirty move, but I have no fucks left to give. I need to feel her. "I'll help her. Ya'll go to bed."

"Thank you both." Dane reaches out and snags Laney around the waist. "Bed, woman. Now."

Bennett and Tate call out a goodbye as the door shuts and Laney and Dane obviously "make up" the whole way down the hall to her room. Emmett and I are alone now and neither of us has moved a muscle, both standing statuesque and silent. I speak first, the words that have been dying to come out all night spilling from my mouth.

"I've missed you."

"Me too," she chokes out. "You're kinda, I don't know, my best friend."

I spin her around to face me. "I'm your best friend?"

Through building tears, she nods. "You're my only friend, really. But that's not why— you'd still be the best one even if I had a million. You're just that cool," she mocks, pushing on my chest.

"Ah, Em." I squeeze her to me, firing off kisses into her

hair like a starved man. "I'm so sorry I yelled at you and pushed you for too much. Let's start over, okay?" I lean back and catch her sweet eyes, inviting her with mine to let me back in.

"K," she agrees, sniffling.

"Come on," I pull her to the couch and sit her down. "Wait right here. Don't move." I hustle to my room, swiping up the gift bag and hurrying back to her with it behind my back. "I got you something."

"You did?" First surprise flits across her face, then wonder, and finally the smile that lights me up. "What? Why?"

"Just a little something. I actually enjoy it as much as you do, I think." I bring the bag around and offer it to her.

She looks to the fancy bag, then me, then back to the gift. "Can I open it now?"

"Well, yeah," I laugh. She's so fucking adorable.

Her tiny hands can't get in it fast enough and when she's made it through all the puff, she gasps. "Red," she breathes, popping open the cap and spraying one wrist then rubbing it against the other.

I clear my throat and sit down beside her. "Were you out?"

Her head turns, beautiful green eyes rimmed with unshed tears, and she nods.

"I thought so. I missed it too." I lift her wrist gently,

bringing it to my nose and inhaling deeply. "There's my Emmett."

"Sawyer, I, you're so—"

"Shh," I give her a wink, "no big deal, Shorty. Now come 'ere." I manhandle her, pulling her to me and situating her on my lap. "Catch me up, what's been going on with you?"

"Ugh." She puts her gift down and drops her shoulders. "You don't want to know. They condemned my apartment building today and we can't go back in until he fixes the air, and the heat, and the locks, and about twenty other things."

I feign surprise. "Where are you staying?"

"I have no idea. Everything just happened this afternoon. I was thinking of asking your girlfriend," she teases me with a sarcastic grin.

"And who might that be?"

"Mariah," she counters defiantly.

"Girlfriend," I scoff, "very funny. Why don't you stay here? Laney won't mind at all."

She scoots out of my lap backwards, mouth agape. "Sawyer, I can't move in with you, don't be ridiculous!"

"Okay," I unapologetically grab her and situate her back in my lap, securing one arm around her waist, "but you can crash here until we find you somewhere else to rent. You don't need to go back to that apartment, even if he fixes everything. Let's find you something nicer."

"You wear me out," she drops her head on my shoulder, sighing loudly, "but I secretly love knowing I have you. How selfish is that?"

"It's not selfish at all, Shorty. You're not taking. I'm giving, freely."

"Can I," she whispers, tilting her head up to peer at me, "sleep in your bed tonight, with you?"

If I wasn't sitting down, that one sentence would have dropped me to my damn knees. "God, yes," I moan, standing and lifting her in my arms.

"Just sleeping, Sawyer," she mumbles into my shirt, where her small, cherubic face is nuzzled.

"It'll be the first time in four nights I get any. Trust me, I'm all for sleeping."

Chapter 11

A TALK TO REMEMBER

-Emmett-

"WHERE ARE YOU TAKING ME?" I ask with a giggle.

Sawyer is behind me, his hands over my eyes, walking me forward less than gracefully. "Almost there, keep going," he whispers in my ear. One hand slides over to block both my eyes as his other does something that causes a rattling noise I can't quite place. "Open." He drops his hand to let me see.

I look around at the empty room, a tad confused. "What am I looking at?"

"Your new place." He bends and kisses my cheek. "Dane owns this duplex too, since it's by Laney and he's insane and all—don't ask. Anyway, this side is yours for the same $450 you were paying."

I spin around and narrow my eyes at him. The little sneak. "There's no way this place rents for that, Sawyer. What have you done? I told you—"

He cuts me off in a placating tone. "Shorty…simmer down and just enjoy, please. And, you're only two doors down, so if you need anything…" He shrugs, not making this feel casual at all.

"I told you." I shake my head. "I warned you, Sawyer, don't give me your heart."

He lifts my chin gently, captivating me with the struggle in his eyes. "I know you did, and I'm not pressuring you, but some things you can't call the shots on. I'm not sure if I gave you my heart or if you stole it, but either way, I don't want it back."

His lips crash into mine before I can stop him, his tongue seeking entry. I try, Lord knows I try, to fight it, but mortals aren't made with that kind of strength. My mouth opens to him at the same time as my heart and I stand on my tiptoes to wrap my arms almost around his neck. Large hands scoop up my butt, lifting me as though I weigh nothing and I wrap my legs around his waist shamelessly. I don't care, I don't think, all I can do in this moment is try to keep breathing.

Our lips wrestle, his large and domineering, mine swollen and grateful. The deep groan he releases in my mouth drives me crazy and I grab his head with both hands, grinding my crotch into whatever part of his hard body it's currently lined up to. "I can't help it," I grunt, then kiss him again, "you're so damn sexy, and wonderful, and—"

"Fucking kiss me, woman." He silences me, completely consuming my mouth with his own.

I don't know how long we go at it for, both of us oblivious to anything but the taste of each other, him holding me up the entire time. But when we break to catch our breath, reality hits me. I have to tell him. I can't fight it off anymore, the pull to him, nor can I "go" for him in good conscience. "Let's go for a drive," I suggest.

The tormented look on his face is almost comical, poor guy, he so thought we were about to screw like animals right here on the ground. Which I would love nothing more than to do, after I tell him…when it will no longer be an option he affords me.

"If you wanna go for a drive, we'll go for a drive." He sets me on my feet and links our fingers together. "Your show, Shorty, lead the way."

—SAWYER—

"SAWYER, THIS IS MY GRAMMA, Katherine Louise Young.

Gramma, this is Sawyer."

I'm not sure what I'm supposed to say to a headstone. "Nice to meet you" doesn't seem quite right, so I remain silent, looking at my sweet angel with what I hope isn't blatant pity.

"Sit down." She takes my hand and guides me to the flat stone bench right behind her grandmother's grave. "My gramma was all I had in the whole world. My sperm donor remains a mystery and my mother took off pretty much the minute I popped out of her." She fakes a laugh and rolls her eyes. "She was the ultimate hair band groupie. Sadly, she never got the memo that the members of Twisted Sister and the likes are now twisted grandparents, and that no one thinks men who use Aqua Net are cool, so I'm sure she's off living her dream of hotel rooms and reunion tour buses." She pops her shoulders. "Who knows? Not important, really. So, when she died a few years ago," she nods her head back to her grandma's headstone, "I was alone."

"Em—"

"No," she stops me with a stiff hand to my chest, "let me say it all at once or I never will."

I nod, scooting back an inch. She takes a deep breath before she continues.

"So when I found out I was pregnant, I decided to look at it as a blessing and make it work. I'll have someone to give every ounce of my love to and they'll love me back, right?

Neither of us will ever be alone."

There are certain moments in life where you'll never forget where you were when you heard. What you were wearing, how she wore her hair, if it was cold or hot out...I know this is one of those moments for me.

The girl I might quite possibly be falling in love with, a fall that started the first time I looked at her, is pregnant. And not with my baby.

"You're pregnant?" I choke out, my tone as level and calming as I can keep it, hoping my face is pulling it off as well. "I saw you in a bikini—you didn't look pregnant."

She rolls her eyes, letting out a small, exasperated laugh. "I'm about fifteen weeks, as far as I can figure. It'll be a while, I guess, before I really show."

My face must have failed at stoic, showing exactly how confused I feel, 'cause she gives me an opening.

"Ask me anything you want, Sawyer."

"Who's the father?" I blurt out. "Do you love him?"

"And then there's that part." She runs a hand through her hair and turns to look at her gramma's headstone over her shoulder. "You might as well hear it too, Gramma. You're both gonna freak, so let me start with," another long exhale, "I'm fine. I've come to terms with it and made my decision, so please don't think I'm crazy or try to talk me out of it."

An eerie feeling rolls over me and I know I'm not gonna

like what she's about to say.

"I don't know who the father is. Calm down, Gramma." Her forced giggle is clearly false bravado and tugs at my heart; I want to hold her and make it go away. I want to kiss her silent so I don't hear what I suspect will be some guy's death wish. But rather, I force myself to remain still and listen, letting her get it out to both me and her grandmother; a cleansing of sorts. "I was a virgin, far from a whore," she continues, turning back to me now. "I went to a party one night and drank way too much. I admit it and I own it—it was stupid. The last thing I remember is watching a girl in a shiny green top do a keg stand, then I woke up on the floor of a dorm room with about ten other people. I was devastated when I realized exactly how stupid I'd been, and so humiliated…" Tears are gushing down her cheeks and she's actually snorting in an attempt to breathe, but still, I don't move to touch her.

I'm frozen; in shock, in anger, in awe…I'm fucking frozen.

"I dug around for my shoes and snuck out, walking as fast as I could to the bus stop. I'd ridden with a girl I knew from school, but I didn't want to look for her or talk to her ever again, so I just walked and walked until I saw a sign."

Make it stop, I can't hear anymore.

"When I got to the hub, I finally took a breath and went to put on my shoes. When I—" Her body racks under the violent sobs and I can't not hold her another minute, sliding across the bench and wrapping her in my arms. "When I lifted my foot, to put…to put on my shoe, I felt it."

I can't ask; I don't want to know. Instead, I hold her tighter, manically kissing her hair as I smooth it down. Rub, kiss, rub, kiss…it's all I can do efficiently right now.

"It hurt, like a pull inside me, and a spurt of something came out." She wipes her nose and looks up at me apologetically. "Sorry, that might be too much. I meant, I knew, I just knew, I'd been with someone."

"You were raped." The words burn my mouth, the sting of venom fresh on my tongue.

"No!" She's quick to answer, but then frowns as her reaction sinks in. "I don't know, maybe. I remember dancing with a guy, so maybe I flirted too much. I was out of it enough to not remember, so maybe I was out of it enough to say yes. I'll never know for sure."

Another moment I'll always remember—I've never been so angry and consumed with absolute hatred in my life. The person I now hate most in the entire world is a stranger; a man with no name or face known to me, who will die the moment, if ever, we meet.

"Don't you ever say that again!" I hope my grip on her chin is gentle as I grasp it to make her meet my eyes. "This was not your fault. You can't say yes and mean it when you're drugged, which it sounds like you may have been, or even passed out. And anyone with it enough to do what he did would've been able to see you weren't in your right mind."

"I know," she pulls her face from my grasp and buries it in my chest, "but my version makes it bearable. Maybe I just drank too much. Sometimes, not very often, I have dreams and see flashes of a scene I don't understand. I'm not sure if it's something I was there for or a nightmare I made up after…it."

"Did you go to the ER when it happened, Emmett?"

"No," she looks up, "and please don't yell at me about it. I thought if I couldn't remember actually saying no, then I couldn't accuse someone, let alone a faceless stranger, of being a rapist."

"Are you worried he knows you?" I ask, because whoever he is, he better hope like fucking hell I never find out. I will kill him, no questions, no chance for explanation. I know myself, what I can and cannot handle reasonably—it would be both his and my "game over"—him underground, me to jail.

"No," she mumbles. "I moved, sold my car, changed schools and jobs, everything, even though I seriously doubt he even knew my name, or cared. I'm sorry, Gramma," she wails, the most agonizing sound I'll ever hear, "but I'm keeping this baby. I don't care if it's selfish, I am! I'm not afraid of the bus or hard work!" She pauses and hiccups. "I'm…I'm afraid of one day looking into the eyes of another child I have with my husband and knowing I didn't do everything I could to love the first one!"

"Shh." I gather her up in my embrace as tight as I can. "No one thinks you're selfish, babe. Wanting to pour all your love onto someone else couldn't ever be thought of as selfish."

"But I worry that I won't be able to give them a good life. Like if I gave the baby up for adoption, maybe they'd get a family with a big house and a backyard, maybe some dogs." She loses it again, succumbing to body shakes and gasping cries.

Sweet girl, her thoughts scrambled but adorable. "We can get a dog, babe," I assure her. "I love dogs."

"So now you know it all. That's why we can never be more than friends. But like it or not, I feel a bond with you. I trust you and I can't bear the thought of not having you in my life. Will you please keep being my friend?" Her bottom lip is quivering as her watery green eyes beg an answer from me.

And I'm a goner—bag me and tag me, I'm done.

"Yes, sweet, beautiful, selfless Emmett. I'll be your best friend."

Chapter 12

NOT CRUEL INTENTIONS

—Emmett—

I HAVE A WHOLE NEW OUTLOOK on life. My steps have an extra spring, my shoulders a lightness I haven't felt in months, and my journal pages have happy little doddles in the corners. Now that Sawyer knows everything and let me keep my job and his friendship, for the first time in a long time, I have hope that everything really will be all right.

Against my better judgment, I moved into the duplex by him. Actually, I quit bitching and smiled as he moved my stuff in it, then made him a sandwich. Then when he looked around and sighed, I made him another one.

I still want him every time I look at him, but we've kept

things strictly platonic for the last two weeks. I'm sure it's not a struggle for him, with the new information he's been given, but it's becoming increasingly difficult for me. My hormones kick in more and more every day and we're together constantly and much of the time he's shirtless, or being cocky, or sexy…or breathing.

He's always with me when I fall asleep, telling me about himself or his day. Constantly, after my eyes have drifted closed, he nudges me when the "good part" is coming up in the movie. And when we drag in from work together, late at night, my bath's usually running before I even have both shoes off. And he, or a sweet note, is always there when I wake up.

So it more than hurts a little and feels like that balloon of hope I'd been carrying around just popped when I round the corner at work Friday night and see Mariah practically lying across the bar in front of him. I stop short and observe from afar, the dagger cutting deeper as he looks down at her and shoots her that sexy grin of his that I so love. She runs one hand up his arm and he dips his head to let her whisper in his ear, then laughs and nods when he pulls back.

I know I'll never be his, or him mine; I'm pregnant and a constant charity case for him to rescue, but he deserves better than Mariah. She's not smart enough to pick up on his quick wit or keep up her end of a late night, snacks in bed conversation. She couldn't possible appreciate his kindness, once you get past the growling and under the breath bossiness, and if she doesn't say "thank you," then he won't get to ask her stuff and they'll never build a real relationship. And his races, which he's almost completely stopped for some reason...but should he ever start up again and take her, there's no way she'll focus and cheer for him rather than skank along the sidelines for her next slut fix. And oh my God, he'll flunk Calc II! He thinks he's good, but he's horrid, so you have to go back and erase his answers and forge in the right ones in sloppy handwriting. She probably can't even add!

I should stomp over there right now and rip her off that bar by her badly bleached hair, for Sawyer's sake and all, but I can't. That'd be more of my selfishness keeping him from being single, young, and carefree, to keep him strangled with my polar opposite drama.

I rub my belly and whisper, "I didn't mean you were drama. I love you and I'm happy you're coming."

As though he can feel my gaze, he averts his attention from Piranha, which sounds an awful lot like Mariah and can't possibly be a coincidence, and stares back at me. Like a pathetic sap, I lift my hand and give him a small wave and a contrived smile.

"You okay?" he mouths to me.

I nod abruptly and turn, not wanting him to see my agony. I've got to stop this, stop begrudging him a life that doesn't include me. I need to stop picturing how perfect we could be in my head. I need to stop thinking about a little boy atop his shoulders laughing and clapping.

I seek Kasey out amongst the mass of bodies, the heat and stench of sweat almost more than I can take. I always try to skirt around the edges, never one to bear the brunt of the epicenter of the club, but I have to talk to him, so I barrel through.

"Hey!" I yell, tapping him on the back.

"What's up?" he screams, cupping around his ear.

I bend my finger and he leans down to me. "I have to get out of here; I really don't feel well. Can you let Sawyer know? Give Darby my tables or let them order from the bar. I gotta go."

"Yeah, okay." He ushers me carefully through the crowd. "Go grab your stuff and I'll walk you out."

I HAVE TO ADMIRE his tenacity. When I shut off my phone after about forty calls and texts, he took to beating on the door. And after I ignored that and heard Tucker, the tenant in the other half of this duplex, come out and ask him politely to stop banging, I can now hear him trying to take the screen off my bedroom window.

141

Creepy? Yes, but I know it's him and not a deranged burglar, just a deranged Sawyer. Even when he gets the screen off, I don't think he'll break the window, so I'm gonna lie here and try my best to block him out.

"Emmett Louise Young, I'm gonna spank your fucking ass when I get in there!" I hear him hiss outside the window.

"Go away, Sawyer!"

"Do you want me to break the glass? I don't want it to fly across the room and cut you, so just come open the damn thing! Or here's a thought, go open the goddamn door!"

"Go home, Sawyer!"

"Not happening, woman," he mocks me in a singsong tone. "I'm counting to three, so if you're not gonna open it, at least get back. I don't want you hurt."

He wouldn't.

"One!"

I don't think he would.

"Two!"

Shit, okay! "I'm coming! Simmer down, you crazy man!" I brush aside the curtains and look out at the man I can't seem to shake, the moonlight a melodic backdrop to his angry, muscular, adorable glory.

The second I have the window latch flipped, he's pushed it open and already hoisted himself through. "You are in some serious trouble, Shorty."

"And you are scarily close to needing medication. What

the hell are you doing crawling through my window in the middle of the night? Did you leave all your brain cells inside Mariah?"

It's the meanest thing I've ever said to someone in my life and I already regret it.

"Is that what this is about? You think I fucked Mariah?"

"You sure as hell looked close to it at the bar!"

He stalks toward me until I'm backed against the wall, the lazy moon our own only light. "I was trying to be distant but polite. I didn't want to cause a damn scene. What do you care anyway?"

"I don't care! You came to me!"

He grabs the finger I'm poking into his chest and pulls me forward with it, coming nose to nose with me. "You leave work without telling me. You don't answer your phone, texts or your door. What the fuck was I supposed to do?"

I like it better when he screams; this low, gritty voice is steering me a bit off course.

"Nothing! You've done enough! My car, my house, my job, everything is because of you! I can't use you anymore. I'm such a goddamn leech I can't even look myself in the mirror! Quit worrying about me, Sawyer, go be happy. Fuck Mariah sideways if that's what it'll take, but leave me be!"

"Fine!"

"Fine!"

I'm not sure which my neighbor, Tucker, will appreciate

more, our volume or our extensive vocabularies.

Surprisingly, I don't cry this time. No, I'm too wound up from being screamed at and pseudo-burglarized to cry. I know the nausea, which you'd expect from pregnancy, is from picturing him and Mariah together, not the hormones. I climb back into bed and curl in a ball, turned toward the wall.

It's not the lack of loud foot stomps or the absence of an opening or slamming door that clue me in...no, it's the charge in the air, the tingling that starts at the base of my spine and slinks its way up until the hairs on the back of my neck stand on end. I know he's still here, looking over me.

"I didn't touch Mariah tonight, nor will I ever touch her again." His voice, now calm and low, cuts through the darkness.

"It's none of my business," I say to the wall. "I'm sorry for what I said."

The mattress squeaks and sags under his weight, but I hold my ground and don't turn over to see what he's doing. "It scares me when I hear you're sick and then I can't find you."

"I just couldn't watch her hands on you, Sawyer. She's not good enough for you."

"Do you really think that?" He lies down behind me, scooting up against my back and curling an arm around my waist.

"Yes. You're the lottery and she's a penny slot

machine—everyone can get a pull. Find someone who appreciates all the extraordinary things you have to offer, Sawyer."

"Like what?" His stubble scratches my shoulder as he snuggles in further.

"You don't really need me to boost your ego, do you?"

"Yes," he tickles my side, "I do. I want to know…what someone as mind-blowing as you would possibly find special about me. Humor me, please."

"Hhh," I sigh, unable to resist entwining my fingers through his resting on my stomach. "Let's see. First of all, you're hot as hell, and you know it, but the sexiness comes from your mannerisms—the cocky smile, the dark blue, all-seeing eyes, the sarcastic smirk—they're all sexy and all you. It's so much more, though, your aura or something. I don't know. I'd bet good money you could even lure in a blind, deaf girl from fifty yards."

Abruptly, he flips me over, no longer satisfied having a conversation with my back. "My turn?"

"No." I silence him with a finger to his lips. "I didn't ask, you did. Want me to stop?"

I hope he says no. He needs to know how incredible he is, and I'm happy to be the one to tell him.

"I guess not." He plays aloof and I snort, not fooled—he's dying to hear the rest.

"You're kind, maybe the kindest person I've ever met.

You're generous to a fault and a fiercely loyal friend. You're protective, but in a non-suffocating way, and you respect women wholly. You're hilarious and clever and pretty easygoing most of the time. And you care and love with all you are."

"Why didn't you go to the ER and report it?"

"Who has ADD now? Where'd that come from?"

"I can't quit thinking about it. The thought of you dealing with it all by yourself makes me crazy angry that I wasn't there for you." He kisses my forehead. "I'm sorry I wasn't there."

"You didn't even know me then, so there's certainly nothing for you to be sorry about."

"Why didn't you go?" he asks again, holding my eyes with his own, a deadly serious conversation brewing.

"And say what? I got smashed and irresponsible at a party and may or may not have rejected sex with one of fifty guys at said party?"

"Or, I went to a party, which everyone should be able to safely do, and someone drugged and then attacked me? Please make sure I'm okay and run the DNA so I can press charges."

"I didn't want anyone to know. I feel foolish and ashamed that I even put myself in that position."

"If a girl wears a really short skirt and dances on a table at a bar, is she 'asking for it'?"

"No, of course not."

"Exactly! It didn't happen because you went to a party or because of what you wore or even that you drank. It happened because one douche thought it was okay to attack a comatose girl. It will only ever be his fault, not yours."

"See, that's why you deserve better than Mariah," I say, running my hand down his chest. "You're a one of a kind man. Hard body, soft heart."

"Can I hold you tonight? I was so worried. I just want to be able to sleep, knowing you're right beside me, safe."

"I should say no because the line is so blurry, but I sleep better with you too," I admit. "So yes, please stay."

"Come 'ere." He pulls me closer, offering his arm as my pillow. "Goodnight, Shorty. Don't ever scare me like that again."

"Night, Sawyer, sweet dreams."

"They will be now."

Chapter 13

PERFECT PICTURE

—SAWYER—

TUESDAY NIGHT we all get a group text, which I'm shocked but pleased immensely to see Emmett is now a part of the list.

The pleased part dies a quick death when I actually read it.

Laney: Laney's 20th birthday party this Sat night at The K, 8 pm. Costume ball— come as Disney Princes and Princesses!!

Whitley: OMG yay! So fun!

Tate: FML. Aren't we too old for this?

Dane: Surely you're not ragging on my beautiful

girl's party idea which she is very excited about. I'm imagining that, right?

Whitley: I call Tinkerbell!

Bennett: Taterbear, be nice. I call Ariel!

Evan: Again, HOW do you u remove yourself from a group message?

Emmett: Thank you so much for thinking of me. I'd love to come but I work that night.

Sawyer: No u don't, Shorty. We'll close down for the bday girl. Will you please come as my princess?

Laney: Ahh xoxo

Emmett: Which princess did you have in mind?

Sawyer: The half-naked one with the long black hair.

Emmett: Pocahontas?

Sawyer: Yes, Pokeyourhontas.

Zach: Good one lmao

Emmett: How about Belle? You can be the Beast.

Sawyer: I don't even need a costume to be a Beast.

Emmett: Well there ya go, Belle it is.

Zach: Who the %!#* am I supposed to bring?

Emmett: Zach, Sawyer could ask his friend Mariah to join you.

Sawyer: EMMETT.

Laney: Zach, take off your shirt & walk to dorm laundry. You'll have plenty of choices in minutes.

Dane: LANEY.

Laney: So excited! Can't wait to c everybody!

Emmett walks in the front door of The K about twenty minutes later, apologizing the whole walk up to me for being late.

"Everything okay?" I ask her.

"Yes, Beast, I just couldn't find my keys. Are you excited about the party?"

"I guess." I pop a shoulder. "If it makes Laney happy and you're excited, then I'm willing to do just about anything."

"Thank you for asking me to go with you. I've never done anything like this—no prom, no dances, so it will be my debut." She does a curtsy then rises back up and smiles at me.

"There's no princess I'd rather take. And you thanked me." I wink. "You know what that means."

"Are we still playing that game? I haven't been paying attention. Okay," she huffs, "shoot."

"Why don't you ever go to the doctor? You should know exactly how far along you are, your due date, and all kinds of stuff. Prenatal care is vital, Emmett, and I haven't seen one clue that you're getting any."

"I take a prenatal vitamin every single day. I don't drink," she's fired up, ticking off on her fingers, "I googled the healthiest diet, I cut out almost all caffeine. And I went to get tested for diseases, just in case he—" She chokes up, seemingly on air, then takes a few deep breaths. "He didn't give me anything. I'm not being neglectful."

"Hey," I come out from behind the bar, "you didn't hear any judgment in the question. If you did, you put it there. I only wanted to mention it because the book says you should be seeing a doctor once a month."

"The book?"

I reach back and pull it out from under the counter. "What To Expect When Emmett's Expecting. Step one is go to a doctor."

"Why do you have that book? And at work?" She darts her head around, making sure no one hears us.

"I want to be able to help you."

This is the part where she reminds me she's not a charity case and I can't get too close and keep rescuing her. I brace for it, ten plausible comebacks already rehearsed.

"Really? You want to help me?"

Ah, read about this too. It's totally natural for her to cry a lot...and tinkle. Two mysteries solved by chapter five.

"More than anything, Shorty mama. That's what friends do, right?" I say with a grin. "So you're not mad?"

"No," she chuckles, "I'm not mad. I'm once again impressed and touched. So I guess I'll start looking for a doctor now that I make good money. I couldn't afford it before, but I did take precautions."

That's my cue—I whip out the card from my back

pocket and hand it to her. "Doctor Pregnant at your service. She takes The K's insurance and we have an appointment at one on Thursday."

She slowly looks from the card up to me, eyes wet but happy. "I'm not sure how I managed before you, but I thank God every single day that I have you now. Thank you, Sawyer."

I hold open my arms and she slides right in, soaking up my hug as much as I relish in the feel of her. "Let's call her by her actual name though, okay? It's Dr. Greer."

"Count your blessings, woman. It was Doc InspectAPuss for a while."

"I will kill you." Her eyes slit and warn me; she actually will kill me.

"I know, I know. Sheesh, those damn pregnancy hormones are suffocating your sense of humor." I release her, evaluating her from head to toe. "Are you ready to get to work? If you get too tired on the floor, tell me and we'll switch you. Your energy level should start to go back up in a week or two, though."

"I'm great and I need the money the floor brings. Don't patsy me, Sawyer. I can do it."

"Okay then." I swat her butt, laughing when she jumps and turns around to give me a surprised visual dressing down.

MAYBE IT'S THE GRACEFUL WAY she glides instead of walks, or her sweet smile and the way it seems like every customer is as important as the last, or perhaps I'm just mesmerized by the way her low cut top seems to be trying to kick her boobs out of it, but work time isn't good enough right now—I want only her and I time, us time, and I want it right this fucking minute. Wednesday nights are always slow anyway, so I put Kasey behind the bar and take Emmett home early. Of course she balks, desperate for the money, but when I point out her one customer and offer up a chick flick and no MSG Chinese takeout on me, she caves.

I take her hand as we walk out and open her door, laughing to myself. My poor bike is sitting under the carport collecting dust most days. I take this car, with its hot little passenger, everywhere more often than not.

When I climb behind the wheel, feeling like the freakishly big man in the circus car, she's already turned on the radio. It's garbage, Top 40 brain-melting bullshit, so I grab my phone and plug it in.

"Got a song, for you, from me," I say with a wink.

She tilts her head and gives me the side-eyed examining look of hers, eyes turning sad and a frown kidnapping her sweet mouth when she figures out what it is—"Savin' Me" by

Nickelback.

"You don't need me to save you, Sawyer," she mumbles through that frown.

"You're right. I don't. You already did. And I'd love nothing more than the chance to show you what I can be."

"You already did," she retorts like the clever little vixen she is.

"Oh, Em, you have no idea. There's so much more I want to show you."

She doesn't respond to that, turning to look out her window instead of at me. We listen to the rest of the album as we go through the drive-thru, the wait taking longer than usual for them to remove all MSG, which I highly suspect is a ruse. Can you really take all that shit out of it and still have Chinese food? I figure it must be kinda like taking the cow outta the milk.

Back on our way, the sounds coming from the passenger seat sound like a football team hitting a buffet. "You saving me any over there, woman?"

"It'z jus wun egwoll," she mumbles, hand under her mouth to catch any food she loses with her excuse.

"Uh huh, are you sure it was the right one, with no MSG?"

"Yez, I chebbed ddu wapper."

"Well then, by all means carry on, my lil' piggy."

She holds up a finger that she needs one more second to

chew, then swallows and gives me a huge smile. "Can we go get ice cream too, my treat?"

She seems so happy tonight, a new air about her, and it's turning me on like mad. "That sounds good, but I'm buying. Ah ah—" I hold my hand up, "talk to the hand, woman."

Her head falls back with a sweet giggle and I shift slightly in my seat, my jeans suddenly a bit crowded.

"Hand, can we make it Coldstone?"

"Your wish, madam, is my command. Birthday cake cookie bash blah blah it is."

"Close." She laughs. "You've been?"

"Nah, Laney. She sometimes makes me take a bite of hers. So sweet it's disgusting."

"What do you like?"

"Moonlit strolls on the beach." I look over at her and smirk. "Oh, you mean ice cream? Good ole chocolate."

"Plain," she mocks a yawn.

"Not plain at all, more…classic. When you know exactly what you like, what you want, you stick with it."

I keep my eyes straight ahead but catch her in my peripheral. She's staring at my profile, short, shallow breaths pausing between her parted lips. "Right," she whispers, "that makes sense."

"We're here!" I turn to her with my announcement, a grin to stop traffic lighting up her face. You'd think I went to Jared.

"Woo hoo!" She bursts out of the car. Skipping, ah how I've longed to see that move again, to the door and flinging it open. "Oh my God, can you smell that? This is what Heaven smells like, I know it."

Buy stock in Coldstone, people—I plan on making a habit of seeing her so tickled. She's gone without so much like a trooper, not a trace of bitterness or self-pity, for so long…all it takes is some ice cream to make her day. I'm in awe of this girl.

She orders something with the word cookie in it (called that) and I go with one scoop of chocolate in a cup. When she pulls out her money, I gently swat her hand and step right in front of her, much to the cashier's amusement.

"Can we eat in the car?" she asks in between licks of her cone as we head for the door.

Oh. Hell. No. I am but a man, after all.

"Hold on." I grumble, walking back to the counter. I grab a spoon from the jar by the register then stomp back to Emmett, jabbing the spoon into her cone like a candle on a cake. "Eat it with that."

"Why? If we can't eat in the car, that's fine. Let's just grab a table."

I huff, holding the door open. "Not worried about the car, woman. Did I say anything when you ate the Chinese food in the car? Come on." As she passes by me I lean in to whisper, "Just keep that little pink tongue in that sweet mouth of yours, okay?"

She turns back to look at me over her shoulder, her green eyes filled with shock...and something that doesn't look anything like rejection.

We're not far from the house, so she's still eating when we pull into her driveway.

"Your house tonight, I assume?" I ask as I turn off the car.

"Laney's gonna think I kidnapped you. You're never there anymore."

"Yeah," I open my door, "but Dane'll love me for it. He can't get her to move in with him, so he's squatting at hers."

I walk around and open the door for her, snagging the bags of Chinese food from her lap. I test their weight, making sure I don't need to call and order a pizza, 'cause the ice cream will not fill me up.

She slaps my gut. "I didn't eat it all, you big baby."

"WHAT'D YOU DO before you knew me?" she asks as I get the DVD ready.

"What do you mean? Same as I do now: work, school, whatever."

"Like all the nights you're with me. If you weren't, what

would you have been doing?"

"Besides pining away?" I poke from head around the TV and wink. "I don't know, maybe a race, or—"

"Stop! Never mind, I don't need a reminder about your checkered flag activities." She holds up a hand and then pretends to gag. "Anything else? Sex takes what, five minutes? You had to have done other stuff—movies, dates, bowling?"

I rise gradually, making my way to where she's lounged on her bed. "I don't date, Shorty. I can watch movies at home and sex should never, and I mean never, only take five minutes. It takes longer than that to get undressed."

"Uh, you know what I mean."

"Actually I don't." I roll onto my back beside her. "I guess I'm a boring guy."

"I don't think you're boring at all." She grabs the remote beside my hip. "What movie did you put in?"

"Enemy of the State." I jump up and flip off the light then get back in bed. "You seen it?"

"No, wh—"

"How many rocks must one live under to not have seen Enemy of the State?" I cry, scandalized. "It's the greatest movie ever."

"So you like it then?"

Lil' smartass.

-Emmett-

"SAWYER!"

"Uh, too early."

"Sawyer, I have to pee. Can you lift your arm?"

I'm going to wet the bed, like actually piss the bed. I've tried to hold it, not wanting to wake the sleeping giant, but my bladder has met its max...and he's got his huge arms wrapped around me so tightly I can't escape.

He snuggles his face further into my hair. "Go back to sleep, Shorty."

"Sawyer," I use my only line of defense and pull hard on his arm hair, "I'm gonna burst. You have to let me up," I whine.

Finally, he rouses, letting out a sleepy chuckle and lifting his arm. "Hurry back."

I run to the bathroom, pulling down my pants as I go; it's a seriously close call. I sit there shaking my head. Who would have thought this is how I'd end up—my pregnant bladder waking me up from sweet slumber in the arms of Sawyer Beckett. Our whole dynamic together confuses me. He's my best friend, we spend all our time together, we sleep in the same bed more often than not...but we'll never be together together.

"You fall in?" His voice through the door startles me; I've been sitting here deep in thought so long I've drip dried completely.

"No, I'm fine, be there in a sec."

Of course he's standing right outside the door when I come out, faced lined with concern. "Everything okay?"

"Yes," I sigh, "I guess I zoned out. Come on," I grab his hand, heading back to bed. "Sawyer, don't you think it's kinda weird, us always sleeping together?"

"I wish we were sleeping together." He scoots in, flush to my back, and pulls the covers up over us. "But falling asleep in the same bed? Nope, not weird," he squeezes me, "comfy, though."

"Toaster." I nudge his feet with mine, our code for him to part his feet so I can slip mine in between them for warmth. He's like my own personal toaster oven for my always freezing cold feet.

"Go to sleep, Mama, we have our first doctor appointment tomorrow," he mumbles, kissing the back of my head.

Our first appointment?

Chapter 14

MR. DOUBTFIRE

—SAWYER—

HER LEFT LEG HASN'T STOPPED bouncing since we sat down on these pocket-sized plastic chairs.

"Here, let me." I take the clipboard from her lap; she's only filled in the top line—in fifteen minutes. "Are you nervous?"

No answer, just more bouncing. Yep, she's wigging out.

Maybe if I get her talking, out of her own head? "What's your date of birth, Em?"

"Huh?" She turns abruptly to me, face pale, masked in fear. "Oh, um, October tenth, ninety-one."

That's right, she mentioned it was coming up during the

interview; I gotta get busy on birthday plans. "Okay, I know your address and phone number." I scan the paperwork quickly. "Who's your emergency contact?"

"Uh…" She thinks, chewing the corner of her mouth, her brow furrowing in concentration. "You," she whispers, "if that's all right?"

"That's more than all right, Shorty." I lean in and give her a quick kiss on that trembling rosebud mouth of hers. "Relax for me, okay? I'm right here. Everything's fine, I promise."

She's a tad calmer by the time we've finished all five thousand forms. I kept waiting for "when did you last fart and what did it smell like?" or "did your last booger come from your left or right nostril?" I mean, fuck me they ask a lot of questions.

I deliver the clipboard back to the blonde behind the window who's eye fucking me like I'm not sitting in a pregnancy clinic with a gorgeous brunette. Rolling my eyes, I set the board down on the ledge and make my way back to Emmett, picking up her hand and kissing it. "One time, not at band camp though, I tried to shave lines in my eyebrows. All the guys had 'em, so I thought what the hell." I glance at her from the corner of my eye—it's working!—a smirk starting at the edge of her lip. "Anyway, the more I tried to even them out, the worse it got, till finally I spent three months of seventh grade with no left eyebrow."

A small gasp precedes her laughter, then she quickly covers her mouth when she snorts. "Oh my God, how awful. So you walked around with one eyebrow?"

"Yep, loud and proud. People learned real quick not to give me shit about it."

"Emmett Young?" We both turn as her name is called.

She stands, wobbling a bit, so I quickly rise and place my hand on her back. Her sweet green eyes find mine and I give her a reassuring grin.

"Let's do this, Mama."

"Can he come back with me?" Emmett squeaks out to the nurse waiting for us.

"Of course he can! Is this Daddy?"

"That's me," I boast automatically.

Emmett's whole body goes rigid, then trembles, under my hand.

I find her ear with my mouth and whisper softly, "It's none of their business, babe, just go with it."

She nods dazedly and I propel her forward with a gentle urging of my hand.

I'll be damned if they're gonna look at her like some too young, no father reject, judging her with pity or condemnation in their glares. No one's gonna look at my Emmett like that ever. And sadly, she can't supply the real father's medical history or anything anyway, so...no, not gonna think about it. She'd probably get real mad if I punched a fucking hole in the wall right now.

"This way." The nurse smiles, extending her arm. Right inside the door she stops us, indicating a scale. "Let's get you weighed."

"Oh, um," Emmett clamps down on her lip, looking at me. "Can you turn around and maybe plug your ears?"

"Hell no." I smirk at her then turn to Nurse Betty. "My guess is 123. 'Bout three pounds in the last two weeks, all in her boobs." I wiggle my eyebrows. "Pretty happy about the weight gain to boob ratio."

Emmett drops her face in her hands and shakes her head, but Nurse Betty thinks I'm hilarious, laughing out loud.

"Well, let's see how good you are. Please step up here, Emmett."

Oh, I get a nasty glare from her as she steps onto the scale. "You haven't ever seen my boobs, and how would—"

"121! Very nice!" the nurse exclaims, interrupting Emmett's tongue lashing.

I wink at the struck silent Emmett, offering her my hand. "What? So I pay attention? Come on, dear, right this way."

The nurse leads us to a room, quietly chuckling to herself the whole way as Emmett tries to break my hand.

"Don't embarrass me," she hisses quietly.

Once the door is closed and it's just the two of us waiting for the doctor, I start whistling "Savin' Me," casually flipping through an exhilarating edition of Parents. Holy shit!

Did you know the biggest baby ever born that survived weighed 19.2 pounds? Good Lord. We won't be sharing that little tidbit with the already petrified Emmett.

I can feel her angry stare boring a hole in the top of my head, but I keep on reading, holding back a laugh. Why is it that aggravating her makes my heart do a jig in my chest?

"You're lucky I can't whistle, or I'd be busting out some choice songs for you right now," she warns.

Huh, microwaves do not pose a threat to the fetus, despite rumors. Fascinating.

"I know you hear me," she throws at me and I can tell she's seething.

Guess what she's not doing right now? Freaking out, shaking her leg, or fidgeting with her hands. Worth it. Keep 'em coming, Shorty. I can distract you with my infuriating appeal all day long.

"You announce my tit growth out loud, but I'm being ignored? Unbelievable," she sneers, shaking her head and trying desperately to kick me from her perch on the examining table.

Yeah right, with her short legs? Not happening. Ah, but dynamite comes in short sticks, and she's getting off the table to come over and attack me when I'm saved by the knock.

"Knock, knock." The doctor peeks around the door. "Emmett? I'm Dr. Greer." The woman doctor (you bet your ass I got a woman) shakes Emmett's hand, then mine. "And you are?"

"Sawyer Beckett, the love of Emmett's life."

"Oh yes, I've been told you're quite the character." She clears her throat. "And how are you doing, Emmett?"

At first she mumbles her answers, never looking up from her lap, but after about ten minutes she starts to feel more comfortable and things start going smoother. I'm surprised to learn Emmett's had a lot of abdominal tweaks and lower back pain. Neither of those sound good to me, but the doctor says it's her body stretching, making room for bubba, and quite normal.

"Okay, let's get you in a gown and we'll examine you. Let me step out and give you time to change."

"I'll, uh, step out too. Good luck," I kiss her cheek, "you're doing great."

"Sawyer." She grabs my shirt and pulls me back.

"Yeah?"

"Thank you." Her eyes mist up, her voice shaking.

"My pleasure." This time I bend my head and kiss her lips. "Have them come get me when you want me back in here. Don't be afraid to speak up."

She nods, her smile holding more confidence now than it has all day.

———— ⌇ ————

"MR. BECKETT?" I look up from my phone when my name is called. "Emmett's ready for you to come back."

I follow her, an odd feeling in my chest. Knowing she really does want me there, that she sent for me, is severely fucking with my heart. When I walk in the room, Emmett's lying back on the table and immediately holds out her hand for me to take. "March tenth," she says with a smile. "We're about to hear the heartbeat. Do you want to?"

"Yeah, babe," I kiss her forehead incessantly, "I'd love to."

"Okay, Emmett, this will be cold." The lady on a stool warns as she squirts sploog all over her belly.

"What the—"

"Sawyer," Emmett squeezes my hand, demanding my eyes on her, "no comments."

"I wasn't gonna."

"I know you, you were so gonna."

My argument is stopped cold in my throat as a loud whooshing sound fills the room.

"Nice and strong," the nurse comments. "146 beats per minute. Perfect."

"PERFECT? FOR A FUCKING STROKE!" I scream.

"Sir," she chuckles with a broad smile.

I'm not sure what the fuck is so funny.

"That's absolutely normal for a fetus. It's in the ideal range."

"We'd like a second opinion. Can you go get Doctor Down Under, please?"

"Dear God," I hear Emmett mumble. She sits up, hands covering her face for a second. "I am so, so sorry. We're having him tested for Tourette's."

"I think it's adorable he's so protective over his baby. Trust me, the daddy stories we could tell," she laughs, "they'd make your man here look calm."

"You ladies do realize I can hear you when you talk out loud, right?" I butt in. "I wasn't kidding. I want to hear someone else tell me that's a normal rate."

"Of course," the nurse stands, "here's a towel to clean up with, Miss Young."

Emmett thanks her, wiping the lube from her tummy blindly, because she's staring at me. "You are insane, and blunt, and embarrassing," she hisses.

"Em, I—"

"Ah, let me finish. And I love it all. There is no one I'd rather have here with me today. Come here." She opens her arms and kisses my cheek, hugging me fiercely. "Love you."

It's not the same as "I love you," but I'll take it.

Chapter 15

AS GREAT AS IT GETS

—Emmett—

"DID HE ROB DISNEYLAND?" I ask Sawyer where only he can hear. The K looks like... well, Disneyland.

"Laney wants, Laney gets." He laughs like it's no big deal. Apparently Dane making Laney's fantasies come to life is the norm.

"Hi!" Laney floats across the room in a white gown, rivaling Cinderella. "Emmett, you make an even hotter Belle than the real one!"

I open my mouth to point out that there is no real Belle, but Sawyer quickly shakes his head at me and squeezes my hand in his.

"Sawyer Landon Beckett, what the hell are you wearing?"

"I'm the Beast."

"Those are you BKE jeans," Laney points, "and a ball cap? Really? And a—a t-shirt?"

"Shorty, tell her. I'm a beast in any outfit, right? Happy Birthday, Gidge." He picks her up and twirls her around.

"Oh, here," I cut in, extending out her gift bag. "Sawyer and I got you something, together. We hope you like it."

"Thank you!" She takes the bag and gives me a big hug. "So basically, Sawyer put in some money and sent you shopping?" she jokes, jabbing him with her elbow.

"Actually, no. We went shopping together and he helped pick it out."

"Birthday girl burn!" Sawyer goads, pinching her nose. "Enough about how awesome I am though, where's Prince Pansy? Shouldn't he be carrying the back of your dress or something? Is he wearing tights? Please tell me he's wearing tights."

"No, he's no fun either. Go find him, you'll see," she pouts.

"Am I really not fun, baby?" Dane sneaks up behind her, slinking his arms around her waist. "Emmett, tell the truth, can you not tell who I'm dressed up as?"

He steps around her, wearing jeans and a t-shirt that reads "Prince Charming" across it. I can't help but snicker, giving Laney "I'm sorry for breaking girl code" eyes. "Prince

Charming?"

"Prince fucking Charming." He points and me and winks. "See, baby, they all know who I am."

Laney huffs and grabs my hand, dragging me over to the cake table. "We are officially playing hard to get. Don't look back at them."

"Okay." I fight to hold a straight face, helping myself to a glass of punch.

As the rest of the guests arrive, the night peps up with Dane refusing the birthday girl's attempt at playing hard to get, and Laney almost pulling off "miffed." It didn't hurt his case any that all the other guys showed up...not dressed up. Evan's in regular clothes with a hook on one hand, the Captain Hook to Whitley's adorable Tinkerbell. Tate's wearing an eye patch...cause Bennett's Ariel? We all took a turn explaining that yes, Ariel is a mermaid, but that doesn't make Eric a pirate, but he argued and told us all to fuck off, repeatedly. And Zach? Zach looks like John Smith anyway, and the girl he brought with him as Pocahontas? Yeah, she's a head-turner for sure.

All the princesses in the land hate her.

"Looks like you got a Pocahontas after all," I grumble as Sawyer and I dance. I'm standing on top of his boots to even make it look reasonable and suddenly feel short, and fat, and pregnant...

I should have come as Winnie the Pooh.

"Who are you talking about?"

"The hot, half-naked, Amazonian girl with Zach? What do you mean who am I talking about?"

"Not you?"

"Are you on crack? No, not me."

"Then I have no idea who you mean. Eyes on Emmett, always. Belle of the ball." He kisses the end of my nose.

I rest my head against his chest, pretending for only a moment this is real, he is mine and I am his, that I'll always be the only girl he sees. "When can we go home?" I yawn into his chest, the rhythm of our bodies swaying and him holding me up suddenly making me very sleepy.

"Now, if you want. You want?"

"Uh huh." I nod, kinda hoping he'll carry me and rescue me from this ridiculous dress.

"Let's go say goodbye and get you home."

"Are you sure?" I protest. "I can go alone. I don't want you to leave your friends because of me. Stay."

"Do you ever hear me, Emmett? When I tell you how I feel, do you ever really hear me?"

"What do you mean?"

"Nothing." He closes his eyes and takes a deep breath. "Let's go home."

"You awake?"

He doesn't answer my whisper and there's no flinch of his body, entwined with mine, to indicate that he heard me.

I'm not sure what's changed, but there's something in the air that hasn't been there the weeks of other nights we've slept in my bed together. Tonight I can't find sleep and each breath is a struggle. Tonight my clothes feel like a barrier rather than armor and my nipples are hard, aching for his hand to come up and caress them.

"What are you thinking so hard about over there?" His sleepy rumble makes my body respond even more.

"I thought you were asleep?"

"Don't change the subject." He manipulates my body like his favorite toy, gently but determinedly guiding me to my side so I now look into curious midnight blue eyes. "What's wrong?"

"I'm trying to understand what you're getting out of this. You have great friends, so you don't need me. And don't you need to uh…"

His sultry laugh draws my eyes back up to his, the mischievousness in them confirming I have indeed been caught staring down at his dick. "Whatcha lookin' at, Em?"

"Nothing." I feel my cheeks flame, darting my eyes to the far wall behind us.

"Nothing huh? I don't think it was nothing, I think you were checking out my—"

"Stop!" I slap his chest and he doesn't miss a beat, placing his hand over my own, securing it there on his taut, heated skin.

"No, you stop. Stop denying this, us." He touches our foreheads, teasing my lips with his. "You know I want you, Emmett, and I think you want me too, but you're scared. Tell me why. What exactly are you scared of?"

Is he serious? Why am I scared? Oh, I don't know, maybe because I'm pregnant, about to be a mother, and sleeping with him will only make what I already know a too harsh reality. I don't want to know for sure what I can't keep. What I've conjured up in my sweetest dreams, ached for in the depths of my unknown, is bad enough.

I'm afraid of what would happen after, when he leaves. I'm terrified I'd never recover, and I'd spend the rest of my life comparing any chance of reasonable happiness with each and every minute of sheer perfection I had with him. But then another voice in my head speaks louder, the voice that says even if I find a very nice man one day who will love me and my baby, they won't ever be able to make me feel the way Sawyer Beckett with only his voice, his looks, his care. So more, allowing my body to take from him what my heart's already latched onto, it's just not smart. If you had to choose between one night of ecstasy or a lifetime of comfortable...which would you pick?

It's inevitable that one day all too soon, I won't have him anymore, that I'll be left with only my dreams and memories to keep me warm at night while he's warming another woman's sheets. I've told him my secret, so he'd be going in eyes wide open; would it really be so bad to allow myself to give in? If only this once, I want to know how it feels to make love with a man, fully aware and wanting. I want to see the passion in his eyes as he takes me and accepts all that I so desperately want to give him.

And being real with myself, it's gonna happen; you don't sleep ever night in the same bed as a man as virile as Sawyer, madly attracted to him, and never give in. So I might as well quit kidding myself and free fall.

"I'm not scared if you're not," I finally answer.

"Liar." He smiles sweetly, kissing my nose, each of my cheeks, then lastly my chin. "But I am too. You scare the shit out of me, beautiful Emmett, with how fast and how hard you completely mesmerized me. One day you might figure out I'm an ass and run screaming, but I'll chance it. I'll risk anything to keep myself by your side as long as possible."

As long as possible. He means on or about March tenth, and I get it, I do.

But right now? Right now it's September.

I take a long, deep breath, turning off the battling voices in my head, letting only my heart and body guide me now. Slowly, I run both hands up his chest, wrapping them around his neck. "Kiss me like we have forever," I whisper, moistening my trembling lips with my tongue.

Tentatively, his eyes flick back and forth between mine, making absolutely sure, and then his arms tighten around my waist. I close my eyes, feeling his breath so close it mingles with my own as he finally delves into my mouth. I moan at the contact, relishing his tender but dominating lips, their large coarseness moving lazily, then fast, open and tasting, teasing with small sucks and bites.

"Emmett," he groans, sliding a hand up my back and into my hair. "So damn sweet." His tongue claims entry, curling around my own. His fingers tangle in my hair, tilting my head, and he eats at my mouth, the ravenous hunter inside him making me feel so alive.

Sawyer kisses are a whole body experience—consuming, like one ember quickly turns to wildfire. Somehow, with only our mouths connected, he makes my whole body feel like part of the act. Not one muscle in me hasn't gone lax, every inch of me his all at once. "More," I beg into his mouth. "Sawyer, more, anything, please."

"Oh no," he tilts my head back further, making me listen, "there is no way you're rushing me. I will take my time on every single inch of you."

If that's not the best argument I've ever heard in my life, I don't know what is. "Show me," I grunt as he pulls on my hair, "show me everything."

"Lie back and let me love you. For every sweet smile you've given me, every sexy outfit you've tortured me with, every night I've held you in my arms, never knowing if you'd be mine... I'm," he licks straight up the middle of my throat, "going," he nibbles down the left side, "to savor you." He finishes with open-mouthed sucking side to side across my collarbone, hitting a sweet spot that makes me positively shiver.

One of his hands leaves my hair, gliding downward, and my girls know he's on his way, my nipples hard and waiting. He stops, asking in a husky pant, "Can I touch you here, Emmett?"

My heart soars at his thoughtfulness, trying to overly ensure my comfort since he knows my past, but my past has no place here now. I grab his hand and crash it on my chest, arching further into his now kneading grasp. "You can touch me anywhere you want, however you want."

He growls, attacking my mouth with a rough, aggressive kiss. The tug on my nipple makes me gasp, even my lower half trying to come off the bed now.

"Are they sore? Too rough?"

"God, no! It feels great."

"Then can we lose the shirt babe?"

"You ask too many questions." I grab his cheeks with both hands. "I want you. I'm not scared or breakable. Take me any way you want, Sawyer."

"Fuck me," he snarls, grabbing the bottom of my shirt.

"I'm trying to!" I giggle, rising so he can lift it over my head.

His eyes take in my bare chest and I force myself to keep

my hands at bay despite the urge to cover myself. I've talked a big game and it's time to back it up.

Leisurely, he moves his gaze back up to mine. "You're so fucking gorgeous, Emmett. Better than anything I've pictured in my head a million times."

I don't know if it's me or my hormone-induced inner minx talking, but somebody says, "Suck them, Sawyer." I grab myself, offering up both achy peaks to him. "Suck my tits, babe."

"Oh, goddamn, I love that mouth, you nasty little girl." He goes for the right one first, his mouth open wide around it, his tongue flicking my nipple. Every time the hot metal of his tongue ring hits the very tip of my sensitive nipples, I jump a bit, sucking in a deeper breath. Sensory overload— yes, please!

My hands are firm on the back of his head, daring him to try and stop. I rub my hands back and forth over his close-cropped black hair. I love it. I mewl, or whimper, or make some other sound I'm sure I've never made before, and feel around for his hand. Finding it, I place it back on my left breast, wanting stimulus on every part of me at once.

"That feels so good," I moan.

He tries to pull away but I push his head back down, grunting my protest. "Just wanna suck the other one, baby; not stopping."

Oh, okay then. Carry on.

I see the smirk on his face as he moves his mouth over, latching on to my left nipple with vigor. "Mhm, Em," he murmurs through licks and nibbles, "you have the best tits I've ever seen. Real and big and in love with my mouth. They're perfect." He leans back on his haunches. "You do crazy things to me, woman." He watches his own finger trail from between my breasts down my stomach, hinting at the top of my shorts. "Crazy fucking things."

The touch of one fingertip exudes the sizzle of a thousand hands, the eyes of one man have me entranced, my toes curling under and my breathing staggering. Without a word, I elevate my hips, bidding him to bare the rest of me. Both hands now find my hips, his fingers curving beneath the edge of my shorts. Eyes never leaving mine, he slips them down my legs, carefully maneuvering first one ankle, then the other, out of them.

"I'll never be the same, will I?" he asks no one, his stare now trained on my wholly revealed body.

I crook my finger at him, wanting to feel him cover me.

He shakes his head, giving me a sexy air kiss and wink, then lifts my left leg. Running both hands up and down my over-sensitized skin, he croons, "I love your short ass legs, baby." That full, sexy mouth of his begins kissing every spot those hands just rubbed, a low hum emanating from him. When he's worked his way up to the spot that has me writhing in anticipation, his mouth is suddenly gone.

"What the—" I rise up onto my elbows, precariously close to devastation.

His low chuckle only lasts a moment before he starts treating my right leg to the same torturously delightful ministrations. God. This man. This patient, willful fucking man. "Relax, Emmett, I'll get there. When I do, I'll be staying awhile."

I can't stand it, the swelling, the tingles, so I literally take matters into my own hand. For three glorious seconds the pressure subsides…then my hand is hijacked by a much stronger one cinched around my wrist. "Don't even think about it, woman," he rumbles. "You'll come soon; in my mouth, on my fingers, then a few times all the fuck over my dick. Those are your only options."

"Please, Sawyer, fuck me."

Now he hovers over me, conscious to shift his weight to one forearm. "One day I'll fuck you real good, Em, but not tonight. Tonight I want to give you what I've never given anyone."

"I don't want your piercing. Nothing but you, ever. Only you inside me."

He buries his face in my neck, laughing faintly. "That's the sexiest thing I've ever heard, but I didn't mean the happydavra, babe." Kissing my neck, my chin, finally backing his face away some to commandeer my half-lidded eyes, he whispers, "I meant making love to you, Emmett. Loving your whole body with my whole body as slowly and gently as I can possibly go."

Don't you have to love someone to make love to someone? It's just semantics, really, because I do…I love his gentle, his crazy, his bossy, his tender, his coy, his playful…I love everything about him.

As far as what he meant, now is certainly not the time to ask for clarification. Not only am I clueless as to what I'd do with whatever his answer may be, but I can feel my need easing down the inside of my thigh.

"Show me, Sawyer, show me what that means."

That one magic finger of his again starts its taunting descent, finding its home in the shameful, embarrassing pool between my legs. "Aw, fuck, babe." He bends his head to my ear, pulling the lobe in his mouth. "That's all for me," he guides said finger up and down, "and I love it. Can I go down there and taste you, sweet girl?"

My holy…who knew sex held so many extracurricular activities? Leg licking, finger sliding, boob sucking…it's a smorgasbord of tantalization and it feels too damn good to be worshipped. I can't wait to have my turn on him; I have no idea what I'm doing, but as he's said before, I'll feel my way.

"Okay." I grab the back of his head, putting his mouth to mine. "But kiss me first, lots and lots."

"Oh yeah?" He chuckles. "Am I grounded from your

mouth after I go downtown?"

"Would you kiss me after coming in my mouth?"

"Shorty, if I could figure out how, I'd kiss you while I was coming in your mouth."

"Ew." I grimace. "We'll see, okay? Put in on our sexual bucket list."

His face goes stone-cold serious. "Do I get to make one of those? Like for real make one?"

I laugh, something extra special about how comfortable we are together—me naked, several things explored…throw in some banter while I'm naked and being explored, yep, that sounds like us all right.

"Shut up and kiss me," I demand. "You've got a trip downtown to get to."

"Yes fucking ma'am." He salutes me playfully, our mouths joining ravenously while his right hand sets off on the trip without him.

"Uh, please," I grovel into his mouth, gnawing his lower lip. "Do that again."

I don't know how many digits he slips inside me, it's hard to tell, but I know it's my new favorite number. The pad of his thumb pressing down and rubbing circles on my swollen clit has me on the edge of detonation. But his words, that seductive mouth of his, is what finally does it. "Ah, Emmett babe, you're so sweet and fucking tight for me. If I survive, I'm gonna make you feel so damn good."

If he survives? My head feels like it's going to explode off my shoulders, right after my pussy shoots sparks. "What...you're...doing...Ah!" I lose my voice, my eyes rolling back in my head.

"There's the spot," he groans, this thumb working miracles while one of however many fingers presses against a spot inside of me that feels unbelievable. "Don't tighten up, baby." He starts sucking on my neck again. "Breathe and relax through it, it'll last longer. Relax, Emmy, go numb with it."

I take big, deep breaths, willing my legs to relax, 'cause currently they're drawn up tight, as is my whole body, almost like I'm having a seizure.

"That's it," he moans around my breast, where his mouth somehow snuck while I was in the throes of my orgasm. "Better, baby?"

"B-better?" My breathing escalates at the hopeful prospect. "It gets better?"

His husky laugh resonates through the bedroom as his fingers slowly leave me. "I meant, do you feel better, did that take the edge off? But yeah, it does."

"When do I get to see you?" I playfully tug on the waistband of his shorts.

"Trust me, babe, the longer my shorts stay on, the longer this lasts for you. I'm only human, and you..." he rubs the back of his neck, his head falling back, "you're out of this world."

While he's got his head back and eyes closed, I quickly get up on my knees, closing the gap between us. "Or," I say, loving that he flinches when my mouth meets his chest, "we could take your edge off too."

"Emmett," he growls out, fisting a hand in my hair.

I worship his torso, so broad and hard beneath my lips, placing kisses everywhere, leaving no spot untouched by my mouth. Teasing both nipples with my tongue, I ask him, "Will you wear your piercings in these for me sometime?"

"Done," he mutters, "anytime you want."

I nod and grin, pleased and ready for more. "You have a magnificent body, Sawyer." I bend at the waist, following the trail of my wandering hands over his abdomen with my hungry mouth. "And this," I lick the groove of his V, "is the sexiest thing I've ever seen."

Straightening back up, I place both hands on his pecs and lean in for a kiss. He doesn't leave me wanting, doing that thing with his mouth where I enter another realm. Which is probably where I find the courage to quickly make it past his waistband and wrap my hand almost around his dick.

When I saw it that day in the alley, he was obviously going soft, having been finished and all, because MOTHER of HELL!

"Em," he growls, his hand on the back of my neck, the other in my hair, both gripping down hard.

"Hm?" I hum against his lips, my right hand exploring him.

An odd time I know, but all I can think about right now are Holly and Erica, two girls in my eleventh grade gym class. One day, while dressing in the locker room, I eavesdropped on their non-whispering, vulgar conversation about the many different male appendages they'd "tried out" and their disappointment. According to them, their quest for a dick that was both long and thick was futile, most guys blessed more so in one facet or the other, but never both. Considering they were admitting to being experts, I've lived for years under this assumption of what to expect.

Well, here's to locker room sluts being wrong, because the pulsing, heated cock in my hold is too thick for me to fully circle with my hand and long enough that the head is peeking out from his waistband.

"You're huge." I flash my eyes to him, mortified I said that out loud.

"And you've got quite the grip." He winks, then places a chaste kiss on my lips. "You win." He scoots back and off the bed, standing before me like the Adonis I just found out first hand, he is.

Languidly, he removes his shorts, no underwear, and remains still, letting me look my fill. He's so damn sexy, his large body made up of deeply cut lines, bulging muscles, and large, broad shoulders, a fine line of dark hair leading to the beautiful cock straining up to his stomach—perfection. I try my finger crook again, gleeful that this time it works as he climbs, one knee at a time, on the bed toward me.

"I'm ready, Sawyer, I want to feel you deep inside me."

"Not yet, Angel. I'm nowhere near done. I still want to—"

"Shh," I lay a finger over his mouth and stare straight into his eyes as I lie back and hold out my arms to him. "Now."

He makes a move for the nightstand drawer but I lock onto his wrist and pull him back. "I trust you, Sawyer. Only you inside me."

"Em?" he says, his grumble and eyes full of doubt.

"Well, we know I won't get pregnant," I chuckle nervously. "And I just want to feel you. No jewelry, no barriers, nothing but the two of us. Is that okay?"

"God, yes," he groans, bending his head to lick up my neck. "Never gone bare, Em, ever. Only with you. Just the two of us."

I lift his head, my hands on his cheeks and stare him in the eyes. "I believe you, you'd never hurt me." I kiss him once. "Now feel me."

Taking his time, gentle and caring, he eases the tip of himself in, back and forth, not even an inch at a time. He kisses my mouth and my neck, asking me over and over if I'm all right, the battle of restraint heavy in his voice. His

186

concern, his scent, his tenderness—they relax me, my gasp matching his rumbling groan when my body fully invites him in. And then he is. Inside me. And it is everything, but nothing like what, and so much more than, I had imagined.

"My Emmett," he murmurs. "My sweet Emmett." He slides in and out of me, gentle and unhurried, kissing my face, my lips, my neck, my breasts.

I've never felt more adored and safe in my entire life.

"I can feel everything, baby," he groans. "You feel like my Heaven. So hot, so tight, so—fuck." His hands grip my ass, maneuvering me up and closer to him and we gasp together.

"Oh God, Sawyer, it feels so good, so good." I clutch the sheets beside me, digging my fingers in painfully. "Sawyer," I whisper.

"Ruined, forever." He thrusts deeper, harder, bending down to run his tongue up my throat. "Nothing like it, Emmy, nothing."

Our moans become grunts and he runs both hands up my arms, lifting them up and beside my head, where he links our fingers. It puts more of his weight on me and I welcome it. With this strong, splendid man covering me, no harm can ever come to me.

The rhythm of his hips changes, no longer a straight in and out, so I shift with him, placing that spot he'd found earlier in his direct target. "Right," I squirm once more, "oh, right there. Hard, you won't hurt me," I pant.

"Like," he pulls almost all the way out, then slides back in, up and to the left, "that?"

"Yes, babe, yes, don't stop. Never, ever stop," I beg as the prickle in my abdomen shoots downward in one big explosion. "Oh shit, SAWYER!" I scream, I yelp, I make sounds that are completely unhuman.

"With you, baby, oh goddamn," he swears, speeding up momentarily, squeezing harder on my hands, frantically finding my breast and sucking hard with a small whimper of his own.

He stills, never letting go of my hands, kissing up from my breast to my mouth. I can feel him, pulsing inside me harder now. "Oh Em," he kisses me languidly, still slowly pushing in and out, as gentle as his kiss, "if that's making love, I don't ever want to fuck."

I snicker, untangling our hands to grab his face, pulling him into me for another soul-sucking kiss. When I've thoroughly thanked him, I come up for air, my chest pumping up and down in sated exhilaration. "That was amazing. Thank you."

He grins that cocky, one-sided smirk that I adore. "You're amazing. You don't thank me when you just gave me the greatest gift I've ever received." He drops kiss to the edge of my mouth. "Emmett?"

"Hmm?"

"I lo—"

"Let's take a shower!" I drop my hands, pushing myself up despite his huge body on top of me and him still inside me. "Or a bath. Either one, your choice."

"Bath'll work," he mumbles, gently pulling out and rolling off me. "I'll run it."

Chapter 16

UNFROZEN

—SAWYER—

I'VE NEVER FELT LIKE THIS. Is this God's way of punishing me for all the women I've fucked and left? All the mouths I gladly shoved my cock in with no reciprocation?

Well played, sir. Point taken.

She made a fool of me. I gave her my all and she changed, taking all we'd built and tossing it aside.

The morning after the best night of my life, she was up before me and I found a note saying she ran some errands. I waited until late afternoon, finally going home, only to see her pull in after dark. No call.

The next day, she drove into work without me and was

completely engrossed in a conversation with Darby, of all people, when I arrived. The whole shift, she'd call off her orders, run off to somewhere she had to be, then come back and hurriedly load up the drinks once she saw they were ready.

As a last ditch effort, I'd finally cornered her on day three of the freeze out at her house. I now have a key, so it wasn't really breaking in, but she was taken aback nonetheless.

"You didn't do anything wrong. I've been busy is all," was her explanation.

So yeah, the cocky, aloof playboy hath fallen. Now what?

"Hey, you're home!" Laney squeals in surprise when she walks in, dropping her bag by the door.

"That I am," I mutter, rising to hug her. "How are ya, Gidge?"

"Can't complain. How are you?" She pats my chest. "I feel like I haven't seen you in years. How's Emmett?"

"How much time do you have?"

"As much as you need. Let me grab a quick shower though, okay? No sense in gagging ya. I just got out of practice."

"I'll start dinner," I suggest. "What do we have?"

"Dunno," she taps my nose, "look." She heads down the hall with a grin.

I'm browning chicken in a pan, sipping my second beer

when Dane walks in.

"Holy shit, a Sawyer sighting!" he shouts. "Should I alert the media?"

"I think they'd be more interested in a dick that can walk and talk. Maybe I should call."

"Aren't you a ray of fucking sunshine? Where's my woman?"

"Shower."

"Where's yours?"

"Where's my what?" I had yet to turn around, but now I have no choice—I need another beer.

"Your woman."

"It would seem," I slam the fridge door and crack open my beer on the edge of the counter, "that I do not have a woman." I take a long, delicious sip of ice cold hops before I continue, looking curiously around the room. "Nope, no woman here."

"Oh boy," he sighs, stepping around me, pulling a bottle of Crown from the cabinet. "Sit down, I'll serve. Coke or Sprite mixer?"

"Sprite," I mumble, taking a seat at the kitchen table.

"So, what happened?"

"I made love to her," I scoff, "should have stuck with fucking I guess, 'cause she ran like she was on fire. Now she acts like I have the plague."

Dane eyes me over the rim of his glass, taking his time to

savor the whiskey and contemplate his response. "She lives two doors down and works for you. How far can she have possibly run?"

"Oh, I still see her, but it's like she's checked out. Everything's at arm's length and awkward; it's not the same. When I try to put my arms around her, there's a tiny flinch she can't hide. When I go in for a kiss, I get the cheek turn. She swears nothing's wrong, but I'm not stupid."

Laney picks this time to walk in, hair wrapped in a towel. "Ah, I see we're drinking our dinner?" She smiles, leaning over to kiss Dane. "Hey, handsome."

"Baby." He pulls her into his lap, getting a better kiss. "You eat, I'm gonna drink with my boy here."

"No way are you hogging him! I haven't seen him either." She scrunches her eyebrows at Dane, then turns a warm smile on me. "Hit me with it. What's wrong, Saw?"

"Emmett and I are," I run a hand over my head, blowing out through my nose, "not good. Going backward instead of forward. I think I scared her with too much too fast. Again."

"Why?" Her face crinkles, truly feeling my pain. "You two are adorable, seamless. What happened?"

I don't miss that she doesn't ask what I did wrong. My Gidge believes in me.

"We made love, finally, and she got weird."

"She ran before you could," she murmurs so low I almost don't hear her. "Self-preservation."

"You really think that's it? I thought when she finally wanted to be with me that meant she was over her fears and she believed in us."

"Sex is different for women, Saw." She leans across the table and pats my hand. "Nothing will open up a woman's floodgates and make her feel vulnerable faster than sex. She probably thought she could handle it, but women are truly, genetically, unable to keep emotions separate from sex. Sounds like she found out too late, and now she's dealing with it."

"That sounds like Emmett. She's got some stuff..." I stop myself, taking a drink. "I think you nailed it, Gidge."

"Green Eyes" by Coldplay comes from somewhere and I knock over the chair I jump up so fast. "That's her, where's my phone?" Scrambling around, searching frantically, I find it behind the couch cushion.

"Hey, Em," I answer with a half-assed bravado. "What's up?"

"Sawyer," she sobs.

Fuck, she's crying.

"Can you come down here? I know I'm an ass and I shouldn't call, if you're busy—"

I don't really hear the next few words, I was off in a dead sprint at "down here." It only takes seconds to get to her stoop. Thankfully, the door's unlocked and I bust it open, anxious and scared of what I'll find.

"Oh uh, you're here," she says into her phone, still at her ear, before she gets her wits about her (me busting through her door and all) and puts it down. Her red, wet eyes track my rush across the living room to where she's curled up on the couch. "You're fast," she tries to joke, wiping her nose.

"Why are you crying, babe?" I've already scooped her up and sat back down with her on my lap. "Emmy, baby," I grab her face, pleading with her for answers. "Talk to me, what is it?"

"I'm, um, bleeding." Her face falls to my chest, frail little body racked with sobs.

"Where?" My hands and eyes run over her wildly. "Em, where?"

"Sawyer," she whispers, not getting me to stop my examination. "Sawyer!"

My head jerks up to her, the frightened look in her eyes squeezing around my heart.

"I need to go to the hospital. I'm bleeding down there."

It takes a second, but it finally registers. I nod. No words would be the right ones, so I just move her off me to stand. "Where're your shoes? Your purse?"

"My room, the table. Sawyer?"

"Yeah?" I drop to my knees, grabbing both her hands in mine.

"I'm scared."

"Don't be scared." I pull her head into my chest and rub her hair, kissing the crown of her dark head. "I got you. Whatever it is, I got you, Emmett. I'm right here and I'm not going anywhere."

She nods and sniffles, bucking up. "Let's go," she says with steely determination.

"I'll drive."

We both startle at Laney's voice behind us and turn like idiots to stare at them.

"You and Dane drank. I'll drive."

"She'll drive," Dane reiterates from his post beside her.

Had I not shut the door? Was I so concentrated on Em that I didn't hear them come in? Who fucking cares. They're both clutch and I'm damn lucky to have them. We're damn lucky to have them.

THESE MOTHERFUCKERS need a lesson in the word "family." The next person who refuses to let me see Emmett or tell me any news because I'm not "family" is going the fuck down. Hard.

Looking around the waiting room, my whole family is here, less the one back there without me. So now the Crew obviously knows Emmett's pregnant, and like I knew without a doubt they would be...they're sitting here like soldiers, one army, praying everything's all right with my girl.

"Which one of you is Sawyer Beckett?" Eight weary heads all pop up at once when the doctor speaks.

"I am." I stand, rushing to him. "How's Emmett? Can I see her?"

"She'll be fine," he smiles, "you can follow me."

I trudge behind him, concentrating on my feet, making sure they remember how to walk. He smiled at me, no frown, no pity...that means she's okay, it's got to. Exam Room Four, that's where he stops, stepping to the side.

"I'll go have the discharge papers drawn up. You can tell her she can get dressed."

Discharge as in go home? Nerves wreaking havoc, I lift a tentative hand and knock...on a fucking curtain. Seriously, I have got to pull my shit together and be strong for my girl. I shake it off and square my shoulders. "Em?" I call through the curtain.

"Come in," her sweet voice answers. "Sawyer," she breathes, holding out her hand to me.

"Hey, Shorty," I make my way to her until our hands connect, "are you okay?"

"I'm fine." Her reassuring smile is genuine and the sudden rush of comfort it gives me feels like the elephant finally stepped off my chest. "I was just spotting, which they say is completely normal. Oh, and I had a bladder infection, which probably didn't help. Apparently," she looks down and blushes, "I should always use the ladies' room after sex."

"I read about spotting," I admit, feeling like a moron for only now remembering. "Not the tinkling part though." With one finger curled under her chin, I bring her face up to mine. "So our baby, she's fine?"

"She?" Emmett's brows go up as tears come down. "Ours?"

"Or he, either's great, but I can't say 'it.' And yes, ours. As in you and me and no more hiding. It'll be hard for you to tinkle in private if I'm fucking handcuffed to you. And that will be my next step if you shut me out again." Gripping both her hands, I pin her with the stare of all that I feel inside, of the inferno that shocked me, then consumed me. "You're making me crazy, woman. I adore you, Emmett." I dip my head, maneuvering her face with my own and licking the seam of her lips. "Quit fucking shutting me out. Let. Me. Love. You."

She fights me, turning her head the other way and squeezing her eyes closed, so I let her have it and keep right on talking.

"I knew the minute I saw you that you'd be the end of me." I nuzzle her neck, lightly kissing up it. "I was right. You're it. You're all I see." I tug on her earlobe and follow with a soft kiss. "You're all I think about." I release one of her hands and let mine feather down her arm. "I love you,

Emmett. And I love our baby."

"Our baby?" She now looks at me, asking again on a gasp. "You love me?"

"Our baby," I confirm, kissing the end of her button nose, "and more than anything." Waiting a moment, it's clear she's not quite ready to respond to my last two, huge announcements, so I go ahead and continue. "My gene pool sucks. I'd trade it in a heartbeat, but it has nothing to do with who I really am. My family is who loves me and helps me be the best me. You are my family, the people out there praying you're okay are my family." I use both hands to cover her stomach. "This baby will be half you, half all the wonderful things you have to give and teach. And the other half will be me, their daddy, the man who worships their mama."

"Y-you can't possibly mean that. You'd take on a baby that isn't yours? A woman who's dirty and damaged?"

That's it. She may be in the hospital, having just had the shit scared out of her, but I snarl and feel my lip curl. "You're gonna want to put that shit on simmer, babe. Don't ever say something like that again. That baby is mine, forever. I. Live. Right. Here," I rub her stomach, "and I. Want. To. Live. Here," I rub over her heart then lay an open-mouthed kiss there. "If you ever, ever, call yourself dirty or damaged again," I grab her chin between my thumb and forefinger and force her face to meet mine, "I will actually be angry with you. You're degrading the woman I love, and I won't fucking hear it. You're not dirty, which we'll work on," I wink, "and you're far from damaged. You're magnificent and I love you, so watch your mouth." I pause, making sure it all sinks in. "Hear me?"

"Sawyer," she touches my cheek, contemplating her next words, "I'm sorry I've been weird. I thought..." A soft, frustrated sigh escapes as she tries to sort her words. "God, you just deserve more than any woman could possibly give you."

"Simple yes or no, Em. Do you hear me?"

"Loud and clear."

Chapter 17

TWENTY-TWO CANDLES

—SAWYER—

THREE DAYS—that's how long Emmett froze after we made love.

Another three days since Bennett, Whitley and Laney found out there's a baby on the way.

Three glorious days booked in a suite at Hillside Manor to hide away with Emmett since the Crew girls now know there's a baby coming.

They've got baby fever Bad with a capital B. Yesterday, I went to get a movie from Red Box—I was literally gone twenty minutes—I get back to see The Sanderson Sisters hovered over my woman, who's flat on her back on the floor, and they're twirling needles on string over her!

After I barked at them to never do voodoo on my baby again, then helped my sweet preggo off the damn floor, I sent them packing with a promise to write them an approved project list ASAP.

Then I got on the web and booked this trip.

Then I made them a list and texted it to them, with a very strict forty-eight hour delay in start time. GO CRAZY, CRAZIES—after I have my Em tucked safely in my arms four hours away.

Emmett falls asleep about twenty minutes into the trip, her head leaning up against the window, which makes me uneasy. "Babe," I fiddle for her hand still watching the road, "Em, I need you to wake up, honey. Lean my way."

"Uh," she frumps in her sleep, shifting toward me, readjusting so her head is on the console between us. "Oh, this is comfortable," she mumbles. "Why'd you move me?"

"I didn't want you to fall out the door, grumpy."

She sits up, giving me a skeptical smirk. "Fall out the door? It's locked."

"You never know."

"I know you're paranoid."

"And you're radiant."

"And you're forgiven." She leans over, kissing my cheek. "How much longer?"

"A while. Why, do you need something?"

"No, no reason."

"Short stuff?"

"Huh?"

"You need to pee, don't you?"

She huffs, shoulders dropping. "Yes, sorry."

—Emmett—

CANCEL THE DREAM COTTAGE I wanted to build—I want to live here for the rest of my life.

Tucked away off the main road and surrounded by dense woods, Hillside Manor is absolutely magnificent. Our room is beyond breathtaking, the humongous bed so high off the ground I have to take a running start or get a boost up from Sawyer. In the corner, there's a mini-kitchenette, ensuring you don't have to leave the room if you don't want to, though you can go downstairs for meals in your pajamas if you feel like it.

The best part is the bathroom, hands down. A Nickleback-sized garden tub is sunk low in the floor, candles at the ready. Which is exactly where I'm reclined, lost in serenity, when I hear music.

I thought he wanted a nap?

Sitting up, I train my ears, making sure I'm right. "Can't Help Falling in Love" by Elvis Presley is playing. What a great song; my gramma loved The King.

Sawyer appears in the doorway and turns off the lights, letting the lit candle he's holding be his guide. He sits on the edge of the tub, putting the candle down on the countertop and dipping his right hand under the water to find mine. "I can't help it, Emmett, I fell. I love you, birthday girl."

Oh my gosh, that's right. With everything going crazy in my life, I'd completely forgotten. How's it even possible to forget your own birthday?

"Thank you," I whisper, completely enchanted by him.

"You're welcome." He winks. "So what do you want for your birthday?"

"You, in this tub with me."

"Em, we—"

"Nuh uh." I squeeze his hand, stopping him. "I'm fine, no problems, and Dr. Greer said it was okay."

"But what—"

I let go of his hand, letting my own disappear under the water. I slump further down in the bubbles, my head falling back against the wall, and blatantly spread my legs as wide as the sides of the tub allow. "Mmm," I close my eyes and moan, "it's okay, babe. I got it."

"Temptress," he hisses.

Eyes still closed, I giggle, hearing his clothes rustle off and hit the floor at lightning speed.

"That water better not be too hot," he grumbles. "You

know that, right? Speaking of which, you know not to get in the hot tub should Laney ask, don't you?"

"Yes, Sawyer," I agree ho-humly. He just can't stand it when I take control of the situation.

"Sit up," he commands, to which I gladly comply. Sliding in behind me, his long, large legs come around either side of me, sending water up and over the edge.

Big hands come under my arms and around the front to massage my breasts. "Feels good. No hotter than this, though, Em."

"I heard you, bossy," I hum, enjoying the feel of his hands on me.

"We gotta get one of these tubs," he murmurs against my shoulder.

"Or we could stay in this one forever," I mumble, purposely squirming, making sure my ass grinds back into him.

His response is to pinch both my nipples, rolling them between his thumb and finger. "Promise me something?"

"What's that?" I get up on my knees, sending another splash to the floor, and then turn and straddle him. Very nice, he put in his nipple rings like I asked. Sexy. As. Hell.

He stops my hands from their journey up his chest. "Promise me that you won't hide. You want my cock again? I want your heart first. Tell me," his always deep blue eyes, now resembling a starless night sky, stare through mine, "that we'll be forever."

It steals my breath, his sweet, sincere plea. I'm done trying to convince him that I'm the wrong one. If he wants me, maybe I should let myself believe I'm the right one. I heard someone once say, "if you know you're gonna get your ass kicked, walk away from the fight before wasting energy on even one punch." Honestly, I've known from day one this was a fight I'd never win, so here it is—my white flag. I'm done attempting not to notice the days he wears Usher versus Obsession. I'm totally over swapping pillowcases every other day so his scent is always most potent under my cheek. And I refuse, for one more minute, to credit pregnancy hormones for what one smirk from the man does to every part of me.

"Em," he breaks into my thoughts, "I need you to promise me."

I nod, smiling from ear to ear. He's taking a huge chance on me because he thinks I'm worth it. I need to do the same for him. "I promise. No running, no hiding. We belong together."

"Mine?" He lifts a hand to my cheek, the thumb tracing my jawline. When I nod, he runs that hand down my body to my stomach. "Mine?"

I suck in a breath and tug at my lower lip, trying not to cry. Yeah, right, like that's possible. Tears stream down my face, but again, I nod.

"I love you, Emmett." He starts to kiss me, my tears, my

eyelids, my forehead, lastly my lips. "I love you so much."

"I love you too, Sawyer," I choke out, chuckling at my pathetic blabbering. "You'll always be my first miracle."

Now he tilts my head, kissing me deeply. I kiss him back with all the adoration and lust I feel coursing through me; this sexy, badass, tender man wants me, and he's always making me feel like the most precious gem in the whole world. I sneak one hand between our chests and give a tug on his nipple ring—scorching hot on him.

"Love these," I praise into his mouth.

"Love these," he answers instantly with a pull on my own nipple.

Ever so slowly, absorbing the feel of every muscle, my hand creeps lower until it's exploring the head of his dick. "Want this," I run my tongue along the inside of his upper lip, "now."

"Yeah?" He sucks on my bottom lip and tugs, opening his eyes and finding mine. He leans back, shifting his hips, and wraps his right hand around himself. "You want this?" he taunts me, holding our locked gaze as he leisurely rubs himself.

I silently nod, giving him my best seductive look.

"Then climb on it, babe," he encourages. "Take it."

One hand braced on his pec, I raise my bottom half and spread my knees out further. I guide myself over him until I feel the tip of him hinting at my entrance. I try to hold his gaze while I slide down him, but he's not looking at me right now. His orbs are DEFCON 5, locked on the exact point where we're about to join, his tongue sliding methodically back and forth along his lower lip.

"That's my girl," he croons, fingers curled mercilessly on my hips. "Take me in you, baby, nice and slow."

Like there's another option; it's a tight fit and more than a tad intimidating. I look down when I swear I feel him poking my ribs. What? Jesus Christ, there's more.

"Relax, babe." He catches my eyes now. "You've had it all before. Relax your muscles and take deep breathes. Take all the time you need." He winks that sexy smirk, telling me he doesn't mind the slow burn one bit. "Lemme help." He releases one hip, the blood rushing back into the spot he's been squeezing, and presses his thumb to my clit, moving it left then right to really get in there. Oh yeah, that instantly makes my pussy moisten, the natural lubricant sliding me further down on him.

"Yeah, Em, good girl, baby," he groans, rubbing harder on my hot spot. "All of it." His head falls back as my skin finally rests flush against him.

I give it a second without moving and bask in the overwhelming feeling of fullness. It's a lot different in this position; a hard, long rod straight up in me, the hint of his coarse hairs tickling my most sensitive spots. Acclimated, I start to rock, up and back, down and forward, and the animalistic groan that rips from Sawyer's chest spurs me on, encouraging me to pick up speed.

"Fucking hell, Shorty, you have no idea how good you feel. Ride my dick, babe, ah fuck yes, Em," he grunts, breathing hard in and out, "ride me." He never stops his ministrations on my clit, and when his left hand guides my hip, showing me how to roll my hips, I get this curve and pop thing going that feels like nirvana.

"Gonna, oh gonna—" I hiss through my teeth, my throat closing up as the sensation grows.

"Yeah you are." He sits up now, sucking one breast in his mouth and biting my nipple gently. "So damn good, Emmy, let go all over me."

And I do; grinding my clit into his thumb, wiggling around to find the right spot, and detonating like the space shuttle at lift off. "Uhh," I moan, never wanting it to end.

It's a whole new kind of orgasm than the last time and I feel the difference again as he thrusts up into me. Leaning over him, I take his nipple in my mouth, tugging on the silver ring there with my teeth.

"Gonna fill you up, baby." He grasps both my hips strongly, holding me down and still, forcing me to absorb the impact of his deep, hard thrusts up into me. "Fuck, fuck," he pants, the last sound a long growl until he's finished twitching inside me.

I rest my cheek upon his chest; playing with the nipple

ring right in front of me. He rubs my back, kissing the top of my head. We stay like that, no words, until the water starts to get a chill to it. Staying inside me, he rolls us to one side, slipping out of me then and kissing my nose. "Stay right there."

When he climbs out of the tub, I take a moment to appreciate his tight, fine ass. I'm enjoying the view immensely, but I'm also curious—how the hell is it as tan as the rest of his body? "Do you go to tanning beds?" I ask.

"No," he chuckles, wrapping a towel around his waist then grabbing another off the shelf. "Why?"

"How is your butt as tan as your arms then?" I pull the plug, then stand, taking his hand offered out to me.

He wraps the towel around me, downright snickering at me. "I have no idea. What about you? Your ass isn't exactly fluorescent. Sexy as fuck, yes. Bright white, no."

I reach behind me to lift the towel, craning my neck to have a looksee at my own rear end. Huh. I'll be, he's right. "Where do you come up with this stuff, anyway?" He chuckles as he asks, smiling at me with warmth and sincerity.

Shrugging, I move around him to brush my teeth and pull back my damp hair. Who I see in the mirror is a stranger, a version of Emmett Young who was only just born.

I look content.

There's no fear or second guessing in my eyes, no hint of fraud in my smile or burden to the lay of my shoulders. My jaw is slack, unclenched for the first time in as long as I can remember, and the blush to my cheeks is the perfect shade.

Scratch that, I look happy.

"I love you." His arms come around my waist from behind, our gazes meeting in the mirror. "Never thought it'd happen to me; maybe even thought I was making you up. Turns out you were better than a fantasy and more than I'd ever been foolish enough to hope to want. You see that absolute beauty in the mirror there?" He points and I shrink in embarrassment, but he quickly moves my face once again. "You think that's gorgeous, you should see this." He moves his hand over my heart. "Most determined, caring, courageous, resilient, loving person I know. And she's all mine."

Behind us on the back of the door are plush robes, so he grabs one, holding it open for me. I loosen the knot on my towel and let it drop to my feet, our eyes still connected in the mirror. Feeling his way, the robe is draped around me, my arms maneuvered through. Then I turn around and do the same for him.

"You ready for bed, lil' mama?"

"Yes." I yawn at the reminder.

"Movie?"

"Nah," I pull him behind me, then stop waiting for his touch on my hips for my hoist into the bed, "too tired."

He climbs into the bed, pulling me right up against his

front, one arm over my waist, loosening the knot on the robe. "I couldn't sleep those few nights, Shorty." He nudges my hair off my shoulder then pulls the cloth off my shoulder. "I missed this."

"Me too," I sigh, tipping my head left to help his cause.

"Then why you'd pull back? You never really told me."

I flip over and grab his cheeks, stroking them and looking him directly in the eye. "I refused to believe I was as great of a package as you seem to think, and I guess I'm a glass half empty girl. When I didn't know for sure all I might lose if you ran, I could deal, pretend we had more time as friends. But once I felt you, really felt the instant you became the other part of me, thinking of how much harder it'd hurt when you ran? It shredded me; all at once I had so much more to lose. I was scared." I pause, collecting my thoughts while sampling his sweet lips. "I thought if I gave you up slowly, and first, by the time you did leave, I'd be used to it. But then, I slept without you. I ate without you. Something was funny and I'd turn to tell you, but you weren't there. I couldn't do it. I'm not strong enough to let you go. I already had a "forgive me" letter written; I was gonna hand it to you and run, but then I had to call about…you know. I'm selfish and scared and new to feeling like this, but I'm hoping you'll love me anyway."

"You're as far from selfish as one can possibly get. And I love you for all you are, not even though." He drops a delicate kiss to my lips. "Never again though, Emmy, promise."

"I promise," I reassure him with a smile, a yawn taking me by surprise.

"Baby, I know you're tired," his hot breath is on my skin, "but can you stay awake for me to give you your birthday present?"

"This trip was my present. That bath was my present."

He kisses the crook of my neck, along the slope of my shoulder, and chuckles. "Pretty sure the bath was my present. Hang on." He gets out of the bed and goes to his suitcase where he pulls out a wrapped package.

"Sawyer, you got me too much," I argue.

"Zip it." He air smooches to soften the blow of his directive. "Happy birthday, Emmy." He hands me the gift and climbs back beside me.

"When's your birthday?"

"May fifteenth. Now open it."

Peeling back the paper, I snicker at the excited man by my side, twitchy with anticipation more so even than me. "Oh my," I gasp, moisture building in my eyes.

It's a black leather journal with "Shorty" embossed on the front, accompanied by a black and gold pen.

"Sawyer," I turn to him, not quite sure what to say besides, "thank you."

"You're very welcome, love. No more tiny notepads in

your back pocket. You deserve a big, badass place for your thoughts."

I go in for a chaste kiss on his lips. "You still can't read them."

"Dammit," he grumbles. "I can see your nipples but not your notes?"

My head falls back on my laugh. "They're not notes!"

"Pussy but not your passages?"

"Better," I set aside the gifts, "but still, no."

Chapter 18

THE SWEETEST THINGS

—Emmett—

THE BIRTHDAY WEEKEND with Sawyer was the happiest I've ever been in my life—and way too short. Driving home, I can actually feel my mood start to sour the closer we get to reality. Not that our real life isn't spectacular, because he makes it so, but still...

He takes hold of my hand. "Babe, we can go back soon, I promise."

"That obvious, huh?"

"Lil' bit." He smiles. "Here, I got something for the baby." He releases my hand to fiddle with the radio while driving. "The book said babies can hear voices and music, so… I give you…La Baby Lullabies."

Me, the mother, should probably think of these things, but I must confess that it does something to me to watch him get so involved, so excited at his discoveries.

The first song is slow and peaceful, something about the moon. Not bad. We smile at each other, an endearing moment of classical music that of course we both find painful to the ears, but good for our baby.

The second song is morbid, about falling out of a tree or a swing or something. "Oh my God," I gasp, shocked someone thought this song would comfort a baby. "That's awful. They said—"

"I heard." He slams the "off" button. "Bastards."

"I think Alex is a Bruno Mars baby." I reach up, plugging in my phone and searching artists.

"Alex?" he asks, turning down "It Will Rain."

"Cute, right? And unisex."

Sawyer goes silent, highly unusual, and drops his shoulders. "Yeah, cute."

"Hey," my hand finds his now and squeezes, "what just happened? The CD was very sweet. We can try some other songs if you want."

"That CD blew—babies falling to their deaths? Fuck Rock-A-Bye," he grumbles, his grip on the steering wheel noticeably tightening.

"Then what's wrong?"

"Nothing."

"Or something."

"I guess I kinda thought we'd pick the baby's name together," he says softly.

Oh. Well, if a Sawyer pout isn't the sexiest, most charming thing ever, I just don't know what is.

"God, you're the best man alive," I whisper, constantly astounded by the many sides of Sawyer. "Babe, I have to call the baby something and we don't know what we're having, so I thought Alex was a cute unisex nickname, for now. I wouldn't pick the name without you. Promise."

He cuts his eyes to me skeptically, that luscious bottom lip of his pulling up in the corner. "Alex works for now."

"You let me know if you think of something better," I suggest, hiding my smirk.

"SURPRISE!"

I look around my living room, startled. There are no balloons and nothing's changed, the only occupants Laney, Bennett and Whitley, who are all three beaming at us and clapping. I'm not sure what the surprise is exactly, but I thank them anyway.

"I take it we're good?" Sawyer asks them over my

shoulder.

"Yes!" Whitley squeals, jumping up and down like we just won the lottery.

"We'll be going," Laney says with a grin, pulling the other two by their shirts. "We hope you like it, Emmett. All Sawyer's idea."

Bennett nods, confirming the credit to Sawyer.

Once he's hugged them all and walked them out, he comes back wearing a huge smile of his own. "Come on." He links our hands and leads me down the hall to the door of the spare bedroom. "Ready, mama?"

"Ready."

He opens the door, stepping to the side to let me enter first. "Wow," he whistles, "they nailed it."

Oh. My. God.

If I closed my eyes and envisioned the exact, perfect space where I would want to lay my sweet baby down each night, this would be it.

He'd planned and executed my dream nursery.

The walls are green, with various critters and trees spread around the room—a few rabbits, a lamb, squirrels and the cutest little deer. And of course, one single butterfly flying toward the ceiling, where the paint becomes a pale blue and turns the ceiling into a perfect sky with clouds. This is what our precious Alex will see when looking up, kicking those tiny feet.

Covering the line between green and blue are swirly, scripted words around the entire perimeter of the room. "Always Kiss Me Goodnight," then a heart, "Our First Miracle," another heart, "Wish Upon a Star."

Sawyer's laugher shatters my trance. "What?" I ask.

He points above the closet. "'Play ball.' Not one I wrote down." He shakes his head and grins. "Good ole Aunt Gidge."

Aunt. I never dreamed it'd actually ever be, and there it is—this baby will have a family. I will have a family, the head of it the exact man I would have hand-picked if granted a wish.

"I can't believe you did this." I stand on my tiptoes, curling my arms around his shoulders. "It's beyond perfect," I take a deep breath, hoping the word pleading to be released doesn't send him packing, "Daddy."

"Daddy," he repeats me on a breath. "Daddy," he says again, as though taste testing it, followed closely by a tender look of delight. His dark blue eyes take on an unmistakable shine and he meets my forehead with his own, grinning. "Very cool."

I fall in love with him all over again in that moment. "It suits you." I pucker, offering my lips 'cause I can't reach his on my own.

He pauses, withholding his kiss. "Do you really like it? I didn't want to overstep, but I saw it in a magazine and thought—"

"Magazine?"

He shrugs. "Doctor's office. They really should be ashamed of how long they make people wait. Why even set appointment times if you're never gonna hit them?"

"I don't know," I giggle at his exaggerated frustration, not at all a cover for the fact he's embarrassed he reads the magazines. "But yes, I love this nursery, and you could never overstep because there is no line."

"No lines, very promising," he teases, pinching my butt.

"You are awful," I titter, shaking my head. "We're standing in the nursery."

"That's bad?" His brows furrow, but he recovers quickly. "I mean, that's bad. Ok, so I thought tomorrow after class we could go pick out a crib together. I didn't figure I'd push my luck, picking too much. And then the name thing. I'm sorry, I didn't even think about being a huge hypocrite." He grabs the back of his neck, ducking his face.

"You know, I never have to worry about being mad at you. You get mad enough at yourself, for nothing, for both us." I poke him in the stomach, unsuccessfully as my finger bends back against the firmness there, but he does lift his head to me now, grinning. "We can go look at cribs, sounds fun. Did you know, my gramma told me a story once, that when my mom was born, unplanned, eleven months after her older sister, they were so poor that they turned a dresser to the wall and used a drawer? True story."

He scowls. "We're getting a crib."

"I know, silly, I've just always thought it was a cool story."

"Cool story, babe, but do not tell it again." He grumbles under his breath, something about babies falling from trees and being shoved in drawers, then finally returns the kiss I've been waiting for…but with a tight, grumpy mouth. "You done in here for now?"

"I guess so," I take another look around, sighing wistfully.

"We can stay in here all night if you want."

"No, I'm good, for now. Hey! Let's walk over so I can thank the girls. This was so sweet of them."

"Yeah, they're pretty great. Remind me to tell you that story one day, how Laney and Whitley met and became friends, it's a classic." He shakes his head and chuckles. "But for now, you go on." He caresses my cheek, kissing my forehead. "I'll unpack the car and meet you down there."

"You sure?" I pout, pathetically not wanting to be without him. After a few days locked away in Wonderland together, you get clingy I guess. "I could wait, and help."

"Nope, you go. I'll even start the laundry. Anything to buy time from hearing the play by play of every brushstroke from three possessed women."

"Fine, but hurry."

His right brow lifts. "Why Miss Emmett, are you jonesing for your man?" One hand snakes around and grabs my ass, pulling me against him. "I can fix that for ya."

"Not in the nursery!" I shriek, disgusted, pushing at his chest.

I'm swept up before I can blink, both his strong hands lifting me and turning to leave the room. "I can fix that too. Pick a room."

Damn he's strong, and sexy…and so sly. I'm tempted, but resist. "Babe, I need to go say thank you."

"He knew you were gonna say that." He sets me down and looks at his dick with a sigh. "Sorry, bud. I was rootin' for ya."

Chapter 19

One Screw Over the

Cuckoo's Nest

—SAWYER—

AT FIRST, I thought Em had a specific crib in mind and knew where to get it and that was the reason she boycotted Babies 'R Us, laughed at Brooke Ashley's Boutique, and refused to exit the vehicle at Four Monkeys. I finally told her just to tell me where to go.

All I got was right, left, straight…which is how she got away with stopping me in front of a resale shop.

Am I snob? No. I wore shoes from The Salvation Army after one of my foster brothers outgrew them.

Am I gonna let my baby sleep on used shit? Hell no.

"Emmett, what the hell are we doing here? That mattress has a piss stain!" It does—the one mattress they choose to display out front and it's been pissed on? Come on.

"Sawyer," her soothing tone tries to placate me, "babies need lots of really expensive things and I have a budget. Alex will never know how fancy the crib was, but I bet he or she would notice if their ear keep hurting or their belly was empty. I have a budget based specifically on priorities."

I love her planning, her organization and sensibility. I also love her, which is why I'm not going to bellow harshly at her. "Em," I mock her calm tone, "there is no 'I' in "our baby's budget exceeds pee-soaked hand-me-downs." Oh yeah, I threw her some air quotes.

"Do you know what diapers, formula and doctor visits cost? Or medicine? Please," she rubs her forehead, "don't fight me on this. Let's go in and see what they have." Quibbling, I get out and walk around to her door, helping her out. "I'm sure we'll find something great, trust me."

An older woman spots the two suckers and zones in on us right when we walk in, and now we're stuck. "Hi, can I help you guys?"

"We're looking for a crib, and a new mattress." She turns and smirks at me.

"Back here." Sanford's...daughter leads us through too tight, cluttered aisles. "Boy or girl?" she asks.

"We don't know. We decided to let it be a surprise!" Emmett exclaims back to her.

Oh, I'm gonna spank her butt, the little twerp, saying it like sunshine rolling off her tongue...now. Lemme tell ya something—she did not agree with me on that without a whole lot of goading. Little in life surprises me, and I wanted this one, bad. And through my powers of prowlsuasion...I won.

"Cribs are pretty neutral and with some plain bedding, you should be fine. Okay, here's some brand new mattresses, still in the plastic. And the cribs," she takes another right turn, "are here. Now the used models are the ones on the floor, put together. But we do have some in boxes, mostly returns or overstocks."

"Mattress in plastic is fine," I pipe in, "but no used or returned crib, so let's see the overstocks."

Emmett's eyes bulge and she scrunches her eyebrows at me. "Be nice," she mouths.

How was I not nice?

"We have the—"

"Too high," I comment. "Baby'd be practically in the air."

"Okayyy, how about this one? It's—"

"Too low. Mama's a shorty. She'd fall over the edge on top of the baby."

"What about—"

"What about that one?" I point. "Em, you like that one?"

"Oh, me?" She glowers at me, muttering under her breath something about her being able to make a decision. "Which one?"

"This one," I walk over and tap my finger on the box, "the Marlowe Sleigh Crib."

"Sawyer," she leans into me and whispers, "it's four hundred dollars! At a resale shop!"

"So? That seems reasonable, babe."

"My budget for a crib is $175 max," she clips.

"That's when it was your budget. Now it's our budget, which we've discussed. Now do you like this one or not?"

"Of course I do; it's beautiful. But that leaves more than half for you to pay. That's not fair, and too much."

"Come here." I snag her and drag her into me, surrounding that teeny frame with my own very large one. "I sold my racing bike for more than I had in it, so I have some extra cash. If you love that crib, I want to buy it for you, for Alex."

"Why?" She tries to escape but I hold her even tighter, denying her. "You love to race."

"I don't love anything inanimate, and I far from love racing, but I do love you," I dip my head and speak to her stomach, "and you. So why would I need bullshit races? They just filled a void until I found you."

226

She's speechless, and that includes insta-watery eyes, so I take charge—which started the minute we walked through the door—in case anyone was still unsure.

"We'll take the Marlowe Sleigh and one wrapped mattress." I smile at the saleswoman.

"Fabulous!" she says happily. "Let's go to the front to check out. I'll have someone bring them up."

"Oh," I stop short, "we're in Mama's car; it's never gonna fit. Do you deliver?"

"Certainly, for a fifty dollar fee."

"Ring 'er up," I say, turning my attention back to Em. "Mad?"

"No, I just think—"

I cut her off with a chaste kiss. "No's enough."

I feel great, like I'm really a part of things, so it really can't be helped when I dip her in the middle of the store and kiss the breath from her. Her face is pink with embarrassment when I raise her back up.

"I love you, Emmett."

"I love you too," she simpers, pretending to straighten her hair back in place.

"And that crib kicks ass!" I stick out my tongue and wave "rock on" hands, not a bit fucking ashamed that my baby got the coolest pad in the land.

"Motherf—"

"Whoa, what's wrong?" Emmett asks from the doorway, sneaking up behind me.

"This crib! I swear to God there're parts missing and there's subliminal messages in the directions. It can't possibly be this hard."

"Why don't you take a break? I have to get to work and don't want to have to worry about you blowing a blood vessel. Specifically," she points, "one of those pulsing out of your forehead right now."

"You don't work tonight." I should know, I make the schedule.

"I do now. Laney called me because your phone is in there on the counter and Dane couldn't get you. Austin and Jessica have both called in sick tonight." She grins and gives me an exaggerated wink. "Interesting development, I'd say, but that puts them way short, so I said I'd go in."

I know Emmett, and she won't turn down the extra money, so that means I'm going in too. Like hell my woman's walking around a bar while I sit at home. "What time did you say we'd be there?"

"We? I didn't volunteer you."

"If Austin's out, somebody's got to run the music.

Nobody else knows how to do that."

So that's a little white lie. Several know how, but I don't want her to think I'm going to "keep an eye on her." Women tend to get all shrieky about that shit, a.k.a. I've seen Laney do it a hundred times.

"As soon as possible was assumed, I think, so I guess you better get ready." She turns and hurries in the bathroom. "I need ten minutes!" she calls.

I'm ready now, so I use the time to stare, dumbfounded, at the instructions again. I refuse to ask one of the guys for help, but damn…good thing I have a while. Maybe there's a hotline you can call, 1-888-Sure Feel Better About Putting My Baby in Here if I Used Every Screw?

"You ready?" She appears back in the doorway and I let the pamphlet fall from my hand, mouth agape with an audible groan.

"New outfit?"

She surveys herself, looking down at the two sizes too small pink shorts with a white tie at the waist and a tight white t-shirt; an outfit guaranteed to rake in the tips. "Not at all, why?"

"You're a walking wet dream. I'd have remembered that outfit." I'm flicking my tongue ring on the inside of my bottom teeth, trying not to go crazy on her and demand she change. Women get shrieky bout that shit too.

"I know the t-shirt's snug, but they all are these days.

And the shorts," she tugs at the bottom of them, trying to miraculously create more material, "it gets so hot in there, you know? But I could change."

Hold up. Does this ever really happen, the girl offers to change rather than throw a shit fit that you said anything?

The Crew girls had not prepared me for this reaction.

"Whatever you're comfortable in is perfect, Em. We'll get ya some bigger shirts tomorrow."

Chapter 20

SAVE THE LAST SONG

—SAWYER—

THE CLUB'S PACKED when we get there, mostly because ladies drink for a dollar all night. Dane's behind the bar, so of course there's a line, and what the hell are we listening to? Is that house music?

"Babe, come back out here with me a sec." I cinch her hand, ensuring she stays with me, and go back to the door. "Sheldon," I call him over to me, "twenty more guys, okay? There are plenty of girls inside. Then max it out and come in to bounce."

"You got it." He gives Emmett the once over and smiles. "Hey, Emmett."

"Hey, how'd you do?"

"Eighty-four!" He beams, giving my mama a knuckle bump.

"Oh yay! The man's a genius!" She giggles.

"K, get inside, Shel, we need ya, man." I grimace slightly, pulling Emmett back with me. "What was that?"

"He was nervous about a big exam. Sounds like he nailed it. What was that?" She crinkles up her face and puffs out her chest, bowing and flexing her arms, badly mocking me, I think. "You jealous?"

"No," I scoff, shaking my head like it's the craziest thing I've ever heard in my life. "No."

"Good," she loops her arm through mine, "'cause that would be a major waste of your time."

"Uh huh," I mumble. "Ok, so Dane's not fast enough behind the bar for dollar night. I'll pull Kasey behind the bar, put Dane and Sheldon on the floor, you and Darby on tables, and I'll get the music. Sounds right, right?"

"So smart." She reaches up on her toes, her short legs begging me to bend to her, which I do, gathering her delicious kiss. "K, I'm gonna get out there. Later, babe." She finger waves, walking away.

I'm burning those fucking shorts. Right after she wears them for just me one more time.

"Hey!" I yell at Dane, chuckling at the relief that washes over his face when he sees me. "I'm trading you out with

Kasey. Shel's maxing and coming in to bounce with ya. Cool?" He nods, removing a female customer's hand from his arm and shooting her an annoyed look.

About twenty minutes later, I finally have everyone situated in the most efficient scenario, so I head up to the DJ booth. The crowd's thinned some, probably cause of this shitty music, but I'm not opening the door again right away; a breather's nice.

From this high perch I can see the whole club. I find and track my girl below, easily found in a sea of women, shining with a light none of the hoard could pray to possess. Damn, she's quick; no wonder the weight I keep expecting to embrace isn't quite coming...that butterfly can't be caught, flitting around faster than any waitress we've ever had.

It takes but a minute to zero in on the table demanding the most of her attention; four guys and one girl, the dick munch in the plaid, yes, plaid, shirt the one who wants her. My fists clench, but I hesitate, watching it play out. Something tells me Miss Emmett is perfectly capable of taking care of herself, and my gut tells me it may just be very important for her to prove that to herself whenever the chance presents itself.

She takes their orders and moves away hastily, checking on three other tables in her path to the bar. When she delivers their drinks, she passes them out from the far side of the table from AssHat, never looking at him. The fucker's mouth moves and then Emmett's head flies up, eyes glaring at him. I watch proudly as she lays into him, one hand on her popped out hip, the other holding up one finger and shaking it at him, a sure tell. She talks a mile a minute, then takes that one shaking finger and gives him smartass duck lips as she flicks it to point right at me.

Hey, fucker. I wave and watch his eyes bulge. Emmett covers her mouth, I assume laughing at his dumb ass, and looks up at me.

"Come 'ere," I mouth, crooking my finger at her.

In the sexiest saunter possible, she makes her way to me, climbing the steps to the raised platform, shutting the door behind her.

"What'd he say?" I snarl.

"The last thing was, 'oh shit, sorry.'" She giggles. "You look big even way up here."

I swivel my chair, turn fully forward, and jut out one thigh, patting it. "I think you earned a break."

The zing in the air can't be mistaken and she feels it too, her eyes growing hungry. She swallows hard before she climbs on my lap, her back to my chest. I spin us back to the front now, looking down and out at the whole club. "Flip the green button," I whisper in her ear, reaching up the back of her shirt and unhooking her bra. "Now the yellow one."

"Sawyer, wh-what are you doing?"

"What do you think I'm doing? Want you."

The club lights are low now, the floor runners providing the only glow. I curl my arms around her waist and pull the bow on her shorts loose. "Any special requests?" I ask, pushing her shorts and panties down, which she automatically helps me with, hoisting herself up.

"Hmm?" she hums in question, letting her head fall back to rest on my shoulder.

"You wanna pick a song?" I clasp her hand and move it to the mouse, spreading her fingers by lacing mine own over and through them. "On the screen, love," I say, focusing her attention. "Anything you want to be fucked to?"

She gasps, looking back at me. "Here?"

I nod. "Here."

"Sawyer, I don't know," she chews her bottom lip nervously and glances frantically in every direction.

"You do know," I nibble on her neck, up to her ear. "You know you want it too, right here, right now."

Without another word, lust and determination both glazing over her eyes, baby girl stands to lean on the ledge, searching out her jam while I flick open each button of my fly. "Motivation" starts to play as she sways her naked ass to and fro, right in front of me. Fuck, it's sexy. I could watch her do that all night, if not for the insistence of my throbbing, rock hard dick. I rip down my jeans and briefs, then pull back on her hips. "Come 'ere and sit on this." The demand thunders from my throat, but she has plans of her own.

She twirls around and lifts one leg, pushing my chair back with her foot. Dropping down to her knees in the space between me and the desk, her angelic face tips up to me. "You ever had a blow job in the booth?"

I shake my head no slowly. "But I'm about to." I wink and grin at her. "You're gonna suck it for me, aren't ya?"

"Yes," she breathes, head bowing to lick me from root to tip.

I cry out when she sticks the pointed end of her tongue into the hole in my dick—never had it like that—love it. "Good girl." I fist her long, dark hair. "Suck me deep, baby, run that tongue up and down that big vein."

Oh, she heard me, doing exactly what I asked.

"Now grab my balls, Em, hard," I direct, that small hand complying immediately. "You're such a good fucking girl." I push her head down, testing her limits.

She resets herself higher up on her knees and bears down, moaning and slurping as she eats my dick like she's starving, rolling my balls as my cock seeks her fucking tonsils.

It feels so goddamn good, but I'm not ready to come, so I reach under her shoulders as Somo starts singing for her to "Ride." I'm a fool for ending the euphoria, but her pussy's even better. "Enough. Get up here, baby. I wanna come in you."

I wrap one hand around the base of my throbbing cock and with the other twirl one finger, "turn around." Emmy likes the sound of that, teeth tugging on her bottom lip, but still looking around hesitantly at the outline of bodies entwining in dance below, knowing they might be able to see us. I see the resolve, then hunger, move back into her eyes before she spins around seductively. Her body searches for me as I guide myself into my reverse cowgirl, the sound of her sweet whimper louder to my ears than the music.

Goddamn, she may be the clumsiest stripper on the stage, but Shorty can lap dance like a champ, her body curling from head to ass in one fluid movement, the hard snap of her hips jerking my dick inside her to the beat of the song. She fucks gracefully, cupping her own large breasts under her shirt as she seductively dances on top of me, up and down my pulsing length, swirling, moaning, panting for both of us.

"How many, songs, uh, you give me?" I pant, trying to still her gyrations before I explode as her hot, slippery and ready, but still devilishly tight, body sucks me in further.

She turns her head, peering at me over her shoulder. "One more."

I run my hands down the tops of her thighs. "Fuck me good, Em, right in front of them."

She bows her back on another soft whimper and grabs my thighs, so I go up the front of her shirt, under the loose bra, squeezing her full tits for her. "The-they can't," she stutters as I sink my teeth in her shoulder, "really see us, right, babe?"

237

They can't see us; no one gets to look at my Emmett with her head thrown back, licking her lips as she comes. But the fear, mixed with temptation, of an audience is turning my girl on something fierce, taking her wantonness to a whole new level. And knowing she wants me so bad that spectators be damned, she has to have me inside her right now makes me want to howl and beat my chest with every punishing thrust into her hot, weeping for me pussy.

"Don't. Give. A. Fuck. Show 'em how I like it. You do know how I like it, don't you, baby?" I lick the shell of her ear and suck on the lobe, causing her to clench her inner muscles around me.

"Mhm…" She grabs one of my hands and drags it down her damp skin to her pussy. "Play with me, Sawyer, make me come."

I tease her, spreading my fingers into an inverted V and running them up and down the outside of her pussy lips as my dick punches through, getting work done in the middle. "Kiss me, now," I growl, flicking her clit once.

She grabs around my neck and smashes our mouths together, sucking my tongue into her own crazed mouth, so I reward her with my rough thumb, the exact thing she craves, crushing down on her clit. She whines for me, loud breaths coming from her nose as she rolls her hips back and down, faster than before.

I feel her coming, every muscle in her already snug core

grabbing onto me, screaming in a pulsing mantra that I come with her. After she's finished that one, I break from her mouth and push on her lower back. "Lean forward, baby." I run my hand all the way up her spine, applying pressure 'til she's bent, ass up, over the ledge for me. I cover her hands, desperately clinging to the table with my own. "Brace yourself."

Pulling almost all the way out and watching my shiny, slathered dick come back out, I warn her one last time. "Push back, babe," I groan before pounding all the way back into her like there's not a floor of people dancing right under us, that we're the only two people here or anywhere. Her sweet pussy...I can't get enough, never enough. "Fucking," thrust, "take," pound, "me." I pull her ass up higher, at the perfect angle, driving down and in to hit the spot I know makes her soar the highest.

"A-again!" she cries, her own hand working her clit so I let go of one of her hips and join her. A flash of pink, then blue, shines in my eyes; she must have hit the button to the strobe light with one of those hands she's slamming against the tabletop as she commands me. "Don't care, don't stop." She pushes back, countering my movements, our bodies banging together as the array of electric lights flash over and around us now. "Sawyer, ah, babe!" she cries.

"One more, baby, then I gotta fucking fill you." I manipulate our entwined fingers now, feverishly flicking and taunting her clit. I feel her tighten, then relax, as she lubes me up like only she can, and I empty myself inside her, thrusting slowly long after I'm drained. I lift the back of her shirt and lick up her spine to taste her sweet sweat. "Love you, Em."

"Love you too," she pants, letting her head fall forward.

EPIC. FUCKING. SEX.

Chapter 21

DOCTOR CRASHERS

—Emmett—

"NICE TO SEE YOU, Emmett, how are you feeling?"

Dr. Greer is wonderful. She has a monotone, soothing voice and a neutral face no matter what you say or ask. Some women might find her sterile or cold, but for me? For me she's the perfect doctor.

"A lot better, actually. I'm not as tired and sluggish all the time and my appetite's back. It was like one day I woke up and was finally over the flu."

"Yes, this middle trimester is usually the part women choose to remember, thus multiple births. You're no longer sick, and not yet large, so enjoy these next few months."

I nod, instinctively looking over my shoulder; for the hundredth time in the last hour.

"Are we waiting on Mr. Beckett?"

"Oh, no," I falter, caught. "He had an exam, so he said he'd try, but," I suck in a deep breath, showing these damn hormone-driven emotions who's boss, "it's fine, we don't have to wait."

"Okay, well unless you have any concerns, a vaginal exam isn't necessary today. Your vitals are excellent, urinalysis normal." She talks with her head down, looking at my chart. "Oh. Oh my."

"What is it?"

"It says here that Mr. Beckett called in with some—" She titters, covering her mouth. "Sorry, excuse me, with some questions. Shall we go over them?"

When she finally raises her head, making eye contact, the humored twinkle where I'm used to stoic professionalism tells me I do not want to hear this.

I cover my face with both hands and brace myself for the oncoming conversation. "All right, let's do it," I mumble through my fingers.

"Emmett!"

"What in the world?" Dr. Greer moves quickly to stand and open the door, sticking her head out in the hall. "Mr. Beckett? She's in here."

An out of breath Sawyer comes barreling through the

door, apologizing as he practically mows over the poor doctor. "Hey, Shorty, what'd I miss?" He comes to my side and kisses me, like everything that just transpired is completely normal and no one noticed he's a lunatic.

"H-hi? What, why?" I'm flabbergasted, shaking my head and starting over. "Why didn't you ask the receptionist to show you back instead of yelling your way down the hall?"

"Excellent question, Emmett," Dr. Greer says from behind him, her toe tapping on the floor a loud, punishing sound in the tiny room.

"She was on the phone and all holding up her one minute finger at me. And shit, babe, I didn't want to miss anything more than I had to. I'm sorry," he turns his head to address Dr. Greer, "but your desk chick wants me, so she was stalling, trying to keep me from my woman."

"My desk chick wants you." She crosses her arms over her chest, repeating him, not asking him. Of course he answers her anyway.

"Yup, she undressed me with her eyes like five times while I waited. Then she eye sucked me before I—"

"I've got it." She holds up her hand, cutting him off. "You certainly are a handful, aren't you?"

"Actually, I'm—"

"Sawyer!" I stop him, shrieking in sheer mortification.

"Sorry," he mumbles to us both, pouting for 1.1 seconds before winking at me and stealing another kiss. "So," he claps his hands and rubs them together, "where were we?"

"We were about to go over the questions you phoned in," I grit out.

"Oh good." He faces Dr. Greer matter-of-factly. "I have a few concerns."

"Oh, I read," she answers with a lilting laugh, her usually stoic face betraying an almost entertained smile.

Holy crap, he's done it! He's cracked her shell—she can't wipe the tickled look off her face.

"Let's see, number one," she clears her throat, "should I be worried about going too far in and hurting her? Should I hold back an inch or two? I don't want to poke the baby."

"You actually called up here and asked that?" I hiss, a hinting sob of embarrassment intermingled with my question.

"Actually, Emmett, many men have that same fear and question. They tend to articulate it differently, but it's the same concern."

"See, babe," he rubs my shoulder, "I'm not the only one."

"Uh huh," I reply curtly.

"No, Mr. Beckett, you cannot poke the baby. It is physically impossible."

"Even if you're like—"

"Physically. Impossible," she reiterates firmly.

"Good to know." He smiles over at me and I have to bite my lip, 'cause he's seriously happy, and it's kinda adorable. He honestly thought his massive manhood was gonna stab the baby in the head.

"Next." She coughs, I think to cover a laugh, and Sawyer's halfway to her to pat her back when she waves him off and recovers. "How hard is too hard?"

"Right." He nods.

"What are we talking about here? Do you mean an erection getting too hard?"

"Nooo, like…" he trails off.

OH. DEAR. GOD. HE'S. DEMONSTRATING.

"You know, going in too hard. Should I hold back some power, 'cause the other night I was really givin' it to her, like hard? I don't want to jar the baby loose or something."

Dr. Greer is scarlet, moving to the sink to wash her hands even though she hasn't touched anything. "Anything that Emmett is all right with, erm, comfortable with, is fine."

"What about bent over?"

"Fine."

"On top? Really bouncing?"

"All sex is fine."

"Yes!" He beams, flashing me a wink. "S'all good, babe."

"I heard." I cringe, pinching the bridge of my nose.

"Any other questions?" she asks the ceiling.

Poor Dr. Greer. He does take some getting used to.

"Hmm," he rubs his chin, "no, I think that covers it."

"Thank God," she mutters under her breath. My

sentiments exactly. "All right then, Emmett," her gaze turns to me, "let's go ahead and do a quick ultrasound today. You may even get to find out the gender if we're real lucky."

"Oh, we've decided to let that be a surprise. But can we still do one anyway, to see everything else?" I ask.

"Certainly. I'll send a tech in." She closes the folder and heads for the door. "And I'll see you in a month. All right?"

"Sounds good." I smile warmly. "Thank you, Dr. Greer."

"Thanks, Doc," Sawyer chimes in, offering his hand, which she pretends not to see as she blazes out the door.

"Shit!" he yells, banging his forehead with his palm. "I forgot to ask about anal!"

"YOU READY?" Laney sticks her head in the front door, finding me in the midst of chaos. It looks like I've been robbed, everything I own flung about haphazardly. "Emmett? Emmett, what's wrong?" She rushes in and skids to her knees by my side, putting an arm around me.

"I can't find it!" I wail, wiping my nose and snorting embarrassingly. "It's missing! Gone!"

"What is, sweetie?"

"The ultrasound picture! I wanted to show you guys today, but it's gone! I looked," my sob shakes my whole body with a shudder, "everywhere. My purse, every drawer, the car. Where could it be?"

"We'll find it, don't worry." She hugs me to her side. "I promise, we'll find it."

"Th-thank you." I inhale a cleansing breath, pulling myself together. "Can we find it before we go?" I can't go out for "girl's day" without laying my hands on Alex's mug shot first.

"Have you asked Sawyer if he's seen it?" She stands, helping me to do the same, then tucking the couch cushions back in place.

In my frantic state, I hadn't even thought of that. Brilliant, Em. "Where's my phone?" I pat myself down, no pockets, ready to yank apart the sofa again.

Laney stops with a hand to my arm. "I'll call it. And then I'll call Sawyer. How about you go splash some water on your face and grab your shoes. Sound good?"

"K." I stumble aimlessly down the hall, as though disconnected from myself. It'd be impossible to explain how many ways pregnancy toys with you to someone who hasn't experienced it. One minute you're fine, the next? The sky is falling.

"Emmett!" she hollers down the hall. "I found your phone. And your picture."

Spinning around so fast I get dizzy, I plant a hand on the wall and settle, then run to her. "Where was it?" I search her hands. "Where is it?"

"Now Emmett, you know I really love Sawyer, so I need you to promise me you're not going to go all pregnant postal and kill him."

I reach up and rub my temples. "Just tell me."

"He took the picture with him to get copies and enlargements made!" she explains with a sigh. "How sweet is that? You're happy with him now, right? It's not at all kill worthy, I think."

"At ease, soldier," I say with a laugh. "It was very sweet. I won't hurt him."

She sighs in relief. "Awesome, now let's go. Whit and Bennett are waiting."

The drive to lunch is interesting; Laney swears if I have an ultrasound picture, I know the gender, and berates me the entire way to "give it up." I swear on everything I know to that I don't, but her cutting eyes tell me she doesn't believe me.

"I'll ask Sawyer. He's like a book and he can't lie."

"I'm not lying to you!" I feign devastation. "And you know that pregnant postal thing we talked about? You're fixing to get it firsthand."

"Oh, Emmett," she gut laughs, "you and I are gonna get along just fine. I'm even gonna buy your lunch!"

Chapter 22

While She Was Sleeping

—SAWYER—

Sawyer,

My eyes are closing as we speak, so I will no doubt be asleep by the time you get home. The girls wore me out today, how fun are they? Oh, and between the four of us, the crib is all finished! (Don't worry, they all pinky swore to give you all the credit.)

Hope work was okay tonight and I'll see you in the morning.

xo Em

Work wasn't great tonight. Mariah came in and tried to show her ass, literally...but the note Emmy left me suddenly makes it all better. The paper holds the slightest trace of her

Red scent and one sniff calms my nerves. I creep down the hall, being as quiet as I can, and find her in bed. She's on her side facing me, one hand tucked under her cheek, the other on her stomach. I'd never mention it first, but lately, there's a tiny bump emerging and I love it. Call me crazy, but with Hayden, Parker's wife, it was like the bigger she got, the hotter she got. Emmett's already the most beautiful girl I know, and adding in the whole growing a baby thing, well...Damn.

Stripping down to my briefs as quickly and silently as possible, I climb in beside her. Remaining still, I make sure I didn't wake her, then scoot down in the bed until my legs hang off the end of the mattress so my face is even with her belly.

"Hey there, sport, or princess, or whoever you want to be, no pressure." Off to a great start. "What I mean is, hey you in there," I whisper. "I'm gonna be your dad. And one day, maybe you'll hear things, like I'm not your dad dad or something, but I'm hoping by then I've taught you how to see through that bullshit. Oh sorry, I mean, that crap. Being a Dad means more than you'll ever learn in Biology. I'm gonna do my damndest to show you what all those other things are. And if you're a son, I'm gonna show you how to love a woman right, the way I love your mama. And if you're a little girl, I'll show you what to expect from a man."

The feel of a hand on my head, rubbing softly, tells me

I've been caught.

"I love you," she whispers.

Kissing her stomach, I shift up even with her. "I didn't mean to wake you. I thought I was whispering."

"You were." She smiles sleepily, stroking my head. "It's fine. That was worth waking up for."

I lean in and touch my lips to hers. "Go back to sleep, babe."

"Who taught you to be such a fine man?" she asks softly. "You've never told me a thing about your family."

"Sure I have, I told ya I wouldn't go there. The Crew's my family, especially Dane."

"What about your parents? Grandparents? Aunts, uncles?" She keeps pushing and the curious sympathy in her voice makes my skin crawl.

"Can we not do this? I just wanna hold you and fall asleep." I wrap myself around her, hoping we're done.

She fights it, probably biting through her tongue for about three minutes until she can't take it any longer. "My story was ugly, but at least I told you," she says through a sigh.

"Em, this is not one of those 'please drag it out of me cause deep down I really wanna talk about it' things, I swear. I simply don't care. I really don't. I had a birth mom, she sucked, mostly for meth. When I got big enough to block a few blows and maybe give a few back to her dick of the day, school saw bruises and I landed in foster care. That was my gig 'til I was eighteen, then I got out, fucked off, met Dane, and here I am."

"I'm so sorry, Sawyer." She tries to roll over but I hold her still.

We are not doing this. I do not want her to look at me like that right now.

"Your story wasn't exactly pretty, babe. Nobody I know has postcard parents, except maybe Evan. Bennett's aren't bad either, but other than that? You and I are the norm, not the exception. Everybody's got their own shit."

"You're right," she relents, "I won't ever bring it up again." She scoots further back against me, pulling my arm around her snugly. "Night, Sawyer."

"Night, babe." I kiss her hair, smelling her girly shampoo. "I love you too."

IN NO TIME AT ALL, we have eliminated thirty-two pages of the baby name book she bought. There's not even one option we both like. I'd love to meet the person who made up half those damn names—are they just gunning for kids to get ridiculed? I mean come on, work with me, people!

Alex is only a nickname, so I'm honestly afraid our baby is going to end up being named "Baby." Every time I bring up this crucial point, Emmett laughs and says "then we can't put them in the corner." I have no idea what that means, but nobody better even think about putting my kid in the corner anyway, lest they want my foot up their ass.

Much like the crib (if anybody asks), I single-handedly put together the bassinet we got for the bedroom, using every single part in the box! And I hid the breast pump straight away. That thing looks like a medieval torture device and will not be going anywhere near my favorite set of beautiful boobs. I will happily milk her.

She didn't like it when I said it, either.

Overall, things have been great, but I'm restless. Every once in a while, I stop and look around. I find my phone, my keys, my Emmett...nothing's missing, but it doesn't help. Something's off and I can't shake it.

"You think I'm just looking for something to go wrong since I've never had great?" I kick my shoes up on the edge of Dane's desk while he stares at his computer screen.

"Maybe, that sounds like you. I wouldn't worry until there's something to worry about, though. You could be me. Laney's harder to pin down than an angry bear."

"I bet." I chuckle, enjoying his predicament.

"Seriously," he runs a hand through his hair, pulling, "I know she's only twenty, but it's not like I'm fifty, and I'm ready. I want to take the next step. She wants to plant her feet in cement."

"What next step? You mean like married? It's only been a year, bud."

"Bullshit," he grumbles, banging on the keyboard.

"Relax, you don't have to get married tomorrow. You guys got a good thing the way it is, don't rush it."

"Says the man about to have a baby?" He stares at me pointedly.

"That was all the universe, brother," I explain, holding my arms out with a flourish. "Fate dealt, I called. What you're talking about is jumping the gun."

"We could have a long engagement."

"You could." I nod, letting my feet fall and sitting up straight. "Maybe ask her to move in? I'll be leaving the duplex officially real soon."

"You're moving in with Emmett?"

"Well yeah, douche. Kinda thought I'd live with my fiancé and child. I'm crazy like that."

"Fiancé? When the fuck did that happen?"

"Hasn't." I grab a mint from the bowl on his desk and pop it in my mouth, standing. "I'm waiting for my moment. Later." I head to the door, laughing the whole way. I think it's hifuckinglarious that the one man always in control, able to make just about anything happen, fell flat on his ass for the most stubborn, independent hellcat of a woman I've ever met.

Hifuckinglarious.

Chapter 23

GOOD LUCK SCHMUCK

—Emmett—

IT'S SATURDAY, Halloween in fact, when I really feel it. Not the usual flutterings, but an all-out kick. "Sawyer! Hurry, come here!"

He rushes in, in his Hugh Hefner costume, full sprint. "Baby, what? What?"

I grab his hand and place it on my stomach. "He—she kicked. You have to—"

"Holy shit!" We smile at each other and fall into a fit of giddy, shocked laughter when the baby kicks his hand. Without moving, he goes to his knees. "Happy Halloween, no name."

"Ah, no name, how sad." I frown down at him. "We're awful parents already."

We wait, neither of us moving a muscle, for another kick…that doesn't come. Halloween night will pack The K, so we're forced to give up for now and head to work, Sawyer in his velvet robe, me, of course, in a bunny outfit. Guess who won the coin toss to pick our costumes.

Laney's not old enough to help work, or even be in the bar, for that matter, but low and behold, she greets us as we walk in, dressed as a referee.

"It's not a costume if you had the shit in your closet, Gidge," Sawyer teases, lifting her off the ground in a hug.

"Hardy har har. I only had the shoes. And the whistle. You look cute, Emmett." She tugs on my ear. "Lose a bet to Hugh here?"

I nod, tickled. "I need to hop to the bathroom before I get started. I'll see you both later?"

"Yeah, right," Sawyer scoffs loudly. "Laney, will you go to the bathroom with her? And who's watching you? This place is crawling with horny college guys, ya'll stay in sight and if you need to go to the bathroom or locker room, go in a pair." He scowls back and forth between us. "I'm not kidding. Em, you take One tonight."

He means Section One, the two straight rows of tables directly in front of the bar, where he'll be. "Okay," I smooch my lips and huff, wanting my kiss before I pee myself. When

I get it, I grab Laney's hand. "Seriously, I've gotta go. Come on, buddy."

Thankfully there's not a line yet at the public bathroom, the closest one to me, but by the time I use the bathroom, wash my hands and walk back out, at least a hundred people have packed inside—it was that quick.

"Dayummm," Laney mutters, staring at the sea of bodies before us.

I mentally pep myself up, squaring my shoulders with resolution. "At least I'll make great money! Let's do this!"

WHEN YOU WAIT TABLES in a bunny costume, you're going to get hit on, I know this, but the comments are growing louder and more crude as the hour gets later. I handle it, in one bunny ear and out the other, always keeping a straight face, remarkably well, I'd say. Not only does a non-reaction discourage them, but it keeps Sawyer at bay.

He's great behind the bar, but even better at never taking one eye off me. If he sees a strong reaction from me, he'll know someone got too far out of line and be in their face before I can blink.

Knowing all this, I still let it happen.

On a night like this, faces blend together and all voices

sound the same, everything an impatient yell over the music. Tables empty and fill without ever seeing the exchange. Sweat drips down the back of my neck, my calves ache, but I suck it up and work for the almighty dollar, eyes on the prize, the only constant awareness the beautiful man behind the bar.

So how I pick out one voice, I'll never know. Apparently, I know the sound of trouble when I hear it.

"What time you get off, cottontail?"

I attempt to ignore him, emptying the tray as fast as I can and trying to scurry around the opposite side of the table, but he's quicker, grabbing me around the waist and hauling me up against his front.

"I asked you a question." He grabs my arm and spins me around, his nails digging painfully into my flesh causing my tray to crash to the ground. "You're awful cute." He's too close to my face, his rancid breath reeking of the Jim Beam he's been ordering all night, and I suddenly feel very nauseous.

"L-let me go," I choke out past the bubble of fear and vulnerability caught in my throat.

"Let her go, man," one of his friends tries to urge him, but it only seems to egg him on.

He leans in close to my throat and loudly sniffs all the way up it. "You smell awful sweet, think I need me a taste."

"Em?" And this is when I really panic, because as relieved I am to hear Sawyer's voice right beside me now, I know this is going to end badly. "Dude, you want to get your fucking hands off her?" Sawyer pushes on his forearm, but the guy doesn't release me, rather firming his grip.

"Not really, friend. We're getting to know each other. Aren't we, sugar?"

I shake my head, my mouth opening and closing, trying to back away. "N-no, not at all."

"Let. Her. Go," Sawyer hisses at the man, his eyes glued to where the grubby, intrusive fingers sting my flesh.

"What's the problem here?" Oh thank God, Dane's here. He'll ask him to leave, Sawyer won't go crazy, and it'll all be okay.

"No problem, man," the guy answers Dane, finally letting go of me and putting up both hands in mock innocence. "Simply trying to talk to the pretty help ya got here. Think big boy there might be a little butt hurt, though," he turns to his table of friends and grins evilly, "seeing as how his bitch wants me."

"Dane," Sawyer snarls, "I need you to take Emmett, now."

"No!" I find my voice, loud and panicked. "Sawyer, no, it's not worth it. Please." I pull on his arm, turning to Dane. "Just kick him out, Dane, please."

I've seen Sawyer's passion, his love, his sweet, his gentleness…if his angry is backed with half as much power as his other emotions, this will not end well.

Sawyer and Dane share a look, as though I'm not even there, begging, and Dane gives him a curt nod. "Let's go, Em," he barks right before I'm scooped up in his arms.

I see Laney scrambling through the crowd, trying to catch us, and I call out to her. "Laney! Laney, help!" I point to where things are about to get very ugly, kicking and struggling against Dane. "Go get Sawyer!"

We whirl around fast and Dane screams at her. "Laney, no! Follow me, now, no questions!"

She looks to Sawyer, then me, back again, then finally to Dane. Nodding, she jogs to us, sheer terror on her face. "I've got her, baby, go help Saw," she says, patting Dane on the back. "The other guy has friends."

"And he'll need every single one of them, I assure you." He sets me down and places my hand in Laney's. "Up to my office, door locked. Don't test me, Emmett," he points in my face, "and don't fight Laney. Now go!"

We both jump at his harsh voice but immediately comply, Laney dragging me toward the stairs. I look back and start to cry; Sawyer's already got one hand wrapped around the guy's throat and is dragging him outside. All I can do at this point is pray Dane stops Sawyer short of killing him.

—SAWYER—

THIS PIECE OF SHIT may not make it. Glaring at him, I see more than just his bad-mannered, prick self, but rather the manifestation of all the wrong that's been done to Emmett at the hands of unmanly men. Her wide, terrified eyes were like windows, showing me that she too was thinking of a time when another man thought she was nothing more than a plaything.

He's struggling against my grip around his larynx, using both hands to grab and pull at mine while his feet drag and try to gain leverage. Dane enters my vision from the side. "Sawyer," he warns lowly. "Outside. I got the friends."

No fucking shit. Where ya think I'm going?

I bash his forehead against the bar on the back door to open it, tossing him outside roughly. He's not even off his back by the time I get my costume off—I'm not fighting in a fucking robe.

"Stand up!" I grab his collar and yank him to his feet. "That woman you put your hands on? That's my woman, whom I love very much. She has rights. Who the fuck do you think you are?"

"Fuck you." He spits in my face. "Why don't you chill

out, man? Just having some fun. No big deal."

The first punch is to the gut. When he bends with the blow, my knee comes up to clock his nose and I revel in the snapping sound it makes, the blood soaking my leg. "That's for touching her!" I yank his head back up by his hair and return the favor of spit in his face. "You can't be a gentleman, don't fucking drink."

He swings his right arm clumsily and I let him land it on the side of my jaw before I laugh. "That all you fucking got? Come on, big man, show me how you overpower people. Grab my arm, tell me what to do!" I push him away from me, letting him regain his bearings. Isn't that what guys like him get off on, the power, the toying with them? "Come on, show me." I wiggle both hands toward myself.

He roars, coming at me, both fists up…and that's as far as he gets, his best effort. One crack, straight out and back, and I lay his lip wide open.

"Come on, Mary, you got it," I taunt him.

All I see is a morph of this pudsmack, putting his hands on my sweet Emmett, and the other guy who thought it was okay to hurt her. I want to show them both what it means to hurt—how fucking dare they touch her! Her fear, her helplessness… She's so tiny, so fragile… I have to swallow a sob of pain at the same time as my growl. I want blood. I want her revenge for her.

I lunge for him, but he's backing up, waving his hands.

"I'm-I'm sorry," he whimpers, wiping his mouth and spitting blood on the ground.

"Yeah, you're pretty sorry all right." Left, right, I make it rain, every blow for Emmett. "You," gut punch, "don't hurt," another to the nose, "women," right hook that puts him flat on his back. I stand over the top of him, pulling him up by his collar again 'cause this kid can't stay off the ground, and rear back my fist, punching him over and over…trapped in a haze of red. Red, my sweet girl. Punches, kicks, rage flows out of me in a rhythm over which I have no control…

"Sawyer!"

I leer down at this worn out, poor excuse of a man, hands on my hips, my chest heaving. I move to go after him again, but Dane stops me, both hands braced against my chest.

"He's done, and so are you."

"He fucking hurt her, he—"

"I know, I know, man."

"Why do they think they can touch her?"

"Sawyer, she's safe, bud. You took care of it. Breathe, man, she's fine."

He gives me a minute to walk around, my head back and my hands on my hips, sucking in fresh air.

"You good?" he finally asks.

I nod, shaking out my hands, consciously directing my breathing back to normal.

"Go on then, driver's waiting. Straight to my house."

"Emmett?" I look around, as though she'll appear. "Where's Emmett?"

"Already on her way there. Go."

"What about," I look to beaten man on the ground, "him?"

"I got it. Go." He hands me my costume and I hustle the hell out of there.

Chapter 24

LIFE AS WE KNEW IT

~Emmett~

LANEY'S HOLDING ME, stroking my hair and singing, as I sob quietly but unstoppably with my head in her lap. She is a terrible singer, truly so bad that I can't even think of a metaphor to describe the severity of her tone-deaf caterwauling, but she certainly puts her whole heart into it and knows every word to every song written for a Disney movie.

"Somebody's here," she whispers, taking a break from "A Dream Is a Wish Your Heart Makes."

I don't even lift my head. I know it can't be Sawyer, he's probably in jail right now, so what's it matter... Honestly,

Dane's house is so big, someone could be robbing the whole bottom floor and I doubt we'd hear it, so I think she's probably mistaken.

"Want me to go see who it is?"

"Not really." I clench onto her leg. "Stay with me, I think you're hearing things."

"No, the alarm chimed, somebody entered the code." Oh, well that explains that at least.

Loud, heavy footsteps start to rumble down the hallway, in our direction, and I pop up. He's here! I know it's Sawyer, Dane doesn't sound like a herd of elephants when he walks. I scramble to a sitting position and quickly swipe beneath my eyes; I don't want him to see I've been crying. He's had a rough enough night without my hysterics adding more stress.

"Emmett? Babe?" he shouts.

"Back here!" Laney yells back for me.

"Em?" His head comes around the doorway. "Oh, Em," he bolts across the room, sweeping me into his massive, strong arms, "are you all right?" His words are muffled, his face buried in my hair.

"Me?" I push on his chest, needing to look at him. "Forget me, are you okay?" My eyes work frantically over, up, and down him, assessing any damage, of which I see nothing more than a small red mark on his jaw. I don't know what I'd been expecting, but minus the barely visible scuff and some dried blood on his left hand, he looks the same as he did before the nightmare started. "Sawyer," I gulp, sobs coming up again, "I was so worried. I thought you'd be in jail, or hurt, or... Well, not really hurt, I knew you'd win, but definitely jail. I'm so sorry."

One hand rubs my back, the other wrapped around the back of my neck. "I'm fine, babe, shh."

"I'll, uh," Laney mumbles, "I'll be downstairs if you guys need anything. Is Dane here yet?"

"No," Sawyer answers her, his lips still touching my hair. "Thank you, Laney, for taking care of her. Are you okay?"

"Of course," she says quietly, and I can hear the tender smile in her reply. "I'm fine, no worries."

The door closes behind her and Sawyer sits us on the bed, my arms and legs tangled around him desperately. I don't ever want to let go. I don't want anyone or anything to penetrate our happiness, tear us apart, or take him away from me. The thought of losing him is suffocating, a sadness so bone deep I can't take a full breath. I don't even remember who I was before I let him in. I don't think I ever want to. The only Emmett I want to be is his Emmett.

"Baby, I promise it's okay. I'm here, everything's fine."

"What happens now?" I lift my head from his tear-soaked robe. I need to see his eyes when he answers me, to make sure he's not softening the blow to not scare me. "Are you gonna go to jail? How bad did you hurt him? What if he presses charges?"

"If he does, he does, and we'll figure it out. He had it coming, Em. Men who prey on women are cowards and need to be taught a lesson, especially if it's my woman. I didn't kill him, just kicked his ass good, and not half as good as I wanted to. You can thank Dane for that. He stopped me." His chest moves my body with it as he takes a deep breath, rubbing his lips lightly back and forth on my forehead. "I just kept thinking about you, how you've been hurt before, stupid, fucking guys thinking they can do whatever they want. No one gets to touch you, Emmett. I'll always protect you, or die trying." He cradles my cheeks and uses his thumbs to wipe under my eyes. "I don't want you to worry, all right? And it's not good for you to get so upset."

I nod, putting on a stoic face for him, and grab the sides of his head. "Thank you," I whisper, kissing his lips softly. "Thank you for being exactly who you are and loving me exactly how you do."

"I don't know about all," he chuckles with a small frown, "but I will always love you the best I know how."

My head rests in the crook of his neck and shoulder, my eyes heavy with exhaustion. I can feel the tension in his tightly drawn muscles dissolve slowly as we embrace in silence.

"You better now?" he murmurs with a kiss on my jaw some time later.

"Mhm?"

"Can I go get a shower and something to wear besides this damn robe?" He shakes his head. "Of all the nights to get in a fight."

"Are we staying here or going home?" I climb off his lap, settling into the bed so he can go get cleaned up, pretty much answering the question for him.

"Do you mind if we just stay here tonight, babe? Neither of us has a vehicle and it's late. I kinda need to talk to Dane anyway."

I'm already snuggled under the covers, he knows I'm fine with it, but he's too considerate not to ask. "Here's fine. Get your shower. You know where to find me when you're done."

He stands, but stops to lean onto the bed and kiss me once more. "I love you, Emmett."

—SAWYER—

"FUCK!" The flesh of my knuckle rips open, blood dripping down the tiles. What a shitstick I am...punching Dane's shower, running around in a goddamn robe almost killing dudes, letting my girl be whisked away to a strange house where she now lies in a foreign bed, crying, worried I'll be taken from her.

Tonight I put everything that's important to me at risk. Going to jail is a real possibility—yeah, that'll help Emmett and the baby out a lot. Fighting at Dane's club—we pay people to stop that shit from happening and here I am the one doing it.

Am I losing my mind? Apparently, since I'm going vigilante at my job with a baby on the way. What if I had killed him, what if I do get locked up…who will take care of Emmett?

Sure, Dane will most likely fix my mess, like always, and I'll probably never spend a day behind bars, but what kind of father has his friends clean up after him? And sign his checks? And loan him cars?

I'm a fucking joke. She deserves better than some half-cocked punk who can't provide enough to keep her from having to serve drinks to handsy pricks in a bar.

A knock on the door saves me from my own mental beating. I know who it is.

"Come on in, Dane."

"Hey," he says quietly and I hear him close the door behind him. "Girls are both asleep; I just checked on 'em. You all right?"

I'm too strung out to give him shit about being a perv and wanting to see me in the shower. I think about it, though, and decide it's a good sign; there's still some "me" left in there somewhere. "Dandy. So?"

"So, broken nose, cracked rib and eight stitches for his lip and above his eye. All fixed up now. He won't be pressing charges and neither will she. Cool?"

"You'll have to make sure that's fine with Emmett, but should be." I brush my hands over my face, pushing the water from my eyes. "Thanks, man, I owe ya one."

"You don't owe me a thing; the prick deserved it. Her car's in the driveway now. Get some sleep."

He fixed it, but I already knew he would. Like it never happened.

If you get used to someone else fixing your little shit for ya, how do you learn how to handle your own big shit?

"Hey, Sawyer?"

"Yeah?" I say too loudly; I thought he'd already walked out.

"You almost lost it tonight, bro, you had me worried for a minute. When'd you get so volatile?"

"When I found something worth fighting for."

"SAWYER, HONEY, WAKE UP." I'm shaken from my slumber.

"Hm? What?" I look around, senses slowly coming to me; Dane's guest room, Emmett beside me. "Wh—you okay? The baby?"

Her warm hand soothes across my chest as she sits up over me. Dark strands fall over her worried eyes so I reach up to tuck them behind her ear. "We're fine. You were having a nightmare."

"I don't have nightmares, Em. Go back to sleep."

"But you were. You were thrashing around and yelling about being a man." Even in the dark, I can clearly see the concern lining her face.

"Only thinking, Em, not a nightmare and nothing for you to worry about. Okay?"

"Okay," she whispers, lying back down and snuggling into my side.

"I got it, babe, I promise. Get some sleep."

Chapter 25

UNSWEETENED NOVEMBER

—Emmett—

SAWYER HASN'T HAD ANOTHER NIGHTMARE, at least not any bad enough to wake me up, but I swear he's not getting any sleep. He's not so much looking tired, but he seems at odds with the world, not absent-minded really, but definitely more distracted. So distracted that half the times I've asked if he's all right, if he wants to talk...I've had to ask twice just to get his attention and often don't even get an answer.

So although he's home early tonight, when he heads to bed still chewing his last bite of the dinner I'd made, I don't even suggest a movie. Instead, I clean the table and load the dishwasher as quietly as possible, giving him time to get settled. With school and work, I understand he's carrying a full load, but a quick kiss would've been nice. I refuse to complain though; I haven't forgotten that I'd been the first to doubt us and withdraw into myself. Sawyer had been sure from day one, so now it's his turn, and I need to keep reminding myself that turnabout is fair play.

I deserve this.

I've stalled long enough, straightening couch cushions and wiping counters for a good thirty minutes before I decide it's time to join him in bed. I tiptoe down the hall to the bedroom, trying to shoo the hope out of my heart.

At least I didn't wake him up. He's lying on his back, hands under his head, staring at the ceiling.

"Hey," I mumble awkwardly, heading to the dresser to find something to sleep in.

"Hey," he turns his head to look at me, "you coming to bed?"

"Yessss," I hitch up the flirt in my voice, totally receptive to anything he's about to suggest.

"Cool, will you turn out the bathroom light?"

I have to stop my jaw from falling open as I watch him roll over, punching at his pillow before closing his eyes. Even with only one case study under my belt, this I know for sure—men are uncomplicated, predictable creatures. Much like a baby, all you have to do is run through the "checklist," and the box left unchecked at the end—that's their problem.

I fed him. He used the restroom earlier. And now he's going to sleep.

The box not checked? The voice in my head is a bit fuzzy, so I'm not sure if it's Gramma or one of the Real Housewives, but somebody says, "If he's not getting it at home, he's getting it somewhere else."

Surely not…said the naïve, stupid woman in each and every Lifetime movie, seconds before she came home unexpectedly on her lunch break and heard suspicious moaning coming from the back of the house.

Seriously though, he hasn't "left early" for class, and I work with him a solid four days a week. His phone is on top of the dresser, inches from me, unguarded, and he doesn't madly dash for the shower right when he gets home. Am I missing something? Again, had Lifetime not taught me all the signs?

Maybe I'm a fool. I debate with myself the entire time I get ready for bed, changing my clothes and brushing my teeth, but find myself confident enough in his character and that he really is just spread too thin and tired that I crawl into bed beside him…after turning off the bathroom light, of course. His back is turned to me, so I lightly kiss his shoulder goodnight.

———————— ∽ ————————

"WHAT THE," I jolt awake and upright from a deep sleep and instantly feel it again. Stretching my arm out blindly, I find and flip on the lamp then push the covers off me hurriedly, not quite sure yet what's happening.

This time, I feel it and see it, a massive bulge rolling across my stomach. My thin shirt hides nothing, rippling with the baby's movements. "Sawyer!" My hand fumbles for him as my eyes stay trained on my stomach in awe. "Sawyer, you gotta see this, babe! Wake up!" Shaking him with one hand, I squirm around, pulling up my nightie with the other.

"Hmm?" he grumbles, rolling toward me. "What is it?"

"Watch this, watch my stomach!"

He sits up and rubs his eyes, a small "hrmph" trying to penetrate my bubble—not happening, buddy. With baited breath, I will Alex to do it again, to show him the fabulous new trick.

"Come on, little one," I urge, tapping my hand on the side of my belly.

I feel like Jacques Cousteau on a whale watching expedition. Any second now, the hump will emerge, breathtaking and majestic, then slowly roll back down, out of sight into the depths.

"I don't see anything, Em," he frumps. "What was it?"

"The baby rolled over, like a huge wave across my stomach." I demonstrate a wave with my hand. "It was amazing!"

"Very cool." He bends his head and kisses my belly. "Do it for me tomorrow," he tells the bump, then lies back down and turns on his away side.

And just like that, before Sawyer's even completely settled, my baby gives me, the patient, anxious one, another show, which I smile upon and watch in silence.

THE LITTLE ORCA I'm carrying around never stops now, clearly visible acrobatics a daily occurrence which Sawyer finally got to see. I've got baby all figured out now, and sometimes, when I'm alone or bored, I purposely eat some sugar and lay flat on my back and watch as the little bundle puts on a full rock show in there. It makes me laugh, and makes me feel like they're right there with me—entertaining Mama.

Dr. Greer got to see it at my appointment yesterday, too—she made a big deal about it, as animated as I'll probably ever see her. She also said I needed to stay off my feet for a few days and see if the swelling there would go down.

I followed my doctor's orders and traded my shift tonight, so here I sit, once again alone and mindlessly bored. I'd already checked and Laney's busy, so I guess it's Steel Magnolias and a fat-free yogurt fest. I hate being bored…I'd take more than my one class if I had the money, and work more if my feet didn't look like water balloons, because stagnant is just plain lonely. I've always been independent, able to entertain myself, but even my beloved books and journal don't hit the spot these days.

I feel invisible.

I feel useless.

And I miss my best friend.

Perking up at the thought of him, I take the chance he won't be too busy at work and text him.

Emmett: Hey babe, how's your night?

After I stare at the screen of my phone for at least five minutes solid, I decide a watched pot really doesn't ever boil, tossing the phone beside me and pressing play on the movie.

Barely past the opening credits, my phone dings and I hurriedly push pause.

Sawyer: All right, yours? Everything ok?

Emmett: Ya, fine. I just wanted to tt you. I miss you.

Sawyer: Me too Em. So you're good, nothing's wrong?

Emmett: I told ya, I'm fine worrywart. Lol

Sawyer: Cool, so can I ttyl? Need to get back to

work.

Emmett: Sure, hagn babe. I may go down n chill w/ Laney in the hot tub for a while.

I shouldn't tease him and get him all riled up while he's working, but I'm a brat when I'm bored. That's not it at all, really, I'm not a brat. I'm desperate for some Sawyer…some "no you don't, because you're my woman."

Sawyer: K have fun.

Or not.

PREGNANT WOMAN with her feet up here, people! I've yelled come in four times, and yet, they do not. Obviously it's someone I don't know, so I grumble, lowering my legs with a grimace and heading for the front door.

On my tiptoes, I look out the peephole to find a young guy standing on my porch, beside him a dolly stacked with red tackle boxes.

"Can I help you?!" I yell through the door.

"Yes, ma'am, I'm Scott from Baby Steps. I'm looking for Emmett Young?"

"What is Baby Steps?"

"We're the baby proofing specialists. I've got an order to safeguard the home of Emmett Young." He holds up a piece of paper so I can see it through the peeper.

Knowing who sent him, and pretty sure the odds on random serial killers taking the time to plan a ruse that coincides with the fact you're actually pregnant are pretty low, I open the door to him.

Holy hormone.

Scott from Baby Steps is not ugly—Scottie Too Hottie indeed.

His smile rivals the sun as he greets me, biceps trying to rip through the sleeves of his uniform shirt. "Hi there," he says in an adorable country accent, "are you Emmett Young?"

My head bobs up and down while my eyes argue with my mind over breaking his beautiful eye contact.

"Okay, well I have a work order to baby proof," he sweeps his brown eyed gaze down to my belly then back up, question in them, "your place today?"

Bless his heart. I blush at his inferred compliment, suddenly not feeling nearly as frumpy and dumpy as I have been lately. "I can guess who sent you." I laugh, stepping aside and motioning him inside. "Come on in."

He springs into action, laying his clipboard on top of the pile and scurrying around to prop up the dolly and wheel it inside. He turns to shut the door for me and wipes his feet thoroughly, smiling the whole time. "All right," he picks up his clipboard once more, glancing over it, "looks like you're set to have all the rooms done. Anywhere specific you'd like me to start?"

I should know the answer to this, being the expectant mother and all, but it was just so cute to let Sawyer read the book instead. Not so long ago, he'd even read in the bathroom, screaming out factoids to me as he took care of business. Perhaps not the cutest of moments I could have referenced, but to me, every time he read about baby stuff was precious.

"We could start with toilet locks. Usually only one or two of those, knock out one item quick."

"Oh," I shake off my reminiscent thoughts, "I'm sorry. Sure, only one toilet." I point down the hall to the bathroom. "Do you need me to do anything?"

"No, ma'am, but when I'm done and mark off each task, I'll need you to initial that I've shown you how to work it. Which I will," he grapples, unable to situate the pen under the clip as he desperately wants to, "show you, I mean." He's so adorably nervous, his voice shaking unsurely through his constant smile.

"Scott, is this your first time doing this?" I ask, sure of the answer.

"Yes, ma'am," he nods his head, "but I swear I know what I'm doing. All three of my sisters have kids and I got their places fixed up water tight."

I giggle, but reign it in fast. I don't want to make the

poor guy think I'm laughing at him. "I'm sure you do. So go ahead and do your thing and I'll just try to stay out of your way."

He nods again briskly, then starts unsnapping the lids of his tackle boxes, getting to work. I leave him to it, finding my phone and heading to the kitchen. If he's going to the bathroom, this puts me furthest away from him as I make my call.

"Hey, Em," he answers, winded.

"What're you doing? You sound out of breath." I steal a peek around the corner, confirming Scott's occupied in the bathroom.

"I'm jogging, late for class way the fuck across campus. What's up?"

I wonder why he's late for class, but don't ask. For reasons that can't be precisely defined, I've let lots of small things here and there go unquestioned lately. It's not that I need to know every move he makes—it would drive me insane if he expected a daily recollection of my whats, wheres and whos, which would take approximately ten seconds with my boring life lately—no, this is more about me and what it means that I consciously don't ask the little things anymore.

"I thought I'd call and let you know the baby proofing guy you ordered is here. Anything special you wanted done, or—"

I wish you'd told me? Asked what I thought? Be here

when it happened?

"Ah shit, I forgot! He's there now?"

"Yep, he's in there locking up the toilet as we speak. I was surprised when he showed up, since I'm not sure what we're having done." I keep my tone nice, 'cause it is very conscientious and thoughtful of him, but insinuating all the same.

"Hey, Sawyer, where've you been hiding?" I hear the girl's chirp in the background.

"Hey," he answers her a tad awkwardly, yet wears a smirk on his face as he does so. I can hear it.

"Sawyer?" I draw him back tersely. "I'll let you go, just telling ya."

"I'm sorry, Em, I should be there. I…" His frustrated breath is loud in my ear. "I forgot. I'm not really sure what else to say."

Lucky for him we don't take the time to play our "I'm sorry" game anymore; he'd run out of facts.

"It's fine, really. It was nice of you to think of it, thank you." The goodbye is tickling my lips, but I pull it back, and try again. "Hey, babe?"

"Yeah?"

"Is everything okay?"

"Em," he sighs, "everything's fine, I promise. Can you try to bear with me?"

"Of course," I whisper, clenching my eyes shut,

squeezing back the building moisture.

"Thanks, babe. I'll see you tonight."

He's gone, hung up, when I open my eyes, composure reclaimed. I can hear Scott on the other side of the wall right beside me, digging in his boxes. Toilet done, he must be ready to move on to the next project, so I grab my current book off the counter and plop down on the couch…out of his way too.

My neck is stiff. I roll my head back and forth and rub my eyes, stretching my arms out in front of me. I've read the same chapter of the paperback I'm holding three times, absorbing no facts of the story, unable to picture the scenes in my head, when Dane breezes in through front door with no obligatory bell or knock.

"Hey, Emmett, how are you?" he says cheerfully.

I look around and behind him, finding no Laney, then back up to him, puzzled at minimum. "Hey, Dane. What's, uh, can I help you?" What else do I say? What the hell are you doing here?

"No, no, don't get up or anything. I was down at Laney's and saw the van parked here. Thought I'd come by and make sure everything was all right." He's not fooling anyone. He's talking to me but staring holes through Scott in the kitchen. "Who's your guest?"

I roll my eyes, setting down my book and pushing myself up off the couch. "Scott," I call out as I do so, "can you come here a minute, please?"

In a blink, literally, he's standing in front of me, smiling politely. "Yes, ma'am?"

"Uh, this is my..." Boss? Friend? I have no idea the appropriate thing to say here, but thankfully the two men save me from having to decide.

"Hi, I'm Scott Barton with Baby Steps," Scottie Too Hottie says, sticking out his hand. "Making your baby's home a safe haven."

Dane eyes him curiously; he probably wasn't expecting the full ad. "Dane Kendrick," he offers his hand, "her man's best friend."

Knowing what little I do of Dane, it seems perfectly within his idea of normal to take it upon himself to stop by, walk in unannounced or invited, and investigate suspicious vehicles. But, it seems more likely that Sawyer sent him to check out the man alone in the house with me. I'd allow it to miff me a bit, except...Sawyer sent him.

Scott glances back and forth between us a few times before shrugging and saying, "Well, it's nice to meet you. I'm gonna go ahead and get back to work?" he questions me with his tone and his eyes.

"Yes," I nod, "thank you."

Dane clears his throat, shifting beside me, so I look up at him. "Can you walk me out, Emmett?"

"Oh, sure." I clear my face of confusion and head to the

door.

One step on the porch and Dane has already closed the front door and placed a hand on my arm, startling me. "You don't have to walk me to my car, Emmett. Do you feel safe with him here while Sawyer's gone? I can stay."

"Wow, that's very nice Dane, thank you. But it's fine, really. I feel perfectly safe. And if I didn't," I just realize I've shifted my stance to somewhat defensive and crossed my arms, "I'd call Sawyer and expect him to come home. He's the one who ordered this, after all."

He runs a hand back through his hair, eyes flicking left, right, down, then back to mine. "Emmett, I may be out of line, if so, I apologize, but," hand through hair again, clearly his coping gesture, "well, is there anything I can do? Or talk to Sawyer about?"

"I don't know what you mean."

"Yes, you do." His eyes aren't cold, but they're serious, as is his tone. "Sawyer's my brother, I love him very much, and I know him very well. I can't stand by and watch him sabotage himself, so I'd like to try and help if I can. Nothing would please me more than for him to be happy, and I know you're his happy."

For some reason, I always find Dane to be very intimidating, and even though his words are kind and his intentions are noble, right now I feel especially feeble to his aura of power and control, so it takes great effort to hold my voice steady and keep my chin up as I say as confidently as I can, "I appreciate your concern, I really do, but Sawyer and I are great. We don't need anyone to run interference. We're a team, together, and we'll find our own way back to good."

He considers me and my answer, rubbing his chin and finally letting a coy grin take over his face. "That's how it should be. Good answer," he says decidedly. "All right then. If anything feels off, you call him right away. All right?"

"All right." I nod and walk back in the house and he heads to his car.

Now I need to convince myself, as I just did him, that I'm confident in my team.

FOR THE FIRST MORNING in what seems like forever, I'm up before Sawyer. Not only will I get to see his face instead of the occasional note this morning, but I'm excited to attempt my first Thanksgiving dinner. I'm hoping for edible and praying for no food poisoning, so anywhere in the middle will be considered a success.

Things have been lackluster, to say the least, between Sawyer and I lately, and there's a distance between us that I feel growing wider every day. I'm not a moron, I see the signs, but one person's slow down is another person's go faster before it turns red. A racecar driver at heart, I continue to try. I'd put up a fight and he continued to fight for me, I'm more than woman enough to do the same. There's still a "we" inside him, I catch glimpses of it every so often; a brush of his hand on mine, a wink here and there…deep down, we're more than just the roommates we've become. Maybe this holiday meal, just he and I, will bring us back to good. Bellies full, snuggled up on the couch with a movie, maybe finally a good heart-to-heart conversation…

"You're up early." His groggy morning greeting startles me.

"I am. Good morning." I go up on my toes for his kiss, but all I get is a chaste brush of his lips then he steps around me to open the fridge. "I had to get the turkey in early if we want to eat by lunch time. I'm about to start peeling potatoes. You wanna help?"

"Oh, um," he falters, eyes flicking around the room, "I didn't know you had a big deal planned. I was gonna go in to work."

"On Thanksgiving?"

"Yeah, Em, on Thanksgiving. I need all the money I can get. I have responsibilities."

"I have responsibilities too, Sawyer. I'm up to my eyeballs in responsibility," I measure that with a sideways hand at my eye line, "but taking today for family seemed pretty important too. Can't we just have today?"

"Sure," he concedes with a small smile that reeks of effort. "What time you want me to be back?"

"Whenever." I toss the dishtowel on the counter, my mood turned.

"No, not whenever." He reaches out and grabs my hand, pulling me to him. "What time, Em?"

I bury my face in his shirt, hiding my teary eyes and disappointment. "I don't want it to be a burden, Sawyer. I want you to want to be here."

"I want a lot of things, Emmett." His face goes to my hair and for a fleeting, hopeful second I think he's going to give me one of his infamous head kisses that I've gone far too long without, but he merely speaks. "I'll see ya at two. Good?"

All I can do is nod, afraid to try and speak any more. If I dare, I'll either cry, burdening him more, or scream out my frustrations, driving him further away. So I nod, lift my head, and release him.

"Okay, I'll be here at two."

Here, not home. No kiss goodbye.

When he's gone, I slide down to the floor, right where I stand, and wrap my arms around my knees. We aren't "playing house" any more and reality's proving to be too much. I've lost Sawyer to his own mind—I've become his responsibility. Who could blame him for checking out? The road to heartache, it would seem, is also paved with good intentions.

"Happy Thanksgiving." I rub my stomach and let go of the hold I had on my tears, watching with a strange detachment as they splash onto my shirt.

I SUCK IN A HARSH GASP, quickly wiping my face and scrambling to my feet. Hoping my mask is in place, I turn, elated that he's come back in.

But no, he hasn't…I hear his voice, but he isn't speaking to me, it's floating through the open window. And damn you all to hell, Georgia, for hosting Thanksgivings warm enough for open windows, 'cause what I hear Sawyer say next reaches into my chest and takes the last hopeful piece of us I had left and snuffs it into the ground.

"Hi. I didn't think you'd answer on Thanksgiving. Can I come over now and talk?"

Chapter 26

MY FAMILY STONE

—Emmett—

"THIS FEELS AMAZING. You're all geniuses."

"All?!" Whitley cries. "Do not even think of giving Laney credit for pedicures! She wouldn't even know that word if it weren't for Bennett and I. Right, Ben?"

"Right." Poor Bennett is breaking a sweat taking the pumice stone to Laney's crusty, ball playing heels. "God, Laney, I hope you wear socks to bed! If not, Dane's not gonna have any skin left on his poor legs!"

"I can hear you bitches when you talk out loud," Laney retorts, her head back on the couch and cucumber slices over her eyes.

I giggle even though I'm only half-listening to their banter. Whitley is a rubbing, scrubbing goddess, performing crazy miracles on my swollen feet right now. I'm so relaxed I might fall asleep.

This is precisely what I needed, an evening with awesome ladies and my aching cankles being tended to. Nowhere in the book Sawyer's reading did it say that the minute you hit 27 weeks your water retention triples overnight and you turn into an Oompa Loompa. If it did, he didn't read me that part.

Then again, Sawyer hasn't been reading me any parts lately. Nor have we watched movies together, and the two times I treated myself to some Coldstone relief, I was alone. He missed the first breastfeeding class, which I understood, since he doesn't need to know how to do that, but missing the last doctor appointment? That spoke volumes. Even louder is the fact that he hasn't so much hinted at, let alone made love to me in weeks. Maybe the person he can "talk to" filled that gap as well...

Lately, I've been regarded with little more than causal friendliness, with pecks goodbye and radio rather than conversation on the trips to and from work—the ones we actually make together, that is. He still finds his way to my bed every night, but he sneaks in late when he thinks I'm asleep and I do nothing to let him know otherwise. In the morning, he's always awake before I stir. He's there, but

ENTICE

nowhere to be found.

I don't think I'm grotesque, my total weight gain thus far is nine pounds, which Dr. Greer assures me is healthy and acceptable. I can still wear almost all my old clothes, even my jeans, if I push the top of them below my baby bump. I haven't spied any stretch marks yet, but I still lather in Vitamin E Cocoa Butter every morning and night.

So I'm not sure what the problem is, or when it officially started, but my Sawyer is gone and left "Dutiful Sawyer" in his place. If he'd just talk to me, confirm what I already know deep down, he'd find that I'd peacefully be more than okay with simply having my friend back.

"Emmett, you okay?" Whitley smiles, drying my feet and placing one on her knee. "Lost ya there for a minute."

"Oh yeah, fine. It's so relaxing, I must've started to doze off. Are you done?"

"No silly! Now I have to clip and paint your toenails. You pick color?" she says in her best pedicure technician voice.

"Surprise me. Before long I won't be able to see them anyway." I laugh.

Bennett's sigh can probably be heard by the whole block when she's finally to the nail painting phase of Laney's feet. "So what's everybody doing for Christmas? I can't believe there's only two weeks left!"

Whitley answers first. "Evan and I are going to Parker

293

and Hayden's, and of course, to see his parents."

"How is Hayden?" Laney's interest now piqued, she peels the vegetable patches off her eyes and sits up. "She should be popping out those triplets anytime now, right?"

Whitley frowns, her lip quivering some. "She's due January 4th, but with triplets, they could come any day. Her doctor's adamant to keep them in there as long as possible, so she's been on bed rest for over a month."

"I should have known that," Laney says softly, a flash of shame moving over her face. "I'll be over to see them too. Dane and I are going to Daddy's. And a trip to Mom too, of course. And let's not forget, a very important visit to Bag N Suds! I have to make sure Kaitlyn's kicked out of college ass is enjoying her new job," she cackles, holding her stomach and throwing her head back.

"No way! I hadn't heard that!" Whitley's face lights up and Laney bobs her head yes very enthusiastically. "What do you know? Karma got something right."

I don't know who Kaitlyn is, and as much as I should be a good friend and ask, I don't really feel like it. I'm such a sadsack lately…stupid hormones.

"What about you, Emmett?" Bennett asks me. "What are your and Sawyer's plans?"

I must look as pathetic as I feel with the three of them scooting closer in on me. "I, uh, haven't heard that we have any specific plans, per se. I'm sure we'll talk about it soon. In fact," I go for exuberance and a subject change, "I need to get a tree up and shop for some presents for you ladies!"

This seems to placate them and all three start rattling off ideas for a Crew Christmas before everyone leaves and maybe drawing names out of a hat for buying.

"Hey, ladies, foot party I see."

Over their excited planning and fight for loudest voice in the mix, Sawyer's arrival has gone unnoticed. Who knows how long he's been standing in front of us.

"You want yours done next?" Bennett teases him, gesturing to the foot spa on the floor.

"I'm gonna pass, B," he barely chuckles. "Em, you here waiting for me?" He levels his quirked brow gaze on me, expecting an answer.

"N-no," stumbles out of my mouth. "The girls invited me down for pedis." He probably thinks I've camped out here, waiting for him to get back, but if he really stopped to think about it…how the hell would I know when he'd be back, or that he'd decide today he comes here instead of mine for that matter? Hard to stalk a ghost, Sawyer.

"Hmm." He nods. "I'm beat, I'm gonna lay down." And then he's gone, walking back towards his room.

"What was that?" Laney hisses when his door shuts.

I pop my shoulders nonchalantly, because I don't even know. "I'm gonna go ahead and go. I have a lot to do tomorrow and I need some rest." Getting up and out of the couch shouldn't be as challenging as it is with only nine extra pounds, but pregnancy does inexplicable things to your center of gravity.

Seeing my struggle, Laney jumps up and offers me a hand. "Emmett, is everything all right with you and Sawyer? He's our friend, but you are too. So if you want to talk—"

"Everything's fine, just different schedules and paths lately. I'm sure he'll be down later." I slip my freshly painted toes into the flip flops I brought in December. "You guys let me know when we're drawing names, okay?"

"Okay," Laney mumbles, wearing a concerned frown, and the other two silently nod.

As I shuffle down the sidewalk back to the home he'd secured me, and maneuver around the car in the driveway that he'd secured me...I feel secure in knowing one thing: I'm stronger than I think...I mean, I manage to get all the way inside my living room before I let even one tear fall.

Chapter 27

ABOUT A GIRL

—SAWYER—

"WHAT'D I TELL YOU about worrying and upsetting Laney?"

"Nice to see you too, brother," I bite back to Dane, standing across the bar from me. "We were low on vermouth and two taps. I put the order in; it'll be here tomorrow."

"Great, thanks. Now back to my original question. Laney's all in a snit about you and Emmett. You wanna tell me what's going on?"

"Nope, none of anybody's business. I can't run my life based on what Laney's gonna think. That's your gig." I turn behind me, starting to load the cooler, so he's forced to talk to my back.

"You're damn right it's my gig. It's the only one I have that really matters and one I plan to stick to. One I made dead sure I was serious about before I ever asked her to be serious about it too."

I slam down the door on the cooler and spin back around, stalking to the edge of the bar. "You got something to say, say it."

"Pretty sure I just fucking did."

Briefly, I try to remember the last time Dane and I faced off. I can't.

"All right, then, what is it you didn't say? My job? I work my ass off. School? Pretty much work my dick in the dirt there too. So you must mean Emmett, which we covered, under the 'none of anyone's fucking business' part. Now, if you're done spewing at the suck, I have to run this club, boss."

I don't give him a chance to respond, rather, I slam my hand under the bar flip and head around the corner to the storage room. When I load up all I can carry and reemerge, he's gone, the key to the Accord on the bar.

Why's he giving me the key to Em's car? To make a point that he has it. Bastard.

Hold the fucking phone…why does he have it?

Sawyer: Why does Dane have the key to your car?

Goddamn women. You need a blink of fucking time to yourself to sort shit out and get your head straight, and they start wildfires—drastic fucking moves over exaggerated drama. And that shit grows, involving everyone in its wake.

Emmett: It was his car, his key. I don't need it anymore, but thank you so much for the help when I did.

Sawyer: Why don't you need it? How are you getting to work tonight?

I'm about to stop this texting bullshit and call her, but stop myself. It's better this way. I don't want to yell in her ear.

Emmett: I have a ride to pick up my new car! Found a great deal on an older Jeep Cherokee on craigslist. This sweet old couple's gonna release it to me and let me pay cash over the next four months! And because of year/model, found insurance that's only due every three months. Pretty excited things are starting to come together.

It doesn't escape me that this is the longest conversation Emmett and I have had in quite some time...over text. Nor do I miss the fact that somehow she managed all this without my help or without me knowing. Right under my nose and I had no fucking clue.

Emmett: I can't thank you enough, Sawyer. It all started because of you, my first miracle. I could make your favorite chicken enchiladas one night as a thank you?

Did my girlfriend, whom I basically live with and is

about to have my child, just invite me to dinner? Oh God, I've completely fucked up. I've been so worried about how to make a life for her, us, our baby…fuck! I'd made her think I didn't want her, us, our baby. Now she's making the life she thinks I left her to, alone… She doesn't need me.

Well fuck me if I don't need her, a sharp pain in my chest confirming it.

It rings three times before she answers. "Em," I swallow down my pride. "Emmy?"

"Yeah?"

"I'm sorry, babe, I didn't realize. I need to tell you…" I grapple for the words, gripping the phone mercilessly. "I've just been so worried, and—"

"Sawyer?" she interrupts me distractedly. "I hate to do this, but can we talk when I get there or something? My ride's here."

"Oh…yeah, okay, sure."

"Okay, so I'll see you in a little while?"

"I'll be here." My exhale echoes in the phone. "Who's your ride?"

"Kasey, why? Listen, he's honking, I gotta go. See you in a sec?"

"Yup."

She hangs up and it takes all I have not to smash every motherfucking thing in this bar right now. Kasey? As in Kasey Munson, the guy who works here? The guy that spouts prophetic about her very discreet tattoo? That Kasey?

Fucking fuming, I do something I've never done before—I pour myself two shots of Patron and down them both—at work. Then I flip on the music and get the house ready for tonight. Oughta be a hella one.

-Emmett-

I'M SHOCKED. Sawyer called, and to tell me something. I swear I heard the faintest hint of caring in his voice. Some small, pathetic part of me almost wants to believe he was jealous of Kasey helping me out. That wasn't my intention, Kasey's simply a great guy that was able to help me since Laney had practice. And while I pray I didn't cause trouble for Kasey, the girl in me, the same one in love with Sawyer, can't help but bask for just a second in the afterglow of Sawyer perhaps caring enough to still get jealous.

Kasey drops me off and I briefly visit with Mr. and Mrs. Rosen, the sweetest couple I've ever seen in my life. They'll never know how much they're helping me, letting me take the vehicle now and pay it off over the next four months. I give them both a hug and jump in my new Cherokee, positively giddy.

It's old and has a ton of miles, but it's mine. It doesn't

smell new and the floor mats are stained, but it's mine. I sing along with the radio on my drive, a bliss I haven't felt in too long about me. But all good things must end and all I feel as I park in front of The K is anxious and unsteady. I have no idea what to expect when I walk in. It could be anger, or worse, it could be more cold indifference.

Alex must feel my nerves, giving me a swift kick right as I pull open the door. I smile and rub my belly. "Don't you start with me too."

So far so good. Everything seems normal. Kasey's unstacking chairs, smiling and giving me a wave. "How does it drive?" he asks when he sees me.

I give him a thumbs up, not ready to announce my presence vocally. Austin's up in the booth getting his stuff ready and Darby and Jessica are standing at the bar counting cash for their aprons.

My shoulders relax with my sigh of relief as I head to the break room to put up my things, but tense back up just as quickly when I see Sawyer standing by my locker. He's leaned in on one hip, arms folded across his chest, and he does not look happy.

"Shut the door and lock it," he directs in an eerily calm voice. His eyes give him away, narrowed and a dark, stormy blue. He is anything but calm.

He doesn't scare me though, not really, and it's probably high time we talk, so I do as he says, shutting and locking the door. Turning slowly from it back to him, I plaster on the most convincing smile I can conjure up. "Hey, what's up? I'm not late, am I?"

"You know you're not late."

"Oh, okay. Then what's up?"

"What's up?" he sneers, moving toward me now in measured, methodical steps. "What's up, Emmett, is why you're giving back and buying cars without so much as a word to me, and especially up is why the fuck you're chummy enough to ride with Kasey!"

His voice isn't anywhere close to calm, and I'm sure every employee out there can hear us without even listening hard. Especially Darby. Yes, I know he's been with her. She very colorfully enlightened me the night she took me home. The bitter venom in her voice told its own story, though…it was only one time and Sawyer never entertained the option again.

"Can I put my stuff up, please?" I step around him to my locker, taking ample time before I have to eventually turn around again.

"Emmett," he's right up against my back, growling low in my ear, "you know I would have taken you. Do I not help you with anything you need? And you damn sure know I wouldn't like you asking another guy."

If he was looking to get my dander up, he succeeded. I slam the locker shut and flip around to get as right up in his face as I can reach. "How would I know that, Sawyer, huh? You don't get to act like I'm invisible then pop up all growly when something doesn't sit well with your male ego! I'm not mad at you for wanting out, hell, I RAN FIRST! Granted, it was only a few days, not weeks, but I did and I own it. So you can run too, but oh wait, you already did!" I hiss in his face, all of my frustration and anger coming to a head. "I freely admit that I had it coming and payback's a bitch, but even before I pulled back, I told you. I told you, Sawyer. I told you from day one that you wouldn't want me. I said it over and over. You finally figured it out and I'm glad! The sooner the better, right? Less damage. But what I don't get, what does make me mad, is why you care what anyone, guy or not, does for me?"

I can feel the heat blazing up my neck and cheeks, the pounding in my temples. That rant took all the breath from me, my chest rising and falling rapidly with my pants. But none of that matters, the tearing at my freaking heart is the worst of it. I just gave him his ticket out, told him it was okay for him to go and I wouldn't be mad.

I'm surprised he's still standing here, glowering down at me.

"I didn't run! I'm there every single day. I sleep in our bed, get groceries, gas up your car, go to appointments with you! How the hell is that running?" He's screaming, eyes wide and pupils dilated, liquor on his breath.

I reach back in my locker and grab the papers from my purse. "This came to my place for some reason. I called. They've been trying to reach you. You need to go take your physical to complete your application." I slap the pamphlet against his chest and fight diligently against the tears dying to fall. "I can't remember the last time you kissed me. We haven't made love in weeks. And you don't come to my appointments—you missed the last one. I kept waiting for you to start screaming down the hall, but you didn't. All that's okay, Sawyer, I get it. You made a valiant effort and helped me more than anyone else ever has, or probably ever will. So run. I'm not going to chase you, but please consider stopping short of enlisting. You have a great job, school, and friends who love you. You don't have to run that far."

But I do. I move as fast as my trembling legs will carry me and have the door unlocked and open with dexterity that came from I don't know where. Only a few tears manage to escape before I'm safely tucked in the back stall of the ladies' room, my feet pulled up on the seat.

If I get through this shift tonight, it'll be a miracle. And right after that, it'll be another change in my life.

Chapter 28

I Have No Idea What I Did

Last Night

‒SAWYER‒

Riding with other guys—what the hell? And speaking of which, Kasey might wanna start looking for a new fucking job.

Getting a car, insurance—she thinks she doesn't need me? Everything I do is for her!

Missed the last doctor appointment? That's because she didn't tell me!

"Run, Sawyer, I won't chase you."

"You finally figured it out, I'm glad!"

I've got Patron in my system, she's cooped up in the bathroom, avoiding me, and I can see Kasey's smug fucking face across the room...I grab the bottle and shove it down the back of my pants, ready to blow outta here.

Sawyer: You in your office?

Dane: Yeah?

Sawyer: All yours tonight. I'm out.

And with that, I head out the back door to my bike. Ah, my beautiful girl, my silver GSX-R. Never talks back, always in the same place I left her and feels so good between my legs.

I fire her up and fly out of the lot, not really knowing where I'm going until I know exactly where I'm going. I need a place to be a miserable, drunk degenerate. Somewhere no one decent I know will find me, where hurting the people you love most because you're a scared fucking loser is acceptable. I take a left at the light and motor to CJ's mysteriously now un-condemned apartment.

Perfect. This is just the circle of hell I belong in. Smoke-filled air, beer cans everywhere, guys screaming at the Xbox and half-naked chicks trying to get their attention. Bitch getting fingered in the corner of the couch? Totally normal for this place, but she needs to put that shit away. It smells like catfish and assholes in here.

But this is indeed where guys like me need to be. Nobody here's thinking about babies or houses in safe neighborhoods with good schools or affordable family insurance. Nobody here cares that the best I can offer is slinging drinks for diaper money in the middle of the night while she's up for feedings alone.

Here? Here I'm actually the most put together person in the room.

"Sawyer!" CJ yells from the couch. "Long time no see! You want a beer?"

I pull the bottle out of my pants (a bit uncomfortable when you're riding, by the way) and hold it up for him to see. "Drinking the good shit tonight. Brought my own."

"You want good shit, come get a hit off this." He raises that creepy ass wizard bong.

"Gimme a minute to get warmed up." I walk into his kitchen and quickly decide not to use his glasses, instead taking a long, burning swig straight from the bottle.

"What are you doing here?" a familiar purr says from behind me.

Mariah. Great.

"Hey, what's up? What are you doing here?"

"No race tonight; have to come to the man's to find the sexy racers. Now what's your excuse? Heard you quit."

She moves closer and I back away, right into a counter. Now I'm pinned between her and a sink full of dirty dishes. FML. I take another shot.

"So did you quit?" She's so close now I can smell her

smoky ashtray breath.

"Ya, I quit," I reply, using a hand on her shoulder to gently urge her out of my space. "Sold my racing bike, too."

Here she comes again, right on top of me, running a hand up my arm and sneering at me. "Did that selfish bitch make you sell your bike?"

"Nah, wasn't like that. Let's..." My eyes flash around, devising an escape plan. "Let's go sit down at the table. Want to?"

She tries to sit on my lap, but I foil that plan real fast, grabbing her hips and moving her over.

"Sit in a chair," I say sternly, "you're suffocating me."

Pouting, and not sexy as hell like when Em does it, she takes the chair beside me and pulls it flush to mine. I ignore her, turning my bottle up once more. This expensive shit will fuck you up quick, which I'm realizing as I start seeing two of everything. When CJ sticks two joints in my face, I only take one of them and hit it. Mariah grabs my face and covers my mouth with her own, sucking the smoke out.

"Shotgun!" CJ cheers.

"Not cool." I push her off me. "If I want your fucking mouth on me, I'll tell you. You know damn good and well I have a girlfriend."

"Do you?" She attempts coy, trying to flirt. She bends down with one hand braced on her thigh, shirt gaping open, showing her tits, and bats her makeup-caked lashes. "Then why are you here and she's not?"

Pot, Patron, despair…I have no idea why I answer her. "Because I got scared. I was so busy worrying and planning, I lost her. I didn't kiss her or love on her!" I slam a fist on the table, sending the bottle on its side. "Now she moved on."

"Ahh." She stands, crushing my head in between her tits and rubbing my cheek. "If she moved on that fast when you were doing everything for her, then she doesn't deserve you. A man like you needs someone who can treat you right; who can make you feel good and reward you for all you do." Now her mouth is over my ear, whispering, "I can make you feel good. I've done it before and I'd love to do it again. Only this time, that bitch won't fuck it up for us. I'll take care of you all night long."

Nothing, not a twitch, slight chub, nothing. All I can think about is Emmett, her words running over and over through my brain.

"Valiant effort."

"I won't chase you."

"I told you over and over you wouldn't want me."

"But I do want her. I love her so damn much. I only wanted some time, some space, to figure things out. I'm the man, goddammit! I need to make money and own a house, all the things she and Alex deserve!"

"I didn't ask you about her." She glares at me now, both hands on her hips. "If you wanna go nursemaid to some short, fat, pregnant chick, go ahead, but I'm sick of hearing about it! My God, it isn't even your baby!"

Oh darn, she stormed off.

I haven't drank this much in years, let alone smoked. My forehead is pounding, right in the center, the spot aneurysms start, I'm guessing. What am I doing? This isn't me. There's not enough weed and whiskey in the world to make me not love Emmett. And I do. God I do.

I take out my phone and scroll blearily through my contacts, waving goodbye to CJ and walking outside.

"Hello?" Evan answers on the third ring.

"Ev, bro, did I wake you up?"

"Yup. What's up?"

"I'm fucked up, I fucked up. Can you come get me and my bike?" I grab a seat on the cold concrete step closest to my bike. "I'm not leaving it here to get stolen."

He grumbles as I hear him rouse, sheets rustling in the background. "Where the hell are you?"

"Briarwood, they're apartments. Don't forget about my bike."

"Stay put. Do NOT drive."

"'Preciate it, man."

Okay, back on track. I'll just go home and tell Emmett I'm sorry and we'll start all over. I admit, I have no concept of time right now, so it may be five minutes or five hours before my ass is numb. I lie back, flat on my back on the hard, cold ground and look up at the stars. Damn, there's a lot of them! Or maybe I'm just seeing two of every actual one; I have no idea.

"Emmy, babe," I talk to the black sky, me, filled with twinkling, bright lights, her, and practice what I'll say. "You had it all wrong. I've always wanted you. Always. I was afraid I couldn't be enough for you. You're so strong and fearless, forgiving and loving—everything I'm not. I don't forgive that man, the men, who've hurt you. It eats at me every damn day that I can't fix that for you. And what if I'm a shit dad? Lord knows I didn't get any formal lessons how to be a good one, let alone an excellent one. I work in a bar, for Christ's sake! You need a house, a yard, that dog you mentioned." I'm screaming at the moon now and sit up, swiping quickly below my eyes before I actually cry and feel like an even bigger puss.

"You need a ride?"

Lurking in the shadows? Who does that? Can you imagine the lengths she'd go to if I'd actually fucked her? "No, I'm good, thanks. I got a ride on his way."

"Sawyer, you've been out here for almost an hour. I don't think they're coming. Let me give you a ride." She walks to stand in front of me, sticking out her hand. "Come on."

I grasp on and struggle to my feet, stumbling into her. "What about my bike?"

"Get it in the morning." She pulls me toward...hell, I

don't know. "I'm over here, let's go."

I really don't want to leave my bike at the mercy of this neighborhood, watching over my shoulder as it gets further and further away, but I need a bed. I'm a mess. I have to sober up so I can talk to Emmett, so regretfully, I cave and follow her.

"I live—"

"I know where you live," she interrupts me haughtily.

Of course she knows where I live, not at all creepy. Told ya I need to buy a house.

"Sawyer!" Bright lights blind me, a voice calling my name. I cover my eyes with one hand, straining to see who's beckoning me.

Oh thank baby Jesus in a manger! Evan's jogging up to me, Zach on his tail.

"Where you think you're going?" Evan asks me, eyeing my chauffeur skeptically.

"I didn't think you were coming. Marcy here was gonna take me home," I slur out.

"It's Mariah, you asshole! My God, you came in my mouth and you can't remember my name? You're pathetic!" she yells, stomping her foot, and shoves on both my shoulders.

Thank you so much, Marcy, for that public service announcement. "Easy on the name callin' there, sassy. You let me come in your mouth without first making sure I'd want to remember your name."

"You what? Sawyer, dude, what the hell were you thinking?" Evan's head drops, shaking from side to side.

"Not just now! A long time ago. Emmett knows." I chuckle, not sure why. "Hell, Emmett saw."

"I don't..." Evan mutters, looking to Zach with a plea of help in his eyes. "Any idea what to do with that?"

Zach steps up and grabs my arm. "Storytime's over. M girl, go home. Sawyer, where's your bike? We're gonna get it loaded and you home."

I point to my bike, I'm almost positive, and let Zach drag me that way.

"You better be so glad we got here in time, you dumb shit," he growls in a low voice, squeezing the hell out of my arm. "If you'd have gotten in the car with some chick Emmett knows blew you before, she'd have never forgiven you."

Zach would know all about the pains of cheating—what's her twin had done a number on him.

"I know, I know. Thanks for saving my ass. Why'd Evan call you?"

"To help load your precious bike. You're no help," he shrinks me with a glare of condemnation, "obviously. We're both breaking curfew right now for this bullshit, by the way. We get caught or benched and you're a dead man."

Chapter 29

ROAD TO REDEMPTION

—SAWYER—

WHEN I WAKE, I'm in my own bed, face down in the pillow. It takes a minute to get my bearings and collect my thoughts, considering my head feels like I used it as a battering ram, but it starts coming back and it's not pretty. Parts of last night are fuzzy, but you'd think I'd remember someone shitting in my mouth, which is exactly what it tastes like. Pushing myself up with great care, at the speed of smell, I turn over and scrub my hands over my face. I feel like busted ass…and what is under my ass? Digging in the back pocket of my jeans, I pull out my phone. Nothing from Emmett.

Evan: Bike under port, key on the kitchen counter.

Good luck!

I delete the twelve from Dane without reading them. I can only imagine the all caps, scathing rants he'd sent. No, thank you.

Now time to bite the bullet.

Sawyer: You home? Busy?

While I wait for her to answer me, I muster up the will to climb out of bed and head for the shower. I start to feel half alive again under the scalding hot water, but the minute I step out, the pounding in my head returns with a vengeance. Wiping a clear spot in the fog on the mirror, I get my first glimpse of all that is Sawyer after a night of self-destruction. I definitely won't have to tell people I'm hungover—one look will answer any curiosity.

I check my phone, still no answer from Emmett. Hungover and haggard or not, this shit ends now. We are gonna talk, she is gonna listen, and it's happening now. After I get dressed and scrub the enamel off my teeth and fuzz off my tongue, I head outside to her house.

Car's in the driveway. She's either asleep or ignoring me.

Gentlemanly is probably the safest route to take right now, so I ring the doorbell rather than busting straight up in. My hand's tapping on the door frame, a lump of unease forming in my throat, when her sweet voice comes from the other side of the door.

"Who is it?"

"Em, it's Sawyer."

"What do you want, Sawyer?"

"I want to talk to you. Please, Em." I'm not above groveling. My whole life's on the other side of that door, so close I could knock this damn barrier down and grasp it, hold onto it, and never ever be foolish enough to let it go again, but still devastatingly out of reach. "Please."

The sound of the deadbolt unlocking gives me a surge of hope, new life springing in my regretful heart. She cracks open the door and her precious face peeks out. "Talk."

"Can I come in?"

"I don't think that's a good idea, Sawyer. You can say whatever you need to from right there." Her eyes won't meet mine, head dipped, raven hair shrouding part of her face.

"I'm sorry, Emmy, so sorry, babe." I bend, both hands now spread on the frame, and dip my head to look up at her. "I never meant to hurt you or push you away. Please let me come in. I need to explain things, make us good again."

"Did you sleep with her?" Green eyes now lift to mine, brimming over with pain, pain caused by my carelessness.

"What? Sleep with who?" I'm a horrible person. I begged for her heart, and when she finally, wholly gave it, I didn't take care of it.

"You know who," she sneers. "Mariah. Last night, did you sleep with her?"

"No, God no! Why would you even ask that?" And

how'd you even know I saw her?

She shuts the door in my face, the lock clicking back in place. I dig out my keys, fumbling for the right one, when it suddenly opens again. She slips two things to me through the crack in the door, first, the empty ring box I put my davra in when I'm not wearing it, and second, her phone, a screen already pulled up for me.

I look at the phone first. It came through at 1:18 am last night.

Mariah: Hate to bother you so late but Sawyer's kinda drunk and wants us to go back to his. Can you text me the address?

I read it again, a sickening, wrenching ache flaring in my gut. I'm not surprised to see it; it seems the definitive move for a scorned, trashy, jealous bitch to make, but I'm shocked Emmett even opened the door to me at all.

Now who can't meet whose eyes?

The crack in the door gets a smidge wider and she sticks out her impatient hand. I have barely enough wits about me to hand her back the phone.

"Did. You. Sleep. With. Her?" Oddly enough, the lower and steadier a woman's voice gets, the deadlier its effect.

"I said no. I didn't sleep with her."

"Why's the box for your junk jewelry empty?"

"I told you, Em, if I don't wear it every so often, the hole will close up. It hurt like hell, I'm not doing it twice."

318

"And I've told you, Sawyer, I'm not interested in any magic tricks. I don't ever want anything but you. So you care if the hole closes up why?"

"I didn't know you meant never ever. Fine by me, babe, consider it gone."

She huffs loudly, the door open just enough for me to see she's rolling her eyes at me and crossing her arms over her chest.

"Wait, you think…" I can't help but bark out a facetious laugh. "You think I had it in for that skank last night?

"If the penis pearl fits…" she mumbles.

"I. Didn't. Touch. Her." Oh shit, another piece of the puzzle that is last night flashes through my lagging mind; the shotgun. True to form, I'm confessing the whole truth before I can talk myself out of it. "She did, uh, she grabbed my face and forced herself, well, her uh, mouth on mine. But I pushed her away immediately."

"You poor thing!" She covers her heart in mock horror. "She just attacked all six feet, two hundred pounds of you? My God, were you hurt?"

One brow quirks and I battle a grin. "You know what I mean. I don't want to lie to you, but I didn't touch her. "Just," I hold up a finger and get my phone out. "Give me one minute." I scroll frantically and dial, then speaker.

"I swear to God, Sawyer, if you're calling her—"

"I don't know her fucking number, Shorty. I'm—"

319

"Afternoon, Sunshine, how ya feeling?" Evan goads with a laugh.

"Fabulous. Hey," I catch Emmett's glare and hold it, "what happened last night, man?"

"Which part?"

"Any of it. How'd I get home? Where'd you find me?"

"Dude, that's just sad. You called me to pick you up at some apartment. Zach and I came and got you and your bike. Any of that ringing a bell? I sent your sorry ass a text. We threw you in bed, unloaded your bike and put the key on your kitchen counter."

"Yeah, I got it. Thanks so much, bro. But hey, was Whitley with ya'll? I thought I remembered a girl?"

Emmett's body shifts, crossing her arms and narrowing her eyes at this part. She's preparing to hear I screwed up major, which I know without a doubt, fucked up or not, I didn't.

"I'm gonna pretend you did not just confuse Whitley for that…whatever the hell she was last night."

"Who was it? Was I with her?"

"Sawyer, seriously bro, don't get that bad again and I mean it. Having to call me to remember a whole night of your life? Too far, brother, too far."

I speak to Evan, but make the promise to Emmett with somber, promising eyes. "It won't happen again. You have my word. But I need to know…about the girl."

"You were standing in the parking lot when we got there, worried about your bike. Some random chick was trying to pull you to her car, but we saved you. It was pretty funny," he laughs, "when you called her the wrong name. She shoved your ass and stormed off. Good stuff."

"That it?"

Emmett and I have been having an entire conversation of our own, with our eyes, this whole time. And hers just softened and said, 'fine, I believe you.'

"That's it, thank God," Evan's reply interrupts us. "You think you need more?"

"No man, I'm good. Thanks again."

"Beckett?"

"Yeah?"

"Fix things with Emmett, okay? That heartbroken rambling of yours the whole ride home? Not your best look."

"Working on it."

—Emmett—

So HE DIDN'T SLEEP WITH MARIAH, which reduces my anger marginally. He did, however, of all the places in Georgia, happen upon the same one as her. And let's not forget her vicious attack, holding his lips hostage.

Puh-lease.

"Fine, I believe you didn't sleep with her. I'm even willing to buy the 'she kissed you' bullshit. And maybe the whole 'Emmett doesn't care about the dick metal but I'm worried about the hole closing anyway' case holds some very coincidental water. But you know what really stings, Sawyer? The one person who you know I wouldn't want you anywhere near, that's exactly who you found your way to. You set out to intentionally hurt me and you aimed for the jugular. Direct hit. Congratulations."

I leave a despondent, tongue-tied Sawyer on the opposite side of the door as I slam it in his face, propping a chair under the knob before throwing myself on my bed. "Sorry," I apologize to my stomach for the crash landing and roll on my side, tucking a pillow under my cheek.

The door's rattling against the chair as he attempts to get in. That'll only hold him out for so long, he is a practiced burglar after all. I figure I've got about ten minutes, tops, before he's lording over me.

My phone dings, incoming message, and like a glutton, I pull it up. It's a video, so I push the play icon, despite knowing better. "Can't Help Falling in Love," our Elvis song, fills my empty room with its melodic plea.

Where was this heartfelt attempt weeks ago when I quickly sucked back my tears every night when he snuck into bed? My life is not my own anymore and I can't allow it to be toyed with! More angry now than hurt, I march to the front door, tossing the chair to the side and flinging it open. There he stands in worn out jeans, a plain gray tee and a hopeful, desperate smile.

"I can't lose you, Shorty. I just can't."

His eyes, his honest, tender, blue eyes, resign me to at least listen, so I step back, letting the fully open door invite him in for me. I turn and go sit on the couch as he shuts it and follows me.

"Emmett," he drops to his knees in front of me and takes both my hands in his, "I swear to God, on my life, I didn't touch her, and I didn't know she'd be there. I felt like a low life, so I went to the trashiest place I knew, and low and behold she was there...you tend to find rats when you hang in trash cans. And the davra? I promise you, Em, it's just a coincidence. I didn't know you meant you didn't ever want it. But now that I do, it's gone, babe."

"I like the nipple ones," I mumble, looking around and not at him.

"Then they stay." His chuckle is fleeting, immediately followed by a loud sigh. "Em, I got lost. All I wanted to do was step up and be the man who deserves you, who can take care of our family. Baby, I got so busy, then tired, and worried, that I forgot the girl I was doing it all for needed to be loved first. I don't want you in a bar full of assholes who think they can touch you. I don't want our family dependent on Dane. I want you to be able to finish school. God, Emmett," one hand leaves mine to try and fist his hair that's still not long enough, "I got so obsessed, so hell bent on making everything perfect, that I ruined the only thing that was already perfect—me and you, together."

"How do I know you won't get scared again and shut us out? Are you going to run back to the dump every time things get hard? Why couldn't you talk to me about it? One day we're in love, the next we're strangers. I can't set myself up to be hurt like that again." I drop my head and inhale the scent of him, not a great idea when trying to resist, but exactly what I need to calm myself, every emotion in me firing off at the same time. "I can't take it, and a child certainly couldn't. We're not your job, your burden, or your responsibility. We're either your choice, your have to have, your die without…or we're not."

"You are," one hand brushes my cheek, "you always were. I need to be able to control our future, be sure, like Dane. He could buy Laney anything she wanted, private schools, vacations, backyards and fucking ponies. You name it. Our baby, our family, deserves no less."

I cover his hand with my own, sliding my fingers in between his. "You know what's wrong with that theory? Dane always loves Laney first and foremost. Neither one of them care about his money. I have no doubt he'd give away everything he has and live on a deserted island with her if she asked."

"No way," he shakes his head emphatically, "without the empire he couldn't be so controlling and possessive. He'd lose his power and be miserable, using all his time and energy to get it back."

My sweet Sawyer. He grew up poor, with no worldly possessions, unloved and unhappy, so he equates all that as one big meshed cluster. He couldn't be more wrong.

"Sawyer, first of all, there is a big difference between being controlling and possessive and making your woman want to be controlled and possessed. You had that part mastered, and if you have that on point, it doesn't matter if you're a pauper. And what about those military papers? Are you doing that?"

"No. I went and saw the recruiter on Thanksgiving. I thought it'd be the best way to make sure I had a job, housing for you, insurance. But I've have to leave you for six weeks of basic." He shakes his head and looks to me. "I'm not sure what the right plan is after I'm done with school, what degree is best, where we'll need to live for whatever jobs we'll have…but it's not that plan. I told them no."

"Thank you," I breathe, glad that's settled. He's right, I have no idea exactly where we'll be in a year, or ten years, but I'm relieved it won't be with him in the military, possibly at war, perhaps never coming home. I don't have what it takes to be a military wife—they're way stronger than me—I'm just not made that way.

His head nods slowly up and down, his processing of all that's been said close to visible. Lost in thought, his thumb strokes my cheek as gradually, he drops his head until it rests on my stomach. "Emmett," he whispers.

"Hmm?"

"Do you still love me?"

"Sawyer, even if I live to be a hundred, I'll love you 'til the day I die. But I don't plan to spend that time convincing you to love me back. I want to be loved by a man that I have to spend my time convincing myself he's real. I had it once, although briefly, and I won't ever be happy again with anything less."

His arms wrap around my waist, holding onto me in tight insecurity. "Em," still a whisper, "I'm so sorry. Please forgive me. Tell me you love me. Please, Shorty, tell me we can be good again."

I bend my head down and place a soft kiss on top of his. "I love you, Sawyer. I never stopped, and I never will."

"But?" He knows me too well, hearing words I don't say.

"But I need you to take some time, all the time you need, and make sure you're sure. There will be no next time like this. You hurt me. You scared me too," I admit, my voice cracking. "You left me. Maybe you were here physically, but my Sawyer left."

"I promise—"

"No, not today. You take that time to be sure."

"But I don't need it." He lifts his head, watery blue eyes boring into mine, touching his forehead to my own. "I may not know exactly what I'm doing all the time. You're my first and only go at love, Emmett, I've had no practice on how not to screw up. The only way I know how to give all I am to one person is the way I am with you. So, babe," he draws back his head to beg with his baby blues and words, "I'm kinda a work in progress, but I'm your work in progress. Only yours, ever, forever." He rubs his nose along mine, his long eyelashes tickling my cheeks as I sigh upon his skin. "I don't want to be away from you, Em. I don't want to miss another thing."

"I didn't say you had to leave. We'll start over, see how it goes. Even if I only ever get my friend back for sure, I want you around, 'cause God, I missed you." The dam breaks and there's a full facial flood. "I missed you so much, Sawyer. Some days I could hardly breathe, and every day was an endless blur of lonely."

"Never ever again, Emmy, I swear. We'll eat macaroni and live in the fucking box, as long as we're together and you're smiling. I love you." He kisses my nose, chin, cheeks, before hovering over my lips. "I'll show you, Mama," he whispers. "I promise. I love you."

I meet him in the middle, placing my lips to his. "I hope you do.

Chapter 30

OUR CHRISTMAS STORY

—SAWYER—

CHRISTMAS' APPEAL for me has always been the break from school, nothing more. I have never bought a woman a present and avoided mistletoe at parties like it was a sport. So to convince my Shorty I'm in it to win it, this year I've gone all out.

I cut my hours at work way back, thus I'm in bed every night before she falls asleep. In the mornings, I don't so much as leave the bed to piss before she's awake beside me. And she's only shaken me awake from one nightmare, where I dreamt the Christmas tree caught on fire. Which is really quite possible, since I took her to a live tree farm and got the granddaddy of all spruces, so big we had to trim the sides with scissors and take a five inch chunk off the top. It's topped with a big ass bow instead of a star, covering the large dent.

All afternoon I lifted her up so she could decorate the top half of said tree, with ornaments and decorations we also had to go buy since neither of us owned a single one. Someday, though, we'll hold our grandkids up to the branches and point out fifty-year-old keepsakes.

Yeah, I went there.

Exhausted from fighting the Christmas Eve crowds, tonight I drive through and get her favorite takeout and some new release chick flick to watch. I don't know what the hell I was thinking before, or how one disappears so far into their own head, but I live again for my evenings with Emmy. When I think of all I missed, off in douchebag-trapped-in-his-own-fears land, I want to severely kick my own ass.

When I get home, the front of the house is dark and still, but light shines from under the bathroom door. I set down our dinner in the kitchen and decide to make my move. Since we're still on "trial period," Em hasn't done anything more than give me a few kisses, so to say my libido is in homicidal range and my dick is massively depressed would be a gross understatement. So the chance to sneak in and catch a glimpse of naked, wet Em in the bath? No brainer.

With the steady hands of a thief, I ease open the door

enough to watch her in the mirror, undetected. Goddamn but she's lovely, her head back against the tub, her eyes closed, a hum on her lips. The bubbles taunt me, clinging to her breasts, showing me only the rounded crests and a hint of one baby pink nipple. Her legs are stretched out, feet on the ledge, tiny toes begging to be sucked. And that sweet little pregnant belly? It turns me on, so fucking sexy, and thoughts of keeping her like that as often as possible cause me to grin.

I can't take it another second, lowering a hand to the buttons on the fly of my jeans. It takes too long to get all five undone, my left hand bracing me against the wall. Zoning in on the perky nipple totally revealed to me now (God bless gravity and the inconsistency of bubbles), I maneuver my right hand into my briefs. Pushing them down some and grasping firmly around my groveling, lonely cock, I thrust into my own hand.

Unaware of her admirer, she shifts in the water, displacing the remaining bubbles perfectly. Now I can see both full, glorious breasts resting just above the water. I imagine them in my mouth, stiff nipples scraping along my tongue, as I pump my cock faster. Fuck, I miss the feel of her warm, tight pussy around me, contracting and relaxing in devilish tandem with the orgasms I give her. Without knowing, she puts on the most seductive show, letting her legs fall more open, and I barely catch the growl that'd give me away.

Eyes now glued to the somewhat underwater, distorted V between her luscious thighs, I swipe my thumb through the bead of cum on my head and spread it up and down my shaft. Yearning for release, consumed by the sight of her, I grope up and down with the fierce grip and speed of all twelve pistons firing. I know it won't take long, it's been forever since I've touched her, so I force my eyes to stay open despite the urge to let them fall closed and get lost in my grossly overdue undoing.

She moans lightly as she succumbs to the hot water, slumping further down and brushing her wet hair back from her face. I clamp down on my lip, painfully so, as to not groan with her and alert her to my pervy presence. The second her little tongue comes out and glides achingly slowly along her bottom lip, I'm done, hot ropes of semen shooting from me, saturating my hand. I relish in it, continuing to jack myself off leisurely now until every ounce is unloaded and my breathing evens back out.

Awkwardly, I back out of the room with my cum-covered hand and open fly, praying I don't bump into anything. When I know I've cleared the bedroom door, I turn and race to the kitchen, putting myself back together and washing my hands.

I begin plating the food and pouring our drinks, whistling as innocently as possible. It definitely eased the threat of backed up spunk-induced insanity, but enflamed the longing to be inside her again. I want to feel her soft, sweaty skin under me, on top of me, to hear the moans and whimpers that only I can pull from her. I miss our tongues entangled, fighting for control as I surge into her and she screams my name and digs her nails into my back. Even more so, I miss holding her afterward, her head on my shoulder, her hand petting my chest as her contented sighs tickle my skin. I miss knowing she's in love with me and that I can have her anytime I want, her wanting it just as badly.

She lets me put an arm over her waist when we sleep, but she doesn't scoot further back against me. I'm allowed to rest a hand on her tummy, but she doesn't cover it with her own. She smiles when I read to the baby, but she doesn't rub my head methodically while I do. I know she's afraid that I'll get scared again and bolt, but I don't know what the ultimate grand gesture, the one that knocks down the whole wall all at once.

"Hey," she smiles as she steps around the corner, hair damp and dressed in a short white robe, "when did you get home?"

"Not too long ago. You hungry? I got your favorite. And," I hold up the box, "some ovaryfest for your viewing pleasure."

"Sounds like the perfect night to me!" She beams, stretching up to give me a kiss on the cheek. "Let's eat on the couch and watch the movie. And thank you."

-Emmett-

"SAWYER?" I whisper in his ear. "It's morning. Merry Christmas."

"Mhmm," he grumbles as he rouses himself, firming his arm around my waist to pull me against his chest. "Merry Christmas." He kisses my forehead blindly, eyes still closed. "What time is it?"

"Time to get up and open your presents!" I can't help it, I'm excited to have someone I love to share the holiday morning with after so long without. "Last one to the tree makes breakfast!" I clamor out of bed and hurry down the hall, already waiting anxiously on my knees as he sleepily emerges. Mussed hair, five o'clock shadow, and wearing only navy pajama pants, he would make an excellent present…if I knew for sure.

"Do I have time for coffee?" He smirks at me.

"Yes, but hurry!"

While he's dragging in the kitchen, I sort the presents into two neat little stacks, stopping short and covering my gasp with my hand. "Sawyer?"

"Yeah?"

"Why does Alex have presents? I don't think babies get

gifts until they're actually born." I'm still talking loudly as he ambles in the room, leaning down to kiss the top of my head.

"My baby, my rules."

"You're crazy." I roll my eyes, merely feigning indifference when inside, my heart is bursting. I grab two of his presents and walk on my knees to where he sits on the couch, handing them to him. I can't wait to see if he likes them. "Open that one first," I direct, pointing to the one on top.

"Hold up, Shorty." He places the gifts to the side and stands, picking me up effortlessly and setting me on the couch. He retrieves my pile and sets them in my lap, then retakes his seat beside me. "There ya go. We'll open at the same time."

He opens his henleys, one gray and one navy, and for me, a bag of Red body spray, bubble bath and lotion.

"Do you like them?" I ask. "You always look so nice in the ones you have."

He snakes a hand around the back of my neck, pulling my face to his. "I love them. Thank you," he husks out before kisses me passionately. Wow, he must really like shirts.

Next he opens his Usher cologne and aftershave package, thanking me with another forceful, but wonderful all the same, kiss, his tongue not having to ask for entrance. He tastes like coffee and all I've needed but resisted for far too many lonely days and nights and I moan into his mouth, eating back at him urgently. One hand runs up my neck, turning my head as he deepens the kiss momentarily, then pulls back too soon. "Open yours before I—" He shakes his head, visibly getting his heaving chest under control. "Just open yours."

Hands still shaky from that kiss, I fumble with the wrapping until I'm looking at a silver heart locket, Mine engraved across the front.

"Open it," his deep whisper slices into my trance.

I do, moisture springing to my eyes when I see a tiny picture of the two of us on one side and the first ultrasound photo on the other. "Sawyer," I squeak, a tear rolling down the side of my nose.

"Turn it over."

Yours is across the back.

Maybe because it's Christmas, or perhaps because of the sweetest gift I've ever received, or quite possibly because he's shirtless, in sexy pajama pants, smelling like Sawyer and kissing me all morning—pick a reason—but I throw myself on him. My lips, my hands, have no rhythm, no grace as I pour into his mouth and onto his body the frustrations of a very pregnant, very sentimental woman who can no longer pretend she doesn't need him to live.

"Sawyer," I mewl, clinging to his shoulders and letting my head fall back as he kisses up my neck.

"What, baby? Tell me."

"Can we?" My hands move, up his neck, around the back of his head, pulling his head down against my neck.

"Can we what?" he pants, clenching both cheeks of my ass in his wanting hands. "What do you want, Em?"

"Ah…" It makes me crazy, senseless to all but his touch, when he uses his teeth to barely nip the tender skin of my neck and underside of my jaw. "Can we do this without forgetting we need time? Just make each other feel good? I need it so bad."

His mouth disappears abruptly, hands sliding off my ass causing me to raise my head back up and meet eyes so dark blue, pupils so dilated they're almost black. "Is that what you want? 'Cause that's far from what it will be for me."

"I don't…" I brush my hair back with both hands and blow out a confused, exasperated breath. "I don't know. I'm not sure we're ready for more, if you're ready for more, but God, I want you, Sawyer. I need to feel you." I take his hand and guide it to the heated, liquid place between my thighs. "Let's just make each other feel good. H-have…" Fearful of the coming answer, I turn away before I ask. "Have you been with anybody else?"

He springs off the couch, glaring down at me with both hands on his hips. His face is red with fury; this situation just went way south, way fast. "How can you even ask me that? The last woman I was inside was the last woman I'll ever be inside! You!" He points one stiff finger at me, his voice

336

escalating. "I'm not gonna fuck you to feel better. My dick's filed for disability and my heart's half-broken, but a," he air quotes with angry, flippant movements, "'let's feel better cause it's Christmas romp' isn't gonna cut it for me, Emmett!" He turns, giving me his back, his muscles bulging angrily, hands now linked behind his neck. "I thought you meant we were finally fixed, that we could make love again," he says softly.

"Oh," is all I mutter.

"I'm going out now. I'm not running, I just need some time to cool off. I know I hurt you, Emmett, and I'm so fucking sorry, but Goddamn if you didn't just hurt me too."

I remain in place on the couch, dumbfounded and curled into myself under the blanket as he stomps around to gather clothes and whatever else he needs. The whole while he mumbles irritably to himself, a few times causing me to jolt when the mumbling turns to a harsher volume and ferocity. When his hand is on the doorknob, he takes one deep breath and turns back to me.

"This is not me running," he says again.

"Okay," I whisper and nod.

Chapter 31

BREAKFAST AT GRANNY'S

—SAWYER—

I DRIVE AROUND ON MY BIKE aimlessly for a while, Christmas clearing the roads enough for me to gun it and avoid having to stop much. The briskness in the air whipping past me stings my exposed fingers, but does little to chill my temper. What a splendid fucking end to Christmas morning. I knew this holiday sucked. I thought she was back, exposed, that she'd finally realized we were meant to be and I never really "went" anywhere, but no. No, she wanted to come, missing the d, pregnant and horny.

Had I been with anyone else? Jesus, how far removed was I, putting that possibility in her head? Yeah, Emmett, I fucked other women and slept in bed with you every night…really?

My stomach's growling, since breakfast was denied. What's open on Christmas? I cruise through the streets of downtown until I find an open sign calling to me like a beacon and I pull over. Granny's Kitchen—no fucking way. I'm not sure I believe in signs, but I believe in this one. I walk in and chuckle at the "Please Wait to be Seated" stand—I'm the only person in here.

A smiling elderly woman, I'm guessing Granny in the flesh, greets me. "One?"

"In all my glory."

"Follow me." She shuffles, back bent with age, to a booth where she seats me. "What would you like to drink?"

"Coffee and a water please. You have a big breakfast special?" There's no way I'm making her walk back and forth to me, poor little thing, so I take a stab at an easy order.

"We do." She smiles and takes the menu I hold back out to her.

"I'll take that." When she scoots away, I rest my elbows on the table, cradling my sagging head in my hands. Maybe I should've gone with it, Lord knows I've been dying to sink into her again, but something snapped and I simply couldn't. I refuse, with all the meaningless dick dips I've had in my life, to cheapen what I found when I found Emmett. I told her once if she wanted my cock, I wanted her heart. I meant it.

339

Granny's back, so I'm forced to move my elbows for her to set down my drinks. "Alone on Christmas? Such a handsome young man?"

"Such a foolish young man is more like it." I shake my head at myself, giving her my best attempt at a grin. "I can't get it right, Granny."

"You messed up with your young lady?"

"Something like that. Then we decided to work it out, but it's taking a while." Why I'm telling her all this beats the shit outta me, but Granny's got kind eyes with wrinkles around them that somehow let me know there's nothing I could tell her she hasn't heard or lived through before. "And then today, she—" I cut myself off before I go too far, debating making love versus fucking with a ninety-year-old stranger. "Nothing, never mind."

I can hear her sympathetic "tsk" as she goes to get my food. Back with my plate, which I have no idea who cooked, as I haven't seen any trace of anyone else in this place, she doesn't walk away. Drawn, I look up at her.

"How much time did you waste messing up?" she asks pointedly.

"A while," I answer quickly. "Too long."

"And how much time have you spent making it right?"

"Not as long I guess."

"Which do you think should take more time, bad acts or good ones? Earning trust seems more time-worthy than breaking it to me. What's that they say, love is patient?"

Damn right. Everybody needs a Granny so wise.

—Emmett—

THE GRUMBLE OF HIS BIKE pulling in the driveway wakes me from a nap; I take a lot of them these days. I'm surprised he's back so soon. My proposition before had been stupid and hurtful. I wouldn't have blamed him if it took a while to want to look at me again. I'm still sorting through the wake of feelings brought about by his rejection, never mind the fact that he turned down my baser need for something real. Right after I finished feeling like a shunned fool, my insides fluttered at the romanticism of it. He doesn't want me unless he gets all of me—and from a sexual man like Sawyer, that speaks heavily on his intentions for our forever. A step in the right direction for sure. Doesn't mean my body's happy about it though.

He's at the bedroom door now. I don't have to roll over to know, my heart rate accelerates and the backs of my knees get clammy anytime he's near.

"Dane and Laney are headed back," he says evenly. "You up for going over there tonight?"

"Sure." I face him now, giving him a smile. I'm way

ahead of him—Laney and I are very sneaky when we want to be.

"You wanna talk?"

I sit up, eager to hear what's on his mind now that he's calmed down. "Of course, if you do."

Taking a seat on the bed says that he does. He slouches, his forearms on his knees, hands clasped in between them. "Here's where I think we're at. You tell me if I'm wrong." He takes a minute, tapping his thumbs together. "I love you. You love me..." He angles his head to me and pauses again.

"Very much," I confirm.

The reassurance earns a brief, but unmistakable, lip quirk and relaxing of his shoulders. "We're together, having a baby, but you're afraid to go back to what we were until you're positive I'm in it for the long haul." Another glimpse to me for confirmation, at which I nod. "All right then. I'm moving in, officially."

He's so cute, firm lip and challenging eyes at his "proclamation." He already lives here, it's really just semantics, but I go with it for him.

"That makes sense," I reply, keeping my face serious.

"We'll tell Laney tonight, or I can tell her, whichever. Not like she has to make up the rent," he chuckles, "but still. I know Dane will worry about her being alone."

These domineering men of ours truly live under some cloud; Dane's at Laney's place more than he's at his own. It's laughable, but I don't say anything. "Right," I agree.

"Now, about the lovin'." He sighs, taking my hand and rubbing his thumb in my palm. "If you ever question my fidelity again, I'm gonna spank your ass, pregnant or not. You are mine and I am yours. I hope you like my cock, babe, 'cause it's the only one you're ever getting for the rest of your life. And that sweet pussy of yours is the only one I want for as long as I live. But," his grip on my hand tightens, "you can't be thinking one thing while you're with me and showing me another, Em. You wanna tell yourself you're holding out, testing me or what the fuck ever is going on in that head of yours, fine, you do that. But you know as well as I do that it's more than just scratching your itch. You want me because you love me and miss me, just like I do you, so when we're together, be there with me, Emmy. Don't let fear or ultimatums or girly stipulations get in between us when we make love."

It's frightening how well he knows me; and he's right. There is no way to be with him physically and still hold out mentally. I'm kidding myself and he just called a spade a spade. He sure can give a speech, and of course, I'm crying...cause that's all I seem to do these days.

"Hey now," he scoots closer and lifts me into his lap, "no tears, Shorty, I wasn't trying to be mean." He lifts my chin and kisses my tears. "I love you, Emmett. I love that you challenge me and make me work for it. I love that you're strong and capable, and that you always weigh the impact of your decisions against our baby's future. But the absolute best thing you can give a child, I think, is two parents who love and respect each other and always work things out. I want Alex to know, hell, I want to know, that we'll always be able to find our way back."

He talks so eloquently, every single word sincere and thought out. I want so badly to throw up my hands and surrender completely, turn off the intermingling voices in my head and free fall again. If we were just dating, I would, without a second thought. If it were just us, I would, right here and now. A torrid, spontaneous love affair with no sure ending, the heat felt by anyone near.

But that's not my story.

Chapter 32

WALK MY LINE

—SAWYER—

"MERRY CHRISTMAS! We missed you guys!" Laney plows into us with a gripping embrace as we walk through the door at Dane's house.

"You too," Emmett hugs her while I scoot around them, arms filled with packages. "How was your trip home? Your family?"

I tune out the rest of their babbling, going in search of Dane and a beer, in either order, finding both in the kitchen. "Merry Christmas, brother." I clap him on the shoulder and steal the fresh bottle out of his hand.

"Merry Christmas, you have a good one?" he asks, going

to the fridge to replace his beer.

"Not bad." I shrug. "Where's everybody else?"

"I don't think any of them are back yet, but you'd have to ask the social director."

"Ask me what?" Gidge walks in, her arm laced through Emmett's.

"Anyone else coming tonight?" I ask her, but focus on Emmett, a sweet smile on her face, but her coloring a bit off.

"No, they're all still back home. Just us four tonight." She shoots Emmett a knowing smirk.

I pull out one of the barstools and pat it. "Come sit down, Shorty. You want something to drink, eat?"

"Maybe a bite of something wouldn't hurt," she mumbles passively, taking the offered seat.

"Emmett!" Laney buzzes to the fridge, slinging out trays to the island hurriedly. "You should have said something. We brought back food! Dear Lord, Dane, get her a drink. Some hosts we are, depriving the pregnant girl. Emmett. What do you want? We have juice, champagne, oh wait, never mind."

Oh yeah, Laney's gonna need some work before she's ever allowed to babysit. She gets flustered and it's all out havoc—a complete one-woman circus.

"Laney, I got it," I step in, suppressing a laugh, "go sit down before you hurt somebody."

Emmett pats her hand, grinning. "Thank you, I'm fine really. A few bites of something to settle my stomach is all I need."

"Can I, uh, feel it?" Laney asks her in the most timid voice I think she's capable of.

"Of course." Emmett sits forward, offering out her belly more. "I can't promise you'll get any action, though." She giggles. "Usually if I eat some sugar and lie flat on my back, things get busy."

"Oh wait! I think I felt something!" Laney's face lights up.

"Trust me, Gidge, you'll know it if you do." I slide Emmett's juice in front of her. "There ya go, babe." I start removing tinfoil off platters. "Have a snack."

"Thank you," she takes a sip then snags a cheese cracker.

Dane's silence is actually deafening, catching my attention. He's watching Laney, like an eagle spots a rabbit, as she rubs Emmett's belly, trying to coerce the baby to move.

"I can't believe we don't know what we're having. Do you know all the stuff we can't buy because of that? Kick me once if you're a girl," Laney barters with the belly. "I really hope you're a girl."

"That surprises me, Gidge. As big of a tomboy as you are I thought for sure you'd be rootin' for a willie."

"That's why I want a girl. I shall lavish her in all things princess, which I'd already be stocking up on if she'd kick my hand already," she pouts.

Dane still hasn't spoken, fixated on Laney's flash of

maternal instinct. I decide to throw my man a bone. "So you want a girl then, when you have kids, Gidge?"

"Oh gosh, yes, a girl and a boy. One of each would be perfect."

The girls show no signs of hearing Dane growl, but I heard it loud and clear. Laney's right, he is a caveman. "Well, what if that doesn't happen?"

Emmett's smirking at me now, totally on to my game.

Laney shrugs and looks at Dane. "I guess we'll keep trying. If we get a softball team before a son, I'm okay with that. You?"

If I've ever known the correct answer to a question, it's this one. He is so okay with that plan. My man is using every ounce of restraint he possesses not to jump across the island and attack her right now.

"Yeah," he takes a pull of his beer, eye fucking her over the bottle, "I'm okay with that."

One step toward her is all he gets before she stops him with a hand up. "Halt! We have company, Caveman."

Emmett's head is jerking back and forth between them, her green eyes sparkling wide as she watches the show. She can't hide her snicker when Dane audibly growls this time, winking promises of later at Laney.

"Are we about ready to open presents? You had enough to eat, Emmett?" Laney changes the subject, saving us from a live porno viewing.

"I've never had enough to eat, but yes, I'm good for now." She struggles off her perch, legs nowhere near reaching the ground, sticking the landing before I scramble around to her.

"I SURE AS HELL HOPE ya'll deliver," I say hours later. "No way is this all fitting in the car." I take in all around me, Dane's living room resembling a nursery more than the actual nursery.

"Damn shame she didn't know what you're having so she could really shop," Dane fires off dryly, giving Laney a wink. "We can bring it over later."

Emmett's no longer gut sobbing, which started at present number two, but the sniffles still echo through the room every few seconds. Laney and Dane showered Alex in presents, everything from a high chair, which I'm pretty sure could've waited, to a crate of diapers.

Obviously we hadn't gotten them near as much, but they both seemed happy with what we had managed: some movies, a sweater and spa day certificate for Laney, City & Colour concert tickets and a handcrafted wooden guitar stand for Dane. I'd struck gold when Jack, who owns Jack's Jukebox music store, needed his bike worked on and traded me the labor for Dane's presents.

But the gift of the night was Emmett's surprise to me. Seems her and Laney were in cahoots to make it a Christmas I'd never forget. Don't catch me lying, I debated crying like a girl, then had a Dane moment and had to force myself not to jump her after I opened it. The present in question is a large, framed picture of my Emmy, sheer white top opened down the front, hands cupping her stomach, head down, her dark hair falling over her face. A beautiful, amazing portrait of my girl and child, with the perfect layer of seduction, reminding me my woman's in the picture too.

Best gift I've ever received.

Now that the room is in complete disarray and the girls are engrossed in chatter, Dane jerks his head for me to follow him. They don't notice as we walk out and he leads me down to his rec room, heading behind the bar to pour us both a short stack of the good stuff.

He raises his glass for a toast. "Another year."

"Here's to it." I clink my glass to his and sample a taste. "Thanks for all the baby stuff, man. You didn't have to do all that."

He throws back his head and laughs. "Yes, I did. Laney was hell bent." He punches my arm. "Kidding. I wanted to." He eyes me and I know there's more he wants to say. "We haven't had a chance to really talk since I laid into ya that day. Where are you and Emmett at now? Better yet, where's your head at?"

Maybe I should get a fucking t-shirt made so everybody knows, all the time, where I'm at. Namely her.

I take another drink, rolling the smooth whiskey over my tongue, luxuriating as it warms down my throat. "I love her. Honestly, between you and me?" He nods firmly and I rub my head nervously. "I'm scared shitless I won't be able to do right by them, to provide enough, but I'll do whatever it takes. Before, what you said, that wasn't it at all. I never didn't want her, the baby, the whole thing—I just worry, ya know?"

"Yeah, I know. So this is what you want, you're sure?"

"Completely."

"I thought so." He sets down his glass and opens the drawer nearest him. "Merry Christmas, Sawyer." He hands me an envelope. "Lord knows I don't have much luck handing people envelopes, Laney in particular," he grumbles, "so I'm warning ya, if you refuse it I may lose my shit."

I eye him questioningly, opening it up. It's a thick document, folded in thirds, a million words covering the pages. "What is this?"

"It's a contract. Have someone neutral look over it for you, but in a nutshell, it's The K." His face is solemn as he sips his drink, leery of my reaction.

"No," I shake my head, "no fucking way, man." I throw the papers on the bar and stand. "I can't accept that. I can do this on my own. I don't need handouts!" Anger, shame, embarrassment flood me at once, reminding me of what I already knew; I'm a never has been, biting off more than I can chew and everyone around me can see it. "What the hell, Dane? You don't think I can take care of my family without goddamn charity? Thanks for the vote of confidence, man."

"Since I knew this is how you'd react, why don't you sit the fuck down and let me explain before you go AWOL?"

"I'll stand." I cross my arms and widen my stance, challenging him.

"That contract appoints you 51% partner in The K, which you've more than earned. You run the place now, with little to no help from me, anyway. You keep doing what you're doing and buy me out, at a very reasonable price, over time. Not charity, but a legitimate business deal. Just like Tate and the gym, this is not a handout, just a stepping stone that was due you anyway."

"Tate's your brother."

"As are you," he deadpans.

"You know what I mean."

"Not really. That baby cooking in her belly? Thought you said that was your baby?"

"It is," I hiss through my clenched jaw.

"And you're my brother."

Fucking Dane, my brother in all the ways that matter, who I wanna punch right now.

"I have more than I can say grace over, Sawyer, you know that. Why would I covet more than I need and watch the people I love struggle? To me, The K is just a club. To you, it's a game changer."

"I just cut back my hours to be with Emmett more. I've got school, a baby coming," I'm grasping at straws now, shocked and overwhelmed and looking for an excuse.

"Do you ever hear Laney complaining that I'm not around?"

I shake my head, thinking back to this exact conversation I'd recently had with Emmett.

"Hire six, work them like they're eight and pay them like they're ten. Things will run themselves and you can keep your input as is. You can do it. Hell, I'm still tossing around the idea of going back to school myself."

"No shit? Good for you, man." I can do, as can he, but... Damn, his offer's so tempting I can almost taste it— some breathing room, some stability. I have worked my ass off at that club…but can I take it with pride?

"Let me think about it?"

"Whatever you need," he walks around the bar, slinging an arm over my shoulder, "so long as you say yes."

Chapter 33

GUESS WHO'S GOING TO

DINNER

-Emmett-

EVERYTHING'S HAPPENING SO FAST, I barely have time to catch my breath. One day it was Christmas, then I turned around and it was the middle of January. Which I guess is a good thing since all I hear the women at the clinic saying is how they feel like their pregnancy is taking forever.

Sawyer's all moved in and back at school...and trying his best to keep his fatigue hidden from me. There's something else going on with him though, a glaring shift in his demeanor I can't quite put my finger on. A certain confident air about him, more determination in his steps. And at work, he's a totally different guy.

Like today for example. I drive myself to work because he had class, and when I walk in, Kasey's directing people for prep and Sawyer's nowhere to be seen.

"Hey, Kasey, where's Sawyer?"

"Office." He points.

"With Dane?"

"No," he looks at me like I've got two heads, "alone."

No part of me wants to climb those stairs, but my curiosity gets the better of me so I tackle the feat. Out of breath, I knock lightly on the door.

"Come in," he answers.

"Hey," I look around, reconfirming he is, in fact, alone, "whatcha doing?"

He rises from behind the desk, coming to hug me and kiss the top of my head. "You shouldn't be climbing those stairs, Shorty, but I'm awful glad to see ya. How ya feeling?" He rubs my belly as he speaks.

"Fat and sassy." I wrap my arms around him, inhaling his sweet scent of man and cologne. "How was your day?"

"Damn near perfect. Listen, I took you off the schedule tonight. I should've called before you got all the way here."

"Okayyyy?"

"I have a lot I want to talk to you about. I thought we'd go out to dinner."

We never go out to dinner, a definite takeout or homemade, both eaten on the couch couple. I'm definitely intrigued. "Okay," I agree with what's apparently my word of the day.

"Let me finish a couple things and we'll head out." He kisses my head once more and heads back behind the desk, sitting as though he belongs there, tapping away on the keyboard.

"I'll just wait for you downstairs then." I start for the door.

"Crap, hang on." He jumps back up, jogging over to me. "I'll walk you down."

I have to snicker and roll my eyes at his chivalry, as though I'm helpless. "I can make it down some stairs, Sawyer. I'm not that big." I slap his stomach with a laugh.

"You're beautiful." He ushers me down with one arm around my back, the other on my arm. "It's for my piece of mind; humor me." When we reach the bottom, he kisses the knuckles of my hand and releases me. "Ten minutes tops."

I was right, something's up, and it sounds like I get to find out what it is tonight. I'm praying, like a hooker in heat, whatever the evening holds, it ends in sex. I watch him take the stairs back up two at a time, his jeans stretching tight across his ass; I could probably come on command if he said it in the right voice…if that was possible. But yes, the hormones are still in full effect.

I'm visiting with Kasey but a moment when Sawyer strides up beside me and lays his hand at the small of my back. "Em and I are gonna go. You got it?" he asks Kasey.

"Absolutely," he salutes him with a huge grin, "don't worry about a thing."

"All right, call me if you do end up needing anything. You ready?" He turns to me now and I nod, rising with his help.

"What was that about?" I lean in and whisper to him as we walk to the door.

"Patience, Shorty, I'll tell you everything over dinner. Let's run home and change first, though. Our reservations are kinda fancy." He leads the way to a truck, four doors, black and shiny.

"What are we doing?" I ask, confused.

"First thing I have to tell you—this is my new, well, newly used, truck. I sold my motorcycle and got this."

"What?" I gasp. "Why?"

"We need two vehicles with a baby. Look," he opens the back door, "I even got a carseat."

I slant around him, never-fail tears burning behind my eyes coinciding with my biting back a laugh. "I can't believe you sold your bike."

"Yep. Maybe one day I'll get another one, but for now, a four-door family vehicle sounds more me. You like it?"

I turn back to him, ever amazed and glossy-eyed. He

loved that bike, but not, as he's just clearly demonstrated, as much as he loves me and Alex. "I love it. And I love you, Sawyer Beckett." I touch his cheek and do something I haven't done in a while, puckering my lips to ask for his kiss.

Dropping his head to mine with a sexy, possessive grunt, he immediately grants my wish, kissing me delicately on the lips. "Cool carseat, right? I got one for your car too so we wouldn't have to be switching all the time."

How to pop his happy bubble? I haven't seen him this aglow in weeks.

"Em, you don't like it? They had different colors. I can take it—"

"No, I do, it's a very nice carseat," I look away and mumble under my breath, "for a two year old."

"Huh?"

I soften the blow, tracing his jaw with my fingertip. "Babies start in an infant car seat, a backwards cradle type."

His brow creases and he twists up his mouth in the most endearing fashion. "But we'll need this one eventually, right?"

"Yes," I smile. "You're ahead of the game. Always prepared."

"I guess," he frumps, sliding an arm around my waist and guiding me to the passenger side. He opens my door and helps me in, both strong hands on my hips, still grumbling slightly as he shuts it and walks back around.

"It was a very sweet thought," I reach over and rest my

hand on his thigh, "and I still can't believe you sold your bike for us. You didn't have to do that, ya know. We'd have figured something out."

"I've got no business with expensive toys until we have everything we need. Priorities, babe." He winks at me and starts the new truck.

At home, I put on the nicest outfit I own that still fits comfortably and freshen my hair and light makeup. A last look in the mirror confirms this is as good as it gets, so I grab my bag and let him know I'm ready. Sawyer looks good enough to eat instead of dinner in dark slacks and a blue button up, a warm smile accompanying his outstretched hand.

"You're beautiful, Em."

He certainly makes me feel that way, cankles and all.

DINNER IS LOVELY, candlelight in the middle of the table, pressed white linens and exemplary food I have trouble pronouncing. But now, waiting on dessert with still no big announcement, I'm more than a little antsy. The thought maybe, perhaps, occurred to me that he might possibly be thinking about proposing...nice dinner out, candlelight and all that jazz. Of course, sensible Emmett says it's too soon and insecure Emmett says it may only be because of the baby, but madly in love with Sawyer Emmett has butterflies in her stomach and an unmistakable pitter-patter in her heart. I'm not sure which version of myself will answer him, should he ask.

"Sawyer, what'd you want to talk to me about?"

He clears his throat, taking a sip of water. "I'll just say it." He lays his arm across the table, his hand up asking to hold mine, which I give him, shakily. "Dane gave me 51% of The K, with a plan to eventually buy him out."

I open my mouth to speak but he stops me.

"Let me finish." He smiles gently.

I nod, closing my mouth, which is just hanging agape in shock, and he takes an intense breath before beginning again.

"The last thing I wanted was charity, some pity donation, and I told him so, loudly. But then I thought about it and he and I talked some more, and I decided to accept. It's not about me anymore, or my ego, or my male pride. All that matters is you and our little bundle you're packing, and this is a key to our stable future. I'll have my business degree soon, I'll pay Dane back, and who knows, maybe I grow from it or maybe I just take The K to new places. But whichever, our family will have a foundation. It's our start, Emmy, to a real life, for our family."

My mouth must open and close like a sucker fish cleaning the tank about ten times before I finally choose words. "He just gave you a club?"

"Yeah," he laughs out loud, "he did. Well, part of a club, which honestly, I helped build. And every month I'll put a dent in buying him out. So now we have solid income, two good cars, and we'll work on getting a bigger place when things settle down. Kasey's the best man I've got, so I made him Manager, right after I told him I'd break his legs if he ever helped you out behind my back again. He does a good job, so don't worry, I'll still be with you more hours than not."

I'm speechless; I couldn't be more so if he'd have starting doing backflips through the restaurant. Actually, this news is more unlikely. I know what it must have taken out of him to accept what does have a certain "charity" connotation. Sawyer's a very proud man. Without us to worry about, he would have said "hell no" and never thought twice about it. But as he said, he swallowed his own pride, much like he'd sold his bike, for us.

A moment of clarity often strikes out of nowhere and every facet that makes up your soul—your head, your heart, your fears, beliefs—they all get together and shake hands when you're not looking, and all of sudden you're bathed in a feeling of true contentment. And true contentment feels nothing short of amazing.

I'm surprisingly okay that he didn't propose, loving exactly where and what we are right this very second. "Let's go home," I whisper, giving him a look I'm positive he knows exactly the meaning of.

THE SEXUAL TENSION on the ride home is, to say the very least, substantial. By the time we reach the driveway, the windows are starting to fog from our heavy, impatient breathing. I don't wait for him to open my door but rather leap out and run for the door, keys already in my hand.

He's behind me in an instant, moving my hair to the side, kissing the back and side of my neck. "You got it there, Shorty?" he teases as I have some distracted difficulty mastering the fine art of getting the damn key in the damn hole.

"Got it!" I squeal, every nerve ending in my body tingling at once.

Barely across the entry, he kicks the door shut and stalks me down the hall to the bedroom. My pulse is pounding in my ears, a loud whooshing sound, as I watch him watch me, predatory and virile. He grabs and turns me, my back meeting the bedroom door, arms pinned above my head.

"Give me the rundown, babe. Need to know where your head's at, what this is."

He wants to do inventory now?

I stretch out my neck to kiss him, but he pulls back, denying me.

"Tell me, Emmy."

He ate his own liver and accepted the club for us. He sold his bike for a family truck, for us. He moved in. He even attempted buying a carseat. I believe him, I trust now that he's with me, not going anywhere. My head finally accepts what my heart's been telling me is true.

We're back to good.

"I love you, Sawyer. And I know you're in it forever, babe. I trust you're sure."

"And?" He smirks, cocking a brow.

And what? I'm at loss. "I don't know and what." My breathing's shallow, I'm desperate to have my hands free to rip his clothes off him.

"And what are we about to do?"

"Make love, Sawyer. Definitely make love."

"No more trial period?"

I shake my head back and forth rapidly, then hold his eyes as I slowly lick my bottom lip.

"Em," he roars, dropping my hands and grabbing under my thighs to lift me off the ground.

Gets him every time.

Only arms as powerful as Sawyer's could make me feel weightless and delicate when I feel more like Humpty Dumpty.

"Put me down, I'm too heavy." I squirm, trying to break free, but he only tightens his grip in refusal.

"I've got you, babe." He pivots, walking to the end of the bed and setting me down gently. A pitiful whimper escapes me at the loss of his body mashed to mine, now instead standing over me. He picks up both my hands and pulls my arms up straight. "Leave them there," he bosses in a deep timbre, tracing his fingertips back down, his touch so light it's torture. Grabbing the bottom of my shirt, he whips it over my head and tosses it over his shoulder, never taking his smoldering eyes off me. My nipples bud tightly, pressing against the sheer white fabric of my bra, begging for relief. "Take it off, Em, nice and slow."

Nice and slow…not sure I can do that. I've missed him, us, this…ravenous and back to good is so…good. Without delay, I unhook the back and drag the straps down my arms as slowly as I can manage, dangling the lace from the end of one finger. He goes down to his knees, those eyes, God, those eyes, dancing with mine, filled with promises. Taking my finger, strap and all, in his mouth, he sucks it back off the tip, now holding it between his teeth. He whips his head to the right and my bra goes flying as I giggle.

Smoothing his hands up the tops of my thighs, eyes on their path, he groans and squeezes. "Lie back, Emmy," he barely gets out before he's bent over me, his mouth caressing my stomach soft and wet. "Missed you, Shorty," he whispers.

"Missed you so much."

I lift my head and rub the top of his with my hand as I watch him unbutton and lower the zipper on my pants. "Me too, babe." Reflexively, I hoist my hips off the bed and let him relieve me of my bottoms and panties in a single, seamless yank, working them around my ankles and placing kisses behind the wake.

Now I lie naked before him, electricity in the air raising every hair on my body on end. No matter how much you watch your weight gain, how many bottles of cocoa butter you practically bathe in, when you're pregnant, totally exposed adds a whole different realm of vulnerability and insecurity. I don't even realize I've covered what I could of myself until he pulls my hands away and traps them at my sides.

"You're exquisite, Emmett. Don't ever doubt, for a second, how much I want you or how incredibly sexy I think you are." He drops kisses over every inch of me, from the insides of my calves up to my forehead, not missing a single spot. "I love your body. In some ways, you're even sexier pregnant. Like these." Both of his large hands cover my breasts, kneading gently. "So fucking gorgeous," he hums, taking the left one in his mouth, my body bowing off the mattress like I've been electrocuted. He "pops" his mouth off and looks up at me, sultry smirk in place. "Sensitive?"

"Mmm hmm," I confirm, reaching for his head to force

it back where it belongs. "Don't stop, though."

He listens, back to sucking on a very heavy, heaving breast while his hands journey downward, pushing open my thighs as they go. "When'd you do this?" He traces the lips of my recently bared pussy with one finger.

"W-with Laney. Spa day," I pant, pushing myself against the teasing digit. "Hurt like hell. You like it?"

"Oh, I like it. I like it very much."

Before I have time to say thank you, his tongue is there, flattened against me, covering me with almost evil, languid licks. That wicked tongue ring tickles splendidly right, doing mind-numbing things when he scrapes it along, then flicks it on my clit. When he kisses my mouth, my body, my breasts with that ring in his tongue—God, I love it—but this, this is new and indescribable.

"Sawyer," I beg shamelessly, breathlessly, "don't tease me."

"Only a tease if I don't plan to deliver," he chuckles, hot breath on my wet flesh chilling me, "which I personally guarantee, on time." His whole face dives in now, mouth open and sucking, stiff tongue darting in and out of my slick center while both hands grip my hips in place. Coming up for air, lips and chin coated with me, he gives me a crazed smile. "You are fucking delicious, babe, but I gotta get inside you soon. So let's," the index finger of his right hand glides down from my hip, "see if my girl likes this." He spears that finger inside me, swirling it in circles then hooking it against my top wall, motioning "come here" repeatedly. His mouth joins the dance, descending to suck my little button until it's pointed out and stiff, his tongue flicking it zealously. Hook, swirl, flick, suck—I lose track, closing my eyes and tensing up rigidly, trying to relax as the orgasm rolls through my body, up from my toes to the ends of my hair.

Long after I'm done, eyes still closed, erratic breathing back in seemingly normal range, he continues to orally fixate, lapping up all of me. "Who always hits your sweet spots?" he asks deeply, crawling up my body. "Hmm?" He bites each nipple, placing kisses along my chest, then heads for my mouth…before swerving at the last second with a chuckle. "Don't move."

He carefully climbs off me, then the bed, and dashes for the bathroom. I lie in bed and giggle happily when I hear him brush his teeth furiously then gargle with mouthwash—he remembered! I want to burst into tears. I'm the luckiest girl in the world.

He comes back in the room sporting a proud smirk. "Ah, kiss me breath once again."

I hold out my arms for him to join me, but he pulls on my hand instead, so I sit up.

"Overdressed here, babe. Wanna help me?"

That's right. Dazed and sated, I'd completely forgotten he was still fully clothed. Using his hand and hip for leverage,

I stand, my hands gliding up his chest, unbuttoning on the down slide. One by one, I free the buttons, spreading out the sides of his shirt. I'm not sure you can say you've seen a chest until you've seen Sawyer's, a lean bulk of defined, cut muscles, golden skin, and pierced nipples. It never gets old, sending my butterflies stirring with every glimpse. I love his tattoos, lining his arms and ribs, but I adore his chest, a large piece of untouched art. He helps with the cuffs, dropping his arms to his sides so I can push the shirt down and off, kicking it aside with my foot. I lavish the beautiful plane with adoration, only lifting my mouth from it to tug on his nipple rings, his head falling back on a groan. Virtually hairless, his dark happy trail might as well be a flashing arrow leading me right where I need to go. Making quick, jerky-handed work of his belt and fly, I strip him down as he toes off his socks, and soon I have a gloriously naked Sawyer Beckett in front of me. We stand so close my nipples brush against his chest, his long, thick erection poking the top of my stomach.

Unmoving but our hands, we do a dance of exploration, reconnecting together; it's been so long, we both study and worship like it's our first time. Fingertips and palms relearn every curve of the other, kisses and moans breaking the reverent silence when certain places are touched. I back up until I feel the bed against my legs and with one hand, bring him down with me.

"Emmy, babe," he croons in my ear, sucking under it,

"we may have to do this a little different."

"Do whatever you want," I murmur, relishing in having him so close, my hands gripping his rock hard ass to pull him closer.

"Roll over, babe, nice and easy," his voice soothes as he helps manipulate me. "Ah Emmy," he gropes, "dat ass, Shorty, I love it." He bites first one cheek then the other and his hands slide to my hips, pulling them up and back, forcing me onto my hands. "Want you like this, Emmy girl," he traces the seam, "ass up, bouncing for me. You want it from behind, baby?"

I crave his dirty mouth, missed it, really. Anyone ever offers him a stick of Orbit, I'll bitchslap it out of their hand. "However you wanna give it to me, babe. As long as it's now."

"That's my girl," he drawls, low and sexy, as he works his crown inside of me. "Damn Em, you gotta relax for me. Don't tense up, babe, you're tight enough already." He fondles my ass cheeks, moving them up, around, out, as he gradually pulls back a bit then forward again as much, building up my natural lubrication and easing his entrance. "Mhm yeah," a bass rumbles from his chest, "there we go. Goddamn, you feel good, unfucking real." Patiently, he gives it to me nice and slow, applying a light pressure on my back, popping my ass up higher for his taking. I'm halfway to another orgasm by the time his groin is flush against my ass, fully inside me, and he must notice. "Not ready, Em, stay with me baby. Lemme feel for a while."

The hair on his legs tickles the back of my thighs, his breath whispering over my spine. Long, gradual drags in and out, his growl with each, turn my insides to lifeless mush as he basks in me, us. I hold off the best I can, and then, he shocks me. I hear the slurp and pop, wondering what the heck, when a wet fingertip starts to tease around my, uh, my ass...hole.

Definite new territory.

He feels me stiffen and lays lightly on my back now, whispering hotly in my ear. "You don't like it, say stop and I will. But I think you're really gonna like it."

I drop my head 'til my forehead meets the mattress, pushing my ass back against his finger. He circles it several times, increasing his thrusts inside me, until he knows I'm once again fixated on the power of his surges into me and not the oncoming experiment. My legs tremble under me as the tip of his finger breaches me there, a sting drawing a hiss from between my teeth. "Relax," pump, "push back into it, baby, trust me to take you there."

As I do as he's said, I can feel his finger go deeper, and it goes from slightly uncomfortable to euphoric in a flash. "Ahhhhhh," I wail, pushing back harder, faster, his hips adjusting seamlessly to my set rhythm.

He takes me hard now, punishing cock in my pussy,

long, seeking finger in my ass, and I peel the paint off the walls as I banshee scream through the most powerful orgasm any woman has ever had. Hope he didn't want me to wait for him, 'cause a cement wall guarded by starving pit bulls couldn't have stopped that explosion.

There's still splotches of color bursting behind my eyes when I hear his pants increase, his balls slapping against me angrily. Somewhere in there he slipped his finger out of me and wrapped that hand, along with the other, on my hips, holding me steady to meet the force of his cock slamming into me.

"Fuckkkkk, Emmett!" he roars, giving a few jerky, final thrusts before he stills, twitching and emptying himself inside me. Kissing up my sweaty back, he bites down on my shoulder. "I love you, Shorty. So damn much."

"Me too, babe. Now help me up, I have a freakin' Charlie horse in my calf."

He laughs loudly, body shaking with it as he slides from me and jumps up to stand by the bed. "Let me massage it out. Which leg?"

I roll onto my back, whimpering with the cramp but laughing too, and point to my left leg.

He lifts it, working magic on the tensed muscle. "You need more potassium, babe. Want a banana shake?"

"With strawberries?" I make puppy dog eyes and poke out my bottom lip.

"I'll see what I can do." He winks, setting my leg back down. "Can you walk to a warm bath? I'll bring it to ya."

And now I know why women go through what I hear is excruciating, unforgettable pain, and yet, still get pregnant again. I mean, besides the whole loving children, miracle of birth thing.

You get to be the baby when you're having a baby.

Chapter 34

DUDE, WHERE'S MY DIGNITY?

—SAWYER—

"CAN I HELP YOU?"

On edge, I startle and turn, sending up a silent prayer that help is, in fact, on its way. Uh huh, I see what you're doing here…can't get the men to just walk in a bookstore, so you make sure the girl who helps you is even hotter than the girl who greeted you at the door. Brilliant marketing—make it an eye candy 'no, sir, you're not really in a' bookstore ploy.

"Fuck, I hope so."

I must scare the salesgirl, because she backs way up, eyes flying wide open.

"So I read the book about what to expect for the

pregnant woman. Can you show me the book about what the hell the guy's supposed to do to cope?"

"Oh, whoa." She reaches out and grabs the bookcase as it teeters from both my hands being braced on it, about to fall. "Let's see what we have. Follow me."

Lady, I will follow you down the stairs to hell if you find me the "Demons Have Taken Over My Sweet Woman" instruction manual.

Literally, almost overnight, she snapped, and now everything I do is wrong. Even Dr. Greer, who thinks I'm insane and usually plasters herself against the farthest wall from me, patted my shoulder with a pitying frown at the last visit.

We search the bookshelves together, her reading titles with her head tilted, me looking at the little pictures on the spine for one of a fire-breathing dragon lady, when an idea hits me. I should write a book. I'll call it "Your Woman's Pregnant, Get Ready. Real Talk" by Sawyer "If This Book's Out Then I Survived" Beckett.

Chapter One: Sleep. If she finally gets comfortable in bed, don't fucking move a muscle. Don't even breathe, 'cause if you disrupt her, all hell's about to break loose and you will be adjusting, rearranging, and searching out every pillow in the house. (This was my night as of last, from approximately 10-11:15.)

Chapter Two: Showers. You're a fucking idiot for even

suggesting men don't have to go to baby showers. Of course your ass has to be there…unless of course your ass doesn't have to be there, because it's "her" thing, for the mother who "actually has to go through the hard part!"

Chapter Two point Five: Addendum. Chapter Two could go either way, and is clearly subject to change on a daily basis, so do not speak of it. Let her tell you what you are and are not attending.

Shit! Baby shower!

"I gotta go, never mind, thank you!" I yell at the salesgirl, hauling my ass outta there full speed. I knew there was something I had to do today. I'm dialing while I start the truck, downright fear enveloping me.

"Hello?" Oh thank God, a sweet voice.

"Hey, Baby Mama. Whatcha doing?"

"On my way to the shower with Laney. You on your way?"

"Yep, headed there now. Just making sure we weren't riding together." My tongue forks as I speak. I thought for sure I was late to pick her up.

"Nope, Laney's got me. I'll see you there."

"K, babe. I love you."

"I love you too, Sawyer."

Well holy shit, score for the men's team! I roll my neck and relax a bit, cranking up some tunes and heading to Dane's. Who needs a book—I got this!

---❧---

I IN NO WAY, shape, or form got this. Mayfuckingday!

Currently, I am being wrapped in toilet paper, the model for the build a diaper contest. I am the only person with a dick here, and it's shriveled up and gone into hiding. "You bout done?" I grumble.

"Hush!" Laney slaps my arm while Bennett walks around me in circles, wrapping Charmin over, around and through my junk drawer. Much more of that and she's gonna expect me to buy her dinner.

I look over to Jessica, the model for the other team and the only invitee besides the Crew girls. I'm happy to see that she's also being tortured. I'll have to give her a raise. Oh, but look at Emmett, smiling, laughing, and having a blast.

All right, I get it.

"Ya'll hurry up, we gotta win this! Bennett, take some of those thingies out of your hair and use 'em as pins!"

"We know what we're doing," Laney barks, "just hold still!"

"You have no idea what you're doing, woman! You're barely a girl!"

Ouch! I don't think a ball punch was necessary.

"Oh. Dear. God." And it just keeps getting better...Dane walks in and catches me in all my pampered glory. Wait, why is he holding up his phone?

"What are you doing with that phone, fucker?"

He waves his free hand at me absently. "Not filming this, don't worry."

"Time!" Laney belts out, stepping back to admire their work. "Oh yeah, we are so gonna win. Dane, baby," she turns to him, "will you be the judge?"

Emmett drops back on the couch with a huff, exhausted, but levels a stare at Dane. "You're gonna want to pick mine," she warns.

He smirks at her then gives Laney an apologetic wink. "Emmett wins."

"Yay!" Whitley squeals, hugging the mummified Jessica. "We won!"

"Let's eat," Emmett suggests, so I rapidly rip off my TP and rush to help her up.

She thinks she's huge, I know this because she mentions it at least twice a day, every day, but I think she's adorable, not a third of the size I've seen some women get. But I learned quickly—don't argue, say nothing, and nod empathically.

"So, I hear you got kicked out of Lamaze?" Dane laughs and I cut a look to Emmett—I can't believe she ratted me out.

"I wasn't kicked out. I was asked not to come back. There's a big difference," I grumble, helping my woman up on the stool at the bar. "What'd you tell them?" I ask her.

"The truth," she simpers, covering her mouth quickly to hide it.

"Why don't you set me straight with the real story?" Dane quirks that fucking brow of his, challenging me as he takes a bite of a stork-shaped cookie.

Total setup—all six pairs of eyes dart to me, the girls leaning in closer to soak up my every word. "Clear cut case of Hag Rag was all it was." I shrug. "The teacher wanted me, got mad she couldn't have me, starting pickin' on me."

"Uh huh." Dane nods, motioning with his hand for me to continue.

"It's a class about your baby coming out, right? Why wouldn't I need to be down between Emmett's legs?"

Whitley sprays me with her mouthful of punch, choking and sputtering. Bennett slaps her on the back, but shushes her, not wanting the story interrupted, I guess.

"Ain't shit gonna be happening up by her head. I went where I was needed."

"And?" Emmett coughs.

"And what? Babe, she obviously didn't know what she was doing. I wasn't 'staging a coup' as she so dramatically accused. I was simply getting the other dads in gear."

Everyone's laughing, but Whitley raises her hand amongst the noise. "Yes, Whitley?"

"Correct me if I'm wrong, but you don't plan to actually

deliver the baby, do you?" She grasps her chest, voice trembling with the last couple words.

"No."

"Then why do you need to be down there? That's where the doctor goes."

Here we go again. I shake my head. Does nobody have an original argument?

Emmett grabs Laney's arm, slinging her thumb my way. "This, you gotta hear."

"There's gonna be a lot happening in one central location—fluids gushing and flying out. I've read a lot about this, you know. I want to make sure my child doesn't slip through her hands like a greased pig and wind up on the floor. I'm the pinch catcher, just in case. I know these babies never miss," I give 'em all my snazzy fingers, "not to mention," I shush their gasps and giggles, "women screaming, mass chaos—I need to make sure nobody gets scissor happy and snips the wrong thing."

Dane's face is classic—stone-shocked silence...he's just mad I think of everything first, 'cause you know his ass is taking notes. "If I could just figure out how to harness and bottle all that into something useful," he swipes his hands crazily in my general area, "we'd all own private islands."

I WAS EXPRESSLY FORBIDDEN to buy any food, chocolate or otherwise, as well as any "I won't be this size forever" articles of clothing and/or flowers, which all of a sudden give her a headache, for Valentine's Day.

Exactly what the fuck does that leave?

No puppy, to hell with that, we've got a peeing, pooping machine on the way. Jewelry? Too cliché. Definitely not baby stuff—between Christmas and the shower, we're all set for like, ten babies. New journal? Not enough.

I'm screwed. Time to call in reinforcements.

"She's busy," Dane answers Laney's phone with a chuckle, but I can hear her grappling with him in the background.

"Hand her the phone, it's important."

"You okay?" His tone goes deadly serious.

"No! What the hell do I get Emmett for Valentine's Day? And before you start naming basic bullshit, let me tell you the forbidden list she gave me."

"Give me the phone," Laney bosses. "Hello?"

"Hey, Gidge, so I—"

"I heard you," she cuts me off. "She wants one of those Kindle reader things, with a light."

She does love to read. Me thinks Gidge may be onto something. "Where do I get one of those?"

"Any electronics place, Best Buy, wherever. Oh, and have them load it up with credit or whatever they do so she can buy books!"

"Ah, Gidge, you know how much I love you, right?"

"Yes, she knows!" Dane yells.

"Bye," I chuckle, tempted to jack with him and keep talking to her. "Thank you."

I handed her the gift at approximately six pm. That's the last time I saw her. The time is now nearing 10:30 pm.

I am a brave, brave man...I'm going in.

"Hey, baby, whatcha doin?"

"Shhh," she hisses, curled up in bed, mesmerized by the screen. "It's at a crucial part."

Yeah, I got a crucial part and he knows it's Valentine's Day and that she bought us new cologne and sunglasses, not a pocket pussy. Stealthily, I turn off the lights and walk around the bed, stripping down to nothing before I pull up the covers and slip in behind her. I brush her long hair off her shoulder, teasing her skin with my nose, kissing softly. I get a backwards hand swat, like a fly's bugging her.

I am not a fan of the Kindle. I flop on my back, huffing loudly, and when she doesn't even flinch, I huff again, punching and rearranging my pillow. "Whatcha reading, on Valentine's Day, baby?"

"Mirage," she sighs wistfully. "It's so good."

I roll over, naked chest against her back, and grab one her hands, shoving it on my hard, lonely dick. "That feel like a mirage to you, Em?"

"No," she sets the Kindle down and rolls over to face me, "no, it certainly does not. It feels very real." She presses her hand down harder, using her whole palm to glide up and down my poor achiness.

I wind my hand behind her neck and roughly pull her mouth to mine, biting her bottom lip and tugging before sneaking my tongue in to caress hers. "I need some lovin', Emmy," I murmur against our tangled mouths. "You got some for me?"

Her thin white nightgown leaves nothing to my imagination, her nipples peaked and hard, and she's not wearing any panties. Fuckkk me. I run my finger under one strap and let it fall down her arm, then the same on the other side. Now her chest is bared to me, showcasing her visible, fluttering heartbeat and two gorgeous breasts. I prop myself on my right elbow to hold my weight and use my left hand to delve down and hike up the bottom of her sleepwear. No barrier, my index finger tests her readiness. She's warm and wet, like she was waiting for me.

By now she's latched on manically to both sides of my head, feasting at my mouth then steering me down to suck on her tits, one of her favorite things. Every day they grow and I'm often tempted to suffocate myself in them. What a way to go.

"Tell me, Em, you want me? You want me inside that pretty wet pussy, don't cha?"

"Yes," she groans, letting her lips fall open.

"Put me where you want me, Em, show me."

She rolls over on her side away from me and hitches one leg back over my hips. Fumbling, her hand comes behind and between us, tiny fingers grabbing my cock. I scoot closer and she lines me up with her soaking center, backing up until the tip pops inside her.

And for the next few hours, 'cause yeah, I got it like that, we consummate our first Valentine's Day together.

Chapter 35

MIRACLE ON FAIR ROAD

-Emmett-

A SECOND-TIME MOM TOLD A FUNNY STORY at Lamaze one night before we got kicked out. Her water broke in the middle of the grocery store aisle, so she reached over and grabbed a jar of pickles, smashing it on top of her puddle to cover it up. Great story, we all died laughing, but totally non-applicable now, here.

I'm sitting in the lobby of Quickie Lube, waiting for my oil change and tire rotation, when I suddenly feel like I just peed on myself. It doesn't occur to me that it's my water breaking right off the bat because I've got 17 days left. Babies don't come that early, maybe a week, but not over two. This can't be right. What if something's wrong? And SHIT, are jackknife pains supposed to immediately follow?

Okay, I can do this, no need to panic. I pull up Sawyer on my phone, anxious, somewhat frightened tears already dripping down my cheeks.

"Hey baby, you get your car done?" he answers cheerfully.

"Not done yet." I huff out a breath. "Sawyer, my water just broke, in the Quickie Lube on University. And the pain, ahh," I yelp, hunching over, holding my stomach, "has already started."

"Ma'am, are you all right?" a pimple faced kid about twelve asks me.

"Nooo," I growl, "I'm not all right. Unless you deliver babies or have a morphine drip handy. I. AM. NOT. ALL RIGHT."

"Emmy, babe," Sawyer frantically screams in my ear, "hand that guy the phone. I'm on my way right now, just hold on, Shorty, Daddy's coming."

I thrust the phone at the poor kid, slumping down in my chair, trying to reposition some of the pressure off my breaking spine. "OH MY GOD," I sob, screaming, "SEROUSLY?"

"Dude," the phone shakes in his hand, "she's definitely in labor, coming pretty fast I think."

"Uh huh."

"Okay, I can do that."

"All right, yep, I got it." He ends the call and hands me back my phone which I rip from his hand.

Sorry kid, wrong place, wrong time. You'll live. "Ahhh!" I may not.

"Your husband said to time your contractions. If they get five or less minutes apart, I have to call an ambulance. He's about fifteen minutes away."

"Thank you."

"Brian."

"Thank you, Brian. I'm sorry I was hateful, but this hurts like a bitch." I lay my head back and try to concentrate on my breathing, what techniques I got time to learn before Sawyer got us unceremoniously removed from Lamaze. "I'm sitting in a puddle of pain, so just ignore everything I say."

"Can I get you a drink or anything?"

A towel would be nice. "No, thank you I'm fine, I, Ohhh my God! Oh my God, owww." I bellow, bent over at the waist. The pain, excruciating pain.

"That wasn't even three minutes, I'm calling." He turns and runs to the desk.

How is this happening? I thought you had time to grab your bag, drive your car and park, walk in and get a wheelchair....this is like a pop and sprint!

Not but a couple minutes pass and I hear blaring sirens getting closer and closer. I try to stand to meet them and instantly drop back down. Not happening. Another contraction hits as the EMTs come barreling through the door and this one lasts what seems like forever. I felt that one in my hair roots.

"What's your name, ma'am?" one of the rescue guys asks, strapping something on my arm that he pulled from some box.

"Emmett Young." In through the nose, out through the mouth.

"How far apart your contractions?"

"Barely three minutes," Quickie Lube Brian chimes in from the sidelines.

"And how many weeks are you?"

"37. Almost 38. Is that too early?" I bite my trembling lip, worried and scared. Where is Sawyer?

"Gonna be fine, let's get you loaded up." He grabs under one shoulder, another man hooking under my arm from the other side. Mid-stride we have to stop as a 47 on the Richter scale rips through me, causing my legs to go weak, and I'm going down if they don't catch me.

"Emmett!"

There he is.

"Sawyer!" comes out a gargled sob.

He's there instantly, hand on my back.

"Sir, step back, please, let's get her loaded. You're more than welcome to ride in the ambulance with her."

"We're going to Regional. 1499 Fair Rd. I called her doctor so they know we're coming." He's so calm, collected, spouting off facts like the man in charge. He picks up my purse off the ground and looks around, spotting Brian. "Someone will be by to pay you and get her car, a guy named Tate or Dane Kendrick. Give it to them."

Brian nods speechlessly, probably traumatized for the rest of his life.

Once we're rolling, Sawyer stretches and grabs my hand, not letting go until they load me. I scream out in pain and clutch my stomach, every breath an effort. Sawyer and one guy jump in, the doors slam, and next thing I know, we're moving, sirens blaring. Sawyer's once again holding my hand, leaned over me with the other stroking my hair, kissing my forehead incessantly.

"Just breath, baby, everything's gonna be fine. I'm right here. I got you, Emmy."

I give him a tearful nod, tightening my grip on his hand.

"I love you," he mouths, blowing me an air kiss and actually getting me to smile.

The ride lasts no time at all and then the doors are flying open and I'm rolling all speedy like into the hospital. A nurse meets us and starts directing traffic, having me taken straight to the maternity ward.

Three contractions later, so ten minutes, and I'm in a robe and bed with a fetal monitor on my stomach and Nurse

Nasty elbow deep in my vag.

"Four." She snaps off her gloves and rolls her stool to the trash, then back. "You've been working. Dr. Greer's been paged. Do you plan to have an epidural?"

Is that supposed to be a joke?

"Yes, please, ASAP, please," I pant, another wave of pain building.

"Ok, I'll go page the anesthesiologist. That'll keep you out of pain while you dilate to go time! Who will be in the room with you? Hospital allows two."

"That would be only me," Sawyer stands and shakes her hand, "Sawyer Beckett, Daddy."

—SAWYER—

I'D TAKE THE PAIN from her if I could. It's unbearable to watch beads of sweat line her forehead and lip with each bout of pain. She's so brave, puffing her lips and breathing through it like a little blowfish, giving me a weak but victorious smile when each one ends.

Chapter Three: Labor. Touch her, support her, but not too much. Mama gets irritable and swat happy and may spit out "don't touch me" in a demonic growl, but she doesn't mean it.

An hour, sixty minutes and nineteen contractions later, the man with the plan walks in, all casual, to administer the epidural. "Bet you're glad to see me," he says with a haughty laugh.

Beggin' for an ass kickin', this guy.

"Very," Emmett moans, shifting uncomfortably.

Chapter Four: Epidurals. Write this down! Do <u>NOT</u>, I repeat, do <u>NOT</u> watch this part. Dr. Evil is gonna shove a huge, I mean grotesquely long, fucking needle in your woman's spine while she's hunched over crying. They will not let you hold her during this. A nurse holds onto her and you get to sit there like a useless asshole. It will gut you and make you want to beat the ever lovin' shit out of him! But then, an eerie solace will move over the room like a warm, just out of the dryer, blanket and baby mama will suddenly resemble a human being again.

And the rest is smooth sailing...not really, but compared to the perfect storm just endured? Tiny ripples in a shallow creek.

"YOU'RE DOING SO DAMN GOOD, Emmy." I kiss her forehead, then pop down for a looksee, back and forth, entranced. "Squeeze my hand, Shorty," and damn does she, "almost there!"

"Bear down, Emmett, push like your tailbone needs to hit my hand," Dr. Greet directs her. "There ya go, couple more like that."

"My strong, beautiful girl, you got it, baby." I prop my other hand behind her back and help sit her up. "I love you, Emmett. You're doing great." I glance over her leg and see it, a furry black head. "Is that—is that the head?"

"That's the head. I need the clamps," Doc barks at the nurse, and she hands her some big ass salad tongs, scarier looking than the breast pump I hid.

Oh, hell no.

"What is that? What are you doing?" Yup—I'm down where the action is now.

"I've got to turn the head, Mr. Beckett."

"You are not putting that on my kid's head. No, no, no." I shake my head, reaching to grab her weapon.

"Perfectly safe." She makes a move but so do I.

"No way, let me in there, I'll do it!" I butt in front of the nurse.

"Sawyer," oh Doc's first naming me now, "back up or and let me do my—"

"Pushing!" Emmett wails out, demanding both our attention.

'Atta girl, Em—one big, hard push and the baby's head comes out a few more inches. I can't help it, I smirk and stick out my hand and get the tongs slapped into my palm.

From that moment, I don't move, speak, or blink, and I'm not even sure I breathe. The most beautiful little person I've ever seen in my life emerges.

Chapter Five: You'll never be the same.

Dr. Greer catches like a champ, scrubbing, rubbing, patting and sucking in a blurred frenzy and a piercing, glorious cry raises the roof. "You have a daughter." She looks at me. "Would you like to cut the cord?"

This is it. I use one hand to steady the other and separate her from only her mother. She's a part of "our" world now.

"A daughter," I whisper, following Little Miss' transfer from the doctor's hands to the nurse's. "Emmy, did you hear?" I choke out, turning to look at Mama once my baby's safely laid in some tray there, only an arm's length away. (I may have reached out and measured.) "We have a daughter."

Exhausted, sweaty, radiant Emmett holds her arms out to me and puckers her sweet lips. "I heard," she answers, tears streaming down her face. "Is she okay?"

As gently as my heart will allow, I wrap my arms around her, kissing every inch of her beautiful face. "Yes, she's perfect. Thank you, Emmett." I turn my head and kiss her hand as she wipes my own tears for me. "God, I love you. Thank you so much, babe." I laugh, happy as I've ever been, crying like my baby with no shame. "I gotta go make sure they're doing everything right over there and count all her fingers and toes. Be back in a minute."

"You do that, Daddy," she smiles at me, cupping my cheeks, with warmth and happiness filling her vibrant green eyes, "go get our girl."

Chapter 36

WE ARE BECKETT

—SAWYER—

AFTER THEY'VE GOT EM ALL FIXED UP and resting comfortably and Lil Bit's been taken, despite my threats, to the nursery, I head to the waiting room. Busting open the doors, I'm greeted by five of my favorite faces, my family. Laney's leg is twitching a mile a minute, a bunch of pink balloons in her right hand, blue in her left. Beside her is Dane, then Tate and Bennett and good ole Zach.

They all stand up at once, Laney rushing forward the fastest. "Well?" she asks animatedly.

"Did ya'll have bets going?" I ask.

"Duh," Tate chuckles. "Better than betting on the

Falcons."

"All right, team girl over here," I point, "team boy over here. And where are Evan and Whit?"

"On their way back from deer camp," Zach laughs, "I'd hate to be Evan right now. You know Whit is pissed she missed it."

"Only two on team boy huh?" I size up Zach and Tate and hear Laney's grunt beside me. Turning to the pink team, I raise my brows at Dane. "You're team girl?"

He grins. "I'm team Laney wants a girl."

I rub my chin, flicking my eyes between both groups, making them sweat. "You guys know better than to bet against Laney. It's a girl!"

"WOO HOO!" Laney screams, letting go of the blue balloons and leaping at me, wrapping the free hand around my neck. "I knew it! Congratulations!"

"Thanks, Aunt Gidge," I kiss her head, putting her down to accept Bennett's onslaught then bro hugs from the rest.

"So, what's her name?" What's she look like? When can we see her?" Laney rapid fires off.

"I don't know yet. Emmett's sleeping, so we haven't talked about her name. And she's beautiful, head full of black hair like her mama. Lil' chunk, I'll tell ya. Eight pounds seven ounces."

I've never seen Laney so excited. I'd barely heard about Parker's triplets being born, but damn if she's not chomping at the bit for my girl. "When can we see her?" she whines.

I rub my head sheepishly. "I don't know, Gidge, they didn't say. But I think there's a window to the nursery. That's where she's—"

And she's gone like a streak of lightening down the hall.

"Okay, then," Dane clutches my shoulder and shakes my hand, "go take care of business and keep us posted when you can."

–Emmett–

"AND THEN, Daddy said, 'no way, woman. I'm your man and that is that.'"

I wake and turn my head to the sound of his voice, silently watching him talk to our baby bundled in his arms. I'm so tired, but I don't want to miss this. She lets out some whines, fussing, and he sticks his pinky finger in her mouth. "I know, I know, you're hungry. Should we wake up Mommy?"

He lifts his head and catches my gaze, smiling sweetly from ear to ear. "Looks like we already did. Mornin', Mama, somebody wants a boobie. It's her," he nods down at the baby and I have to chuckle at his need to clarify, "I told her I'd share."

"Bring her here." I push myself up, stomach fluttering. I'd taken classes, but I don't think you can prepare for the feeling that comes when you're to feed your child for the first time.

Sawyer laughs as I unsnap the breast flap in my gown. "Well isn't that handy? I'll be stealing that for home." He wiggles his eyebrows at me. "You got her?" he asks, carefully placing my daughter in my arms.

I nod, eyes blurring with tears as I really look at her for first time. "Look at this hair," I sniffle, fluffing her mop of dark fuzz. Her little head flops around, no control, as she searches for my breast. "Hold on, little piggy." I help her, and it takes her a minute, but naturally, like a baby bird just knows to flap and leave the nest, she begins feeding.

Sawyer leans over and kisses first my head and then hers. "Beautiful," he murmurs almost under his breath. "Have you thought about a name?"

I had, nothing that I had to name her though, and no way am I leaving him out of this, so I shrug. "A few ideas. What do you like?"

His face lights up with hope, then quickly recovers, attempting a see-through mask of nonchalance. "I mean, I had a few ideas too, here and there."

"Sawyer," I goad, "I can tell by the look in your eyes that you know exactly what you want to name her."

"Well," he fidgets, "since we've been calling her Alex all

this time, I thought maybe Alexandra would be cool for the middle name? Too uppity for the first name, though."

I nod encouragingly. "I love it, perfect, we keep Alex. Now what about the first name?"

"She's our first miracle, together, so I was thinking about us, something special. Lots of things always make me think of you and me, but above all, is one song in particular." His feet shuffle on the floor, his hand behind his neck rubbing nervously. "What do you think of Presley?"

"Presley Alexandra Beckett," I breathe out as he sucks in a loud breath.

"Beckett?" He smiles through watering eyes. "Really?"

I'd been nervous about that last part, feeling presumptuous, but seeing his face now, that worry disappears. "Of course," I whisper.

"Goddamn, Em," he says, then winces. "Sorry, bad Daddy." He kisses her sweet head and looks up at me. "You cripple me, woman. I love you." He gulps, collecting himself. "I love you so much. And I love you, Presley Alexandra Beckett. Our girl. And just so you know," he lifts my chin, "Beckett sounds good with Emmett Louise too."

Epilogue

—SAWYER—

MY DAUGHTER IS AMAZABABY, defying all laws of gravity, digestion…and Pampers.

"Good Lord, Princess P! You dropped a bomb on your daddy, didn't you?"

One "P" fits all with her—Presley, Princess, Poopy Pants…

"We gotta switch diapers, baby, this is ridiculous. How do you get it down your leg?"

I swear she saves 'em up for me. Emmett is all the time kissing her naked lil' hiney—no way she'd do that if she'd ever gotten one of these gems! Quite proud of herself, she coos and gurgles little spit bubbles out her mouth, arms and legs flailing wildly as I wipe…and wipe…in vain.

"That's it, shower time!"

I refasten her diaper and wrap a blanket around her, snatching her up and heading for the bathroom. Presley and I seem to take a shower every time I watch her alone. She is the cleanest baby ever, except for the few minutes of mass destruction before the shower. Today Emmett's at her "Body after Baby" class, which puts her gone two hours round trip, and this is already our second shower today. Presley loves it, though, and it's the easiest way I've found to get her clean when she surprises me with one of her "treats."

Dr. Greer was sad to see me go, I'm sure, but my new best friend, Doc Horton, the pediatrician, says Presley and her Pooprotechnics are totally normal. I'm shopping second opinions, but in the meantime, I've got this down to a science.

Turning on the water to let it warm up, I turn the shower head to spray at the bench seat, then lay P down on a towel while I take off my shirt and slip on the still-wet trunks hung over the bar in the shower. Yes, Emmett laughs too, but I just don't know the rules on that, so.... Next, I take all Presley's poop-covered accessories off and sort into two trash bags, which I cleverly now keep a box of under the bathroom sink. I pick up the culprit and in we head to sit on the shower seat. No way do I stand and risk dropping her, so we chill on the bench while the water hits her bottom, doing its job.

Her little hands, going a mile a minute, swat around as we play the "can Daddy catch and eat your fingers game."

She gets in a good hit on my chest, right above my heart, right on my newest tattoo. "That's right P, that's you and your mommy, huh?"

Emmett says I'm crazy, but I think Presley's consciously drawn to it. Over my heart is the profile of a Queen Alexandra butterfly—right where they both landed.

ENDURE, THE FINAL BOOK IN THE AMAZON BEST SELLING EVOLVE SERIES, SUMMER 2014!

Twitter: @emergeauthor
Facebook: https://www.facebook.com/S.E.HallAuthorEmerge
Emerge book trailer, by Lisa at Pixel Pixie:
http://www.youtube.com/watch?v=uWooZtXiQN8
Goodreads: http://bit.ly/19xitqD
Dane facebook:
https://www.facebook.com/DanefromEmerge
Evan facebook: https://www.facebook.com/pages/Evan-Mitchell-Allen/409174755862025?directed_target_id=0
Sawyer facebook:
https://www.facebook.com/pages/Sawyer-Beckett/227467650737311
Emerge playlist:
http://www.pinterest.com/emergeauthor/emerge-playlist/
Embrace playlist:
http://www.pinterest.com/emergeauthor/embrace-playlist/

Other works by S.E. Hall—Emerge on
Amazon http://amzn.to/18nKceN
Amazon UK: http://www.amazon.co.uk/Emerge-Evolve-Series-ebook/dp/B00CTYIWGO

Acknowledgements

This part is always harder than the book itself. A lot has changed since I wrote these for Entangled...new readers have come into my life and are now more; friends. Authors named my books in their own, blogs formed and pimped my books lovingly....so many rocked my world!!!

Again, there is NO way to name every single person, by name, who touched my heart and life, so I won't even try, for the ONE I forget would forever haunt me. If I do my job as a person, I've said thank you to you, shown you in some way how much I appreciate you. If not, you have my permission to come kick my ass.

My husband, Jeff, is forever my real-life prince, my best friend and my rock. He's the best thing that has, or will, ever happen to me. If I could marry anyone in the whole world tomorrow, I'd pick him again. I love you, babe!

My girls. Even if they weren't my kids, I'd think they were cool- cause they are! You know your Mama loves you more than her laptop ladies...I do it for you!

My family. Again, one of those categories where you do NOT start singling people out and chance forgetting anyone. My family is crazy, loud, obnoxious, borderline psychotic and so much fun society can hardly stand it when we congregate in groups. But they're all mine and I adore them. Cheers to floating tables! By the way..."You got grill up?"

Angela Graham, my dear friend, my CP. I couldn't do any of this without you. It's so wonderful to have another writer as passionate and OCD as myself to brainstorm with! Your eye for quality and detail keeps me grounded and I thank you, always. I love you, girl. Here's to another year filled with more of this crazy journey we started together!

Ashley Suzanne, my twin soul, my friend, my BBFFL. Shit, I haven't even started typing actual stuff and I'm crying! Woman- you are my heart's song. Forgive me if I call you sugar, or ask about David, or bark at you to "come"...but that's just how we roll! If I felt like the world hated me- you're the first call I'd make. And your support of my books, which even means IN THE WORDS OF YOUR OWN, yeah, people don't do things like every day. You're my ONE in a million! You are the chapter naming Queen, the "ohhh my God, what if we did this...." Master. Please, I beg you, keep mind fing me for the rest of my life! I DARE you to blow me away with your phone calls and grand ideas more so in 2014 than last year!

Jessica Adams- You always make my life easier and I thank you so very much! Every time you say "get out of my brain," I know we were a match made in Heaven! Thank you for rocking out my first signing with the organization and precision of a drill sergeant, and for the gift bag, and the Diet Dew run, and....well, you already know!

The Dynamic Duo of Toski Covey Photography and Sommer Stein, Perfect Pear Creative Covers. For loving my work enough to take it under your wings and give it a fresh, amazing face!! The two of you are so wonderful I can't thank you enough! I am but the humble recipient of your visions...I just sit back and prepared to be awed! Once again, you guys knocked it out of the park with Entice! Your work and dedication is flawless and I'm beyond lucky to have you both!

The Erins: Gotta Have 'Em!

Erin Roth, my editor, who has the eyes of an eagle and does the best job editing, even if she won't let me say "awnry." LOL. And bless her sweet heart, still holding out hope I'll learn all those weird "dialogue tag" and "period not a comma here" rules she's always spouting. #youlovemethewayIam

Erin Long, my formatter, who I swear hears my emails coming in even if in the middle of the night while I'm in full blown panic mode and begging her to change something right that second. She's a speedy lil' lifesaver!

BLOGGERS—there is NO way I am naming you off individually. Knowing me, I'd forget one and it would keep me awake at night to have possibly hurt any feelings. Collectively—YOU ARE AMAZING!!!!!!! You change the lives of independent authors who had a story buzzing in their head and their heart, and took a chance on it. You take a chance of them, put your own jobs and families on hold for that spot of time to read their book and give back. SO many of you supported me, *Emerge, Embrace, and Entangled*….and I'm proud to call you friends. Your ethics, integrity, selflessness, kindness and professionalism are recognized and appreciated!!!! And the 2013 polls, well let's just say, every time a new one went up where I was nominated, I cried more happy tears!!!

My "Crew" aka "S.E.'s Elite" and "Dane's Dolls and Evan's Pretty Girls"—you know who you are and, I hope, what you mean to me!!! I should be making you feel special every chance I get and I sure hope I do just that! You're always there when I need a quick fix, an idea, an opinion, a laugh, a cry… If I never wrote another book, I'd still need you in my life. I love you ALL! And the newcomers, Welcome, and thank you for loving the Evolve Series! And to the "founders", my old-school girls who changed my life the night they had a group read….ladies, you ever need an alibi or bail money, you know who to call!

Sawyer's Sensuously Sinful Betas- GREAT group of ladies who helped me every step of the way with Entice. I'd love to name by name, but if you look real close in the books…I try to do just that in "my way." I love you all, you did a great job, and I hope you're proud of Entice because there's at least one piece of each of you in it!

Toski the person, not the photographer- I've told you before, but I'll say it again, loud and proud. The day you fell in love with Dane and Emerge, my life, my family's life, changed. You took it under your wing like your own book and did it proud! I can't ever thank you enough, ever! I love you dearly!

Samantha Stettner- Always. I know that's all I have to say and you get it, just ALWAYS.

Stacy Borel- So I start Touching Scars, and I see it- 27%- and I start to cry! THANK YOU lovely lady!!!!! Xoxo forever

Erin Noelle- the shout-out in Euphoria? Lezzz be honest, I love you!!!!!!! Can't wait to rock Philly with ya baby girl!

***I reserve the right to amend, make excuses for, beg forgiveness on, or act clueless in general when it comes to this message *IF* I did forget anyone.

THANK YOU ALL!!!!!!!!!!

xoxo S.E. Hall

Entice
Playlist

Hurt- Johnny Cash

Shook Me All Night Long- AC/DC

In Luv Wit A Stripper- Somo

Savin' Me- Nickelback

Green Eyes- Coldplay

It Will Rain- Bruno Mars

Can't Help Falling In Love- Elvis Presley

Motivation- Kelly Rowland

Ride- Somo

INDULGE

Prequel to The Harmony Series

Angela Graham

Coming February 10, 2014

Predictable, as always. "Relax, doll." My lip twitched up in a smirk. "I am very much single."

"Oh," she murmured, a pink blush returning to her gaunt cheeks. Her tongue peeked out, skimming her top lip. Her eyes locked on mine as she released the sheet. "In that case…"

My erection grew as I watched her seductive performance. She ran her fingers down over her breasts as her legs opened, inviting me in.

Unfortunately, I knew better. There was no time. "You can see yourself out."

She wasn't taking no for answer, stepping down from the bed on her tiptoes and strutting toward me confidently. It was one I'd seen far too many times. The morning-after show usually played out one of two ways, but the fact that never changed was that I always had the upper hand. As much as women hated it, I never had a problem turning them away when I was done.

"There's money on the dresser for a taxi."

She released a provoked whine when I turned around and entered my bathroom, closing the door behind me.

The force of water hammering down over my shoulders eased the final stiffness from my muscles. The club I'd ended up at the previous night with Caleb had been a new one with an over-the-top opening, and still I was surrounded by all the same faces—all except that of the woman now scouring my room for her clothing. She'd been a pleasant distraction from the monotony of the evening, but as with all the rest, my curiosity about her was sated.

The predictable creak of the bathroom door sounded around me as I massaged soap into my scalp. After a quick rinse of my head, I opened my eyes, watching her climb in and shut the shower door.

She gave a sweet-but-far-from-innocent smile, judging by the mischievous gleam in her eye. "I can help," she offered.

She reached for the bar of soap resting on the ledge and lathered it in her hands. I waited, a smirk growing, pleased that like all the others before her, she was eager to make sure I had my fill. Her eyes held mine as she encased my solid erection in her soapy hands and began stroking.

Her tongue peeked out, tracing along her lips as she rinsed the soap away under the spray. A slow smile emerged on her lips and I knew exactly what she was thinking—what she wanted.

"Show me what that pretty mouth can do," I said.

She stooped down on her knees and held my cock firm in her hand. Her tongue swirled around the head a few times, firing my senses to life, before gliding down and swirling around the base. Another lap back up caused my hips to nudge forward, urging her to take me in.

She pulled her gaze from my cock and looked up at me through long, dark lashes before opening her mouth and plunging down over my dick, skimming it over the roof of her mouth. She sucked hard before popping her mouth open and drawing it in again.

Her hand gripped my thigh, digging into the skin while she moved her other hand to the base of my cock, stroking me for added pleasure. I threaded my fingers into her hair, thrusting my hips forward and taking full power.

Her ravishment grew wild, her hand pumping and her mouth taking me deeper, over and over. Her head bobbed frantically. The girl knew what she was doing; she was damn near a pro.

A breath hissed from my lips. "Fuck," I ground out when she scraped her teeth down gently, then slid her tongue back over the sensitive flesh.

I slammed my eyes shut, focusing on the vibrations of her lips humming over my hard cock, nearing release. Her mouth moved faster, rougher. I grasped handfuls of her hair tightly with both hands, holding her lips in place suctioned at the base of my cock as its shaft pumped into the back of her throat.

A rough, gratified moan tore from my throat, clearing away any lingering stress in my thoughts. My mind was wiped clean as I lost myself in the feeling of her warm lips milking me into my morning release.

MIRAGE

Ashley Suzanne

The picture frames that once lined the table in the hallway are now scattered across the floor, in shambles, like the pieces of my heart. Anger and sadness flow through my veins as I look at the broken glass, shattered like my soul. I'm sitting on the cool hardwood floor with my back to the couch and hands tangled in my hair. Tears stream from my eyes and my chest heaves up and down as I try to catch my breath. All I can do is think back to the best day of my life and try to figure out how it completely fell apart.

"You're it for me, Pea," Danny said. *"I can't wait to spend the rest of my life with you. We're going to be so disgustingly happy, our friends are going to hate us,"* he joked.

"Don't I know it! I already see the girls making faces when we're together. This is going to push them over the edge," I teased. *"Do you think we should make a group announcement? Head out on Saturday night, like usual, then BAM, look at my ring, we're getting married."* I was going to get my fairy tale happily ever after and I couldn't wait to tell everyone and show off my ring, a classic princess cut ¾ carat diamond on a white gold band.

"We can do it however you want, Pea, as long as you promise me forever and always." How could I not swoon when he said stuff like that?

"I'm yours as long as you'll have me," I said as I crashed into him, pulling him in for the most passionate kiss of my life. Even though I instigated the kiss, it wasn't long until Danny took control, claiming my mouth for his own, just like he did my heart.

In that moment I thought to myself, 'I'm hopelessly in love with this man. Please dear God, don't break my heart.'

I can't remember his voice. I have been calling Danny's phone just to hear his greeting and his sultry timbre and now I can't. Why can't I remember? The way he would say my name would send me into a frenzy. I'll never hear those words come from his lips ever again. If I would have known how short our time would be, I would have burned every event to memory. Now I only get bits and pieces. As much as I want everything all at once, I'll take what I can get just to see him in my mind.

We finally reached the night of our college graduation. I was in my apartment with a few girlfriends, Kylee, Marisol and Lena, getting ready to hit the after party. Knowing Danny would be here soon, I decided to wear something that would tease him in just the right way. My Danny is a boob man, so I put on my black lace corset top that was meant more for lingerie, but God I looked amazing in it. I paired the top with a pair of dark washed jeans and my favorite black peek toe pumps. I was ready to celebrate the end of four years of study groups, aggravating professors, finals, midterms, and lack of sleep with my friends and my man. This was the beginning of the rest of my life …

Danny shows up a little after nine on his bike. "Hey Pea, you ready to go?" he calls from the hallway leading to my apartment.

"Yeah, I heard you pull up. I guess since we're on the bike, I'm not bringing a purse."

"You know the rules, Pea. No purses or heels on the bike. Change your shoes, please. You can put your heels in my backpack, if you want," Danny says annoyed.

I headed back into my room, exchanging my pumps for a pair of black leather knee high boots that fit perfectly over my jeans. Looking at myself in the mirror, I was surprised. I don't know why I didn't think of this earlier. This looks so much hotter. "Damn, Mira," I said to myself.

I grabbed a thin black hair tie from my dresser and used my fingers to brush back my long brown hair and place it in a low ponytail. I was glad I decided to curl my hair tonight because the wind would have really mess up my hair and knotted it if I would have straightened it.

Giving myself one more glance in the floor length mirror on the back of my bedroom door, I walked out of my room and shut the door behind me, "I'm coming." I slipped on my leather riding jacket and left the apartment, walking downstairs.

Danny was waiting for me on the front stoop of my apartment building. I don't know if it was just an emotional day or what, but Danny looked somewhat more mature. He was wearing light faded jeans and an all black button up shirt with the sleeves rolled up to his elbows, exposing the tattoo on his right forearm.

Last summer Danny and Skylar got matching tattoos. Danny's right forearm displays the word 'Smash' in Old English lettering. Skylar's is in the same spot and says 'Axe' in the same lettering. Skylar's uncle used to call them Smash and Axe while they were growing up. Boys will be boys. I think it's silly, but these boys are two peas in a pod. I'm surprised I'm not dating both of them.

Kylee had just finished putting her helmet on and climbed onto the back of Skylar's bike when I reach where Danny's bike was parked. Danny was riding his beloved GSX-R. Again, the boys have matching bikes. I swear these two did everything together. The only difference in Danny and Skylar's bikes is the color of the seats. Where Sky's was purple, Danny's is a dark midnight blue. Everything else was all black. I think the boys call it "murdered out" but I have no clue what that means. It's just looks like flat black paint to me.

I pulled on my black helmet with pink pinstripes and jumped on the back of Danny's bike. This was my favorite part. I could just lay on his back, rest my head on his shoulder and go along for the ride. No talking, no music, nothing but us and the road. Some girls get off on buying shoes. Me? I get off on the sound of a bike. There is just something about the rumble of a bike that makes me want to flip around the front and madly kiss the man I'm so in love with.

Maybe it isn't all bikes. Maybe it's just Danny's. I know the sound. Even though it's identical to Skylar's and many other bikes around this town, something about the sound of this bike screams Danny and nobody else.

We left the parking lot and headed towards the highway. My legs were squeezing the life out of Danny's and I was almost lying down on top of him. We were going so fast, as if we were flying. This was where I got my thrills in life and I was so happy I got to do it with my future husband.

My future husband. Oh hell. In a few months, I will to be Mrs. Daniel Thomas. Mira Rae Thomas. That sounded like music to my *ears.*

I was totally in my zone on this ride. I didn't even notice when a car came swerving into our lane. Danny's bike started to sway beneath my legs. I gripped his waist even tighter and tried to remember everything he ever told me. There was an art to being a passenger on a bike.

"Don't fight against me. Don't lean into turns with me. Keep your body centered. Hold on tight. If we go down, try to stay on your back with your head raised. Try not to tumble."

Ok. Alright. Trying to keep my body centered, gripping tight and not fighting against Danny, the bike continues to sway beneath me. Before I knew it, we were heading right towards the guard rail in the middle of the highway.

Panic set it. "Danny ... Danny ... What do I do?" I screamed and I know he can't hear me over the traffic and the roar of the bike.

We hit the wall. The sound was so loud; I felt it in my bones. The sound of metal slamming against concrete is a sound I will never forget. Nails on a chalkboard don't even compare.

I flew off the bike. The pain of hitting the cement of the highway at over sixty miles per hour was excruciating. I felt my bones in my leg snap as I tried to keep on my back without tumbling.

"Aaaaahhhhhhhhh!!!" I screamed out in pain. Every inch I slid down the highway was terrifying until I hit my final resting place. I had no idea what is going on around me.

My body finally won out against me as my head slammed hard against the cement and pain shot through my entire body.

I assumed I blacked out. When I finally came to, I was in the back of an ambulance with medics looking over my body and starting an

IV, their faces looking grim.

"Danny?" I asked, my voice coming out weak and barely there.

The blond medic just looked at me with blank eyes. He slightly shook his head.

"No," I cried, "no, please no."

Out of all the memories we had built during our time together, this is the one I can't shake. I can vividly recall each and every detail of our last moments together. Why can't I remember the things that helped mold me into the woman I wanted to become with Danny by my side? Why am I only able to remember the day that turned me into the woman I am now?

Love stories are for suckers. Life doesn't happen like it did in *The Notebook*. Or should I say death doesn't happen that way? You don't meet the person you're supposed to be with until your time is up and then slowly fade away together. Real life is a bitch and it hurts. The real story isn't pretty or romantic it just breaks you to the point where you don't want to go on anymore. You pray that this isn't the way your story ends.

My Danny didn't survive. They said he had too much trauma and died on the scene. My body screamed in pain as I tried to get off the gurney to go to where ever Danny was. The other medic, who I didn't remember too well, grabbed my shoulders softly and pulled me back to stay on the gurney. The blond medic inserted a syringe of medication into my IV and within seconds, I felt my body relax and go lifeless.

In that moment, my world came to a screeching halt and that is it for me.

Skylar came to visit me in the hospital for the two days I was admitted while I was being treated for my road rash and broken leg. Surprisingly, I didn't have it too bad. Because my injuries were minimal, I was released on the second day, with crutches and a wheelchair that Skylar had "borrowed" from the hospital. I had a pretty bad bump on my head, some scrapes and bruises and a broken leg, but I was alive. Which was more than I could say for Danny…

It's perfect weather for a funeral. Ugly and raining with no sign of bright skies in sight. At the service, his mom asked me to sit with her. She told me that I was practically family anyway, being engaged to Danny and all. It did feel a little weird not sitting with my friends and parents, but it was nice to be able to sit with Mrs. Thomas, who looks so much like Danny it's scary.

Immediately following the burial, we all head over to Danny's mother's house. People are coming and going. Friends, relatives, faculty from the school and members of the community.

I don't remember eating much today, or any day since Danny died, for that matter. I hear my stomach growling. I know it needs some sort of sustenance if I plan on taking the pain medication the doctor prescribed, but the thought of consuming anything makes me ill.

"Mira, honey, you have to at least eat something. Trust me, I know how hard this is, but you have to take care of yourself," Danny's mom pleads with me.

"Mrs. Thomas, I promise I will eat something later. I just can't right now," I respond back emotionless, not even making eye contact with the woman.

Everything seems to pass by in such a blur. I don't even realize that I am being wheeled out the door with Kylee on my side and Skylar pushing the wheelchair.

"Where are we going?" I ask them.

"We're taking you home, Mi. You have had enough for one day. You need a shower and some sleep," Skylar says.

"And something to eat," Kylee chimes in.

When we get back to the apartment I share with Kylee, Skylar pulls right up to the door so I don't have to walk through the parking lot. While he parks the car, Kylee helps me inside. I immediately see the long thin table by the front door lined with pictures of my past. Some of the happiest days of my life captured in film. I will be forever haunted by these images in my memory, let alone having to look at them every day.

"This isn't fair. Why did you leave me?" I yell as I swipe my arm across the table, sending the pictures crashing to the floor and the glass from the frames flying off in different directions.

The floor is cold under my bare legs and I can feel my heart harden with each breath I take.

"Mira, honey, come on and let's get you up and into bed," Kylee says. I see the pity in her eyes.

"I'm so sorry Ky. I don't know what that was about.

Today was just an emotional day," I say apologetically.

"Mi, we all miss him," Skylar says as he walks in, surveying the mess I have just created.

"I'll clean up this mess, hun. Just go," Kylee says.

I try to get up from the ground but it's not as easy as it might look. This cast makes every movement awkward and I know that I'm probably exposing more than I should, especially with Skylar in the room.

"Come on Sweets let me help you to bed," Skylar says, as he picks me up off the ground and carries me to my room, saving me from the embarrassment of trying to do it on my own.

"Ky, can you just put the pictures up somewhere safe? I don't want to lose them, but I need some time before they are shoved in my face."

Kylee grabs a shoebox that hasn't been taken out in the trash and starts putting my memories away. "I'll just put them all in here, until we can buy new frames," she tells me as lean into Skylar's chest.

As soon as my head hits the pillows, the stress of the last few days overcomes me and I immediately close my eyes. Skylar's voice is the last thing I hear before drifting off to sleep, hopefully to see Danny in my dreams.

Made in the USA
Charleston, SC
03 June 2014